HIS WHITE MOONLIGHT

ALSO BY
MELISSA HAAG

THE JUDGEMENT WORLD
(swoony wolf shifters!)

JUDGEMENT OF THE SIX

JUDGEMENT OF THE SIX COMPANIONS

THE MANTIRUM WORLD
(hot shifters of all kinds!)

OF FATES AND FURIES

BY KISS AND CLAW

IN FIRE AND ASH

HIS WHITE MOONLIGHT

A DOMINANT CEO SHIFTER ROMANCE

MELISSA HAAG

Shattered Glass
PUBLISHING

Version 2025.08.12

To everyone living in survival mode…
"Sometimes life is harder than it needs to be."
Nothing stays hard forever.

.

CHAPTER ONE

THE PILOT ANNOUNCED the final approach, and I felt a surge of nervous anticipation.

"Is there anything else I can get for you?" the flight attendant asked. After I shook my head, she smiled. "You made my job easy this flight."

Since Mom and Dad had bought all the seats to ensure I was the only person in the first-class section, I could see why.

"I hope you enjoy your stay in Motan."

"Thanks. I hope your next flight is as easy."

She buckled into her seat, and I looked out the window at the city I barely remembered. A city that was supposed to feel like home but didn't.

Don't think about it, Wrenly, I silently told myself. *Focus on the positive. You'll finally get to see Aiden and Karter in person again.*

It'd been so long—seven years since I'd been home.

I studied my reflection in the glass, proud of how I'd managed to retain who I was, despite the time away. Rather than a fashionable twist, which would have helped me blend in at school, I wore my shoulder-length light brown hair back in a ponytail. Not a bit of makeup covered the smattering of subtle freckles along the bridge of my average nose or my grey eyes fringed by brown lashes. I felt makeup robbed me of an air of innocent cuteness that usually kept me out of trouble.

My full lips curved at the memory of how many times Aiden and Karter had taken the blame for our trouble because I'd looked too innocent to scold when I was younger. I hoped it would be the same now, even though I was officially and legally an adult.

An adult who still has zero control over her own life, I thought bitterly.

The airplane touched down several minutes later. While everyone sitting behind first class started to collect their belongings, I stood with my tote bag. Almost everything I'd accumulated while at the boarding school, which wasn't much, had been packed and shipped three days ago, so I only had my one bag to worry about.

Debarking was quick and easy, and I power-walked to the security checkpoint, where Mom had said someone would be waiting for me.

I spotted a man with greying hair who wore a suit and held a sign for "Wrenly Belak." Definitely not either of my brothers, whom I'd been expecting.

"Hey," I said. "I'm Wrenly. What's my mom's first name?"

"Pardon?" the man asked, sounding surprised.

"Just because you have a sign with my name on it doesn't mean I'm going to jump into a car with a stranger."

He smiled, showing I'd amused him rather than offended him.

"I don't know your biological mother's name," he said, "but Mrs. Wulf's name is Christine. Mr. Wulf sent me to pick you up. You can call him to verify. My name is Milo."

"Hmmm…I like your level of calm, Milo. Any chance you'll let me drive?"

He folded the sign as he studied me.

"Do you have a license?"

"I do." Not that I'd ever gotten a chance to use it. But I flashed my most charming smile at him as I pulled out my wallet to show him my ID, which I had received courtesy of private lessons and a private, in-school exam.

He glanced at it. "Do you know where you're going?"

I was twelve when I left. What twelve-year-old paid attention to directions?

"That's what GPS is for, Milo."

He chuckled and motioned for me to walk with him. The black Benz he led me to looked sleek with its chrome accents. A car worthy of the high-maintenance girls who'd attended the last all-girl boarding school with me.

Milo crushed my dream of driving it, though, by opening the passenger door for me. I stuck out my bottom lip, but it didn't work.

"Maybe next time," he said. "City traffic is no joke, and you're expected at home."

"Fine. But you just lost some points, Milo."

"I will try to earn them back."

With a sigh, I got in and waited for him to join me.

"So you're employed by Mr. Wulf. Through the business or personally?"

"Personally."

"Where do you live?"

"In the big house with my wife, Sandy. She manages the household."

"Mmm. How many people work there now?"

"Staff has been temporarily reduced to Sandy and myself."

I turned to look at him. "What? Why?"

"Mr. Wulf will discuss it with you when you return."

I stared forward, not liking how that sounded. Rather than wait for an explanation, I pulled out my phone and texted the only group chat I had.

Me: What gives? Why am I being picked up by some old guy and not by either of my two favorite people? Do you want a demotion?

3

Karter: Sorry, Princess. Orders. We've been reassigned.
Aiden: No demotion! We're owed favorite status.
Me: The favorite title needs maintenance. Be prepared to
compensate me for this level of neglect. He wouldn't even
let me drive!

Both sent back laughing emojis. I tucked my phone away, leaving the rest of what I wanted to say until I saw them.

It took an hour to reach "the big house," as Milo called it. It wasn't that big. The Wulfs weren't showy with their money like that. It was just the biggest house in the expansive gated community known as Alpine Run. Surrounded by lawns, gardens, and trees, the house had been a dream come true for six-year-old me when I first arrived. During my childhood, I'd gone on countless adventures with Aiden and Karter, who were three years older than me.

I waited for Milo to park in the circle in front of the house drive before I bolted out of the car. The oversized front door banged against the wall as I rushed into the foyer.

Breathing in deeply, I turned a slow circle, taking it all in. The house was exactly as I remembered it.

Home. Finally.

"I'm home," I called out.

"So I see," a deep voice returned.

I spun around toward the stairs and saw Bennett descending.

He wasn't the first person I'd hoped to see. Or the second...or third. Honestly, he was almost at the bottom of the list. Not that I hated him or anything. He was just...Bennett. Seven years my senior, he'd always been distant and stuffy, not fun like Aiden or Karter, his younger brothers.

Bennett had changed a lot since I last saw him.

Seven years.

He'd been about nineteen, my current age, back then. He also might have even gotten taller by an inch or two, which wasn't fair since that meant he towered over me by an unreasonable fourteen inches.

He looked handsome…and even more uptight now than he had the last time I'd seen him.

He no longer wore high-end athletic clothes, but a tailored suit that showcased his broad shoulders and narrow waist. However, some things hadn't changed. His dark hair was still neatly styled, and his expression still didn't give away his thoughts as his dark brown gaze locked with mine.

The pack girls had all raved about how hot he was even back then. They hadn't lived with him, though. I pitied the poor pack girls who had their sights set on him now.

"Where is everyone?" I asked.

Mom and Dad had let me know they wouldn't be home, which was why they'd sent someone to pick me up. But I thought Aiden and Karter would have been there at least. Granted, it was just after noon on a Wednesday, but still…this was my first time home.

"Out," Bennett said, continuing down the stairs.

"Out?"

"Out."

Yep, still the same Bennett, I thought.

"Okay, then."

Milo entered behind me with my bag, which I took from him.

"Thanks for the ride," I said. "Don't forget I get to drive next time."

He looked over my shoulder at Bennett.

"If there's nothing else today, Sandy and I will leave early."

"Thank you, Milo," Bennett said.

I watched Milo leave then looked at Bennett, who was watching me from the base of the stairs. I wanted to ask where Milo was going since I thought he stayed at the house with his wife, but Bennett didn't look too happy, so I swallowed my question.

How exactly had he gotten stuck being my welcoming committee? Not that he was giving much of a welcome.

With a mental shrug, I started walking across the foyer.

When I passed the base of the stairs, he asked, "Where are you going?"

Where did he think I was going?

Rather than answering nicely, I said, "In."

Damn, that felt good.

Smothering my smile, I went to my old room on the first floor.

When I opened the door, I froze. My bed...my things...they were all gone. The room was now an office space, which didn't make sense. Mom and Dad both had offices on the other side of the house on the first floor. Why did they convert this room? *My* room?

I was confused and trying hard not to feel hurt by what I was seeing so that Bennett wouldn't smell it.

Obviously, a lot had been happening at home that they'd kept from me.

"Why bother making me come home if I don't have a place to stay?" I asked, knowing Bennett was behind me.

"You have a place. It's at the end of the hall upstairs," Bennett said behind me.

"The hall to the right or left?" I asked.

"The left."

I turned around without looking at him and made my way back to the stairs. He caught my arm and took the bag from me.

"You're angry."

"You think?" I said, annoyed I hadn't suppressed my emotions enough.

Not fighting him for the bag, I marched up the stairs.

He followed closely, not saying anything until we reached the door.

"Mom made sure everything was the same."

She truly had. From the wallpaper to the posters to the way my bed was situated. Yet, there were changes, too. She'd added a vanity, and I saw I had an en-suite bathroom and a huge walk-in closet, where someone had already unpacked the things I'd shipped.

My modest wardrobe was either hanging or folded in the custom cabinetry drawers. The section dedicated solely to purses and shoes was empty. I didn't look forward to explaining what happened to the gifts she'd sent over the years.

Bennett walked past me and set my bag in the closet.

"Do you need help unpacking?" he asked, sounding borderline impatient.

"No."

He stared at me for a long moment before walking away. I watched him pull his phone from his pocket as he left my room. He was probably giving Mom an update, confirming he'd done his duty.

I sat on my bed and looked around the room again. Then, I sent a message to the group chat.

Me: If I'm no longer wanted, all you need to do is say the word, and I'll leave.

Aiden: What are you talking about?

Karter: What happened? You've only been home ten minutes.

Me: Stop stalking me. Why does everyone get to see where I am all the time, but I can't know where you are? Which is NOT HERE, by the way. Traitors. I thought you missed me.

Aiden: We do.

Karter: Life's been boring without you. Do you know how many pack parties we had to suffer through alone while you were gone?

Me: Good. It was pre-karma for sticking me with Bennett as soon as I got home.

Aiden: What'd Bennett do? Did he hurt you?

Hurt me? Is Aiden insane?

Me: He's just being his usual uptight self. When are you coming home?

Karter: Not sure. We're being "groomed" for management.
Me: Okay. Then, I'll come see you.

Aiden laughed at the message.

Aiden: Nice try. You just got home. Stay out of trouble until
we can see you.

I was so annoyed that I tossed my phone onto my bed and went to unpack my bag. Once I finished, I checked out the vanity and the bathroom. Mom had thought of everything, as usual. I was still bothered that they'd moved my room without telling me, though. I'd been counting on the freedom of having a bedroom farther away from everyone. Or was that why they'd moved me? Did they already know I didn't plan to stay?

Grabbing my phone, I sent another message.

Me: Thanks, Mom. The room is beautiful. I would have
been fine with the downstairs room, though. It's not like I'm
going to be here that long anyway.

I bit my lip and waited for a reply.

Although I hadn't come home in seven years, Mom and Dad often visited me at school to ensure I was doing fine. I never doubted their love for me. It drove every decision they made and every rule they established. But freedom from their suffocating love was something I really wanted. No, it was what I *needed*.

Which was why I wanted to leave for college…a school they hadn't agreed to.

I didn't belong in Alpine Run. They knew it as much as I did. I wasn't one of them. I was normal. Human. And I never forgot that, no matter how much they treated me like a pampered pack princess.

The private boarding school that had been my home for the past four years had almost killed me. Like here, I hadn't belonged. I didn't care about nine-thousand-dollar purses or gem-encrusted heels. No, not true. I did care about heels, but in a loathing, "they could burn in hell" kind of way.

I didn't want to be dressed up like a pretty girl, only valued for how she looked or what she wore. I wanted to be a wickedly smart woman who didn't take crap from anyone. The boarding school had helped with the "take no crap" part. A lot. The wickedly smart part, too, honestly. I'd already completed an array of college-level classes because of that school.

For my next life phase, though, I just wanted a regular education. Normal friends. Normal interactions.

My phone buzzed.

Mom: I'm so happy you're home and can't wait to see you! And what do you mean you won't be there long? We already have a job lined up for you. No refusing until you give it a try.

With a groan, I flopped onto my back again.

Mom was a master life manager. As the pack Luna, she needed to be. But after a lifetime of her gentle handling, I knew her tricks. First, she'd pull me into a pack-arranged job with pay too good to turn down. Then, she'd talk me into enrolling in one of the private colleges in the city so I could be close to home. Once I graduated, she'd probably start arranging dates that wouldn't be called dates, but probably meetings or even family dinners, where some guy would "happen to pass by."

Her tricks to pull me into the life she had planned for me wouldn't work this time, though. After seven years of obediently doing as I was told, I had developed my own life management plan.

I popped up from my bed and looked around the room for my laptop, which had been among the things I'd shipped ahead. It was sitting on one of the bookshelves. I grabbed it, closed my door, and returned to the bed to log into my University account for a state school five hours away from home—close enough to drive to but far enough away to avoid daily family visits.

Thanks to my excellent grades, I'd been accepted without a problem, and thanks to the bags and shoes I'd managed to sell in the last four months at disappointingly low prices, I had enough money in my secret account to cover tuition for the first year and a half.

Was I nervous about having a roommate after seven years of having a private room? Yes, but probably not for the reason most people would be. I'd already had plenty of mean-girl experiences and desperately wanted a friendly one for a change.

Sophia and I had been chatting on and off for weeks, and she seemed genuinely nice. And normal. I wanted normal so badly.

After checking my school email, I logged out and sent Sophia a message that I was finally home and could meet up with her in person before move-in day. We'd both discovered we lived in different suburbs surrounding Motan. Thankfully, she'd never heard of Alpine Run.

I put my laptop away and considered my options. Wait at home like I was expected to, which would set a precedent I didn't want, or go out?

The answer was easy.

I left my bedroom and jogged down the stairs. Everything was quiet as I hurried through the kitchen and out to the garage. The keys to the cars were kept in the same lockbox as before. Grinning, I entered the code I remembered and almost squealed when it still worked.

Randomly grabbing a set of keys, I hit the unlock button and watched the lights on a Lexus flash. I ran for it and quickly got in.

Would I get into trouble for taking a car without permission? Not really. I'd get a lecture about safety and talking to them before making plans, but nothing more serious than that. But if I were caught before I left, they'd find a million reasons I shouldn't go.

The garage door rose with a touch of a button as the engine

purred to life. I pulled out of the garage and down the long, winding driveway.

My phone rang before I reached the road, but I didn't stop to answer it. Everyone in the family got an alert whenever their tracking app detected I was moving locations. After all these years, I had grown so accustomed to it that it no longer bothered me. It was fun, actually. Like playing "Guess what Wrenly is up to now." They had no idea how many times I'd left my phone behind to do things I didn't want them to know about.

As I rounded the last bend in the road leading out of Alpine Run, I saw the closed gate and guard waiting outside the guardhouse. Slowing to a stop, I rolled down my window since I didn't have super hearing like he probably did.

"Just heading out for the afternoon," I said with a friendly smile.

"I'm afraid not. Mr. Wulf called ahead and said you're not permitted to leave. You'll need to turn around, Miss Belak."

"That's odd." I glanced at my phone and wallet. "I didn't forget anything, did I?"

"He didn't say."

"All right. I'll go back and find out."

I smiled, waved as I rolled up the window, then executed a fairly crappy Y-turn because no one ever let me practice.

A minor setback, I told myself. *Nothing you can't overcome.*

After rounding the bend so the car was out of sight of the guardhouse, I parked on the shoulder. Leaving my phone behind on the seat, I jogged across the road. The air in the woods was slightly cooler in a nice way. I picked up my pace.

While the other girls at the boarding school hadn't seen the point in physical education other than to look good, I'd viewed it differently. I'd grown up with people who ran fast without even trying. People who liked to play tricks to make me bleed. I'd known that, if I didn't want to bleed again when I went home, I would need to be as fast as humanly possible.

However, the boarding school had changed my motivation. I'd

learned so much there, including how I needed to be strong and fast to protect myself from more than the people in Alpine Run.

The boarding school had been a test of survival.

And I had survived.

So, I ran through the trees toward the south, where the wall curved in enough to give me cover from the guardhouse. By now, everyone in the family had seen that the car was stopped on the road. What would they do? Probably nothing for a few minutes. They'd likely think I was mad and just sitting there, stewing.

I grinned all the way to the wall. When I reached it, I didn't stop to try to catch my breath; I ran faster, using the momentum to plant my foot on the wall and leap up. My fingers caught the top stone. I planted my other foot higher, ready to leverage myself up.

A hand gripped my ankle and pulled down hard.

I landed on my back with enough force that I struggled to breathe as I looked up at a familiar mocking face.

Storm, my childhood nemesis, hadn't changed much. She still looked like she belonged on a fashion week runway with her svelte build and perfect, long blonde hair, which was ornately braided with pearl accents. The thick lashes around her light brown eyes and pouty lips demanded attention, just like their owner.

"If it isn't our resident normie," she said with a sneering tilt to her mouth.

I exhaled slowly, then successfully inhaled.

"I heard you'd returned," she continued. "You should have stayed away."

"And miss our lovely conversations, Storm? I could never deprive myself of that."

She stepped onto my shoulder with her sneakered foot and leaned into it. It hurt more than I would have liked to admit. The two girls with her, whom I didn't recognize, laughed.

Storm sniffed and glared at me. "Why do you smell like Bennett?"

I grinned up at her. "So it's Bennett you're head over moon for now?"

She stepped down harder then backed away. I got to my feet and brushed off my butt.

When she opened her mouth to say more, I cut her off.

"Let me save you the trouble. 'Stay away from the Wulf boys, Wrenly. They're mine.' Still noted, Storm. By the way, did you make any progress during my absence, since I was the only obstacle to your plan for Wulf domination? Did you get Aiden's number? Did Karter finally cop a feel? We both know nothing happened with Bennett. If you're not a profit margin, you don't exist in his world."

Her pupils dilated, a sign of a pissed-off shifter, and she snarled at me.

"Ah, still have some pent-up sexual frustrations, I see."

She drew her hand back, but I didn't back down. Instead, I leaned in tauntingly.

"When the Wulfs see I'm hurt, who do you think they'll smell on me?"

She snarled and dropped her fist to her side.

"Smart choice," I said. "If you leave now, we can both go our separate ways with no one the wiser."

Storm opened her mouth, but then looked in the direction of the road. Her face's transformation from mean-bitch to one in heat gave me hope.

Please be Aiden, I silently pleaded.

It wasn't Aiden, Karter, or even the guard I'd spoken to striding through the trees, though.

It was Bennett, and he did *not* look happy.

CHAPTER TWO

"BENNETT," Storm cooed, catching his tailored coat sleeve. "It's been so long since you came out for a run."

He dislodged her breast-pressing arm hug.

"Unfortunately, I'm not out for a run." His gaze shifted to me, and his pupils flared a little like Storm's had. "What are you doing out here, Wrenly?"

I knew better than to lie. He'd smell it a mile away. So I smiled innocently.

"Running. Exchanging barbs with Storm."

"I caught her trying to climb over the wall," Storm said as if she were some kind of hero instead of a girl so desperate for a guy's attention she looked two seconds away from leg-humping him.

"Careful, Storm. You're close to panting."

Her simpering gaze filled with rage as she glared at me. I grinned unrepentantly until Bennett grabbed me by the arm—the shoulder she'd stepped on—and started towing me back toward the car.

Storm's whine followed us. I wanted to do the same, but for a different reason. My shoulder was still aching, and I didn't want to go back home with Bennett and his disapproving stares. Or, worse, his mind-numbing interrogations.

He didn't say anything by the time we reached the road, which just meant he was bottling up all his annoyance. He went straight to the car and opened the passenger door for me.

"I can drive us back," I offered.

"Get in, Wrenly."

With a sigh, I plopped into the seat. He closed the door and walked around the front of the car. He'd been smart not to put me in the driver's seat. I would have been too tempted to run him over.

"Are you going to tell me why you were trying to leave?" he asked once he got in.

"And bore you with the inner workings of my insignificant mind? Never."

He started the car and pulled away from the shoulder. "Why do you think you're insignificant?"

"I don't. You do." I felt the weight of his glance, so I met it with an arched brow.

"I don't think you're insignificant, Wrenly."

Of course, he didn't. He found me to be a significant pain in his ass and had since as far back as I could remember. I didn't say that, though, because I knew he'd feel obligated to prove otherwise.

Since I wanted to avoid the second Spanish Inquisition, I gave him what he wanted—an answer.

"I was going to surprise Mom, Dad, Aiden, and Karter at the office." I purposely didn't think of all the other things I'd also wanted to do so that I wouldn't smell like a liar. In the few years I'd lived at home, I'd perfected how to lie-not-lie. It was a skill I'd kept honed.

Bennett didn't say anything more until he'd parked the car in the garage.

"Aiden and Karter aren't at the office."

"Okay. Then where are they?"

"Away."

He opened his door and got out. I scrambled to get out and follow him into the house.

"Away where?"

"Where doesn't matter. They're busy."

If there'd been a pan on the stovetop, I would have tested my backswing on Bennett's head...once I stood on a chair.

"I never thought I would miss school," I said under my breath.

He paused and glanced back at me. "Because you can't chase after Aiden and Karter?"

"No. Because I have the joy of experiencing house arrest and death by boredom. Welcome home, Wren."

His pupils did that dilation thing again, letting me know I'd struck a chord.

Good. He could go tell Mom and Dad that I was already wanting to leave. Maybe they'd be more accepting of the "I'm going away to college" bomb I planned to drop later.

"If you're bored, follow me." He left the kitchen without looking back.

I glanced at the pot rack hanging over the island and cursed my five-foot-two-inch T-rex reach before following in his wake.

He took the hall leading to my old bedroom. I narrowed my eyes when he walked through the door, fully understanding why I'd been displaced.

Bennett.

I entered the office and watched him unplug the second laptop from the desk.

"Here," he said, handing it to me. "Twelve subsidiaries are operating at a loss so far this year. Look at their expenses and find a way to mitigate further loss."

"Why didn't you just tell me to slam my head in the door?"

He sighed heavily. "I know you're smarter than you pretend to be. Do the work."

"What's in it for me?"

"What do you want?"

My attitude did a quick about-face. Bennett *never* negotiated. That was what made him so boring. Had he actually loosened up a little while I was gone?

I considered him as I thought about what I needed most. Backup, inarguably. But could I count on Bennett? No. I needed to start small with him and build up some trust that these negotiation tactics were safe...then BAM. I'd own him.

"My dear, *dear* Bennett, you've asked the right question."

His pupils flipped out, dilating and contracting at an alarmingly non-human rate, serving as a reminder that blatant flattery annoyed him. So I quickly toned it down.

"Going through five months of expenses for even half those subsidiaries is going to take forever. How about one, and you call Aiden to tell him I broke his moon lamp."

Bennett's typically stoic expression cracked a little, and I saw a very brief frown.

"Are you going to break his lamp?"

"Of course not. I know he loves that thing. I just want him to experience a little emotional damage. A teeny amount of harmless revenge for standing me up today. That's all."

"No deal."

I set the laptop on the desk and turned to walk away.

"One subsidiary, and I'll take you for a drive."

I whirled around. "With me behind the wheel?"

"Yes."

"You have yourself a deal."

Did I want to drive Bennett around? No, I did not. But this wasn't actually about getting something I wanted. This was about opening negotiations with the resident dictator.

I scooped up the laptop and settled sideways into the oversized chair positioned near the door. He didn't say anything about my choice of location, which was good. I knew I'd have questions he'd be able to answer.

The accounting classes I took in school helped me figure a lot out

17

on my own. I exported the expenses and created a spreadsheet with several pivot tables—by vendor, account, and user.

I immediately spotted several places where savings could be made. Office expenses were extremely high. Who still needed that much printer paper? It was called email. Save some trees. And why were there so many meals expensed? It was a car dealership.

Was Bennett messing with me?

I snuck a glance at him. He had his elbows on his desk and his hands clasped in front of him, putting his shoulders in a position that seriously strained his suit coat as he read something on his screen. Whatever it was, it couldn't be good. His jaw was clenched, and his pupils were wide.

Was he ever in a good mood? I doubted it.

Even if he was messing with me, I knew to let it slide until he looked less angry.

I typed up all the "misappropriations of funds" in a separate documentation, summarized my recommendations, then minimized those screens to download an old-school Minesweeper game for Bennett to find on the hard drive later.

When I stood, he looked up from his screen.

"What are you doing?"

"Getting a snack and moving around. Want something?"

He looked down at his screen without answering.

I shrugged and left his office with a better understanding of why he was at home and not at the main office. Wulf Enterprises would lose employees left and right with Bennett's cold presence.

Since it was already past five, I raided the fridge and found a square of lasagna that I could pop into the toaster oven. Mom didn't believe in microwaves. She said it changed the taste of food. My taste buds weren't as advanced as hers. Neither was my patience. Using the toaster oven took forever.

So, I set the timer and wandered my way upstairs to spread some torment via text.

Me: Well, that's disturbing.
Aiden: What?

I grinned, glad he was the one to take the bait.

Me: What I found in your room.
Karter: You're that bored that you're going through our rooms?
Me: Yes! Bennett made me do loss analysis on a subsidiary.
Aiden: I pity Bennett.
Karter: May he rest in peace.
Me: You should pity yourselves.

"What are you doing?"

Since I was lying on my back with my head toward the door, I had to arch my neck to see Bennett.

He didn't look happy. Again. Or maybe still.

He glanced at my neck. It probably was a little bold to expose my throat to someone who looked like he wanted to rip it out, so I sat up.

"Harassing Aiden and Karter while I wait for my dinner to warm."

"And the analysis?"

"Done."

"All twelve?"

"We agreed to one."

"You said it would take forever. It didn't." He stepped back and gestured for me to follow him.

"After you," I said with a smile.

His gaze narrowed on me in a way that looked like both a threat and a promise, and my brows shot up. He growled something I couldn't hear and stalked away.

Me: Bennett's in a mood. Come home soon.
Mom: We will. Love you.

"Soon" turned out to be ten at night. I was already in bed with Bennett's dumb laptop. I'd analyzed another subsidiary and had a good start on the third when I heard voices in the hallway.

I looked up as Mom and Dad walked in, smiling.

"Wrenly, I've missed you so much," Mom said, coming to hug me.

"I missed you, too, Mom. Dad." I smiled at him over her shoulder, and he smiled back. Mom was the touchy, affectionate one. Dad was the loving-from-a-distance one. I knew it was a mate thing.

"Sorry we weren't here to welcome you," he said.

"Is something bad happening at Wulf Enterprises? Milo said staff was cut, you've been at work all day, and Bennett has me doing expense analysis on loss-leading subsidiaries."

"Oh, sweetheart, no," Mom said, hugging me harder briefly before pulling back and meeting my gaze. "Everything is fine. I promise."

I didn't believe her for a second. She looked nervous, and if I had the nose she did, I'd bet my hard-won savings she'd smell nervous too.

"Okay. Fine. Don't tell me what's going on then."

She glanced at Dad, and they shared a look.

"Bennett said he gave you something to do because you were bored."

"I was. I was also unable to leave. Am I not allowed to take a car?"

They shared another look. This time, Mom's expression conveyed a hint of annoyance. Good. I hoped she gave Dad an earful for being too controlling.

"Of course you can take a car," she said. "Just let us know where you're going before you leave, okay? You know we worry."

"Okay. Tomorrow I want to take a car to go shopping."

"Tomorrow?" Dad said. "We were hoping you could start that job your mom mentioned tomorrow."

"Where am I working?"

Dad grinned. "Wulf Enterprises."

"Give it a try before you say no," Mom said quickly.

"Fine." I needed summer work for college expenses anyway.

"Perfect," Mom said, giving me another hug, then standing. "Bennett will drive you in at seven. Make sure to set your alarm."

"I can drive myself," I said.

"He's going to the office too. Why waste the gas?"

"Why can't I go with you then?"

"We worked late so that we can take tomorrow off." Mom smiled and waved goodnight before closing my door.

I stared after them in disbelief. They wanted *tomorrow* off? What about today, the day I came home for the first time in forever?

Closing the laptop with a snap, I set it aside and turned off the light.

It doesn't matter, Wrenly. Earn the money and reclaim your life. You've got this.

MOM AND DAD were already gone when I came downstairs for breakfast. Bennett sat at the table, reading a tablet and eating his omelette. He looked up when I entered.

His sweeping gaze was so neutral as it traveled down the length of me that I wasn't sure how to interpret it.

Then, he spoke.

"Don't you have something more...business casual?"

I looked down at my jeans and T-shirt, which were similar to what I'd worn the day before.

"I lived at a boarding school with a uniform for four years, Bennett, and I wasn't expecting to be pushed into working at Wulf Enterprises on my second day home. How would I have business casual clothes?"

"Mom sent you clothes. Purses. Shoes."

"Those weren't business casual, and I sold them for drugs and alcohol."

His gaze narrowed on me. "You're lying."

"And you're annoying. I guess we can't help ourselves." I pulled out a chair and reached over to steal a piece of toast off his plate. "How soon are we leaving? Do I have time to ask for an omelette too?"

He watched me take a bite of his toast and glanced at the door a second before a woman entered with another plate.

"Sandy?" I asked as she set it down in front of me.

She nodded. "It's nice to meet you, Miss Belak."

"Please call me Wrenly."

"I've made ham and cheese omelettes this morning. If you have any preferences in the future, let me know."

"I'm not a picky eater, so I'm happy with whatever you make me."

When she left, I dug in, eating quickly since it was close to seven. Once I finished, I stood with my plate in hand.

"Leave it. Sandy will get it. Are you ready?"

"Give me two more minutes."

I set the plate down and ran upstairs to gather my things and brush my teeth. Bennett was still in the same spot, minus the dishes, when I came back downstairs. I followed him through the kitchen, saying a quick word of thanks to Sandy, and out into the garage. He pulled a familiar key fob from his pocket and unlocked the car I'd taken the day before.

"Am I driving?" I asked.

"Not today. We need to make a stop on the way to work."

I didn't argue about the driving since I knew Wulf Enterprises was in the city and didn't care about the stop.

Bennett walked around the car and opened the door for me. It felt weird, but only because courtesy wasn't something I'd had much of over the last few years.

My phone buzzed as he shut the door.

Mom: Have a great first day, Wrenly. We'll see you after work.

Instead of responding, I set my phone on my lap and stared out the window as Bennett drove out of the garage. I loved Mom and Dad, but they made it so damn hard to like them at times. How could they not see that they'd abandoned me? Again.

Bennett didn't talk on the way into the city, which was fine since I was paying attention to the route until he reached a bustling area and turned into a parking garage. I didn't question it and got out.

He gave me a strange look as he joined me.

"Next time, wait for me to open your door."

I glanced around the parking garage. It was well-lit, clean, and in a business area. Did he think something would happen to me with him standing on the other side of the car?

"Wrenly."

He said my name with enough irritation and warning that I knew not to start anything with him.

"Yeah, sure. Next time, I'll wait."

Like a bodyguard, he walked beside me out to the sidewalk.

The cool breeze swept my hair to the side. It felt nice. Actually, it felt nice just to walk around in public. I looked up at the tall buildings, trying to figure out which one was Wulf Enterprises. I didn't know much about the family business, except that it and its subsidiaries employed thousands of people. That seemed pretty big to me.

Bennett walked so close to me that his hand brushed mine twice. Did he really think this area was dangerous, or did he think I was that clueless? When he caught my arm, I jumped and looked around, thinking there was something wrong, as he steered me toward a glass door.

Too late, I saw the mannequin in the window next to it. Resistance was futile against Bennett's determination to guide me into the upscale boutique store.

"Good morning, Mr. Wulf," a woman said. "We have a selection ready in the fitting room."

"Thank you."

My steps slowed as I navigated through the sparsely stocked store and around a wall that separated the storefront from the fitting rooms. Another woman waited for us there and indicated the rack of clothes outside an open door.

"The grey one first," Bennett said, sitting on the sofa there.

The woman took the suit jacket and matching skirt off the rack, along with a pair of matching heels.

I stared at the heels.

"Wrenly?" Bennett said, his tone laced with impatience.

I struggled to suppress the anger simmering beneath the surface.

"No."

"What?"

I met his gaze. "No, I'm not changing into that."

"Put it in the changing room," he said without looking away from me.

The woman did and then quickly excused herself, leaving me alone with Bennett, which was just fine by me.

Locked in a silent battle of wills, neither of us looked away from the other. Then he slowly stood. His movement had an animalistic, barely restrained edge that set off all my warning bells...as I knew he intended.

He crowded into my space.

Rather than back down, I crossed my arms and tipped my head back to look up at him.

"I will become your worst nightmare if you push this," I said, meaning every word.

He took a slow, deep breath. "Will you tell me why you don't want to change?"

"Tell me why I need to."

His jaw ticced. "Why are you nice to everyone else, but defiant or rude to me?"

"You reap what you sow, Bennett. When have you ever been nice to me?"

He frowned slightly, studying me, then backed up a step.

"Mom and Dad asked me to take you somewhere right after work. It's supposed to be a surprise. You'll feel out of place if you go in jeans."

I uncrossed my arms, hating that Mom's manipulations were already starting.

"Thank you for telling me. How dressy do I need to be?"

"Business casual is fine."

"What will the other women there be wearing? Business casual or something dressier?"

"Dressier."

"Okay." I turned to look at the rack, and the saleswoman magically reappeared, proving she'd probably been listening from the other side of the wall.

"Do you have any cocktail dresses and flats?"

She hurried to bring me two options—a dusky blue and a mauve. I tried them on and decided to go with the blue one, along with a nude flat, strappy sandal that didn't hurt my feet. When I left the dressing room in jeans, Bennett didn't comment. He just paid the bill and carried the bag back to the car with me.

The drive to the office only took another ten minutes. We were late when we pulled into the underground parking garage, but I didn't think it would matter much.

To show that I could be cooperative, I waited in my seat until Bennett opened the door for me. I even threw in a thank you to prove I was the bigger person. He still had the nerve to be annoyed, though. I saw his pupils dilate slightly before he looked away.

Whatever.

I followed him to the elevator, which required a badge to operate. The doors opened to a lobby teeming with people and a bank of main elevators.

People said good morning to Bennett but gave me curious side glances—whether it was because I was with him or because I was wearing jeans while everyone else was in skirts or slacks was up for debate.

We rode the elevators up to the twelfth floor. A reception desk sat just inside a set of glass doors.

The woman smiled at Bennett and said, "Good morning."

Her sweeping glance at me bordered on rude, and I internally sighed. It was going to be a long summer.

Did I need the money that badly if I had already saved the first year's tuition? Unfortunately, I did. I wasn't sure what Mom and Dad's reactions would be when I revealed my plans, and I wanted to be financially prepared for complete independence if necessary. That meant tuition and living expenses. Possibly a car payment too. And experience working at Wulf Enterprises would look good on my resume if I had to work somewhere else next summer.

Bennett didn't even acknowledge the woman as he opened the door to the right of the reception desk. It led to a larger area filled with desks. He continued along the wall, reaching a hallway that had a few conference rooms and connected to another area filled with cubicles and desks.

He stopped by the first one, where an impeccably dressed brunette woman sat in a pantsuit that hugged her curves so tightly that it probably gave her back support. Her caramel gaze lifted to Bennett's without even a flicker in my direction.

"Milena, this is Wrenly." He looked at me. "Milena will show you around and get you set up with an access badge. Let me know if you run into any trouble."

"Yep."

I heard a disbelieving snort from the nearby sea of desks. Bennett looked away to stare at the offender. Some poor idiot would be lucky not to be fired by the end of the day.

"Seriously, I got it. You can go," I said, hoping to spare whoever it was.

He glanced at me then left with his jaw ticcing.

Milena waited until he was out of hearing distance to say, "Let's save ourselves time and skip the tour since we both know you're not here to actually work."

I turned to her. "Oh? Then what am I doing here?"

Someone laughed quietly.

"Making the Wulfs feel good about their philanthropy. Why else would they employ the normie they adopted?"

Mom's voice rang in my head. *Don't say no until you give it a try.*

I knew the Wulf's loved me, but couldn't they see how much I didn't fit into their world?

"Does this mean you're refusing to give me the tour then?" I asked. "It's going to be hard to explain why I don't know my way around or have an access badge when my benefactors ask me."

Her pupils pulsed larger with irritation as I held her gaze.

"Useless," she said under her breath as she stood.

If she meant the tour, she was right. She showed me where the break room and bathrooms were, got my badge from Human Resources, and then led me to my desk, which was located in the exterior part of Bennett's split office suite. I knew it was his suite because of the big nameplate screwed to the wall beside the door.

"Just do whatever you're told to do," she said before leaving me there.

The desk, which was fully stocked with writing implements, paper, and fancy leather-bound notebooks, in addition to a laptop and a large monitor, was positioned adjacent to the glass wall that separated my area from Bennett's main office area.

The blinds were currently closed, along with the door, so I didn't know if he was in there or not.

I sat at the desk and called Mom.

"Hi, Sweetheart. Are you settled in at work?"

"I guess. What exactly is my job?"

"Didn't Bennett tell you? You're his assistant."

"Excuse me?"

I couldn't have heard that right...

CHAPTER THREE

"You want me to spend my summer fetching coffee for Bennett?" I asked in disbelief.

"Of course not. You're not his secretary; you're his assistant. It's a much higher-paid position."

While I liked the idea of more money, I knew better than to fall for her trap.

"Mmm-hmm. Why am I really here, Mom?"

"Because he needs your help."

"And I'm betting there are at least a dozen more qualified people to help him. Why me?"

"First, because you've already proven you're qualified. We saw the analysis reports you finished, Wrenly. It would have taken someone else twice as long. You're smarter than you realize."

She sounded like Bennett.

"And second?" I asked.

She sighed. "Bennett's been struggling lately. I think you can bring a smile to his face."

"I think the last time he smiled was when he had gas as a baby."

Mom's startled laugh was cut off when Dad took the phone.

Though he tried to muffle it, I heard him say, "You're only encouraging her to misbehave."

When Mom came back on the phone, only a hint of humor lingered in her voice.

"I don't want to hide anything from you," she said. "Bennett's been through five assistants in the last four months."

"Sounds like the problem is Bennett, not the assistants."

"You're right. Females keep throwing themselves at him, and his patience is…well, it's thin."

"So find him a male assistant."

"We tried. It didn't stop the attention he doesn't want."

"And you think having me here will stop it?"

Mom chuckled. "Bennett isn't the only prickly member in this family."

"Ouch, Mom," I said without really meaning it. I knew I hadn't been the nicest to them in the past and that they didn't understand why. But that was my problem, not hers.

"Fine. I'll try, but don't blame me if I'm fired on the first day."

"He won't fire you."

"Right…"

"You have a good day, Sweetie. We'll see you tonight."

I hung up after saying goodbye and wondered what she had planned for tonight. Probably nothing I'd like.

Rather than sit and do nothing, I got up and knocked on Bennett's door. I didn't hear anything from inside and was going to go back to my desk when the door suddenly opened.

Bennett had taken his jacket off and loosened his tie. He looked a little wild in the eyes, too.

Huh. Maybe Mom hadn't been lying.

"Good morning, Mr. Wulf. Is there anything that I, your lowly assistant, can help you with?"

His pupils pulsed in time with his heartbeat.

"You're going to give yourself a stroke if you can't calm down," I said. "Seriously, what do you need me to do so you don't start beheading people at the office?"

He studied me for a moment, and I thought he was going to say something not so nice to match his mood. But he didn't.

"Keep going through the subsidiaries, and if my door's closed, I'm not seeing anyone. You're the exception. If you need something, knock and then come in. If I'm on the phone, give me a moment."

"You got it. What time do you take a lunch break?"

"I don't. We can order something in."

"Okay. I'll order something for twelve-thirty then."

He nodded and, after a brief pause, closed the door in my face.

Mentally shrugging off his moodiness, I returned to my desk and resumed reviewing the expenses. It soon became apparent why Bennett's patience was thin.

"Is Mr. Wulf in?" a woman asked.

I tore my focus from the numbers in front of me and looked up at a petite blonde who was holding a contract folder.

"He's in but unavailable," I said.

"Really? I checked his schedule, and he didn't have any meetings or calls."

I shrugged. "He said he was unavailable if the door is closed." I gestured to the door. "As we can both see, it's closed."

"But I need this contract signed right away."

I held out my hand. She looked at my hand, then met my gaze.

"Let him know Andri has a contract that needs his attention."

"Will do," I said.

She stared at me, and I stared back.

"Aren't you going to call him?" she asked impatiently.

"No. Either hand me the contract so I can pass it to him, or try calling him yourself to set up a time to hand it off in person."

Her eye twitched. "I've tried. He doesn't pick up."

Rather than continue to debate with her, I dismissively looked at my screen. She got the hint and went away. Another woman showed up thirty minutes later. Then another...and another.

It kept the morning entertaining when it would have been otherwise mind-numbing.

When the receptionist from the main entry arrived just after twelve-thirty with the food order, I was more than ready for a break.

"Is Mr. Wulf inside?" she asked.

"I'll take that for him," I said. "Thanks for bringing it back."

She didn't argue but did give his office door, which had remained firmly closed all morning, a sad look before leaving.

I got up and knocked on the door before opening it. He wasn't at his desk or reclining on what looked like a tempting nap-sofa. The other door in the office, presumably the bathroom, was closed. So I left the food on his desk.

Then, I slapped a sticky note on the outside of his closed office door, grabbed my things, and headed out for my lunch. I received the same side-eye leaving as I had when I'd arrived. But once I was on the street outside the building, I easily blended into the crowd, happily walking until something to eat caught my eye. Since I wasn't sure how long I had for lunch, I got it to-go and even ordered an extra dessert for Bennett. Maybe something sweet would improve his mood.

My phone rang as I was checking out.

I looked down, saw Bennett's name on the screen, and debated my approach before answering.

"Hey, Boss. Do you like strawberry or lime better?"

I knew the question threw him off whatever he'd been about to say when he didn't immediately answer.

"If you say nothing, you get nothing," I said.

"Strawberry," he finally said.

"Good choice. I'll be back in ten. I left a note on your door so they leave you alone."

"I saw the note. 'Knock and Die' seems a little extreme."

"Has anyone knocked?"

"No."

"Then, I'd call it effective. I'll be back in ten."

I hung up before he could say anything else and happily window-shopped my way back to the office.

Bennett's door was closed, and the note remained affixed. However, the blinds to his office were open in the section that gave him a direct line of sight to my desk, which meant he knew I'd returned.

I purposely didn't make eye contact as I set my to-go bag down and took out his strawberry dessert.

A hand reached around me and plucked the bag from my grasp.

"Inside," Bennett said.

I hadn't even heard him open the office door. Smoothing out my unhappy expression, I turned around and followed him into his office.

"Close the door," he said.

Obviously, I thought.

If he were smart, he would install one of those devices that automatically closed the door on its own. Maybe even something that would deliver a mild shock when someone knocked on it.

"Sit." He pointed at the chair across from his desk and started taking out the food I'd bought. "Why didn't you order delivery for yourself?"

I accepted my lunch from him and sat.

"Because I wanted a break. The number of women I've fielded for you is impressive. They weren't all bad. The receptionist seems nice."

He didn't comment.

"Personally, I'm not a fan of Milena or Andri. By the way, Andri said she had a contract that needed your attention. Not sure how real it was but figured she could email if it was important."

"It's not. All contracts that come in are forwarded to me digitally."

I nodded and watched him sit with his fancy strawberry-laden treat in a cup.

"So what am I going to do once I'm done with the expense evaluation?" I asked. "I doubt it will last me the rest of the day."

"There are more subsidiaries."

"Yaaay," I said flatly.

"I could use your help taking meeting notes this afternoon if you'd rather do that," he said as he scooped out his first bite.

"Does it include protecting your virtue? Why are they so obsessed with you?"

The scowl he gave me carried a hint of hurt.

"I mean, besides the obvious—wealthy heir to Wulf Enterprises and likely future pack Alpha."

"Isn't that enough?" he asked.

I shrugged indifferently and started eating my lunch.

"What are the meetings about?" I asked between bites.

"Buying companies. Some will be our people pitching companies to acquire, and some will be with company owners to get to know their businesses more in depth."

"Sure. I can take notes."

The meetings saved me from having to answer the question I'd been answering all morning, which was whether "Mr. Wulf" was in his office. I began to learn more about Wulf Enterprises and Bennett, too.

Wulf Enterprises was huge, and Bennett could be personable when he chose to be. He greeted men with a handshake and introduced me as "the most important person in his life," his assistant, Wrenly. Everyone he met was super respectful of him, too. It was a little weird to see that side of Bennett instead of the serious, strict side I remembered.

I sat next to him and took the best notes I could, which I was sure weren't that great, considering how many times he watched me make them.

After the final meeting wrapped up and Bennett went to walk the guy out, I headed back to his office suite.

Andri was waiting by my desk.

"He's not in," I said before she could ask.

"I know. That's why I'm waiting."

He rounded the corner, and she was quick to latch onto his arm.

"I don't have a ride to the reception tonight. Can I ride with you?"

He smoothly detangled himself from her, gave me a hard stare, and continued walking toward his office.

Andri took a step to follow him.

"Wait a second," I said.

She paused to look at me. It was enough time for him to close his door.

"He's in, but he doesn't want to be disturbed," I said.

Her face flushed, and she turned around and walked away.

I waited until she cleared the outer door to knock and let myself into Bennett's office. He was standing at his desk with his back to the door.

"What reception?" I asked.

He sighed and lifted the bag he was holding. The one with the clothes he bought this morning.

"The one we're going to. Go change."

He indicated the bathroom door. I snagged the bag on my way past him.

If staff are going, maybe it's a paid reception, I silently told myself as I changed.

Although I'd selected the most modest option of the two the associate had given me, the skirt was more form-fitting than I would have liked and showed my underwear line. I could have ditched them, but I imagined the emotional and mental trauma I would have if Dad figured out I'd gone commando. It didn't matter that shifters group-stripped for pack runs. *I* wasn't pack. So I ignored my underwear lines, grateful that at least the sandals were okay.

I stepped out of the bathroom and endured Bennett's scrutinizing gaze with an unhappy frown.

"You don't like it," he said.

"No kidding. Please tell me I won't need to suffer in this for long."

"You look pretty."

"It's tight, and it's uncomfortable, but yippee for looking pretty. Why can't we just go home and say we forgot?"

He sighed, and I caught a glimpse of his frustration.

"Ugh, fine. Is there any way we can skip out early? Can you pretend to have an appendicitis attack? Heart attack? A lazy eye? Anything?"

My humor wasn't appreciated.

He rubbed his hand down his face, which I found pretty funny.

"Don't even try lying to me and say you want to go," I said. "If Andri is going, that means all the women who were trying to get your attention today will be there."

His jaw muscles twitched.

"Fine. I'll help you if you help me," he said.

I wanted to crow.

"Name your terms and name your price," I said.

"You keep every female from touching me, and we'll leave within an hour."

"Exception being Mom, of course," I amended.

"You and Mom and Grandma."

"Grandma's going to be there?"

He nodded.

"What are the rules? Can I offend people?"

"You will have to deal with the consequences of your actions."

I made a face and sighed. "Fine. Polite-bitchiness only then. Does the timer start now, in the car, or when we get there?"

"When we get there," he said.

I groaned but agreed and let him lead me out of the office. Most of the people were already gone—the few who remained called out a farewell to Bennett. The elevators were less crowded leaving than they'd been arriving.

However, the garage had a few more people than Bennett would have liked. Five women waited around the car.

"Bet you wish the timer started now," I said with an innocent smile.

Bennett growled. I laughed and strode forward through the women waiting by the passenger door.

"Sorry, ladies, I called frontsies in perpetuity thirteen years ago. I think the back seat's open, though."

Bennett grabbed my upper arm, stopping me from opening my door, and opened it for me. Once I was in and he was outside with everyone else, he said something that had them all glaring at me and walking away.

I didn't comment on it when he got in and started the car.

"Is there going to be good food there, at least?" I asked as he drove.

"Mom arranged everything."

"That doesn't answer my question."

He didn't respond.

I glanced at him, wondering why he'd reverted to his usual sulky self. It hadn't been bad working with him today. He'd answered questions and had acted mostly like a normal person.

Was Mom right? Was his patience that thin because of the women chasing him?

If he were Aiden or Karter, I would have asked if he was dating anyone and how serious the relationship was. But I wasn't as close to Bennett as I was with them. I'd never played with him growing up— he'd been sent off to school not too long after I'd moved in—and he'd never called me while I was at school like they had. To be fair, I'd never called him either.

I could ask Mom. She'd know. She knew everything about us... for the most part. Maybe if he liked someone and made it public, the women in the office would back off a little. I made a face. If he liked someone, Mom would have already thought of that.

"What's wrong?" he asked.

"Not liking the direction of my thoughts," I said, turning to look out the window.

"What are you thinking about?"

"I'd rather stop thinking about it if it's all the same to you. How much longer until we get there?"

"Soon."

Fifteen minutes later, I walked up the flight of red carpeted steps to the freaking *museum* while wishing the car would have broken down.

"New deal," I said. "We go home, I'll take the blame for not showing up, *and* I'll work for you for free all summer."

"No deal," he said.

"Come on, we'd both come out winners."

"Are you going to walk, or do I have to carry you?"

"Princess, backpack, fireman, or over the shoulder?"

He arched a brow at me, and I pouted. His gaze dipped to my mouth, and his pupils flickered.

"Princess," he said without looking away. "Mom would kill me if I tried any of the other three. But we both know I'm not carrying you in." He offered me his arm.

I rolled my eyes and slipped my hand around his impressively firm forearm, letting him guide me up the stairs.

Inside, people mingled in the sectioned-off main lobby where tables had been set up with appetizers and drinks. The body count was high enough to necessitate my hold on Bennett. It kept him unavailable to other potential companions and prevented us from being separated.

Mom and Dad stood off to the side, chatting with another couple. I spotted Grandma sitting at a table. But Aiden and Karter were nowhere to be seen.

"Wrenly," Mom said, weaving her way to us. "Welcome home, my sweet girl."

I released Bennett long enough to let Mom hug me and then reclaimed his arm. Considering the long looks he was getting from around the room, I understood his need for protection.

"You really didn't need to throw a party for me, Mom," I said.

"Of course we did. We want everyone to know you're ours."

Not to welcome me home, but to claim me. Was I some kind of toy?

"Trust me, everyone is well aware of what you've done for me over the years."

Mom frowned, and I smiled to take the sting out of my comment.

"I'm a person, not a possession you need to claim, Mom. I know you love me, and that's enough. Now, who do you want me to meet?"

"Meet?"

"Isn't that the point of this? You're trying to set me up with some guy?"

Mom's surprised gaze flicked to Bennett, and I suddenly understood. It wasn't me who needed to meet someone. It was him. My party was just an excuse to get Bennett to mingle with the single pack-females. I wanted to smack my forehead for not seeing it sooner.

He was going to owe me big after this.

"Before Bennett takes me around the room to mingle, why don't we start with a drink?" I said to smoothly transition from my question to appeasing Mom without throwing Bennett under the bus.

I looked up at Bennett. "I could go for a glass of wine. What about you?"

"One glass," Mom said firmly before he nodded.

Legal age wasn't strictly enforced at these kinds of things, thankfully.

"Have fun." She kissed my cheek, and he led me toward the temporary bar.

While he asked for a glass of something that sounded French, I looked around the room. A few familiar faces blended in with the sea of unfamiliar ones. Storm and her crew were off to one side, talking and laughing. They all looked like they belonged at the party, with perfectly styled and accessorized hair, makeup, and dresses. Not an underwear line in sight.

"Are there any friends you'd like to talk to?" Bennett asked as he handed me my glass.

I took a sip to distract my face from subtitling my thoughts.

Did he seriously think I had any friends here? I'd been gone for seven years. And before that, only Aiden and Karter had ever hung out with me. Elementary school with the pack girls had been a brutal game of "make Wrenly cry."

"Why don't we check out the art first?" I asked instead of giving any direct answer.

I held my glass in one hand and his arm in the other and let him lead me to the first sculpture. Neither of us talked as we looked at it. I wondered if he was counting down the seconds like I was.

"Bennett," a woman said from behind us. "If you needed a companion for tonight, you should have called me."

I glanced at the brunette with startlingly silver eyes, saw the challenge in them, and turned us to face her.

"Your dress is stunning," I said. "I'm sorry I stole Bennett tonight. I'm sure he'll think of you next time, though."

Her gaze flicked to me, assessing. I kept my neutral smile firmly in place.

"There won't be a next time," Bennett said.

I saw the desperation flicker across the woman's face. She was closer to Bennett's age than I was, and I'd bet she'd been holding out hope that he'd pick her as a mate during a pack run.

"I'm Wrenly, Bennett's sister," I said, holding out my hand to her.

"You're not my sister," Bennett said before the woman could decide to take it.

His words didn't hurt me. Not anymore. It wasn't the first time he'd said that, and it wouldn't be the last. But the label seemed to appease the woman because she took my hand in hers.

"I'm Mosslyn. It's nice to meet you, Wrenly. We'll need to stay in touch."

I nodded and watched her walk off, knowing damn well the only reason she would contact me was to try to worm her way into

Bennett's graces. Unfortunately for her, I was the wrong person for that.

"Ready to move to the next piece?" I asked.

For the next thirty-five minutes, we repeated the process. Women approached. I politely shielded and then softened any cold rejection Bennett uttered.

And I drank all my wine.

Feeling only slightly buzzed, I glanced longingly at the server weaving through the room.

"Don't even think about it," Bennett said.

"Can I think about a two-minute bathroom break, or is that against the terms of our agreement?"

He actually looked like he was debating it.

I wanted to threaten to pee on his shoes, but there were too many people with much better hearing than I had, and I didn't want to embarrass Mom or Dad.

"Two minutes," he said.

"Aye-aye, Captain." I gave him a small salute and made a beeline for the bathroom. When I exited, a server happened to be by the door with one flute left on his tray.

"Perfect timing." I snagged the flute, downed the contents in a few large gulps, and set it back on his tray.

CHAPTER FOUR

BENNETT WAS STILL where I'd left him. He glanced at his watch before he spotted me, and I made a face at him. Was he seriously timing me?

"Did I miss anything interesting?" I asked.

"No." He reclaimed my hand and wrapped it around his arm.

I moved to stand beside him, but he suddenly captured my chin with his free hand and leaned in, bringing his face close to mine.

My eyes went wide, and I tried to push him away.

"What are you doing?" I whispered harshly, which only called more attention to us.

"What did you drink?" he demanded.

My face started to heat, and the urge to kick him warred with the need to run and hide from the embarrassment of the moment.

"Wine, remember?"

His gaze narrowed. "Wrenly."

The warning in his tone spoke volumes. I was poking his wolf. Why then weren't his pupils going crazy? I had no idea. Nothing about Bennett ever made much sense to me.

"Let go of my face while I'm asking nicely," I said.

His gaze dipped to my mouth.

If he leaned in and sniffed, I would not be responsible for my actions.

He leaned in...

...and brushed his mouth against mine.

My eyes nearly popped out of my head. I jerked myself out of his hold so hard that I stumbled into someone else. A few giggles rang out around us. I barely noticed as I spun around and pushed my way through people toward the exit.

Mom caught me before I reached it.

"Come with me." She steered me toward the sectioned-off area of the museum.

A guard nodded and unclasped the rope for us to pass. She kept leading me along a hall until we'd turned several corners and entered an office with a sofa.

"I'm sorry," I said as soon as the door shut. "I didn't mean to make a scene. It won't happen again. I promise."

She hugged me hard. "It's okay, Wrenly. I brought you here so you could calm down, not to scold you. What happened?"

She didn't know? She didn't see?

My face heated further at the thought of her having witnessed my supposed brother kissing me.

"I snuck a second glass of wine, and Bennett embarrassed me because of it." One hundred percent true. "Do I have to keep working for him?"

Mom smiled and walked me over to the couch.

"He's a bit difficult, isn't he?"

"Very."

She nodded and patted my hand. "I heard today went well, though. No one cried, and nothing was thrown."

"Does he seriously throw things?"

"Sometimes," she said.

"He's completely ridiculous. But I get why he's prickly. If I had that many women trying to climb me like a tree, I'd have mood swings too." I sighed and leaned back into the couch in a very unladylike way that had Mom smiling. "Their attention never seemed to bother Aiden or Karter, though. Speaking of...why aren't they here?"

"They're meeting and mingling with other packs."

I studied her face. Mingling? Hadn't Karter said they were being groomed for management?

"They're looking for mates, aren't they?" I asked.

She just smiled.

"Why doesn't Bennett go do that then? Won't he be a lot calmer once he finds his mate?"

Mom chuckled and smoothed back some of my hair.

"Our males typically don't 'calm down' until the first child is born."

"Lovely. I pity the girl who ends up with Bennett."

"I don't," she said. "He's more patient than most. He'll give her the time she needs, even if it drives him crazy."

"Well, that sounds awful for everyone around him since he's already crazy. Wait...he's already found her and is purposely waiting, isn't he?"

She smiled. "If you're curious, ask Bennett."

"That feels like a setup. No thanks."

"Are you feeling better?"

"Nope. I want to leave."

"If you ask Bennett, I'm sure he'll take you home."

"Bennett is the last person I want to ask anything. He's the reason I want to leave."

She chuckled and tugged me to my feet.

"Then he owes you."

When she opened the door and walked out, I saw the person in question waiting for us.

"I'll leave you two to make peace." Mom said with a glance at me before leaving.

Bennett stayed where he was in the hallway, his hands in his pockets as he leaned against the wall. His calm in the face of my lingering discomfort annoyed me.

"Why, Bennett? I was *nice* to you today. After the shopping incident, I did everything you asked, without question or complaint, no matter how mind-numbing it was. Even keeping the women away, like you wanted. Why did you embarrass me like that?"

"Embarrass you?"

He pushed away from the wall and stalked closer, stopping inches from me. His jaw ticced, and his pupils were reacting now...as if *I* were the problem.

I stomped on his foot as hard as I could with my heel.

Surprise flashed across his face.

I retreated a step and managed to look contrite as I said, "I acted rashly and hurt you, Bennett. I'm sorry." Contrite left my demeanor as I poked him in the chest. "Do you see how that's done? It's called an apology."

He had me pinned against a wall with my hands over my head a second later.

All the air vanished from my lungs as I stared up at him.

"Am I acting rashly, Wrenly?" His eyes searched mine.

I struggled to make sense of what was happening. Bennett had me pinned against the wall, and he was looking at me like he...

Nope.

No.

Not today, man-devil.

I took a slow, deep breath.

"I don't know what game you're playing, but you have two seconds before I scream for Mom and embarrass the whole family."

He didn't react like I thought he would. No anger flashed in his eyes. He simply let me go.

"Maybe you'll be interested in playing later," he said.

He was a psycho. That was the only explanation.

"Take me home, Bennett."

THE CONFUSION and tension from the evening followed me in my dreams until an unfamiliar-sounding alarm woke me.

It's not mine.

My eyes flew open, and I bolted upright, ready to deflect and throw a punch.

Bennett's stoic expression cracked as he took in my balled fist and raised arm. I saw worry and immediately pointed to the door to prevent him from asking any questions.

"Out."

He didn't move. Instead, his gaze searched mine.

"What did you think was happening, Wrenly?"

"Someone with bad intentions was waking me up. And, look, I was right. I'm not going to work today."

"Grandma is downstairs. She wants to talk to you."

He left the room without saying anything else, and I flopped back onto the bed for a minute so my pulse could return to normal.

Those days of waking up in fight or flight are over, Wrenly, I told myself. *Let it go, or they will never let you go.*

My thoughts went back to what Bennett had done the night before. After some rest, I could see it differently.

He didn't kiss you, Wrenly. He was just being an ass and trying to figure out what you drank. It's not a big deal. None of this is a big deal. Stay focused. Nothing else matters but convincing them you're independent and can manage your own life.

I got out of bed, quickly showered, and dressed.

Grandma and Bennett were sitting at the table. Both had already finished eating as I sat and accepted a plate from Sandy.

"I heard you get to work with Bennett," Grandma said. "If he gives you trouble, let me know, and I'll break his legs for you."

I paused with my fork halfway to my mouth, unsure if she was serious or not. Shifters healed remarkably quickly after all.

"A clean break or something that's going to need pins?" I asked.

She laughed so hard she cried.

"And that's why you'll always be my favorite, Wrenly. Don't you ever change."

I still wasn't sure if she'd been serious, so I just smiled and listened to her scold Bennett while I ate.

"If you drive Wrenly away, you'll have more than me to worry about, Bennett. Six in three months is going too far."

"It wasn't six in three months, Grandma," he said calmly. "And no one complained."

She snorted. "Only because some of them were female and desperate. Heard you tried to throw one out a window."

I looked at Bennett in shock, waiting for his denial. He didn't say *anything*.

"Instead of getting him a different assistant, you should have gotten him therapy," I said to Grandma.

She grinned at me. "Doubt that would have helped."

"So are you just here for a morning lung workout? Not that I mind hearing you lay into Bennett," I added quickly.

"No. I'm going to work with you two. It's been a while since I visited the office, and I thought we could chat on the way."

Skillfully managed yet again, I found myself in the backseat with Grandma, going to work like I didn't want to, while Grandma told me about her neighbor's vacation mishap that had landed her in the hospital.

Honestly, I loved Grandma. She treated me like I was her favorite person. Whenever I'd gotten into trouble with Aiden or Karter in my youth, she'd always sided with me. Not that Mom and Dad hadn't, they'd just tried to be a tiny bit more impartial. Grandma was blatant in her favoritism. And it never bothered anyone in the family, even though I occasionally felt guilty about it.

When we arrived at the office, she rode the elevators with us to the administrative floor, but as soon as she saw me to my desk, she excused herself to visit Mom, saying she'd return later.

I shook my head and sat down, knowing full well she wouldn't be back. Her only purpose today had been to ensure I went to work. She'd been like that when I'd gone to boarding school, too. I hadn't wanted to go, but Grandma had shown up that morning, and I'd found myself on a plane anyway.

Mom was a master manager of people and situations, and she'd learned it all from Grandma.

Sighing, I opened my laptop and got to work. Movement in the glass drew my attention. I looked up at Bennett's office and saw him standing behind the glass, the shade wide open. He crooked a finger to beckon me.

"What do you want?"

He shook his head and tapped his ear.

As if I believed for even a second that he couldn't hear me. With a sigh, I stood and poked my head into his office.

"What do you want?"

He caught my wrist and pulled me in, shutting the door firmly and leaning a shoulder against it so I couldn't leave. His pupils were doing their thing again as he stared at me. Saying nothing, I waited.

His jaw started to twitch. "Why are you being so difficult?"

"Difficult? You beckoned, and I came in. You're the one being difficult, pulling at me and scowling for no reason."

The tic in his jaw grew more pronounced, and he looked away from me.

"Why don't you just say whatever is eating at you so we can both move on with our day?"

"Why are you avoiding me?" he asked, his gaze locking on mine.

"How exactly am I avoiding you? I ate breakfast with you and drove in the same car. And I'm standing here, aren't I?"

"You didn't want to do any of this."

"No kidding. But I don't think you're one to talk. You've avoided stuff you don't want to do, too."

"Like what?"

"You could have talked to some of the women there last night. Or the women here."

He averted his gaze again, and I sighed. "You're right. Not my business. I'll work on being more tolerable at work to make this summer go faster if you're willing to do the same. A little bit of patience and cooperation and then I'll be out of your hair."

I didn't particularly like the way he straightened away from the door and took a step closer to me.

"What do you mean?" he asked.

"Physical intimidation stopped working on me three years ago. Save your effort. Now, if you don't mind, I'd like to get back to work. You should do the same. The faster we finish, the sooner we can leave."

I walked around him and opened the door. "Let me know if you need a Xanax laced coffee or something."

When I sat at my desk, I didn't check to see if he was still watching me. Whatever bug had climbed into his brain wasn't my problem. I set to work and didn't look up again until my phone buzzed with a reminder at ten to order lunch.

I was a little surprised that no one had tried bothering Bennett yet until I glanced up and saw him pacing in front of his desk.

Yeah, they're smart not to interrupt whatever that is.

I placed an order with a nearby grill and got up to stretch my legs. On the way to the bathroom, Grandma spotted me through Mom's office windows and waved. I waved back and continued to the bathroom, knowing very well that her wave hadn't been a greeting but a summons. She was waiting in the hallway when I exited.

"How's Bennett today?"

"In a mood, but you already knew that, or you wouldn't have been at the house this morning."

She grinned at me.

"He's a prickly one, but he's easy enough to manage once you know the secret."

"What's the secret?"

"Flattery."

"Pfft. Been there. Tried that. It only makes him more annoyed."

"Then you're not doing it right."

She hooked her arm around mine. "You're really pretty today, Wrenly. That top makes your mischievous eyes sparkle. Your backside looks good in those jeans, too. It'd look even better in a skirt with some heels."

I snorted. "I'm not sure if you're flattering me or hitting on me, Grandma."

She shrugged a little, but her grin said it didn't matter which she meant. She'd proven her point because, even though I knew she was playing a game, I'd liked what she'd said.

While I was pondering that, she neatly navigated me back to my desk and walked right into Bennett's office, ignoring his scowl and the fact she'd interrupted his pacing. She shut the door and closed the blinds.

Shaking my head, I went back to work until she reemerged almost twenty minutes later.

"I'll see you later, my little Wren. Don't forget what I said."

"Yeah, yeah." I watched her leave and wondered if I could get away with sneaking out with her. Probably not.

I picked up my phone.

Me: Do you know what some people my age do after graduating?

Karter: What?

Me: They travel. I wish I'd switched my ticket to Iceland instead. I hear it's lovely this time of year.

Aiden: Don't you like being home?

Me: I feel like this conversation is going to be screenshot and sent to Mom and Dad.

Karter: Nah, we're just trying to figure out what's wrong.

Did he honestly not know? My only two friends weren't here. What was the point of coming home? Just so Mom and Grandma could manipulate me into doing what they wanted?

I tossed my phone onto my desk, leaned back into my chair, and closed my eyes.

Just eleven weeks, Wrenly. You can do this. Eleven weeks and then you'll be moving into the dorms at—

Something tickled my nose, and my eyes flew open at the same time my hands came up.

Bennett choked and coughed, grabbing his throat, which I'd hit, as he straightened away from me.

"One, I didn't mean to do that. Two, being tolerable means not sneaking up on people."

He stopped coughing, studied me for several seconds, then pivoted on his heel and retreated to his office. The slamming door didn't even make me jump.

I picked up my phone from my desk.

Me: How much am I making an hour?
Mom: Administrative assistants start at ten dollars above minimum wage. However, since you're working with Bennett, we added another five dollars.
Me: Add another five for the person who comes after me, or they'll never make it past a week.
Mom: I'll talk to him.
Me: Don't bother. It only makes him worse.

I tossed my phone onto my desk again and happened to look up and catch him staring at me through the window. With slow grace, I lifted my hand and flipped him off. He closed the blinds.

Psychopath.

And Grandma wanted me to flatter him? It would never work. Any flattery that didn't send him into a rage would probably only stroke his already unstable ego.

"Is Bennett in? I need these documents signed."

I looked up at the woman and debated my answer.

"Bennett's in...sane. If you open that door in the hopes of gaining his attention, it'll work, but probably not the way you want. He's extra crazy today, and I heard he likes making people cry. So you do you."

She looked from me to the door.

"You're not going to stop me?"

"Even if I could, I'm not sure I'd want to today. He's being an ass and deserves some irritation."

She looked torn.

"There's a better opportunity. His food is being delivered at twelve-thirty. If you're willing to deliver it, I can go to lunch early."

"Deal," she said quickly.

A few other women attempted to approach Bennett as the morning progressed, and I gave them the same "Bennett's insane" speech as the first one, but without mentioning his lunch. Only one of the women dared to knock on his door and enter. The folder she'd carried in sailed out of the room before she ran away in tears.

Bennett stormed from his office to glare at me, which I purposely ignored. His door slammed in response.

Noontime couldn't come fast enough after that.

As soon as the clock hit twelve, I bolted from my desk and rode the elevator to the main floor with a crush of other people. The street was just as busy as it had been the day before, which I didn't mind. I strolled in the other direction this time and ended up at a little cafe that had delicious-looking croissant sandwiches.

While waiting for my order, a man walked in. He was about Bennett's age, with lighter brown hair and blue eyes. Our gazes met. He smiled, which turned him from average-looking to attractive. I nodded, and he went to order. Afterward, he stood beside me to wait.

"Wulf Enterprises, right?" he said. "I saw you on the elevator yesterday. You must be new."

"I am. Started yesterday in administration."

"I've heard mixed things about that department. How do you like it?"

"It's a summer job, so it's okay."

"I'm at Founders, a Wulf Enterprises sublet on the third floor. My name's Walt."

"I'm Wrenly. Nice to meet you, Walt." I shook his hand.

"It looks like you're doing fine if you already know this is where to eat."

"Random luck. I ate at the place with the fancy desserts in the Steele building yesterday."

"If you like desserts, there's a place two blocks over you need to try. Worth the walk."

We chatted until my order was ready, and just as I was going to leave, he called my name.

"Rather than taking that back to your desk, check out the Aspen Knoll Park. Perfect spot for a break on a day like today."

I thanked him and used my phone to find the park as soon as I was outside. It was only a ten-minute walk, so I decided to go for it. The park wasn't simply an expanse of lawn but a maze of flower beds, trees, winding paths, and sculptures with benches scattered throughout. I wandered for a bit until I spotted Walt at a bench. He smiled, waved when he saw me, and put his sandwich aside at my approach.

"What do you think?" he asked.

"It's really pretty. Relaxing to walk around. I think I could lose track of time here."

"I set a timer, and I eat first." He motioned to the seat next to him, and I sat. While we ate, he explained the park and how each sculpture had a plaque describing the piece.

"It's worth taking the time to read them," he said.

"I will. Thanks for mentioning it." I collected my garbage and stood. "Maybe I'll see you around."

Standing, I waved and turned to leave. Bennett was there, ten feet away. My stomach dropped to my feet.

Mom and Dad had one very firm rule for me: No boys.

They were so serious about it that, when I'd admitted to having a crush on a boy in grade school, I'd been immediately transitioned to an all-girl school. Lessons had been learned. Since then, I'd never let myself feel anything for the opposite sex. Ever.

So I hurried toward Bennett and grabbed his arm.

"Random stranger," I said softly.

"You smell like him."

"I was sitting next to him. We were talking about the sculptures."

He looked down at the ground, and I could feel his arm shaking under my touch.

"Do you like him?"

"Of course not. I just met him, Bennett. And he's *your* age."

His gaze flew to mine, and he looked...shocked. I didn't know why, but it was an opening. I wrapped my arms around him like I had tentacles and gave him my saddest, pleading face.

"Please don't tell Mom and Dad. I promise there's zero interest."

He glanced over my shoulder, gently untangled my tentacle-hold to clasp my hand, and led me away without saying anything.

"Please," I begged. "I promise to eat lunch at my desk all next week to guard your door."

"Not good enough," Bennett said.

I wanted to kick him in the shin. Instead, I tried what Grandma suggested.

"You look really handsome today, Bennett." He stopped walking, and that perfectly stoic mask he liked to wear slipped into place as he looked at me. Hopeful, since it wasn't anger, I pressed forward. "And..." Shit. I couldn't compliment his ass and tell him to wear heels. What else? What else!

"And that shirt nicely accentuates your shoulders. A sleeveless one would be even better." I reached up and squeezed his muscular arm.

"You'll eat lunch with me until the end of next week," he said.
It worked? I couldn't believe it.
"Deal," I said quickly.

CHAPTER FIVE

THE SOFT SOUND of crying greeted my human ears as we neared the desks on Bennett's side of the floor. When I slowed to see what was going on, he caught my arm and led me to his office suite, where a scattered trail of papers created a path from my desk to his.

"I have a meeting for the next hour. Clean up this mess, and wipe everything down to remove her scent. She sat on the couch. Figure out a way to get rid of her scent from there, too."

He turned on his heel and left without his laptop or anything else, including an explanation of who "she" was.

With a sigh, I started picking up papers. Rather than sorting them right away, I placed the stack on my desk and searched his private bathroom for cleaning supplies. Wiping off the surfaces she'd likely touched didn't take long. Debating how to remove a scent from a cloth-upholstered couch did. His cleaning supplies were natural and not heavily scented for obvious reasons. That meant using any of the sprays was out, even if they were fabric-safe. What options did that leave me?

Mentally shrugging, I closed the door and blinds and started doing jumping jacks. When I felt suitably warm, I kicked off my shoes and sprawled on his napping couch. In theory, my scent would smother hers. It wasn't like Bennett would have let her sit on his couch for long, and I highly doubted she would have gotten away with lying on it.

Would Bennett like *my* scent on his couch? Probably not. But if he was fine brushing his lips against mine to find out what I drank and dragging me from the park by my hand, I didn't think he'd have a violent reaction to my scent like he had to whoever'd been in his office. And if he did throw another fit, the worst-case scenario was that I'd lose my job.

Oh, darn…

Smiling to myself, I glanced at the time on my phone and wiggled around on the couch, trying to spread my scent around as much as possible.

Light, rhythmic tapping wormed its way into my brain and slowly woke me. I heard a quiet buzz, Bennett's softly spoken "later," and knew I was in trouble.

I'd fallen asleep on his couch.

The tapping resumed. Typing. He was working while I was napping. What did it mean that he hadn't woken me up?

Deciding not to put off whatever consequence he had planned for me, I opened my eyes and sat up. His jacket fell off my shoulders, and I quickly picked it up from the floor.

He'd covered me?

"It's a comfortable couch, isn't it?" Bennett said.

I looked up at him and managed a weak smile. "Yep."

"Are you ready to get back to work? I have a call I need to make."

I draped his jacket over the back of the couch before fleeing.

The stack of papers was missing from my desk, and when I glanced back at the closed office door, I saw the note I'd written the day before.

Knock and DIE!!!

Had he actually let me sleep on purpose? I snorted. Of course he had. I'd acted like a scent sponge. Now his napping couch didn't smell like random hoe anymore. Just me. At least I knew he didn't hate me, despite all of the times he'd refused to acknowledge me as family.

Idly, I wondered which woman had been daring enough to sit uninvited. The one who'd delivered lunch seemed unlikely. She'd been too timid to knock.

Too curious to let it go, I got up and slowly made my way to the bathroom, trying to listen for office gossip. However, everyone was quietly focused.

Disappointed, I used the bathroom. Two women entered before I finished.

"If he would just pick already, the rest of us could move on. How is it Lily's fault that Olivia already interrupted him? And it wasn't like some made-up reason. She was just bringing him his lunch that the normie ordered."

"You mean the normie who set this all up? She knew what was going to happen when Lily brought his lunch."

I recognized the voice and rolled my eyes before opening my stall door. Neither woman looked surprised to see me, which made sense since they'd probably known who was in the bathroom the moment they entered.

"Sorry to disappoint you, Milena, but this normie did not set anyone up. Lily wanted a reason to interact with Bennett, and I offered the lunch delivery option *after* warning her that he was in an extra insane mood. She took the chance anyway. How is that my fault?" I turned on the water to wash my hands. "And neither is the fact that Olivia interrupted him first. You've all worked with him longer than I have and know he doesn't want anyone around him. Yet, you keep trying."

The other girl crossed her arms and glared at me. "How can he be okay being around you but not the rest of us?"

"Gee, maybe because I'm not trying to molest him every chance I get."

I saw her reach for me from the corner of my eye. Reacting instead of thinking, I had her arm twisted around her back before either of us knew what I intended. Our gazes met in the mirror as I stood behind her.

Her pupils exploded wide, and I could feel the tremor running through the arm I gripped. A second later, I was pinned face-first against the bathroom door.

"At some point, the Wulfs will forget about their charity case," she said. "When that time comes, I'll find you."

She pushed me hard into the wood and then released me. I could feel where I'd have bruises from the encounter but didn't show how much it hurt as I backed up a step so they could leave. Once they did, I leaned against the counter and stared at myself in the mirror.

Eleven weeks, then you're free, Wrenly.

After splashing some water on my face, I left the bathroom. I could hear the whispers, which meant they wanted me to hear.

"Useless normie."

"Charity case."

"Even her real parents didn't want her."

"Oh, look," I said aloud. "I dropped my give-a-fuck."

The chorus of growls faded behind me as I made my way back to my desk. I waited until I was sitting to rub my shoulder and ear, which had taken the brunt of the door contact. How stupid could I be to use that move on a wolf? How long would it take for me to remember I'm not at that school anymore?

Wolves didn't hurt humans unless in defense. Humans did that.

I leaned back in my chair and started to close my eyes before I remembered what had happened last time. Sitting up straight, I resisted the urge to look at Bennett's window and instead focused on the spreadsheets I was working on.

The rest of the afternoon passed in relative silence. I found myself so lost in a spiral of numbers that I didn't realize Bennett had left his office until he grabbed my chin and turned my face toward him.

"What happened?" The question was more growl than words.

Still thinking of the numbers I'd been working on, I had no idea what he was talking about.

"You're going to have to give me more context than that. It's been a long day."

His gaze narrowed on me, and his thumb whispered over my cheek, which I noted ached more than it should have.

"What happened, Wrenly?"

"What happened?" A disbelieving laugh escaped me, and I jerked out of his hold and stood as I closed my laptop. "Due to someone's little temper tantrum, I wasn't paying attention like I should have been, and my face met a door."

He studied my gaze, and I watched him inhale, searching for the lie, but he wouldn't find any. I'd been a nosy idiot, and my face had paid the price. I wondered how bruised it was.

Bennett exhaled heavily and clasped my upper arms.

"I'm sorry."

"Don't be sorry. Do better so your co-workers don't need to walk on eggshells around you. Wulf Enterprises is lucky to have any employees left."

Something dropped to the floor with a thud, and I turned to look at Andri, who was scrambling to pick up a pile of documents.

"Leave it," Bennett said without a hint of anger. "I'll pick it up."

She straightened, looked from him to me, then fled.

"Go get an ice pack for your cheek," Bennett said, reclaiming my attention. "I'll meet you by the elevators."

I found the first aid kit in the break room. The ice pack against my cheek felt amazing as it cooled.

"I'm telling you what I saw," I heard someone whisper. "She talked down to him, and he *did nothing*. If it'd been one of us, our heads would be rolling."

The voices moved off, and I shook my head that they were jealous over his lack of reaction instead of happy that I'd stood up for them. Were werewolves required to be ridiculous?

Bennett was waiting by the elevator and pulled the ice pack away to check my cheek when I joined him.

"You should have done this right away. I think you're going to have a bruise for a few days now."

"I'll live."

His finger brushed over my chilled skin. "Keep this off until we reach the car, then put it on again for a few minutes."

Did he honestly think I didn't know how to use an ice pack? After my time at school, my skill for nursing bruises was PhD worthy.

We entered the elevator alone and rode it down to the seventh floor, where more people got on. Bennett moved me in front of him like I was some kind of shield. Big baby.

When the elevator stopped on the third floor, everyone made room for the next batch of people getting on, which included Walt. He smiled when he saw me, but the smile quickly vanished when he saw my face.

"What happened? Are you okay? You didn't have that when I saw you earlier."

He briefly glanced at Bennett.

Did he think Bennett hit me? That was laughable. If Bennett decided to backhand me, my head wouldn't be attached anymore.

"I'm fine," I said. "My face had an untimely meeting with a door, which I know sounds like a cover-up, but it's not. Bubblewrap might be in my future once my mom sees this."

Or better yet, maybe she'll say I should quit.

My thoughts were whirling on how to spin my bruise for the best outcome possible, and I wasn't thinking of Bennett until his hands closed over my shoulders.

"Wrenly is none of your business."

My brows shot up at the same time Walt's did. However, the

elevator dinged, and before I could say anything, Bennett steered me out of the opening doors.

"Wrenly, do you need me to call security?" Walt asked, following us.

I felt Bennett's hands twitch on my shoulders as I glanced back at Walt.

"This is my older brother. He doesn't hit. He mostly ignores. I'm fine. I promise."

Walt nodded and watched as I got into the parking garage elevator with Bennett. I gave a little wave to reassure him. Bennett captured my hand as the doors closed, and a second later, I was pinned against the wall with my hands over my head.

Bennett leaned down so we were eye to eye, and I could see the level of his annoyance in his eyes.

"I am not your brother, Wrenly."

I made a rude noise. "Fine. You're not my brother. I should have let him believe you're my abuser, instead, so he called security on you. It would have been highly entertaining for me, irritating for you, and embarrassing for Mom and Dad. Don't you think calling you my brother was the best option to defuse the situation?"

His gaze swept over my face as we reached the garage. The elevator dinged, and the doors opened, but he didn't let go. He continued to look at me.

"If we go back up, I'm definitely calling security."

His lip curled at the corner, not in a smiling way, but the start of a silent growl kind of way, and he released me.

After a silent ride home, I fled to my room and closed the door. My room wasn't the sanctuary it'd been in my youth, and I hated that even as I went to my vanity to look at my face.

When I saw the bruise, I snorted in annoyance. It was a mark barely even the size of a dime. The red patch from the ice pack was bigger. Setting the ice pack on my vanity, I sprawled out on my bed with my phone and put my earbuds in to watch a movie.

I was almost to the end when the door to my room burst open

and Mom swept in, looking uncharacteristically murderous. I sat up and tore an earbud from my ear.

"What's wrong? Did something happen?"

She calmed visibly and joined me on the bed. When she reached out to touch my cheek, I made a face.

"Bennett told you I was hurt, didn't he?"

"He did. What happened, Wrenly?"

I withheld my sigh.

"Bennett lost his cool today and made multiple people cry. Being the curious person that I am, I went to the bathroom to see if I could find out who. I wasn't paying attention and face-planted into the door."

She searched my gaze, trying to find a lie that wasn't there. I took her hands in mine and gave her my best sad eyes.

"Working is obviously dangerous for me, Mom. Maybe I should do something else this summer. Like travel around Europe. I heard it's fun."

Her worry vanished, and she gave me a dry look.

"If I find out you hurt yourself on purpose to get out of work, you'll be in trouble."

"Like grounded and can't go to work kind of trouble?"

She groaned and pulled me into a hug.

"I've missed you so much, Wrenly."

Then why did you send me away in the first place? I wanted to ask, but I already knew the answer—Bennett.

Since the day they'd brought me home, he'd had a problem with me. I'd been six and he'd been thirteen. From a distance, he'd watched me play with Karter and Aiden and had tattled any time we'd done anything even remotely fun.

Bennett, the fun killer.

He hadn't changed much in that regard.

When Mom pulled back, she held my hands in hers. "Bennett didn't just tell me about the bruise. He said you were acting off today. Afraid."

"You mean when he came into my room this morning without me knowing and woke me out of a dead sleep, or at work when he snuck up on me again?"

She tilted her head, studying me. "Is that all it was? Surprise? He said he smelled fear."

"Mom, I'm not wired like you guys. When I'm startled, fear is pretty common."

"Okay." She gave me a small smile, leaned in, and kissed my cheek.

When she would have left, I kept hold of her hand.

"I overheard some of the girls at work. They're bugging Bennett because they think he's still looking for his mate. If he's found her, even if he's giving her time, can't he tell them so they leave him alone?"

Mom's smile grew a little sad.

"They stopped believing him years ago, sweetheart. Until he can show her to the world, they'll keep trying."

"Then he's an idiot for waiting."

"I think so too, but he's deeply afraid she'll reject him."

"Really? Why?"

"She's never shown any interest in him as a mate."

A mental image of Bennett rose to my mind. His dark hair. Dark eyes. He was attractive…if the girl liked a serious guy.

"What are you thinking?" Mom asked.

"Since he's not ugly, it's probably his personality holding him back. You said it yourself. He makes people cry and throws things. What girl would want that?"

Mom tried to suppress her smile and failed.

"He mentioned that you told him people will start quitting if he keeps it up. I think it opened his eyes a little "

"Good."

She patted my hand. "You're a good influence on him, Wrenly. Are you hungry? I brought some pizza back with me."

"Seriously? What toppings?"

"Pepperoni."

It was such a normal food item and not something I'd gotten at school. I started salivating and beat Mom out of the room.

I woke with a leisurely stretch and rolled over, not yet ready to get out of bed. For the first time in years, I had absolutely nothing to do on a Saturday. No homework or extra classes. No secret meetups to sell or buy things. No hiding from mean girls. Nothing.

My smile faded as I realized how boring that sounded, and I reached for my phone on the nightstand to send Mom a message.

Me: If I wanted to drive into the city to shop, what are the chances you'd say yes?
Mom: Of course you can. You're not a prisoner. I'll let Bennett know.

Ha! I couldn't believe my luck.

Bounding out of bed, I hurried through my morning routine and flew out my bedroom door only to crash into Bennett. I would have rebounded with a pained grunt, but he wrapped his arms around me and trapped me against his chest instead. Turning my head to the side, I grabbed my nose. My eyes were watering profusely.

"I think I broke it."

He immediately had my face between his hands and was tipping my head back so he could see.

"Is it bleeding?" I asked.

"No. I don't think it's broken either. I'm sorry, Wrenly." He wiped away my tears with his thumbs then leaned in to kiss my cheek, right over the bruise.

I froze.

He pulled back and searched my gaze.

Was he trying to be *nice*? If so, it was oddly…affectionate. Even Aiden and Karter, the two people I was closest to, had never kissed my cheek.

Was this because of what I'd said yesterday? I'd meant Bennett needed to be nice to *other* girls, not me. He was weirding me out.

"I didn't think you'd come out of your room that fast," he said after a prolonged silence.

I stepped out of his hold and said, "Mom said I could leave."

"I know." He held up the keys. "My car and I are at your disposal today."

My excitement imploded. "What?"

"Mom said you wanted to do some shopping," he said. "What are you interested in? Handbags? Shoes? Jewelry?"

"None of the above." I tried to take the keys, but he held them higher, out of my reach, which would have ignited my temper if I let it. However, I knew getting mad would be counterproductive.

"I asked Mom if *I* could drive to the city, not if *we* could drive to the city."

"You drive; I navigate."

"Why can't I just go by myself?"

"It's my car."

I wanted to kick him so badly. Instead, I pulled out my phone and called Mom.

"You said I wasn't a prisoner."

"You're not, Wrenly."

"Then why do I have a warden?"

Mom sighed. "Wrenly, please be reasonable. You've been home for three days, and your face is bruised. We're worried about you. Bennett promised he wouldn't stop you from doing anything you wanted. Think of him as your wallet with legs. This is a way for him to atone for yesterday, too."

Throughout the call, Bennett didn't move. His face didn't give away what he was thinking or feeling, either.

"I can do anything I want?" I asked while meeting his gaze.

"Of course," Mom said as Bennett gave a single nod.

"Okay."

"Have fun, sweetheart."

"I will."

I hung up, grabbed the keys from him, and started down the stairs.

Was I happy to have a chaperone? No. I'd wanted to meet up with Sophia, my future roommate, today. Thankfully, I hadn't tried setting anything up in advance.

When we reached the car, I learned that Bennett's door-opening rule didn't only apply to when I was a passenger or in a parking garage. He opened the driver's door for me and closed it again. He stayed next to the door for a moment.

Don't do it, Wren. Don't look at him, or you'll be more tempted to run him over.

Bennett seemed to sense my mood because he didn't attempt conversation as we left the house and approached the gate. The guard from last time was there and didn't open the gate until he saw Bennett in the passenger seat.

"Yeah, definitely not a prisoner," I said under my breath.

"Is that really how it feels to you?" Bennett asked.

"I'm nineteen. I can vote for the next leader of our great nation, but I can't go anywhere without permission first. Does that sound right to you? Because it doesn't to me."

He was quiet as I took the route he'd taken the last two days to get to the highway.

Driving wasn't bad at first, but the closer I got to the city and the more cars there were around us, the more nervous I got. My palms started to sweat, and my chest grew tighter.

"Take the next exit," Bennett said.

Rather than try to fight for the right to keep driving, I signaled and pulled over to the shoulder before reaching the stop sign.

"Wait there," he said.

He walked around the car and opened my door.

Without a word, I got out and took the passenger seat.

When we were in the car again, he pulled away from the shoulder and got right back onto the highway.

Frustration, anger, and the growing need to cry had me looking out the window for the next thirty minutes, until Bennett asked, "Where do you want to go?"

"Home."

CHAPTER SIX

LYING on my stomach on my bed, I stared at my closet, which was devoid of any new purchases because Bennett had turned around like I'd asked him to.

And now everyone was worried.

Mom had tried calling me twice. I hadn't answered. Aiden had tried next. Then Karter. Like I wanted to talk to any of them. They wouldn't understand.

How could I *possibly* be sad? I could have anything I asked for. A luxury car? No problem. Purses that cost over nine thousand dollars. No big deal. Freedom to do what I wanted when I wanted? Hold on…let's not get crazy. How could I be sufficiently smothered if I had any freedom whatsoever?

The muffled sound of Bennett's voice reached me through my door. "I don't know." There was a brief pause. "I tried."

Tried knocking on my door a million times? He wasn't lying.

"She said she wants to be alone."

Also true.

"Fine."

A few moments later, he knocked on my door again.

"Mom wants you to call her when you're up for it. Okay?"

"Got it." I knew from all the previous attempts to communicate with me that if I didn't answer, he would just come in anyway. Answering at least meant he stayed in the hallway.

"I'm going out for a run," he said.

"Okay."

I rolled onto my back to stare up at the ceiling and willed myself to shake off my current mood. If I wanted freedom, I couldn't have a meltdown whenever things didn't go my way. Was it upsetting that I'd gotten that nervous while driving into the city with Bennett and that he'd *smelled* it? Yes. Was it the end of the world? No. If Bennett had been willing to let me drive once, he'd probably let me drive again. I just needed more time behind the wheel and to have better control of my emotions.

Rather than shut him out, I needed to pull him in...for more than just driving, too.

I needed to win him over so he'd be on team "Let Wrenly go to human college" when I brought it up to Mom and Dad again. Instead, I was being a pain in his butt because Mom was worried and making him babysit.

"Why is everything so hard?" I mumbled, getting up.

After making faces at myself in the mirror, I left my room.

The house was quiet, which was fine. I glanced at the clock in the kitchen and started putting together a sandwich, hoping that Bennett would appreciate the effort enough to listen to my apology.

His run wasn't very long because he strode in ten minutes later. His expression didn't bode well for my apology. It didn't stop me from lifting the plate and giving him my best smile, though.

He stopped walking, and the irritation in his expression melted away, replaced by his stoic mask.

"I made you a sandwich," I said, trying to sound upbeat. "I'm sorry about before. Since getting my license, I haven't had much opportunity to drive. I thought I would be fine in traffic, and when I wasn't, my frustration got the better of me. If you're willing to let me try again—maybe not into the city yet—I promise not to get moody with you."

"You shut yourself in your room because you were frustrated?" he repeated.

"Yeah." I watched him inhale deeply. "You think I'm lying. Why?"

He shook his head slightly and took the plate I was still holding out to him.

"Thank you for the sandwich."

"You're welcome." I moved around the island to get him a drink. "What are your plans for the rest of the day?"

He considered the glass I set on the counter and slowly sat with his food.

"I don't have any plans."

"Is that normal for you on a Saturday?"

"No. Usually, I work."

"Did you take today off to relax, or did Mom and Dad ask you to babysit me?"

He took a bite of his sandwich, which was answer enough.

"Okay...so do you want us to work from home, or should we have some fun together?"

He paused mid-chew to look at me. When I wriggled my eyebrows with a mischievous grin, he swallowed hard and choked. I hurried to pat his back.

"Don't panic. I promise the fun I have in mind isn't anything crazy, and Mom and Dad won't get mad about what we do together...if you say it's your idea."

A slow flush consumed his face, and he took several gulps of water.

"I need you to tell me what you want to do," he said, his voice rough.

That bite really had to have gone down the wrong tube. I patted his back again in sympathy, even as I smiled.

"Let's go to an arcade."

Everything about his curious demeanor changed. He completely shut down.

"No."

"Oh, come on. It'll be a fun way to unwind." I pinched the loose material on the side of his shirt and tugged on it like a kid. "Please. You'll have fun. I promise."

He slowly turned to look at me. His pupils started to expand, and I scrambled to find something flattering to say to defuse his annoyance, like Grandma had suggested.

"Do you know how many women would kill for eyelashes like yours? It's just not fair that you look so pretty."

His pupils calmed, and he frowned slightly. "Pretty?"

"It's a compliment," I said quickly. "And you're right. We need to ease you into fun. Too much too quickly could shock the system. You might actually get funstroke. You need introductory-level amusement." I thought about it for a second, then smiled widely. "You like dessert, right? Let's walk around downtown and find this dessert place I heard about."

Dessert to sweeten his mood, a big dinner to appease him and stall for time, and then lure him into the arcade to loosen him up. And once he was suitably relaxed, I could begin my interrogation to determine what Bennett wanted so we could make a deal that benefited both of us.

"Okay," he said finally. "I'll go change. But you have to promise you'll be with me the entire time."

I held up three fingers and promised. He didn't quite look convinced but eventually left with his partially eaten sandwich. I quickly pulled out my phone to call Mom.

"Sweetheart, are you okay?" Mom asked, her voice laced with real concern. The level of her love for me was both a blessing and a curse.

"I'm fine. I just got frustrated and emotional while driving and wanted to come back home."

"Are you feeling better now?"

"Yep. I made Bennett a sandwich to apologize, and since he doesn't have anything else to do, he said we can go have some fun at an arcade."

"Bennett said that?"

"He did. You can call him yourself and ask."

The beat of silence that followed made me nervous until she said, "I don't know, Wrenly. Those types of places are usually really crowded."

"Which isn't a problem. I'm not allergic to people, and I already promised Bennett that I'd stick to him like glue. It's not like an arcade is that much different from shopping, and he was willing to do that, right? Besides, I've been locked away for seven years, Mom. Why can't I do normal people things?"

She didn't immediately say anything, which I knew meant she was seriously debating the matter.

"And it's not just for me, Mom. It's for Bennett, too. He needs to stop making people cry at work. Maybe a little bit of fun time on the weekends will help with that."

"It's Bennett I'm worried about, Wrenly. You know how he is. Are you going to be able to smooth things over at the first sign that he's about to lose his temper?"

"Yes," I said confidently.

"Oh? How?"

She had me there. I'd never witnessed him losing his cool, only the aftermath.

"Different situations require different responses," I said smoothly. "I won't know the right one until I know the situation. I promise it'll be fine."

She said something under her breath that I didn't catch, then said, "If he looks like he's going to lose his temper, hug him, Wrenly. Okay?"

Weird and a little awkward, but doable. He couldn't exactly throw things or people if his arms were full. Well, he could throw me, but...nah, he wouldn't throw me too hard. Mom would get mad.

"Deal," I said.

"All right. You two have fun. I think Dad and I will stay in the city tonight."

"What are you two up to?"

"Nothing you'd care to hear about."

"You're probably right."

"Goodbye, sweet girl."

"Bye, Mom."

I hung up and washed off the counter. By the time I finished, Bennett was back. He'd showered and changed into a pair of well-worn jeans paired with a white T-shirt and an off-white button-up. I had to admit that with his dark hair and eyes, it looked pretty good on him.

"If you want less female attention, you might want to change. The shirt you're wearing accentuates your shoulders and chest."

He stared at me. I stared back. It felt like he was waiting for me to connect the dots on something, but I had no idea what.

He looked away first, and I noted his jaw muscles starting to twitch. Some games and sweets would hopefully help improve his mood.

The drive into the city center was quiet since I was plotting how to sweet-talk him into the arcade if the desserts failed. But he surprised me by parking near the arcade instead of the dessert place.

When he opened the door for me, I looked from him to the arcade hopefully.

"Are you sure you want to go in there?" he asked.

I smiled brightly, knowing then that he'd either heard what I'd said to Mom or she'd messaged him. Either way, he wasn't going to fight it.

"More than I want to draw my next breath. Come on. Let's go have some fun."

The arcade was filled with flashing lights, loud music, chaotic game sounds, and people. So many people. And I loved it.

However, no matter how hard I tried to pull Bennett in, he didn't know the meaning of the word fun. He scowled at the games...at the people playing them...at anyone who even looked in our direction.

After twenty minutes, I gave up.

"Let's go get something to eat."

He followed me out of the arcade like a six-inch string attached us.

Mom had been right to question the wisdom of the outing. Since Bennett was relatively okay at work—except for when his female coworkers were trying extra hard to gain his attention—I'd thought he'd be fine out in public. However, he'd looked ready to tackle everyone in the arcade and on the sidewalk.

How did he manage to go to work every day?

I used my phone to navigate to the dessert place and then tried to send him to find a table while I waited in line to order. He wouldn't budge from my side.

"Seriously, Bennett, you're being ridiculous, and I'm starting to regret leaving the house with you. Please just find a table for us. Or, better yet, you order, and I'll find a table."

"We'll get it to-go and eat at the park," he said.

If he meant the one by Wulf Enterprises, there was no point. If we had to drive to that, we might as well drive home. I didn't say that, though. I just stood in line and placed my order. He declined to add anything for himself.

Yep. Definitely regretting it.

I waited until we were outside to say, "Let's just head home."

He didn't say anything on the way back to the car or on the long drive home, which was just fine by me. I pulled out my phone and sent a message to Mom.

Me: I'm happy to report that there were no rage-fueled outbursts, so public hugging was successfully avoided.

Then I sent one to my group chat.

Me: In the seven years since I've been gone, neither one of you could manage to teach Bennett how to have fun? My first time ever going to an arcade, and he sucked the fun right out of what could have been a great afternoon. I blame both of you.

Aiden: Us? Blame his mate.

Karter: We tried teaching him. All he can think about is her.

I would have pitied whoever his mate was, but I knew werewolves lived for finding their mates. Whoever she was, she would just as likely be as obsessed with Bennett as he was with her, which made his hesitation to claim her even more confusing…unless she truly was that much younger than he was. If that was the case, I did feel sorry for him. Not enough to excuse his crappy behavior, though. Only sorry enough to keep my questions to myself so I didn't potentially rub salt into any wounds.

He pulled into the garage and parked but didn't get out. Risking his wrath, I opened my door to give him the alone time I thought he needed.

Inside, I put my dessert in the fridge and went upstairs to shut myself in my room.

My phone rang just as I sat down on my bed. I glanced at the number, hurried to turn on some music in my bedroom, and closed myself in my bathroom.

Once I had the water in the sink running, I answered with a quiet, "Hey, Sophia. What's up?"

"A few friends and I are heading downtown to a dance club my uncle owns. Any chance you want to meet us there?"

"I'd love to, but I'm not sure I can manage it."

"Still under house arrest?"

"Something like that."

"Can't you sneak out?"

"Probably not."

"Well, if you decide to, give me a call. I can pick you up wherever.

Whenever. And I talked to my mom. If you need a place to stay until the start of the semester, we have a spare room."

"Thanks. I hope I don't need it, but if I do, I'll call."

We said goodbye, and I turned off the water.

I wasn't expecting Bennett to be standing on the other side of the door when I opened it. Rather than scream like an afraid, normal person would, I punched him right in the face, then cried out in pain.

My whole hand throbbed, and I tried to shake it out. Bennett grabbed my hand and immediately turned on the cold water, sticking it under. It helped.

As the pain receded, clarity bloomed, and I glanced at Bennett's face. His nose was actually bleeding, the drips falling to the floor unnoticed by him.

"I'm sorry," I said. "I didn't mean to hit you. It was reflex."

He didn't look at me. Instead, he focused on carefully moving my fingers.

"Any pain?" he asked as he worked.

"Yeah. I hit your face, Bennett. Of course, it hurt. But nothing's broken if that's what you're asking. You're bleeding, by the way."

He stopped moving my fingers and just stared at my hand for a long moment. I grabbed the hand towel and held it to his nose. He took it over after a second and straightened.

"Who were you talking to?" he asked.

"A friend."

"I didn't know you had friends."

The comment made me want to punch him again.

"Yeah, thanks for poking where it hurts. Did you need something other than to invade what little privacy I have?"

He frowned slightly as he studied me.

"No? Then get out." I grabbed his arm.

It annoyed me to know that everything—turning him, pushing him toward the door, and even punching his nose—was because he allowed it all. He could've dodged or blocked any of it, but he didn't.

Once he was in the hall, I slammed my door in his bleeding face and turned off the music as I replayed my conversation with Sophia in my head. I hadn't said anything to explain who I was talking to or why or what we were talking about.

The explosive sound of a fist hitting the other side of my door was followed by a split in the wood. My eyes went wide. I backpedaled then bolted to the bathroom for my phone.

I hurriedly called Mom. "Bennett's really mad."

"What happened?"

"I accidentally hit him and made his nose bleed."

"Are you okay?"

I loved her for asking that first.

"Nothing's broken. He made sure before getting mad."

"Why did you hit him?"

"It was an accident, Mom. I was on the phone with someone, and when I opened my bathroom door, he was in my room. I wasn't expecting him there and just reacted without thinking."

"Were you talking to a boy?"

"Are you serious? Bennett's wrecking the house, and you're worried I'm breaking your no-boys rule?"

Something crashed in Bennett's room, which was right next to mine. Whatever it was, it was big enough to shake the floor.

"He's throwing things, Mom."

"It's okay, Wrenly. He'll calm down in a bit."

"Before or after he destroys the whole house? When are you coming home?"

"We're still in the city. It would take us over an hour to get to you. Go talk to him."

"Are you crazy? I just hit him. I'm pretty sure the last person he wants to see is me."

"I think you're the only person he needs to see. Apologize and try hugging him. Call me when he's settled down."

She hung up.

I looked at the phone in disbelief.

Not for the first time, I wished I'd been fostered by a human family instead of a werewolf one. Life would have been so much easier.

As soon as I had that thought, I felt guilty. Mom repeatedly told me how much she'd dreamed of having a daughter. Both she and Dad loved me unconditionally. I could do no wrong in their eyes—unless I even looked at the opposite sex. That was their bottom line, and I'd never been brave enough to touch it, not that they'd given me access to boys to try.

Play nice and make peace, Wrenly, so you can leave and have the freedom you want.

Releasing a long, calming breath, I squared my shoulders and left my room.

Bennett's bedroom door stood open. He was standing beside a large, tipped-over dresser. A broken drawer lay farther away with clothes scattered around it. One of the floorboards was cracked, too.

I wanted to turn around and walk away like I hadn't seen a thing, but I made myself knock on the doorframe instead.

His head turned, just an inch toward the side, proving he'd heard even though he didn't speak.

"I'm sorry for hitting you, Bennett. Do you...Do you want a hug?"

I felt so stupid for saying it.

Before I could feel truly uncomfortable, I was pinned against Bennett's chest.

One hand was on the back of my head, with his forearm pressing into my shoulders, pinning me against him, while the other caged my waist. My ear was trapped against his chest. I could hear this thundering pulse over the sound of my harsh breathing. His bicep was crowding my face.

Unable to move, I couldn't draw enough air. Fear bloomed with my growing panic.

"No, Wrenly," Bennett said against my hair. "Please. Don't. Don't fear me. I won't hurt you. I promise."

My fingernails dug into his arms as I gripped them, trying to push him away. He only held me tighter.

"No. Shh. It's okay."

It wasn't okay, though. Nothing was okay. I was trapped. I couldn't breathe.

A low wail filled the air, and I realized it was coming from me.

I was falling apart.

Again.

Bennett loosened his hold.

Able to move, I lashed out. My fear-filled cry turned into one fueled by rage and desperation.

Get away.

The second he removed his hands to block mine, I bolted.

Hide.

I made it to my room, locked my door, and tipped a bookshelf in front of it all within seconds. Without waiting, I ran into the bathroom, turned the lock, and then slowly backed away until I stood in the shower. The harsh sound of my breathing filled the space, and I tried to quiet it so I could listen. My hands shook as I wiped the hair from my face and stared at the door.

They won't follow me here. They won't have the advantage now that I'm awake and free. They...

Catching my spiral, I slowly crouched down and hugged my knees. Then, I took a big breath and filled my lungs until it felt like I couldn't do more. Rather than exhaling, I added little inhales to force even more in until more wasn't possible. Bit by bit, I released that breath and started the process again.

While I worked to bring my panic back under control, I silently coached myself.

It's okay to be afraid, Wren. What they did to you was shit. But you're not at school anymore. You're safe. Bennett wasn't trying to hurt you. He was hugging you. Hugs are good. Hugs are nice.

I wasn't sure how long it took to calm down my racing pulse, but it was long enough that my legs went numb. After a final, steady breath, I carefully stood and shook some feeling back into them.

My gaze never left the door.

Was Bennett waiting on the other side again? If so, I couldn't allow a repeat punch. Two episodes of erratic behavior in one day were more than I could afford to show. With my luck, he was probably already on the phone with Mom, telling her that I needed therapy. I probably did, but I didn't want *Mom and Dad* to know that, or they wouldn't ever let me leave, which would only add to my trauma.

After listening at the door, I cautiously opened it. Bennett wasn't in my room. The bookshelf was still in front of the door, but it'd been moved almost a foot, the same width as my door stood open.

I slowly approached the mess I'd made. The sturdy bookshelf hadn't broken, thankfully. I picked up a few books and stacked them on my bed. When I had enough room to move, I tried lifting the bookshelf but couldn't.

How had I tipped it over?

Fear-induced strength.

I looked at the narrow door opening. It was enough to slip through, but did I want to? Knowing I couldn't put it off forever, I climbed over the shelf and peeked out the gap. The section of the hallway I could see was empty.

Anyone unfamiliar with this family would think they'd gotten a lucky break. I knew better. Bennett was out there. Waiting. Probably listening.

"I don't like feeling trapped," I said. "It's a thing for me. Like claustrophobia."

"Since when?" Bennett asked, sounding calm.

"For a while now."

"Why didn't you say anything to anyone?"

"Do you announce your weaknesses to the world?"

I heard him exhale heavily.

"I'm sorry I hit you, Bennett. Again. Is there any chance you can help me with this bookshelf? I'm not sure how I managed to knock it over. It's heavy."

"Sit on your bed."

I scrambled away from the door and watched the bookshelf slide across the floor with a wood-on-wood groan until Bennett had enough room to wedge himself through the door.

He righted the bookshelf then turned to look at me. His hair wasn't neatly styled anymore. The chaotic disarray didn't make him look disheveled but dangerously appealing, which was not how I should be viewing any man, especially Bennett.

I glanced away.

Keep your head straight, Wren, or they'll never let you go.

"You startle easily, and you don't like feeling trapped," he said. "What else should I know?"

CHAPTER SEVEN

SHIFTING NERVOUSLY ON THE BED, I debated how to respond to Bennett's question. Did he honestly think I was going to open the darkest corners of my soul to him just because he asked? By the serious look in his eyes, he did, and I knew I needed to tread carefully.

"Are you going to tell Mom and Dad what happened?" I asked.

"That depends."

"On what?"

"On your answer and your level of cooperation," he said smoothly.

Something about the way he watched me cautioned me against avoiding the question again. So I gave him what he'd probably already guessed.

"I hate dressing up. It feels fake, and I don't like myself when I feel fake."

"Okay. Anything else?"

"I don't like blue cheese?"

My attempt to defuse the tension of the moment didn't go over well. Bennett crossed my room and crowded into my space, forcing me to recline until my back hit the mattress. His dark gaze held mine as he leaned over me, caging me in with his arms.

I watched him inhale and tried not to feel anything, but it was impossible not to feel something.

He was too close. Too intense. Too unpredictable.

"You're starting to panic. Do you feel trapped?" he asked.

"No."

Uncomfortable and unable to take any more of his direct gaze, I closed my eyes. It only enhanced my other senses. I could feel where his legs pressed against mine. Heat radiated from his chest, making my heart race. Why was it getting harder to breathe?

The sound of my pulse filled my ears, seemingly overly loud in the otherwise quiet room.

His exhale teased my neck, stopping all thought. The gentle brush of his lips against my neck was unmistakable.

My eyes flew open, and I pushed at Bennett's shoulders.

He wrapped his arms around me, holding me closer.

"Do you feel trapped?" he asked against my skin.

"No! Yes! Get off me, Bennett." I pushed with all my might, but he didn't budge an inch.

"Please," I said desperately.

"Cooperate, Wrenly," he said softly. "Do you feel trapped?"

"No."

"When do you feel trapped?"

"When I can't move my arms, and when something is too close to my face."

I hated that I'd admitted it, but I needed him to back up. Fast.

"Like this?" His lips skimmed my neck, trailing up toward my jaw...my chin...

It felt like my heart flipped over in my chest. I turned my head away from him in panic, but not the same kind as before.

He was making me feel things I shouldn't.

Why was he doing this? Was it payback for hitting him? What if Mom and Dad came home and saw this? I don't want to be locked away again.

I started to shake, and my nose tingled ominously.

"Stop. Please, Bennett. Please."

The floodgate opened, and I started to cry in earnest.

He growled and set his forehead to mine.

"Did you feel trapped?" he asked again softly.

"N-no, you ass."

He sighed and got off me.

"I won't say anything to Mom and Dad, but we *will* talk about this again."

About what? How I'd hit him or how he'd tortured me because of it?

I kept my eyes closed, waiting for the sound of him leaving. Instead, his arms slipped under me, and he picked me up to settle me on his lap. He hugged me to his chest, careful to keep my arms and face as free as possible. That consideration, combined with the way his hand rubbed my back, kept me right where I was as his rocking sway broke what remained of my composure.

In terms of ugly cries, it was at least a seven. He didn't say anything, though. He just held me until the tears dried up on their own.

In the silence, I felt numb and drained. But also indescribably *safe*, which was so confusing since he'd been the one to make me cry in the first place.

I wanted to tell him to leave because of the inappropriate things he'd done, especially how he was cuddling me in his lap. But I couldn't bring myself to mention any of it. If I did, it would make everything he'd done more real. So, I said nothing. I just untangled myself, grabbed a clean pajama set, and closed myself in the bathroom. It didn't matter that it wasn't even dinner time yet. I was done for the day.

When I reemerged, freshly showered and changed, everything in my room was back in its place. The bookshelf didn't even look like I'd tipped it over. Best of all, there was no sign of Bennett.

He remained absent for the remainder of the night, but still made his presence known by leaving dinner on the dining table for me, by the muted sounds of typing coming from his office, and by the echo of his footsteps on the stairs after I went to bed for the night.

His presence was more comforting than disturbing, which I refused to overthink as I drifted off to sleep.

GOING to bed early meant I woke early the next morning. Rather than lounge around and dwell on the previous day's mistakes, I got up to make breakfast.

I was cooking eggs for myself when Bennett entered the kitchen.

"Whatever you're making smells good," he said. "Can I have some?"

Since he'd made dinner the night before and seemed in a reasonable mood, I agreed. However, that meant he lingered in the kitchen and watched me work.

Everything that happened yesterday repeated itself in my mind: Being startled by him when I came out of the bathroom. Punching him in the nose. My panic attack because he'd hugged me when I'd tried to apologize for it. Then what happened after...

"Did Mom and Dad come home last night?" I asked.

"No. They decided to stay in the city for a while."

Finally, some good luck for me.

"Good. That'll give you time to get my door fixed."

"And the scratches in the floor."

I wrinkled my nose at the reminder of what I'd done, which outweighed what he'd done, and silently mocked what he'd said while I was turned away from him.

His hand closed around my jaw from behind, and I was suddenly pulled back against his chest. Spatula gripped in one hand, I stared at the stove top with wide eyes until he tilted my face to the side.

"This doesn't scare you," he said, his gaze searching mine.

"No." However, the fact that he was pushing my boundaries again and wouldn't just let it go was making me mad.

When his gaze dipped to my mouth, my answer changed. He *was* scaring me again. I spun out of his hold and held the spatula out like a weapon.

"Keep your hands to yourself, Bennett. Didn't you learn that in primary school?

He tucked his hands into his pockets and shrugged.

Something about that move—the careless grace or maybe even the casual disregard—made me even more suspicious of his intent. I quickly glanced at the eggs still frying in the pan and pointed toward the island with my weapon.

"Go sit, or I'm serving you burned eggs."

Rather than going to the island to sit, he leaned against the counter near the stove.

I gave him a warning glare.

"My hands are to myself," he said.

Reluctantly, I moved close enough to flip the eggs, one of the few normal cooking skills I'd mastered while away.

"You've changed a lot since the last time you were home," he said as he watched me. "You weren't afraid back then."

"I'm not afraid now," I said. "I just developed a few...quirks, same as you."

"I have quirks?"

"What else do you call your temper tantrums? You hate anything that's not your mate, right? And you throw a fit about it? Well, I hate being held down, and I throw a fit about it, too. See? Same thing."

I felt the weight of his gaze as I worked but didn't turn to look at him until I had his eggs and toast plated and ready to hand to him.

When our gazes locked, it felt different. Off. As if he were waiting for something.

Did he think I was going to apologize for mentioning his absent mate? He could choke on his eggs first.

As soon as he took his plate, I went to sit at the island. He joined me, taking the stool next to me. His leg brushed mine, and I moved over to give him more room.

"If you don't have any plans this morning, would you like to try driving to the city again?" he asked. "There should be less traffic this early."

I'd planned to hide away in my room and avoid him the whole day, but the carrot he was dangling was too tempting.

If I wanted Mom and Dad to view me as independent, I needed to prove that I could be. And to do that, I needed more practice driving without freaking out.

"Yeah, I'd like to try again."

"Good."

The way he said it, like he was relieved, had me pausing to glance at him.

He ate half his fried egg in one bite.

Catching on to his need to leave quickly, I picked up my pace.

He began to clean up once he finished and took my plate from me after I was done.

"Go get ready. I've got this."

I hurried upstairs to change. The selection in my closet was pathetic. Shorts weren't allowed at school except for the athletic ones that had been trashed the week before I graduated—that left jeans, which would probably be too warm after a while. I tugged them on and jogged back down the stairs.

It'd taken me only a few minutes, but Bennett was already changed and waiting by the door in the kitchen. He wore a pair of jogging pants that hugged his thighs enough that I could imagine the pack girls whining when he passed. The shirt he wore snugly encased his arms and chest, probably adding whimpers to their whines.

"Ready?" he asked, holding out the keys.

"Yep."

Before I could grab them, the doorbell rang.

"Are you expecting a delivery?" I asked.

"No."

He pulled back the keys and walked around me, heading out of the kitchen.

I hurried after him, curious because it was before eight on a Sunday morning. No sane person would ring a doorbell that early on a weekend.

When he reached the door, though, he didn't immediately open it. He looked down at the floor for a moment, like he was debating. Whatever decision he'd reached had him jerking the door open with enough force that the wood creaked.

"Why are you here, Storm?" he asked, radiating impatience.

She was either oblivious or dumb because she smiled at him and reached for his arm.

"I thought you might want some company."

He stepped back out of her reach and nodded in my direction. "I have company."

Storm's gaze never wavered from Bennett's. "If you're this caring about your sister, I bet you'll be an amazing dad too."

I rolled my eyes at her desperation.

"She's not my sister," Bennett said.

Storm's smile grew a little brighter at his attitude toward me. "Which is why I thought you might like a little break and a change in company. We can go for a run."

"No."

He started to close the door on her, and she had the guts to put out a hand and stop it.

"Bennett, I've heard what's happening at the office. You're pushing your luck. You need to choose soon, or you'll risk your position in the pack. Aiden and Karter aren't the leaders you are."

"Excuse me?" I said. "That's a shit thing to say to their brother."

Her gaze shifted to me, and she shrugged. "They spent their childhoods playing with you, and Bennett spent his training and studying. Who do you think has more skill? I'm just stating facts."

Bennett's hand fisted at his side, a telltale warning sign. Although part of me wanted to see him physically toss Storm to the curb, the other part of me knew we couldn't afford any more trouble.

I heard Mom's voice in my head.

Are you going to be able to smooth things over at the first sign that he's about to lose his temper?

…Try giving him a hug…

Forget hugs. Those did not end well for me. Bennett needed a tranquilizer dart shot in his ass.

Stepping forward, I grabbed his shirt, just a pinch of material between my fingertips that I tugged gently to get his attention.

He looked down at me like he couldn't believe I'd grabbed him.

"You need to stop making people cry."

His expression shifted so quickly, I almost didn't catch the flash of guilt I saw. He took my hand in his and looked at Storm.

"If you heard what happened at work, you know I don't like uninvited guests. Please leave while I'm asking nicely."

Storm's gaze shifted from Bennett's face to his hand, which was holding mine prisoner, then to my face.

"Asking nicely is overrated sometimes," she said. Her gaze shifted back to his. "I'll see you at the pack run."

He didn't wait until she stepped back to close the door.

I tugged my hand free of his.

"As much as I hate to say it, I think you should listen to Storm and just claim your mate. Everyone around you will breathe easier then."

"Not everyone," he said, watching me.

He was right. There was one person who might not breathe easier, but I didn't think his mate would turn down the type of hard breathing he probably had in mind.

My heart skipped a beat as I recalled last night, and I quickly pushed the thought away.

"Are you ready?" I asked.

Again, his expression shifted, but he wasn't as quick to hide his shock, and I realized he'd misunderstood me.

"To leave, Bennett, not to claim your mate. Dragging your feet on that is your business, not mine."

I turned away from him, wondering if that was why he'd done what he had last night. Was he so strung out and desperate that he'd used me as a substitute for a few seconds? It wasn't like we were blood-related or anything, and I'd never really viewed Bennett as my brother, just as he'd never viewed me as his sister.

But even if that was what had happened, he needed to pull himself together because it couldn't happen again. Imagining Mom and Dad's various shocked reactions to learning Bennett had kissed my neck yielded the same result. They'd be furious with both of us. Probably Bennett more than me, but maybe not. After all, he was struggling for his mate, and a wolf's mate was the end-all be-all of his existence. I was the one with the no-boys rule.

In the garage, Bennett beat me to the driver's door and opened it for me. Once I was in, I set up the GPS on my phone to guide me to the nearest lower-class clothing store.

"Any specific destination in mind?" he asked, getting in.

"Yep." I didn't say where, though. If we made it there, it would probably offend his high-end tastes.

The second time driving into the city was much better than the first. The number of cars on the road didn't seem that different, but they weren't driving as aggressively as the commuter crowd had been.

I successfully navigated us to the first exit before things got more stressful. Knowing what lane I needed and figuring out which exit was next when they were right on top of each other wasn't easy.

"If you miss your turn, it's okay," Bennett said as if reading my mind. "You can turn around and try from the other direction."

It helped that he was calm and understanding about it because I did end up missing the turn and had to circle around.

By the time we arrived at the store I wanted, my hands were sweaty. I parked, turned off the engine, and looked at Bennett.

He was watching me.

"You amaze me, Wrenly. You were nervous, but you kept going. You always keep going, no matter how hard things get."

I thought of school again, where I hadn't had any choice but to keep going. Every second had been hell, and I hated that I'd had to endure it. I hated that I'd had a safe home I hadn't been allowed to return to. I didn't want to keep fighting through what was hard because it was expected of me. Easy sounded good.

Unfortunately, easy didn't play with the princess card I'd been dealt. I always had to fight for everything, just like Bennett said. And I felt no pride in it. I was too tired for pride.

"Ready to shop till you drop?" I asked him.

"Ready."

The store was bright and loud, filled with people who dressed as if they would never be able to afford a custom-made suit in their lives, and I *loved* it. Bennett stuck close to me like he had at the arcade, but he seemed fairly impassive about all the people this time. He occasionally asked why I liked a particular item or why I put an item back, but never with any tone to suggest he was impatient, only curious.

Normal clothes shopping was probably a novelty for him. It had been the same for me the first time I'd ventured out. Before that, the only clothes I'd ever owned had been given to me by Mom since as far back as I could remember.

Once I had a few pairs of shorts to try on with some spaghetti-strap tops and sports bras, I headed to the changing room. Bennett stood right outside while I did my thing. Each of the outfits showed more skin than ever before, and I felt like I looked *normal* for a change.

When I emerged once more dressed in my jeans, Bennett looked up from his phone.

"I'm all set," I said, holding up my selections in one hand and discarding the others.

He glanced at what I put on the rack but didn't comment as he followed me to the registers at the front. He paid for everything,

MELISSA HAAG

which was both good and a little disappointing. It saved me money, but it also robbed me of the joy of buying my own clothes. I was smart enough to know, though, that I couldn't draw attention to the fact that I had money they didn't know about yet.

Bennett carried the bags out and opened the back door to put them in the car.

When I moved to get into the driver's seat, he put his hand out and closed the door, trapping me between him and the car as he planted his other hand on the other side of me.

I stayed facing the car, unwilling to turn around. I didn't trust what he'd do.

"Are you going to tell me how you knew how to do all of that, Wrenly? The changing room, the return rack, and removing the hangers to make checking out quicker. You haven't been shopping for your own clothes your entire life."

My mind raced as I struggled to find a way to explain how I knew that wasn't the truth and wasn't a lie. I couldn't tell him that I'd walked through stores and watched people. He'd want to know why and, more importantly, how, since I'd been at a school with a locked-down campus.

"Talk," he said roughly.

"I hate my life." The words were out before I could stop them, and my eyes went wide.

I watched his hands fist against the door and felt him rest his forehead on the back of my head.

"Don't say that," he said, sounding strained.

I bit my lip, unsure how to take back what I said without making things worse. Then I decided honesty was the only thing that might save me.

"Where to go. What to wear. Who I can talk to. I've never had any freedom, Bennett. I know Mom and Dad love me, but it's…"

Bennett grabbed my shoulders and spun me around. His pupils had devoured his dark irises, and his jaw was tense as he stared at me.

"It's what?" he demanded, his voice rough.

"It's not living, Bennett. It's a suffocating cage, and I want out."

He closed his eyes.

Desperate for him to understand, to win him over to my side, I cupped his jaw, gently smoothing my fingers over the muscles that were twitching.

"Please help me convince them that they should let me go to school this fall. Please. I just want what everyone else my age has, what you had. A little bit of freedom to decide my own life."

He hit the door so hard that the metal groaned. I jumped at the sound, and my forehead hit his jaw. It hurt enough that I automatically rubbed the spot.

Bennett's arms wrapped around me.

"I'm sorry. Forgive me."

"I'm fine, Bennett," I said, feeling the panic start and pushing him. "You're holding me too tight."

He immediately loosened his hold and pulled back enough to look at me. His gaze searched mine, then lifted to my forehead.

"Are you okay, Miss?" a man asked, drawing my attention away from Bennett.

He caught my chin to stop me from looking at whoever was there.

"She's fine."

"I'm not asking you," the man said.

The way Bennett slowly turned his head to look at the guy rang all the warning bells. I reached up and covered Bennett's eyes.

"I'm fine," I said.

"The bruise on your cheek and the way he just hit the car say you might not be. I can call the police."

Bennett's growl was soft enough that only I heard it. At least, I hoped that was the case. I removed my hand from his eyes and grabbed his chin so he faced me, and I gave him a warning look.

"I appreciate you cared enough to stop and ask," I said to the man as I held Bennett's gaze. "And so will the next girl, who might be in trouble. I'm not. At least, not from this guy. He's overbearing all of the time, but he's not a bully, just protective."

Bennett winced and closed his eyes.

"Sometimes, that's how it starts," the man said. "Don't justify bad behavior. If someone really cares about you, they'll find every way to lift you up, not break you down."

"Thanks," I said, finally glancing at the middle-aged man. He nodded at me and walked away.

I waited until he was gone to nudge Bennett away from me.

"If you're done acting like an insane person, can we please leave?"

He opened his eyes and shot me an annoyed stare.

"I'll drive home."

He walked me around to the passenger side of the car. Once I was seated, he leaned into the car suddenly, invading my space, with his face once again inches from mine.

"Don't hate your life, Wrenly. Fight to make it what you want until you love it."

My seatbelt clicked into place, and he withdrew, closing the door for me.

I exhaled shakily and hoped Bennett's words meant he understood and was on my side. I really needed someone on my side.

CHAPTER EIGHT

SILENCE REIGNED ALL the way home. I thought maybe he was mad, but he grabbed my bags from the car and carried them up to my room. Then he left without a word.

Closing my door, I breathed a sigh of relief, grateful for a break from his mercurial mood swings, and went to put my new clothes away. They weren't anything fancy, but they were one hundred percent my choice. I ran my fingers over the material, relieved it wasn't a school uniform or something ridiculously expensive that would make people question who I was. I wanted to blend once I left here. Blending and escaping notice would be a nice change.

My phone buzzed with a new message.

Karter: What's your favorite color?
Me: Any color except blue and white. Why?
Karter: You hate blue and white? Weren't those your school colors?
Me: When are you going to tell me where you are so I can visit? I miss you!

My phone stayed silent.

Don't hate your life, Wrenly. Fight to make it what you want.

I tossed my phone onto my bed and used my laptop to log in to the university portal and check for emails from my professor for the online summer class I had registered for. There weren't any new communications after the introductory email explaining his expectations and requirements, which I'd already read. Bored and ready to take a step toward the future I wanted, I'd hoped for something more.

Unfortunately, the start date wasn't until next week.

With a sigh, I logged out and went to change into one of my new outfits. Dressed the way I liked, I jogged down the stairs and crept down the hallway toward Bennett's office.

I could hear the rumble of Bennett's voice through the closed door and hoped whoever he was talking to was loud enough that he wouldn't hear me. Being as silent as possible, I crept past to the back door, eased the handle down, and slipped outside.

The backyard had been my oasis as a child—a safe place I could play where the pack girls wouldn't pick on me. It hadn't changed much. A single swing still hung from the thick branch of an old tree. The lawn spread out around it, broken up by the occasional landscaping bed. The ones closest to the tree had flowers. The rest mostly had ornamental grasses and decorative trees. A dense body of trees defined the yard's border.

I walked toward the swing and gave it a test tug before sitting on it.

Bittersweet feelings surged as I reminisced about all the times I'd played right there with Aiden and Karter. Happy times broken by confusion and hurt. I still didn't know what to think of my childhood. Back then, my six-year-old self had been so grateful the Wulfs had taken me in. But it hadn't been easy.

From the start, Bennett had rejected each of my efforts to be his sister. He'd gotten so mad about it that Mom and Dad had sent him away to school at the start of the next school year. But it'd been too late. The pack girls had picked up on his standoffish attitude toward me.

Whenever I'd left the yard without Aiden and Karter, the girls had made my life hell. Hair-pulling, scratches, and name-calling had been a core part of my childhood and left a deep belief that I was unwanted, a belief that Mom had seemed to sense. She'd done her best to reassure me. The teasing had eased up a little after I told her what had been happening. During those first six years, I'd learned to avoid the pack girls.

Then, I'd been sent away for a new group of girls to bully me.

And why?

I'd broken their no-liking-boys rule. But in my heart, I knew it was also because Bennett had come home, and he'd seemed to hate me even more than he had before he'd left. I'd understood why. They'd sent him away because of his attitude toward me. I would have resented me for that, too, which was why I didn't hold any grudges for being sent away myself when I was twelve.

However, seven years was a long time to be locked away. Longer than Bennett had to endure.

With a sigh, I held onto the rope and tipped myself back to look at the blue sky peeking through the leaves.

Our family was complicated, no doubt about that. But my relationship with Bennett was even more so. He wouldn't acknowledge me as family, but other than that, he wasn't mean to me.

Before coming home, he'd never talked to me. Now, Mom and Dad had stuck him with me. I knew it was probably their way to force us to figure out how to get along. After all, we were both adults now. We should be able to manage a cordial relationship at this point in our lives.

But Bennett wasn't easy. Even Mom said as much. And after my attempted apology for hitting him in the face, I wasn't sure I wanted to keep trying with him.

"Some things just aren't meant to be," I said softly.

"Like what?"

Bennett's voice, so close behind me, startled me enough that I lost my grip on the rope and tipped backward. He caught me and swung me up into his arms. His pupils were dilated again as he looked at me.

"I didn't do that on purpose," I said.

"I know. What's not meant to be?"

Was I dumb enough to say, "any type of civil relationship with you" out loud? Hell no.

"Growing another four inches so I don't need to stand on a stool to reach the pot rack in the kitchen," I said.

He breathed in.

"I'm curious. Do you think I'm a liar, or do you doubt everything I say all the time?" I asked.

"I'm trying to understand you, Wrenly. You say things that are true, but not what you're actually thinking. Why?"

"How long are you going to keep holding me like this? That's what I'm really thinking. But it would have been rude to ignore your question and annoy you more than you already are, especially while you're holding me."

"You think I'm annoyed?"

"Aren't you always annoyed? Are you going to put me down, or are we going to work like this tomorrow?"

His gaze searched mine.

"I get it...a human shield is tempting. But if you really want the girls to leave you alone, you'd find a guy to carry into work."

He frowned and put me down. Then he had the gall to set his hand on the top of my head and level it out to where I measured up to him on his sternum.

"Ever heard the term small but deadly? Pick on my height, and the gloves come off."

"I wasn't picking on you. I was trying to figure out if four inches would be enough to reach the pot rack. Are you hungry?"

"Always. Any chance you want to go for a run first?"

"You want to go for a run? With me?"

His shock was almost comical.

"A horrible suggestion, right? But I think Mom and Dad would be happy if we tried to get along, don't you?"

The truth was that I wanted to go for a run but wasn't brave enough to go solo through the neighborhood now that Storm and the others knew I was home, and especially not after her visit this morning. Her veiled threat hadn't been that veiled.

Bennett studied me, his expression once again unreadable.

"So…"

"Go get changed," he said. "I'll meet you at the front door."

I pivoted and ran inside, not believing he'd actually agreed but excited to do something other than sit around for the rest of the day when it was so beautiful out.

Taking the stairs two at a time, I raced for my room, already pulling my shirt off. Something thumped behind me. I didn't glance back, not wanting to witness his censuring gaze when I was so happy.

I changed into a pair of shorts I'd purchased just for running and the cute sports bra that matched. School had required shirts, and I'd hated them. When I ran, I ran all out, as if I was being chased, because sometimes I was, and I got hot and sweaty. I looked forward to running the way I wanted. It might still be all out, but this time, it wouldn't be for my safety, and I wouldn't have wet material sticking to my lower back.

As soon as I was changed, I pulled my shoulder-length, light brown hair into a ponytail and jogged down the stairs. While I waited for Bennett, I started my active stretches until I heard him.

He walked down the stairs slowly, staring at me like I was a bomb about to go off. Some of my excitement started to fade.

Bennett, the fun killer.

Was he going to tell me to get a shirt? Or, worse, tell me he'd changed his mind?

My mind started racing with possible ways to negotiate for his willingness. Our neighborhood was large, with each house having at least ten acres of land. The road meandered through properties that all belonged to members of the Wulf pack. I needed him.

I watched him breathe in deeply as he crossed the entry.

"You were happy, and now you're not," Bennett said. "Why?"

"I'm waiting for you to kill the fun again."

He tilted his head, studying me as I frowned.

"Is that how you see what I do?"

"Isn't it? I got nervous yesterday, and you made me pull over. I found a cool spot to eat lunch, and you told me I needed to get back to the office because I happened to be next to a man. I wanted to go to the arcade, and you treated it like I'd taken you to a street fight. When we're at the office, you're giving orders and making people cry.

"But you were a fun killer even before this.

"Every time I started laughing with Aiden and Karter, no matter what we were doing, you'd tell on us, finding a way to spin our fun as something dangerous or against whatever rules you had in your head."

A flush heated my face. I hadn't meant to say all of that, but I was so tired of having everything I found just a little bit good taken away from me.

He reached out and trailed his fingers over my hot cheek.

"I didn't know that was how you saw it. I'm sorry, Wrenly. Do you still want to run with me?"

"Yes."

I waited, unsure whether he'd actually go through with it, until he dropped his hand to his side and stepped around me to open the door.

Heart surging with happiness, I bounded outside and spread my arms wide to breathe in the fresh air.

"Which way should we run?" he asked, watching me.

"Which way? Don't we have to stay in the community?" I asked.

He shook his head. "We can leave if we're together."

"Then that way," I said, pointing in the direction of the gate.

We started out with a light jog until I realized he was purposely keeping pace with me. Once we were outside the gate, we picked up the paved trail, and I lengthened my stride, which was considerably shorter than his.

I focused on my breathing and waited for that moment where everything warmed up and the usual euphoria swept through me. Running was something no one could take away from me. It was necessary.

Bennett stayed even with me as I settled into my long-distance pace. It felt so good to run all out. He didn't attempt to make conversation until we slowed to a walk on the way back.

"I didn't know you liked running. You weren't in track."

Still breathing hard, I glanced at him. "If you show what you like, people will find a way to take it away from you."

He frowned again, and his pupils dilated.

"Do you know they're doing studies regarding the correlation between anger, stress, and early-onset dementia?" I asked.

"Pardon?"

"You need to figure out a way to manage your temper." I gestured down to his fisted hands. "You're going to end up in a memory care facility before Mom and Dad if you don't."

"I'm upset that you think people will take away what you like."

I snorted, since he was one of those people, and started jogging again. Alternating between jogging and walking was part of my cool-down process. However, Bennett caught my arm to stop me.

"Talk to me, Wrenly. Why do you think you can't have what you want?"

"Because I can't even leave the community without permission, Bennett. Do you need it? Do Mom and Dad? Aiden or Karter? No. Just me. I'm only allowed to do what I'm allowed to do. Not what I want to do. Not since the day I—"

I looked down the path, hating what I'd been about to say. I loved Mom and Dad, but sometimes, I hated them too.

"Please let go of my arm," I said. "You're going to leave a bruise."

The uncomfortable pressure of his grip vanished.

"I don't know you," he said. His words carried pain and disbelief, which I thought was laughable.

"Of course you don't. I've been gone for seven years. Before that, you were gone for five. We're pretty much strangers, Bennett."

I started jogging again, uncaring if he was with me or not, until I reached the gate. There, I paused to make sure he was close. He stopped jogging, only a few steps behind me.

We stared at each other. For the first time ever, Bennett looked like he had no idea what to do.

"Do you want to keep running, or should we head back?" I asked. His shirt wasn't even a little sweaty, while I could feel my sweat running down my back.

"What do you want to do?" he asked.

"Head back. It was a good run. If you're up for one after work tomorrow, I'm game."

He nodded, and we walked together through the gate.

"Did you run often at school?"

"Yeah," I said.

"Where?"

I glanced at him. "That's a weird question. Where do you think I ran?"

"They have one track, and you never used it. So where did you run?"

"How do you know I never used it?"

"It's monitored, and the instructors said you never used it with the other students."

I shook my head in a combination of disbelief and amazement. It didn't surprise me that Mom and Dad had gotten updates from school, monitoring my activity from afar. It surprised me that they shared the information with Bennett and that they, along with the staff, had been so damn clueless.

"Yeah, well...there are a lot of places there that weren't

monitored," I said, thinking of our rooms and how there'd been dead spots in the halls and grounds. Especially the one near the section of fence that I'd gotten really good at climbing over.

"Are you really not going to tell me?" Bennett asked.

"What does it matter?"

"I feel like you're keeping secrets from me."

"Who cares if I am? It's not like you tell me every little thing about your life."

"If you want to know something, I'd tell you."

"Oh?" I stopped walking and faced him with my arms crossed. "Then who's your mate?"

His gaze dipped to my crossed arms, and he said nothing.

"See? We all keep things to ourselves, Bennett. They're not secrets, there's just parts of us we don't feel like sharing."

He didn't look happy with the valid point I'd made, but he wasn't angry.

"Tell me where you ran, and I'll make sure you can leave whenever you want as long as you have your phone with you."

"Deal!" I said, not hiding my excitement. I couldn't believe he'd actually initiated a deal first. My plan had actually worked. "I ran on the road outside of school."

He frowned. "How? You didn't have permission to leave, and they monitored the gate."

"That bit of information would require another deal," I said.

"What do you want?"

"I'm not sure yet. I'll let you know when I think of something."

He didn't say anything else until we reached the front door.

"Did you think of something?"

"Not yet."

His pupils dilated, and I shrugged.

"I think I'll wait to see how good you are at keeping your first promise before making more deals."

"You don't trust me?"

"Nope."

He scowled at me and then stalked off to the study.

Too happy from the run to care about his grumpiness, I jogged upstairs and closed myself inside my room to take a shower.

As I washed off the sweat, I considered my next move. If Bennett kept his word and I had permission to leave, that meant I could meet up with Sophia.

Giddy at the idea, I hurried to blow dry my hair and rushed out to my bedroom, only to stop short at the vast emptiness where my bed once resided.

It was gone. Not just the mattress, but the whole damn thing.

"Bennett!" I yelled angrily.

He appeared in my open doorway and opened his mouth, but no sound came out. He just stared at me as his pupils slowly grew.

"Where is my bed?" I demanded.

He stuck his hands into his pockets and leaned against the doorjamb.

"I took it."

"I already figured that part out. Where is it?"

"How did you leave school?"

"I already told you. I'm not making a deal until I verify the first one." Stomping my way to my closet, I grabbed a pair of underwear and slipped them on underneath the towel I had wrapped around my torso.

A second later, my back was against the closet door, and my hands were pinned over my head by one of Bennett's. I could feel the edge of the towel I'd tucked in above my breasts loosen.

"Cut it out, Bennett. Save your tantrum for when I'm dressed so I don't embarrass both of us."

His gaze raked down my body in a way that set off the warning bells in my head.

He breathed in deeply.

"Stop smelling my emotions!"

"You're frustrating me," he said.

"Me? You took my bed!"

"What do you see me as, Wrenly?" he asked with a level of calm that made me want to hurt him.

"Probably not the best time to ask me because you *won't* like the answer."

He growled and dipped his head so I felt his exhale on my neck. My eyes went wide as I realized what kind of mood he was in, and I started fighting against his hold.

The towel came loose and pooled around my feet.

I froze.

So did Bennett.

Closing my eyes against the swell of embarrassment and pure rage, I said, "Leave before I do something that will see one of us bleeding again."

"I'm not giving up, Wrenly. I'll never give up."

Then he released me. I quickly opened my eyes as I covered myself, but he was already gone.

With my temper flaring, I slammed a drawer closed…or I tried to. It was one of those silent kinds that wouldn't slam, which only made me madder.

What did it matter how I left school? Why was he being so obsessive? He needed to get a life. No, better yet, he needed his dumb mate.

In the middle of my silent rage-fest, doubt crept in.

What if he told Mom and Dad I'd snuck out of school? The thought worried me. I needed their trust if I wanted to attend the University of my choice.

I let out a frustrated growl.

Bennett was right. We weren't done with this topic.

I hurried to finish dressing then found him in his bedroom. He was facing away from the door, just standing there like a lunatic with his hands fisted at his sides. At least, he hadn't thrown his dresser this time.

"If you say anything to Mom and Dad about me leaving school without permission, I promise I'll tell them what you just did."

He was in front of me so fast that I never even saw him move.

"What did I just do?"

The anger in his gaze had me second-guessing my threat, or at least the timing of it.

I retreated a step, but he followed.

"When are Mom and Dad coming home?" I asked.

"They aren't. You're stuck with me, and I'm out of patience."

He was out of patience? What about *me*?

Realizing we couldn't both be out of control, I purposefully emptied myself of the storm of emotions I was feeling. Once I shut that afraid and angry part of myself away, I looked at Bennett with a calm gaze.

"What do you want?"

His hand cupped the back of my head, and I felt the tremble in his fingers as he drew my face toward his. My heart stuttered with fear and panic, though I tried not to feel it, and I turned my head away from him.

He set his forehead against my temple.

"I want you to stop seeing me as your enemy," he said softly against my ear. "Please."

The 'please' confused me. Bennett never said please to anyone. At least, not that I'd ever heard.

"I don't see you as an enemy," I said, resisting the urge to pull out of his hold.

"You don't trust me."

"I don't know you, just like you don't know me. Do you trust strangers?"

He was quiet for several long, tormenting seconds.

"You're right. I'm sorry." He sighed and released me, looking more in control.

Bennett definitely wasn't stable. No one stable could switch moods that fast, could they?

"Will you give me a chance to get to know you?" he asked.

"Sure. Just don't expect me to tell you everything like we're at some weird, girl slumber party."

"Is that what you did at school?"

I snorted. "Not my school. Were you serious that I can leave whenever I want now? By myself?"

His expression closed. "Why? Where do you want to go?"

"I'm not sure yet. I think I just want to see if I can."

"Okay. Then, I was serious. I'll call the guard now and let him know."

A smile erupted on my face. "Thanks. Can I borrow your car too? I promise to be the most responsible and sensible driver and return it in one piece."

He looked down for a second. "You'll need to talk to Mom first."

"What? Why? I thought you said you could make it so I can leave whenever I want."

The intense way he looked up made me want to retreat a step, but I held my ground.

"You can. It's just that...Mom will worry and want to know where you're going and who you're meeting."

I stared at him, certain that, if I had his sense of smell, I would have caught him in a lie.

Without looking away, I dialed Mom and put her on speaker.

"Mom, can I borrow a car?"

"Of course, sweetie. Where are you going? Do you want company? Bennett could go with you."

"Bennett's busy, and I don't know where I want to go."

She was quiet for a long moment. "You just got home and don't know the area well. I would feel better if you waited until Bennett wasn't busy."

"And I would feel better if I were treated like an adult and not a child who has zero common sense."

"Oh, sweetie, that's not what—"

I hung up on her, turned around, and walked out of his room.

Something crashed behind me, but I didn't care about his poor, rich-boy meltdown. I was trying to avoid my own.

CHAPTER NINE

Mom tried calling me a million times. So did Grandma and Dad. Apparently, they hadn't involved Aiden and Karter yet because they didn't call. Not even once. Bennett knocked on my door countless times, though. Thankfully, he never came in, even when I didn't respond to him.

Was I sulking? No. I was plotting.

They thought they could keep me caged...controlled...but I was done living like that.

I spent the remainder of Sunday making plans to meet up with Sophia for lunch on Tuesday. It was the only guaranteed time I would be able to get away without someone noticing I was gone.

Since I had no bed, I slept in Karter's. It didn't smell like the person I remembered, which made me sad and made me wonder if that part of my life was gone for good.

A soft repetitive sound brought me out of my sleep enough to recognize someone pacing. The low murmur of Bennett's voice assured me who it was and lulled me back to sleep.

In the morning, Karter's door was open, but the hall was empty.

I quietly crept back into my room and started to get ready for work. When I emerged from my room, I interrupted Bennett's pacing in the hallway.

He was impeccably dressed as always, but the look in his eyes was unsettling. Not angry exactly. Definitely a little off kilter—understandable since he'd been pacing in the middle of the night and was probably only running on a few hours of sleep.

Which was why, when he took a step toward me, I retreated one and grabbed my door.

He held up his hands and took a step back.

"I just wanted to ask if we should stop to get something to eat on the way to work, and if you wanted to drive."

"I can drive?" I asked, surprised.

"Of course."

"You say 'of course' as if things are a given, but we both know they're not. They literally have to be given to me."

He bared his teeth for a second. I didn't think it was at me, but more at what I was saying. I didn't know why it mattered to him so much. Had Mom and Dad bribed him? Were they paying him to make nice with me or something? Make Wrenly happy so she'll stay? It wasn't going to work.

"I know you're disappointed," he said slowly. "I swear I'm trying to find ways to make things better. Please give me a chance."

I wasn't exactly sure what he was talking about, but I nodded anyway because he looked like he was two seconds from throwing something again. Since I was the nearest object not attached to the house in some way, I figured it'd be wise not to provoke him further.

"I'll pass on driving to work, and I'm not really that hungry yet."

"You didn't eat much yesterday."

"I'm aware. Are you telling me I have to eat?"

"No," he said quickly. "If you change your mind, let me know."

"Okay."

The ride to work seemed more tense than it had the week before. The silence was the same, but his white-knuckled grip on the steering wheel wasn't. We rode up the elevator together, and Walt happened to join us again on the lobby elevator.

When he said good morning, I smiled and nodded, very aware of Bennett's disapproving presence.

On our floor, Bennett motioned for me to go first. The women we passed eyed me and said good morning to him. He didn't say anything back.

It felt like I was walking to my execution instead of my desk. The note and breakfast croissant that waited for me didn't ease the feeling.

Sighing, I crumpled the note after reading it, tossed it in the garbage, and grabbed the bag to take with me. It looked like food wasn't optional anymore either. I felt Bennett's gaze as I headed off to Mom's office.

Her door was closed when I arrived, and through her office blinds, I saw she was on the phone. She saw me and motioned for me to come in.

"I understand," I heard her say as I opened the door. "Stop worrying. Goodbye."

She hung up and stood, coming around the desk to hug me.

"I apologize for yesterday, sweetheart. I didn't understand what was happening."

"Oh? And what do you think was happening?"

Mom pulled back to look at me, probably surprised at my tone and that I hadn't said everything was okay.

"You want to live independently, and we're stifling you," she said immediately.

That she understood almost brought tears to my eyes. She saw and hugged me again.

"My poor girl," she said soothingly. "I know this isn't easy on you, and I'm sorry for that. I promise it will get better soon. It's hard to let go and give you the freedom you need when we worry so much. If anything happened to you…"

She hugged me harder, and I finally hugged her back. It was hard

MELISSA HAAG

to stay mad when I knew they weren't restricting me to be mean. They truly loved me.

"Life is meant to be lived, Mom. You're worried something will happen to me, so you're ensuring nothing happens. That's the same as being dead to me."

She sniffled, and I rubbed her back.

"Please don't cry, Mom. I'm not asking to join a gang or get a tattoo on my face. I just want to be able to come and go as I please, like everyone else in the house."

"I know. Please give us a little more patience. You've only been home a few days."

The comment reminded me of something else bothering me, and I eased out of her embrace to look into her teary eyes.

"I've been home for five days, Mom. But you and Dad haven't. Neither have Aiden or Karter. Why not?"

"Dad and I have a place in the city to make entertaining a little easier. And you've already guessed that Aiden and Karter are visiting other packs to find their mates."

Which meant they probably wouldn't be back for a long time, and once they were, they wouldn't have time for me. Knowing that hurt. That unwanted, abandoned kid feeling roared forward again.

"Can I stay with you and Dad?"

"Why? Don't you like your new room?"

"I love it. But the whole point of coming home was to be with my family, wasn't it?"

She didn't look away or change her expression, but I still saw a subtle shift that let me know the question made her uncomfortable.

"Of course it is. And you are with family. Bennett's there."

"He's never seen himself as my family."

"That's absolutely not true, Wrenly. Bennett loves you."

I snorted and turned to take a seat on the couch as I opened the bag.

"How long do I need to work here? And when are you and Dad

112

free to have a conversation about college? I found several that I like with the programs I'm interested in."

Her silence spoke volumes, but I didn't verbally backtrack as I opened my sandwich and took a bite. As I chewed, I waited her out.

"We're doing a lot of entertaining in the evenings and meetings during the day," she said finally. "I'll check our schedules and let you know."

"Okay. I've gotten acceptance from all the universities I applied to. Before I make my selection and send the first payment, I'd hoped for your opinion."

I took a bite as she digested that bit of shocking news. And it was shocking. I didn't need a shifter nose to tell me that. Mom sat next to me and stole the sandwich from my hands to claim my attention.

"Where did you apply, Wrenly?" Worry laced her tone.

"Me going off to college isn't something you should be afraid of, Mom. And your reaction right now is why I want to have a real conversation about it. Let's wait until Dad can be here, too, that way I won't interrupt your already busy day." I removed my hands from hers and grabbed my sandwich. "Thank you for breakfast. It's good."

She didn't stop me from leaving her office.

When I closed the door, I saw she was already reaching for her phone. Probably to tell Dad I was veering from whatever plans they'd set for me.

When I returned to my desk, Bennett's door was closed, but the blinds were open. I could see he was on the phone. He wasn't talking. He was listening to what looked like bad news.

Internally sighing, I sat at my desk, finished my breakfast, and waited for whatever hellstorm Bennett would unleash today.

"It makes no sense that they picked you for his secretary," Milena said.

I didn't bother looking at her as I responded, "Didn't we already go over this? He finds your desperation annoying."

She growled.

I looked her in the eye and shrugged.

Her pupils dilated. "Watch your back, Charity."

"Wipe your drool, Bin."

"Bin?"

"Bitch In Need."

She was over the desk before I knew she was coming and had me pinned against the wall by my throat. From the corner of my eye, I saw Bennett move. The door banged open, and she was ripped away from me a second later.

I crumpled to the floor, holding my neck, and as I wheezed for air, I watched Bennett pin her to the wall like she had done to me.

"She is a Wulf. You will extend her the same respect you extend me, or you and your family can find another pack. Am I clear?"

"She—"

He slammed her against the wall. The drywall indented with a snap.

"Am I clear?"

People gathered at the opening of the office suite, watching the drama unfold. No one spoke, but I could feel their accusing gazes as Bennett waited for her answer.

"Clear," she rasped.

He dropped her like a hot stone and turned toward me. He offered his hand, which I ignored as I got to my feet.

"In my office. Now," he said.

Without looking at any of them, I marched into his office. He was right on my heels and closed the door behind us. Then he closed the blinds so they couldn't see.

He grabbed my shoulders and tipped my chin up to look at my neck.

"Does it hurt to swallow? Can you speak?"

"I quit."

He released my chin and looked into my eyes. "It won't happen again."

Was he an idiot? It might not happen where he would see it, but it most definitely *would* happen again.

"You're right...because I quit."

"You can't."

"Are you going to drag me into the office every day?"

"We made a deal. You said you'd eat lunch with me if I didn't tell Mom and Dad you were eating next to a man last week."

I stared at him, knowing damn well what would happen if he told them that before I had a chance to talk to them about college.

"I hate you."

"Then hate me. But you're not quitting."

With a final glare at him, I left the office, making sure to slam his door as hard as possible.

He left me alone for the rest of the morning but kept his blinds open so he could watch me. Did he think I'd run? I had to admit I was tempted. How much would it cost to take a ride-share home? I checked. Thirty dollars. I had that.

But I didn't do it. I sat there and worked, thinking about how a little patience now would bring me freedom later. Because Mom was right. I'd only been home for five days after years of being away. They needed to know I could successfully survive as an adult on my own.

An hour before lunchtime, I left my desk to use the bathroom. As I'd anticipated, several of the office girls entered behind me.

"You want Bennett?" I asked before any of them spoke. "Have him. I'm leaving for an hour. Good luck. Tell him I called him an asshole before I left and that I plan on spitting in his lunch."

They all stared after me, open-mouthed in shock.

No one else bothered me on my way out. On the street, I walked several blocks down and then over without any destination in mind. I just wanted the air and the time away.

My phone buzzed with a voice message.

"If you want to spit in my lunch, that's fine," Bennett said, "but you're going too far to do it. A bento box from the place next to our building is fine."

I sent him the finger emoji in return. He immediately replied with another voice message.

"You have ten minutes to get back here, or I will bring you back, and you won't like how."

The people walking toward me gave me a wide berth as I called Bennett every bad name I could think of. Then I turned around and started back.

I bought two bento boxes, and when I got outside, I shook his like it was a dice cup. It was more satisfying than spitting in it.

He was waiting for me by the elevator doors on the twelfth floor. He didn't look as mad as I thought he would. Just relieved. He stole the lunch bags from me and motioned for me to lead the way.

Mom was out of her office, talking to some of the workers. When she saw me with Bennett, she smiled. I flashed her a smile I didn't feel. Her smile faltered, and the women noticed. Of course they did. From their point of view, it looked like Mom was being loving and supportive and I was just being a bitch. Whatever.

When we reached the office suite, I noticed my laptop was missing from my desk as we passed it. Its location had changed to the coffee table in Bennett's office, where he set the lunch bag. He brought out both boxes and looked at me.

"Which one is mine?"

"The top one."

He nodded, sat on the couch, and watched me expectantly.

Rolling my eyes, I sat next to him and grabbed my lunch along with the chopsticks. He opened his at the same time I opened mine and paused. Staying focused on my lunch, I didn't let myself feel any glee or satisfaction—just annoyance.

"You didn't spit in it," he said.

I chewed my mouthful of rice and cucumber. When I swallowed that, I took another bite, making it clear I wasn't going to answer him.

He looked down at his mixed-up box and started eating.

I finished first, dumped my garbage, then moved to take my laptop. He put his hand on top of it, stopping me.

"Lunch is an hour. Minimum."

"Whatever," I said, moving to sit in his office chair.

His jaw ticced. I wished I could make mine do the same.

"If you don't like me sitting here, switch spots with me. I'll take the couch."

He stood, and I kept my word. Only, instead of sitting, I lay down and turned my back to him.

MY NECK WAS STIFF, and I didn't immediately remember where I was as I sat up and saw the shaded office windows. With a frown, I turned my head and found Bennett leaning back in his chair, watching me.

He seemed pretty relaxed for a change.

"What time is it?" I asked.

"Two."

"Good." I grabbed my laptop and left his office, making sure to remove the "knock and die" Post-it note from the door after I closed it.

I'd barely settled into my chair when one of the office girls peeked around the corner.

"What do you do in there for two hours?" she asked.

"Me? As little as possible. If you have any tips on how else to get fired, let me know."

She gave me a surprised look. "Why would you want to get fired?"

"Do you honestly think I asked for this job? I wasn't given a choice. I'm never given a choice. I'm told where to go and what to do. Do you know I picked out my own clothes for the first time this weekend? So, by all means, figure out a way for me to get fired, and

I'll leave this desk so all of you can be someone else's pain in the ass because I don't need it!"

The blinds suddenly opened.

I spun around, flipped Bennett off, and left my desk.

Every word I'd spoken was the truth, but I didn't really care as much as I'd portrayed. I'd purposefully gotten myself worked up so everyone would smell my anger and realize I wasn't the actual stepping stone in their path to Bennett. He was.

Bullies tended to give up once they no longer had a reason to bully. Unfortunately, sometimes the reason was a personal grudge. Those never went away.

After using the bathroom, I returned to my desk and found a piece of chocolate on it. I picked it up, looking at it closely. It didn't appear that it'd been unwrapped already, but that didn't mean anything. I'd been fed laxatives once under the guise of friendship and learned the hard way not to trust gifts from frenemies.

I glanced at the door to the office suite, but no one was there. When I glanced at the office window, Bennett was standing in front of the couch, watching me. I gestured to the chocolate then to him. He nodded.

That he'd left a piece of chocolate for me after I'd flipped him off confused me. Was it a peace offering?

At least, if it was from Bennett, I knew it wouldn't be a laxative. Well, it shouldn't be, but if it were, I would be able to leave early. So I unwrapped it and stuck it into my mouth. It started melting almost immediately and was so damn good.

He smiled slightly and turned away to go back to his desk.

A little less annoyed, I sat at mine and got to work. The rest of the afternoon passed quickly. No one tried to bother Bennett, which meant that no one bothered me.

By the time his office door opened a few minutes after five, I'd finished analyzing another subsidiary's expenses, which I sent to Bennett's email.

"Ready to go?" he asked.

"Yep."

I followed him out of the office and noticed more women were lingering at their desks than usual. He didn't even look their way. But they weren't watching him. They were watching me.

Shrugging it off, I continued to follow in his wake.

"Did you like the chocolate?" he asked once we were in the elevator alone.

"Yeah. It was pretty good. What kind was it?"

"It's handmade from a shop downtown," he said. "I'll get some more."

"Kay."

"Do you have any plans tonight?"

I glanced at him, wondering if being a dick just came naturally.

"What do you think, Bennett?"

His jaw clenched briefly.

"Do you want to go out for dinner?" he asked after several seconds.

"Sure. Did you have somewhere in mind?"

"Depends. What types of foods do you like to eat?"

"What...didn't the school instructors give Mom and Dad a rundown of everything on my plate for the last seven years?"

"I'm learning not to trust the information they provided."

"They seriously tracked what I ate? Unbelievable." I shook my head.

"Did you have a favorite food?"

Since he wasn't angry and asking nicely, I thought about it for a second. "Honestly, I was too busy eating fast to pay attention to what was on my plate. The instructors probably noticed more than I did."

"Didn't they give you enough time to eat?"

"Lunch was free time, and I had other things to do."

"Like what?"

I shrugged lazily. "Where's my bed?"

"How does some brick oven pizza sound?" he asked, not even missing a beat.

"I'm willing," I said indifferently.

The pepperoni pizza Mom had brought home a few days ago was the exception to the pizza I'd eaten over the years, not the norm. Whenever the school tried doing pizza, they always went for overly complicated chef creations. Rich people's food. What was wrong with pepperoni, mushrooms, and onions?

It didn't take us long to reach the restaurant. However, they already had an hour waitlist, so Bennett put his name in and suggested we walk around a nearby park. I quickly agreed. Moving around and seeing something new sounded great.

We walked side by side on the sidewalk. There weren't many people out, but he still grabbed my hand and pulled me closer...and he didn't let go.

Did he honestly think I was going to wander off?

His hold shifted, and his fingers twined through mine. The way my heart tripped sent a ripple of shock through me, and I quickly pulled my hand from his.

To cover the awkwardness, I pointed at the park sign again with the hand I'd reclaimed.

"Is that the one?"

The weight of his regard made my panic want to grow, but I breathed through it as I dropped my hand to my side and quickened my pace.

That wasn't what it seemed like. Just shake it off. No boys. Especially not Bennett. No more cages called "private school."

I blamed all the togetherness over the last few days. And the way he kept doing things that could be easily misunderstood. Not that I misunderstood. I knew Bennett didn't see me as anything. He'd made that very clear. I was just a safe female he could be affectionate with in place of his mate.

The park entrance was prettily landscaped with flower beds that were between their spring and summer blooms. The paths were new, wide enough that we could walk with space between us, and winding—a perfect distraction.

"What toppings did you usually have on your pizza at school?" Bennett asked when a few minutes of silence had passed.

"I'm not sure. I didn't really pay attention. It wasn't the traditional stuff like a pepperoni, mushroom, and onion, though, that's for sure."

"Pepperoni, mushroom, and onion sounds good." He waited a beat. "My favorite is probably pepperoni, sausage, mushrooms, and bell peppers on a New York-style crust."

I nodded.

His fingers caught the tips of mine, stopping me.

"Do you still hate me?"

"Does it matter?"

"It does."

I sighed. "If I say I don't, will I get my bed back tonight?"

His eyebrows twitched like he couldn't decide whether to frown or be surprised.

"It'll take more than that to get your bed back," he said. "It'll take even more than knowing how you left school now. I want to know why you rushed your meals. It wasn't just lunch. It was every meal. Where did you go? What did you do? You completely disappeared from all the security cameras."

It took a few seconds for what he was saying to sink in. He'd known when he'd asked about my favorite foods.

I ripped my hand free of his.

"You had them check?" I asked in disbelief.

CHAPTER TEN

BENNETT'S dark gaze searched mine as he breathed in. He knew I was angry, but he still nodded.

"Why, Bennett? I graduated. I'm done with that place. What does it matter?"

"I'm trying to understand you."

"Why? I've already told you everything you need to understand, but you're not listening. What more do I need to say?"

"Why won't you talk to me about your time there?"

"Because it was hell, Bennett! And I don't want to revisit it."

This time, he did look shocked. "Hell?"

Angry, I fisted my hands at my sides.

"Are we taking a nice, quiet walk before dinner or giving up and going home?" I asked.

His frustration with me peeked through as his gaze searched mine.

"We'll walk," he said finally.

"Good." I started walking, my stride long and fast to convey my irritation.

I shouldn't have let him provoke me into saying what I'd said. What if he went back to Mom and Dad? Would they think that school in general was the problem, and not want me to attend university?

Does it matter what they want anymore? I asked myself.

I'd listened to them for thirteen years. Couldn't I be just a little selfish and decide for myself what I wanted to do with the next four? It wasn't like I would cut ties with them when I left. I'd be home at break and for the summer...if they wanted me to.

Unless it was like it was now. Then, there was no point in coming home to be harassed by Bennett.

"We should head back to the restaurant," he said after we'd lapped the park several times and my steps had slowed.

"Okay."

He held out his hand to me. I glanced down at it before looking at him.

"I stopped needing to hold hands when I was seven," I said. "If I remember, you're the one who pointed out to Aiden and Karter that I was too old to need handholding. Still don't need it now."

He fisted his hand and pulled it back to his side.

The walk to the restaurant was silent. Thankfully, we only needed to wait a few more minutes before we were seated.

When the server came to take our order, Bennett looked at me.

"Would you like to order for us?"

"Really?"

He nodded, and I ordered the pizza I wanted.

"The food comes out pretty quickly here," he said. "Is there anything you want to do after?"

His question ripped me out of my giddy anticipation spiral.

"Why are you being so nice to me?" Was he worried I'd still quit? We both knew that wasn't an option if Mom and Dad didn't want it to be an option. What was his motive then?

"Is this still about how I got out of school? I climbed a wall, okay? Now let it go and give me my bed back."

The corner of his mouth lifted slightly. "I already told you it would take more than how you left school to get your bed back."

I shrugged. He could keep my bed. Karter's had been comfortable.

"What was your favorite thing about school?" Bennett asked.

"Leaving it."

He sniffed, smelled the absolute truth of my words, and his eyebrows lifted.

"It was the best school in the country. The instructors said you excelled at every class."

"If you want me to stay sitting at this table, I suggest you change the subject," I said.

His pupils pulsed larger briefly.

"Do you like shorts, pants, or skirts better?"

"Clothes preferences, Bennett? Really?"

"I honestly don't know what questions to ask you to get to know you better that won't result in annoying you."

"Me neither," I admitted. Then I sighed and added, "I guess I don't know what I like. I've been told what to wear for so long that I've stopped thinking about my own preferences. Shorts are good for running. Pants are good for cold weather or climbing. Skirts and dresses are probably my least favorite since they aren't meant to make me feel comfortable; they're meant to make everyone around me comfortable."

He cocked his head. "What do you mean?"

Since his tone was curious and his body language was calm, I spoke my mind, not a filtered version that brushed the truth.

"Women are supposed to wear skirts to look good. To be presentable. To appeal to men. But I'm not supposed to appeal to men, am I? So, to me, skirts are the physical representation of all the rules that have stifled my life up to now.

"Giving me a skirt is like telling me to shut up and look pretty because that's all I'm good for. But not too pretty or I'll get sent away again."

He breathed in deeply and let it out slowly, and I got the feeling it wasn't to test my scent to see if I was telling the truth. He was upset.

"Are you really that disappointed I'm not a fan of skirts?"

"I thought we were giving you everything, Wrenly. Unconditional love. Safety. Anything you wanted."

I let out a loud "Ha!" that drew the attention of the nearby tables.

"Unconditional love? Are you serious? Because you couldn't stand me, you were sent away to fucking boarding school, Bennett. And when you graduated, it was my turn to be shipped off somewhere. In what universe does that say unconditional love?"

He swept his hand through his hair, and he looked like he was about to say something when the server appeared with our pizza.

Grateful for the distraction, I reached for a slice.

"Wrenly, I—"

"Drop it, Bennett. The past is in the past, where it belongs. Dwelling on it won't change it. We need to move forward. We're doing what Mom and Dad wanted and working together. We're talking like adults, most of the time. In a few months, I'll be out of your hair again, and we can both live our lives the way we want and only have to see each other on the holidays.

"Now dig in, or I'm shoving a piece of this pizza into your mouth myself."

His jaw tensed—he was going to crack a tooth clenching that hard —and for a moment, he didn't do anything but stare at me. Then he reached forward and took a piece of pizza.

It was the best damn pizza I had in my life. I hummed along happily with each bite, uncaring if people heard or what Bennett thought.

His temper seemed to fade with each piece I consumed. We'd ordered a large to share, which wasn't actually that big, and I ate almost half of it. He didn't say anything when I went for the last piece. He just turned the tray so I could reach it better.

"That was the best thing I've ever eaten," I said.

He waved for the check.

"Better than the chocolate?" he asked.

"The chocolate was the best sweet I've ever had. The pizza is the best savory."

He smiled—a real, honest-to-moon smile. And for a moment, I saw exactly why all the girls flocked to him. Bennett was devastatingly gorgeous.

I quickly looked away.

"Thanks for dinner," I said when he paid and stood.

"You're welcome. If you want, we can come back here tomorrow, or try another place I know."

"We'll see how annoyed with you I am tomorrow."

"Deal."

We walked back to the car together, and he opened the passenger door for me. It still felt weird, especially after going out to eat with him, but I didn't make a big deal out of it. I just got in.

"Do you want to turn on some music?" he asked on the way home.

"Sure."

He glanced at me as I glanced at him.

"Oh, you mean I should turn it on?"

"I don't know what kind of music you like."

"The instructors didn't tell you?" I asked, mostly teasing.

"They never noticed you listening to any."

"That's because I didn't." Music masked the sounds of people trying to sneak up on me.

"What about when you run?"

"Just the sound of my surroundings." Even when I'd left school grounds, I hadn't let my guard down.

"Then tell me if a song is pass or fail."

We played that game all the way home, and it was kind of fun. He laughed a few times when I made a face at a few songs I really didn't care for, which I found a little disconcerting. I couldn't recall Bennett ever laughing before. But it sounded nice—a slow, deep sound that wrapped around me and begged for attention.

By the end of the ride, I decided that "happy Bennett" was

dangerous. I let my guard down around "happy Bennett" and actually answered a few simple questions about school, like which subject I'd liked learning the most and what was my favorite kind of running shoe.

"Thank you for today," he said when he parked.

"Why? I didn't do anything."

His expression closed off again. "You spent time with me without getting mad."

I wanted to correct him, since I'd actually gotten mad several times, but kept my mouth shut since he'd actually been pretty decent the whole day.

He got out while I stayed in my seat for a moment, thinking back. Had my guilt about his being sent away to school skewed my view of Bennett? Had I reacted to him defensively when he'd come home because of it? I didn't think so, but that had been years ago, and so much had happened since then that those memories were a little fuzzy. What I did remember was that he'd always been disapproving and had never accepted me as a sister. The latter still held true.

My door opened, and Bennett stood back so I could get out.

"Thank you," I said.

I glanced at him twice, debating whether or not I should ask what I wanted to ask and risk creating a rift again.

As we walked through the kitchen, I decided I needed to know the truth.

"Does this mean you see me as your sister now?"

He stopped walking and looked at me.

"No. I will never see you as my sister, Wrenly."

It didn't hurt. It'd stopped hurting a long time ago. But it didn't let me know where I stood, either. He watched me, waiting. For my reaction or for a question I would never ask?

Turning away from him, I went to my room. My bed was still missing—no surprise there—so I sat on the floor with my laptop in my lap and checked my bank balance. That reminded me that I hadn't filled out any paperwork when starting at Wulf Enterprises. Where, then, would my promised wages go?

I grabbed my phone and sent Mom a message.

Me: When is payday, and will it be a check, or do you need my banking info for auto-deposit?
Mom: Auto-deposit. I've already filled out everything for you.
Me: Can you please change it to a check?
Mom: Why? Do you need something?

A little independence, but I didn't say that. It would just fall on deaf ears. I also couldn't tell her that I wanted to deposit the check into an account they didn't have access to.

Me: I don't need anything. Did you open an account for me?
Mom: Ages ago. Ask Bennett about it.
Me: Okay. So, no chance on the paper check then?
Mom: It would be more work for our finance department.

"Right," I said to myself. "It would have been more believable if you said you were afraid I'd give myself a paper cut."

Bored and annoyed, I tried calling Karter. It went right to voicemail, and I got a message a few seconds later saying that he couldn't answer but could text. So I tried calling Aiden. I just wanted someone to talk to for a little while to pass the time. And it'd been ages since I talked to them on the phone. However, Aiden sent back a message almost identical to Karter's.

I rolled my eyes, wondering if it was revenge for all of the times I'd been unable to answer the phone to talk to them while I was at school. So I sent a group chat.

Me: I was just bored. You're both lame for not picking up. Guess I'll need to call my other friends.

Karter: Girl or guy?
Me: Non-binary
Aiden: Not funny. Are you talking to guys?
Me: Yeah. Two of them at the same time. I hope your mates take one look at you and run away screaming.
Karter: That's mean. What did Bennett do to make you mad?
Me: He said I'll never be his sister, but I'm not mad about it. His hate is his problem, not mine.

They both replied that Bennett didn't hate me, that he just didn't see me like they saw me. They'd said the same thing their whole lives. It'd never taken the sting out of Bennett's rejection when I was younger. It didn't make things better now, either.

Not wanting to think about Bennett and how he viewed me, I checked the social feeds I followed, which included a few of the girls from school. It was always good to keep an eye on your enemies. After graduation, they'd returned home, like me, which meant they were scattered across the states.

The one I was most worried about, Lindi, lived in the city.

I studied the pictures she'd uploaded from her welcome home party. It wasn't the level of renting the museum, but only barely. It looked like one of the five-star hotels downtown that would drain my bank account to rent for the night. Not that it was a problem for her or her family. Her dress screamed money, as did her string diamond earrings and pendant necklace.

"Perfect makeup. Perfect hair. Perfect smile," I said softly. It all hid the angry, vicious woman she really was.

Thankfully, I would be even farther away from the city once the semester started, and she would probably be off to some Ivy League university somewhere.

Out of curiosity, I flipped to Aiden's feed and saw recent pictures of sunsets, forests, and clubs. Dancing girl pictures, I could have understood. After all, they were supposed to be out there, finding their mates. But not the pictures of a bunch of guys laughing and partying. I checked Karter's and saw more club pictures mixed in with food pictures.

I was so mad that I blocked them both and was tempted to do the same to Mom and Dad. What happened to consistent parenting? Why did the boys get one set of rules, which was to do whatever the hell they wanted, apparently, but I got another? The unfairness of it all rankled until I realized why I was different.

"Charity case," I said, tossing my phone to the side.

I got off the floor and started getting ready for bed well before it was time to. Once I was in my pajamas, I tiptoed to Karter's room. However, the bed was missing.

Silently cursing out Bennett, I checked Aiden's room and wasn't surprised to find that bed missing as well.

"I don't hate you," Bennett said.

Turning, I crossed my arms and leaned against the wall.

"You have a funny way of showing not-hate," I said.

He tucked his hands into his pockets and looked down at the floor for a moment.

"You can sleep in my bed."

"I think I'd rather sleep face down in a puddle."

His pupils dilated as our gazes met and held for several seconds.

"Well, this has been fun." I pushed away from the wall and started down the hall. "I look forward to whatever new hell this family drops on me tomorrow."

"Wrenly, that's not—"

"Save it, Bennett, or you'll need to explain an ER visit and my broken hand to Mom and Dad."

He didn't say anything else as I walked away.

After closing myself in my room and locking the door, I pulled the winter comforter from my closet and settled in on the floor. I'd slept in worse places and survived. I would survive this, too.

THE SOFT SOUND of pacing tickled my awareness.

"She doesn't understand, Bennett," I heard Mom say. "I think you should tell her."

"Now? She hates me. What do you think she'll do? She already threatened to punch me and put herself in the hospital."

"Because she doesn't understand. Talk to her."

The pacing stopped. "I'm trying. Everything I say makes her mad."

"You've been making her angry since she came here, and it's never upset you this much."

"It's different this time. This time, she's home for good."

My heart thumped heavily in my chest.

"Shh," Mom said. "We're disturbing her sleep."

I listened to their footsteps fade as I lay not on the floor but in a bed. Bennett's bed. He'd moved me.

How had I not woken?

Fear overwhelmed me, and not just because I'd been uncharacteristically vulnerable. Bennett *knew* I wanted to go to university. So did Mom. Why did they say I was home for good as if it were a sure thing?

What didn't I understand?

It took me a long time to fall back asleep.

WHEN I WOKE UP, a note was beside the bed.

> We don't have to go to the office today unless you want to. We can work from home. I'll be in the study.
> Bennett

He was giving me a choice of where to work, but not whether or not to work.

Shaking my head, I got out of his bed and checked the time. We were already an hour late. And since today was the day I was supposed to meet Sophia for lunch, I wasn't skipping work. However, another hour wouldn't hurt anything. I really needed a run to clear my mind.

I left Bennett's room and went to mine to change into my running clothes. Then, I jogged downstairs and checked the kitchen for something light to eat.

Bennett walked in a few seconds after me.

"Good morning," he said.

"It was."

"How did you sleep?"

"Like shit. I dreamed that some guy carried me to his bed against my will. It was all rapey and very disturbing."

"I'm sorry I moved you, Wrenly. You looked uncomfortable on the floor."

"I was. But I don't have the first-class privileges of the other members in this house, so apparently, I'm not allowed to own a bed."

Grabbing the apple I'd found, I faced him.

"Did Mom have anything to say about the missing beds when she visited last night?"

His brows rose.

"You heard us."

"I heard you say I'm here for good. We both know that's not what I want, though, right?"

He looked down at the floor. His gaze shifted around like he was searching for something.

"Don't bother. I won't trust anything you say anyway."

I moved to walk past him, but he reached out and blocked the way with his arm. Staring straight ahead, I waited.

"If you give me a few minutes, I'll change and run with you."

"Now that I can leave the community on my own, I don't need

you." I turned my head to look up at him. "Unless that was another fleeting privilege I'd been allowed."

His lips pulled back in a silent snarl, and he dropped his arm.

I marched out the front door and angrily munched my apple as I walked down the driveway. Once I finished it, I threw it into the woods and started a brisk walk to stretch my legs before jogging to the gate.

The guard nodded to me as I went through, and I felt a sense of relief that they hadn't taken this small freedom from me. Climbing walls was a pain in the ass that I didn't want to have to go back to doing.

With nothing but a clear path in front of me, I lengthened my stride and settled into my run. I'd barely reached the pruned tree line when something caught my toe and I fell face-first onto the pavement.

Storm's laughter rang out around me as I picked myself up. I was bleeding in various places—knees, thigh, heels of my hands, forearm —but thankfully not my face. That still had the bruise from the office bathroom. Plus, the neck bruises from yesterday.

"Stop pretending to be one of us, Wrenly. You can't run. You can't hunt. And you will never be a wolf."

"Like I ever wanted to be a bitch in heat," I said.

She pulled back her teeth to snarl at me. "We're not on pack land anymore."

"Exactly."

"What does *that* mean?"

"You want to beat me? Trip me? Make me bleed? Great. Do it. Where is the shower you're going to use to wash your scent off of me? Or are you just going to kill me and try to hide the body somewhere? Pretty sure Bennett will give me another ten minutes of freedom before he comes to check on me. And this," I motioned from me to her, "is what he's going to smell when he reaches this spot. Do you have an explanation ready?"

Hate filled her gaze, and I smiled through my pain because we both knew I was right.

"I'm sure I'll be seeing you around, Storm. I look forward to your fake apology."

With a wave, I started walking back, grateful I hadn't made it very far. Each scrape was burning like hell.

When I reached the guardhouse, I stopped and told the guard to call Bennett.

"Already did when I saw you were hurt."

"Thanks."

Bennett arrived a few seconds later. On foot.

"You didn't bring the car?" I asked, letting my annoyance show. "He said I was hurt. What are you going to do? Ca—ah!"

I glared at Bennett from my position in his arms.

"Put me down."

"Not a chance." He started jogging with me. "Want to tell me what happened?"

"Nah, I'll let you sleuth it out on your own. It'll be more frustrating for you that way."

He glanced down at me.

"Can we go back to how we were last night?" he asked as we reached the house.

"Of course. Tell Mom you agree with me going to the university of my choice and having the same freedoms my brothers have. It looked like they were having a great time with friends at a club recently."

Bennett remained silent as he carried me up the stairs and into his bedroom. He sat me on the end of his bed, told me not to move, and came back with salve, swabs, and bandages.

"Hold up. Before you play doctor, let me shower. I think there's a bit of pavement in my knee. You can take a jog and find out what happened while I'm doing that."

He hesitated, and his pupils went wild as he considered my proposal. Was he already mentally strangling whoever had done this to me—I hoped so—or was he dreading having to report it to Mom and Dad?

He lifted me again and carried me to my bathroom. When he set me down, he captured my chin.

"There are only two places you can be when I get back. Here or on my bed. Understood?"

"I'm curious...what would you do if I said I didn't understand?"

His gaze swept over my face, studying me.

"Are you testing me, Wrenly?"

"Wouldn't dream of it. It'll take me a while, so I'll be in here when you get back. Happy hunting."

CHAPTER ELEVEN

ONCE BENNETT LEFT, I dropped my act of indifference and made all the sad faces as I checked my scrapes. They weren't that bad, but they throbbed with every heartbeat. I knew rinsing the dirt off wouldn't be fun.

Every move hurt something, and I silently cursed Storm. But honestly, it wasn't all her fault. I hadn't been paying attention. If I had, I might have heard her. Maybe not. It was hard to say because I hadn't been focused. I'd thought I would be safe off the pack land.

As I'd expected, the water burned. So did the soap. I gritted my teeth and muttered curses under my breath as I cleaned one scrape after another. Once I was sure I'd gotten them all, I turned off the water and carefully towel-dried.

Two steps from the door, I heard Bennett say, "I'm waiting in your room."

"Well, don't. I need to get dressed."

"Open the door, Wrenly. I heard you swearing."

"You're going to hear me swear again if you don't leave."

My bathroom door opened, and I glared at Bennett as he came in. I would have tried closing the door in his face, but I knew not to start a battle I couldn't win.

"Do you mind? I'm in a towel. You could at least let me get dressed."

He picked me up. Again. Rather than fight it, I put my hands in my lap as he started walking.

"Which ones hurt the most?" he asked.

"My palms. I put them out to catch myself as I fell. I'm lucky I didn't break a wrist. I should have ducked and rolled; then I could have come up on my feet and broken my wrist hitting her in the face."

"No hitting shifters. Storm will be handled."

I snorted. "Like she was handled the last time I was home? Or the time before that? Talking does no good when neither party is listening."

"What do you mean?"

"She's just acknowledging the same thing you did from the beginning."

"Which is what?" he asked, entering his room.

"That I don't belong here."

"You don't belong anywhere else but here, Wrenly."

I wasn't sure if he was saying that because I didn't have any blood relatives left or if he was speaking for Mom and Dad and the rest of the family. My guess was the former, which made him a dick.

He set me on the edge of his bed and took a knee in front of me as he looked at the scrapes on my legs. It was a tempting pose.

"Do you know how much I really want to push you over right now?"

"I can smell your frustration and anger. Is it all for me?"

"Most of it. Some of it is for the rest of the family, then Storm and this place."

He dabbed salve on a scrape and then gently blew on it.

This wasn't the first time he'd doctored me. I had a fuzzy memory of him helping me with another knee scrape when I'd been younger. After that, the tattling had started.

"Does this mean I lost my freedom to run?" I asked as he dabbed salve on the other knee.

"If I ask you to promise only to run with me, would you see it as limiting your freedom or an attempt to keep this from happening again?" He bent his head and started blowing on my knee as the salve melted into the wound.

"Had you not asked, probably the first thing. Are you saying you'd run with me to keep me safe and not to restrict me?"

"All I've ever wanted to do is keep you safe."

I stared down at his dark head of hair and let my doubt show on my face. He looked up then, his pupils blown wide as he took in my expression.

"It's the truth," he said.

"Well, there are better ways to keep me safe than by making me feel like a prisoner."

He took my hand and applied the salve to it as well.

"Let's make a deal," he said.

My skin tingled when he blew on my palm.

"What kind of deal?" I asked to distract myself from the sensation.

"When you feel like you're being restricted, tell me. Let me try to find a solution that won't break any rules, will keep you safe, and will give you a way to feel free."

My chest ached, and my eyes started to water. He noticed and blew on my palm a second time.

"And what do you want in return for helping me?" I asked after swallowing hard.

"No more running away from me."

Technically, I'd never run away from him; I just avoided him as much as possible.

"Okay. You have a deal."

He finished with my second hand and brushed my wet hair back from my face. His pupils were still fully dilated.

"So if running away isn't allowed, what do we do when we're

annoyed with each other?" I asked. "Fight it out?"

His lips twitched like he found that the funniest thing ever, and he started placing the large bandages he'd brought.

"I'd never win," he said.

I snorted. "Only because Mom and Dad would have your hide when I break my hand hitting you."

"You'll have to find a way to fight without hitting, then," he said. "To keep things fair."

Since I was creative when angry, I nodded in agreement.

"Do you need help dressing?" he asked after he placed the last bandage.

"If I did, I wouldn't ask you, Bennett," I said, waiting for him to move so I could stand. "That'd be more of a Mom thing."

He nodded after a moment and rose with a fluid grace I envied.

"Give me twenty minutes, and I'll be ready to head into the office," I said.

"You want to go?"

I shrugged. "At least there, I can walk to the park with less chance of being purposely tripped. With my face and neck bruises and whatever stern lecture Mom gave everyone at the office yesterday, I'm sure the women there will leave me alone for a while at least."

"When you say things like that, it makes me want to put you in a bubble."

"Putting me in one won't keep me safe. It'll just stop me from learning the skills I need to survive once it pops. Because bubbles always pop, Bennett."

I walked out of his room, pinning the towel to my torso with my forearm to hide a minor scrape he'd overlooked. Once I was in my room, I dropped the towel and added a few more adhesive bandages.

Dressing wasn't fun. I chose lightweight, loose clothes that wouldn't aggravate anything. My hair was a mess. Holding the hairdryer hurt. Attempting to comb out my tangles was extra hard, and…it hurt. Trying to tie my hair back hurt.

Giving up, I left my bedroom with my hair down and partially wet.

Bennett was waiting for me in the hallway. He wore his usual suit and tie for the office, but he looked a little less uptight this time. I looked at his hair and checked his tie, but both looked as precise as they always did.

While I was studying him, trying to find the difference, he took in my wet, mostly uncombed hair and the extra bandage on the underside of my forearm.

"What kind of deal would we need to make for you to come to me when you have a problem? From the minor stuff like you have a hangnail to the major stuff like someone hurting you?"

"I wouldn't need a deal for that. I'd need to trust you."

He nodded, grabbed the tips of my fingers, and led me back into my bathroom.

I didn't protest when he picked up the hairdryer. It felt really nice to have someone run their fingers through my hair without trying to pull it from the roots. I closed my eyes and let myself enjoy the moment.

The hairdryer shut off, and he ran the brush through the strands, carefully gathering it all back to tie at the base of my skull.

I opened my eyes and caught him staring at my neck.

"Is it another bruise, or did I miss some dirt?" I asked as I started to reach back and wipe the spot.

He caught my hand. "No. You just..." He leaned in as he breathed deeply.

Did he smell Storm? She hadn't touched me other than to trip me.

His nose brushed my skin, and a jolt of awareness struck straight through me, sending me into a confused panic.

I whirled away from him, but I didn't get far. He caught me around my waist and had my ass on the counter before I registered he'd touched me.

With his hands gripping the counter on each side of me, caging me in, he crowded close.

"I thought we agreed, no running. Why did you panic? Do you think I'm going to hurt you, Wrenly?"

My heart was beating fast in my chest as I stared at him with wide eyes.

"Breathe, Wrenly. You're not in any danger. You're safe."

Safety was a relative term in this situation.

"You're too close," I managed to say.

"You said you didn't like it when you can't move your arms, and when something was too close to your face. I wasn't holding you at all."

I glanced away as my mind raced for a truthful reason for my panic that wasn't the truth: I'd felt something when I'd thought Bennett would kiss me again. No, not again. He hadn't kissed me ever. That time at the museum, he'd just checked what I'd been drinking. And what he'd done in his bedroom had been revenge. Maybe a test. I still wasn't sure.

"Don't you believe in personal space?" I asked.

"Not really."

"I'll be sure to tell the girls in the office that."

He made an annoyed sound and plucked me off the counter.

"Is your hair all right?" he asked.

I nodded and let him lead me out of the bathroom.

When we reached the entry, he had my runners waiting. He helped me into them and tied them for me.

"You didn't eat much for breakfast," he commented as we walked through the kitchen. "Do you want to stop for something along the way?"

"No. It's almost lunch anyway."

As soon as we walked out into the garage, I noticed the grey sedan. It wasn't anything fancy, so it definitely didn't look like it belonged. I glanced from it to Bennett. He was watching me closely.

"Whose car is that?"

"Yours. Do you like it?"

I stared at it again, struggling with a storm of emotions, mostly hope.

"Are you serious?"

"I am. Milo dropped it off last night. I thought you might want to drive it to work, but with your hands—"

"I can drive!"

His lips twitched. "Does that mean you like it?"

"Yes. I love it." I loved it so much I couldn't stop staring at it.

In all my planning, I never dreamed Mom and Dad would get me a car. They'd been so adamant that I didn't need one. That there was always someone home to drive me anywhere I needed to go.

I looked at Bennett.

"Mom and Dad didn't get this for me, did they?"

"No. I bought it."

Some of my joy faded.

"It's yours, Wrenly. No one will take it away from you."

I wanted to believe him, but I'd learned the hard way not to trust gifts. They always had conditions.

"Why did you get me a car?"

"To prove this isn't a prison like you said. You're free to come and go. It would make everyone more comfortable if you could ease into your freedom, though."

"What does that mean?"

"Don't take the car without me for a little while. The city's still new to you. And once we're both comfortable, always let me—us— know where you're going so we don't worry."

I wanted to point out that they already tracked me, but I decided it would be like beating him with the olive branch he was extending.

"You have a deal. Thank you, Bennett."

"Just words? I bought you a whole car."

I'd known there would be strings. But he was right. It was a whole car. I could give a little for that. But what? I would have said I'd leave him alone for the rest of the summer, but he'd already made me promise to stop avoiding him. And I doubted he would see any offer to drive him to and from work as a gesture of thanks, considering how inept I was with city traffic.

"What do you want?"

He bent forward, putting us closer to eye level.

"How about a kiss?"

Instinct and self-preservation had me shifting back half a step. I couldn't have heard right.

"What?" I asked faintly.

He turned his head slightly and tapped his cheek.

"Show me you don't hate me like you said."

Was that what this was about? Relief flooded me, and I quickly darted in to kiss his cheek. Then I moved to the key locker and found the keys to my very own car.

When I turned, he was already standing by the driver's door and opened it for me as I approached.

"I'm worried about your hands," he said. "Can we switch before we hit downtown?"

I nodded, willing to compromise with him since he'd bought the car. Five minutes into the drive, I was glad I did. The car was perfect. However, gripping the steering wheel wasn't fun. I hadn't realized how much I would need to use my palms when driving.

When I took the next exit, Bennett's only comment was to wait for him to open the door for me. He walked me to the passenger door and opened that for me, too. He even leaned in to buckle me, which I appreciated.

We arrived at the office just before lunch. Perfect timing.

"Can I still take an hour lunch break? If so, I'll go get us something. I need to stretch my legs anyway." When he seemed about to object, I added. "I won't go far, and I promise to message you if anything starts hurting. Okay?"

He silently read my pleading expression and then nodded.

"Thank you," I said before rushing away.

Several of the office girls watched me as I hurried past. I didn't miss the way their gazes flicked from my bruised neck to my bandaged knees. The Wulf pack was large. Over five hundred members. How many of them knew Storm? How many of them had already heard the story?

As soon as I was out of the building, I sent a message to Sophia that I was on my way. She replied that she'd already gotten us a table and asked if she should order anything for me. I declined and said I'd be there in a few minutes.

I jogged, wanting to make the most of my time.

When I arrived at the cafe, I was grateful for the low ponytail and lightweight clothes because I'd broken a sweat. The AC was a relief as I went to the counter and ordered my takeout.

Turning, I scanned the tables and saw Sophia waving from hers, making it easy to find her.

She stood and hugged me. A real hug. Like Mom's, but filled with a lot more excitement and a little bit of squealing.

"I'm so glad we could finally meet in person," she said, pulling away from me.

Her gaze immediately caught on my cheek and neck. Her excitement faded.

"What happened?"

"A door," I said, pointing to my face and then neck. "A chokehold." Finally, I held up my hands. "Tripping."

"You said your family was controlling, but that's not control. That's abuse."

I couldn't stop my smile. "Oh, this isn't from my family. This is from co-workers and a neighbor. They're the main reason I want to attend the school of my choice this time. The last one was full of mean girls, too."

"Your office and your neighborhood are full of mean girls?"

"Yep. But let's not talk about them; let's talk about something good. Like orientation week. Have you looked through the events they posted? Did any interest you?"

She nodded, regaining some of her enthusiasm, and we talked about the dorm room, moving in, and the general roommate agreement rules. Time slipped by fast, and I never heard my phone buzz with messages, but I did hear it ring.

When I saw Bennett's name, I cringed.

"I need to get this."

Without waiting for her reply, I stood and answered it on my way to the takeout shelf, where my order had been waiting for a while.

"Tell me you're all right," Bennett said, sounding angry.

"I'm all right. I just lost track of time."

"It's been an hour. You didn't answer any of our texts. What have you been doing?"

I understood he was worried, but the question grated on my nerves.

"Not breaking any rules." I grabbed the bag and waved at Sophia, motioning that I needed to go. She nodded and waved goodbye. "Can we talk about this when I get back?"

"Who is she?" Bennett asked.

Panicking, I scanned the cafe and spotted Bennett outside the wall of windows near the cafe's entrance. He didn't look angry, just worried. But that didn't make me feel any better.

A warning tingle started in my nose, and my chin trembled. To hide it, I looked down at my phone to hang up on him. Then, I swallowed hard and tried to relax everything as I started walking toward the door so Sophia wouldn't know how fucking messed up my life was.

He opened the door when I reached it and took the takeout bags from me.

I couldn't look at him. If I did, I'd lose what fragile hold on my control I had. I was good at keeping things in. I'd done so for years. But I'd started to trust Bennett. Trust that he'd been listening to me despite what I'd heard the night before. All because of his dumb offer to listen.

"You're not okay," he said. "Did she do something to you? I can smell her scent on you."

His voice carried a warning growl, and he turned toward the door.

I grabbed his arm, ignoring the pain, and started towing him away from the cafe.

"*She's* not the problem, Bennett. Why are you here? Why can't I have an hour to myself? Why does it feel like I did something so wrong that I can't even breathe without someone monitoring me?" I stopped walking and spun around to face him.

"You asked me to come to you when I'm having a problem. This is a problem. I'm feeling very trapped and very angry right now because you were standing outside that cafe like some kind of stalker."

He cupped my face and wouldn't let go even when I tried knocking his hands away.

"This," he said, rubbing over my cheek bruise with his thumb. "And these." He gently touched the bruises on my throat. "And these." He caught my hand and held it so we could both see the bandage.

"All of these within six days, Wrenly. When you didn't answer any of our texts, I panicked. When I saw you inside, smiling and talking, I thought I was keeping my word and giving you space by calling instead of going in to make sure you were all right. Tell me what I should have done instead."

His words and imploring gaze hit my guilt button hard. Everything he said was reasonable, and I knew that if Aiden or Karter had been hurt like I had, the rest of the family would have reacted the same way to an hour of no contact.

So I told the truth. I said what had really set me off.

"You shouldn't have asked who she was."

He searched my face.

"Why?" His confusion suddenly vanished behind a stoic mask. "Do you like women, Wrenly?"

People on the other side of the busy street probably heard my frustrated "gah" as I turned around and walked away from the most annoying man on the face of the planet. He followed me back to the office in silence. However, even knowing that I was upset with him, he insisted that I join him for lunch in his office again.

"Why?" I asked, sitting on the couch. "What do you get out of this? It certainly isn't my cheerful presence."

He set the food out on the sofa table in front of me and then went to his desk. I watched him pull a piece of that wrapped chocolate from the drawer.

Was I bribable? Not really. Yet, I didn't get mad when he held the chocolate out to me. Actually, it kind of made me feel better. A little calmer. But only a little.

While I ate my piece of chocolate, he set out our lunches and sat next to me.

"I asked who she was because I was genuinely curious. We both know that I'm completely clueless about your life despite all the information your teachers sent. I know you left the school grounds. I don't know why or what you did. So I was curious how you knew her well enough to look relaxed when you talked to her. Something you've never done with me once during the thirteen years we've known each other.

"And that's not an accusation. I'm not trying to start a fight. I just want to fix this distance between us—the misunderstanding that I hated you because I went away to school."

CHAPTER TWELVE

THE CHOCOLATE in my mouth prevented me from interrupting and forced me to listen until the end. And I was glad for it.

Bennett didn't hate me.

That didn't erase all of our history, but it helped me see that I *had* been reacting to everything based on that assumption, which contributed to the broken relationship we had. That didn't mean Bennett was completely blameless in my anger toward him—he'd relocated every bed in the house except for his. Yet, most of the anger I'd felt toward him since coming home was based on my misunderstanding of his intentions.

"So, will you tell me how you know her?" he asked.

He was certainly persistent. But trust like he wanted needed to be earned.

"She's a friend I've been talking to online for a few months now. We've video-chatted before, but this is the first time I've met her in person."

"She's not from school, then."

I knew he meant the one I'd graduated from, so I said, "No."

"Can I ask why you were upset that I asked who she was?"

I looked down at my sandwich and thought over the question. Was Bennett truly extending an olive branch? If he was, I needed to grab onto it. I needed an ally so I could leave. But there was still a chance everything I said would be repeated to Mom and Dad. I needed to be careful.

"Because I'm afraid of being told no," I said. "No, I can't have her as a friend. No, I can't meet anyone outside of work or home. Just no. Everything is a no."

He was so quiet next to me that I gave up playing with my sandwich and looked at him. He was watching me again, but I couldn't read anything in his expression.

"I don't like it when you do that," I said.

"Do what?"

"Go quiet. Hide behind that mask. I can't tell what you're thinking or feeling and don't have a supernatural nose to figure it out like you do."

"Why do you want to know what I'm thinking and feeling?"

"So I can prevent another moody outburst. They're exhausting."

"Do you want the couch? You can take another nap."

"If it's pre-paying for a mood swing later, I'll pass."

"No. You look tired."

"Do I get paid for napping?"

"I won't tell if you don't tell."

I almost smiled. This version of Bennett was breaking rules, which was a step closer to toeing the fun line. But more importantly, he was listening, and he seemed to actually care about me.

The scrapes and my throat hurt, and I was emotionally exhausted, not that I would admit any of that to him.

"A nap isn't the worst idea."

Like the day before, I ate lunch then stretched out for what I thought would be a power nap. Two hours later, I woke up covered by his suit jacket. My knees felt bruised when I swung my legs over the edge to sit up.

Bennett caught my wince since he was leaning back in his chair, watching me again.

"Are we both taking a two-hour break when I nap in here?" I asked, rolling my shoulders.

"No. I was working until your breathing changed. Do you need a pain reliever?"

I shook my head and stood. "Do you know how much I'm getting paid per hour?"

"Why are you asking?"

"I'm trying to decide if I should feel guilty about taking a two-hour paid nap."

He grinned. "Definitely not."

I couldn't stop my answering smile. As I moved to leave, I remembered my conversation with Mom and turned back to him.

"Mom said that my paycheck would be deposited in an account she started for me ages ago. She told me to ask you about it."

As soon as I said it aloud, I realized how weird that sounded. "Why would she tell me to ask you about it?"

"The paperwork is still at the big house."

"Ah." Having me ask him made more sense now, since I was living there and they were in the city. "Can I have it?"

"It's at home."

I rolled my eyes at him. "I didn't mean right now."

"Ah."

His response got a second eye-roll from me before I left. I removed the Post-it note from the door. When I turned, I saw Miranda, the woman who'd pinned me to the bathroom door, sitting at my desk.

"Another long lunch," she commented. "Anything exciting happen in there?"

"If you consider a nap exciting, then yes."

She stood suddenly and forcefully. "He slept with you?"

"Don't be dumb. That couch isn't big enough for two. I napped. He worked."

Seeing her slow inhale, I made an annoyed sound and gestured at myself.

"If you all want me to spend less time with him, maybe cause fewer injuries. Pity gets this poor little charity human a longer lunch break and access to Bennett's napping couch."

"People might be nicer to you if you weren't such a bitch," she said.

"Doubtful since none of you are interested in my personality, only my proximity to the Wulf brothers. Now, is there something you need, or are you just looking for a place to avoid working?" I motioned to Bennett's closed office door. "He wasn't angry when I left, if you want to give it a try."

She scowled at me. "I thought you were supposed to keep us out."

"Pfft. An entire office filled with resentful she-wolves is way more dangerous than an angry Bennett."

"And why is that? He wasn't even tolerating Aiden and Karter these last few months."

"What do you mean?"

She shrugged cockily. "Ask him yourself if you're brave enough."

I spun on my heel and opened Bennett's door, avoiding my palm. He was on the phone and looked at me.

"Did you do something to Aiden and Karter before I got home?"

"I'll call you back in a few minutes," he said. Once he hung up the phone, he added, "Come in and close the door, Wrenly."

"I don't think so. You tell me now, or I'll ask people who will answer me honestly."

He sighed.

"Aiden and Karter stuck their noses where they didn't belong, and I reacted," Bennett said.

"How did you react?"

"After putting them in their places, I suggested Mom and Dad send them out to find their own mates."

"What business of yours didn't they stay out of?" I asked, trying to give Bennett the benefit of the doubt.

"My mate."

I blew out a long breath and shook my head at him. He remained silent as I closed the door and turned to Miranda.

"What did he leave out?"

"He threw Aiden out of his office so hard it took three days for them to fix that wall." She pointed to the wall beside the entrance to the office suite. "And Karter had a broken nose. It healed quickly, but it was still a serious enough fight...from Bennett's standpoint."

"What did they say about Bennett's mate that set him off?"

She shook her head slightly, losing some of her resentment. "I don't know. Something about him waiting too long."

Even as a human, I knew the longer a wolf-shifter waited to claim his mate, the more volatile he got. Grandma had told me about the whole shifter mate thing during the human birds and bees talk she'd given when I'd been younger. Curious about the differences between myself and them, I'd asked questions she'd been nice enough to answer, maybe a little too openly.

"They aren't wrong," I said.

The resentment surged in Miranda's gaze and in the way she crossed her arms. I held up my hands and stepped away from the door.

"I'm not your roadblock. By all means, go in and have your way with him."

"Do you really not know who his mate is?" she asked.

"How could I? I just got home last week. They don't tell me anything."

She made a face and glared at the door. I could see her thinking about going in. The blinds suddenly snapped open, and Bennett's gaze flicked from me to her.

"I think whatever call I interrupted ruined his not-so-angry mood," I said to Miranda. "You might want to try later."

She left without another word, and I went to my desk to start another spreadsheet.

Before I numbed my thoughts with endless numbers, I checked my messages. Bennett had messaged once, close to the end of my hour break, and six more times the minute the hour was up. Mom had messaged twice about ten minutes before Bennett had shown up and called.

He'd respected my hour break.

Feeling a little guilty, I sent a quick text to Mom that I'd lost track of time and everything was fine, then I got to work. My productivity wasn't the best because of my hands, but I still managed to get something done before Bennett opened his door at five.

"Hungry for pizza?" he asked.

"Not really. Are there any good burger places around here? I haven't had one of those in forever."

"Sit down or fast food?"

The question surprised me, mostly because I knew the Wulfs weren't fast-food kind of people, not with the sensitive noses they had.

"If you honestly don't have a preference, I'd like a fast-food burger. I don't think I ever had one. At least, not that I can remember."

I had another motive for fast food, too—getting home sooner. It'd been a long day, and I was ready for it to be over.

A few more women lingered at their desks when we left today. They didn't talk, but they watched. The way they watched was a tad...unsettling. Like those creepy pictures on walls with moving eyes.

They needed hobbies that didn't involve chasing men.

I looked forward to suggesting fur-crocheting to Miranda the next time she sat in my chair.

When the elevator doors closed, I felt Bennett looking at me.

"What?"

When he didn't say anything, I gave in and looked at him. His gaze swept over my face.

"Would I be an ass if I said today was a good day?"

"Only if you're saying it because I was tripped this morning and we got mad at each other."

"No, it's good because you're less angry at me."

"Give it some time," I said, facing forward. "I'm sure you'll do something."

The elevator doors opened, and Walt got on along with two other men. I wanted to laugh so badly.

Walt caught my smirk and smiled back before his gaze dipped to my neck and new bandages. His humor faded.

"Those weren't there last time," he said.

"Yeah, I need to stop picking fights with stronger people." I lifted my hands. "And get better at running from them."

"Or maybe just keep better company," Walt said, not unkindly.

"Oh, I'm working on that part."

Bennett's fingers caught the tips of mine, tugging them in warning.

"Making friends is easier said than done, though," I continued. "I don't have a lot of free time to socialize."

Bennett stopped tugging.

"If you do get time, there are some decent clubs close to downtown. Just avoid the ones on the south side. A lot of women have had their drinks spiked there."

"Thanks for the warning. I appreciate it."

The elevator doors opened, and he nodded to me before getting off with his companions. I finally glanced at Bennett, who was thoroughly pissed off, based on his dilated pupils and trembling fingers that were still lightly holding mine. At least, he was staring down at the floor so the other people hadn't seen.

"It's called polite small talk, Bennett. Useful to normal people who are put into social situations, and something I haven't had a whole lot of practice with. Now, are we still getting me a burger, or is it tantrum time?"

"Burger," he said roughly before motioning that I should exit first.

He followed me to the next elevator and then to the car so he could open the door for me.

"Are you okay driving?" I asked when he got in behind the wheel.

"Yeah."

The ride was quiet, only interrupted by the stop for food. By the time we reached the house, though, Bennett seemed a little less on edge.

"Can I ask something and get an honest answer?" I asked when he opened the door for me.

"Sure."

"Why is talking to the opposite sex so bad? I mean, I can understand when I was younger. Stranger danger and all that. But why is it still a problem? Do Mom and Dad really think I'm incapable of judging a person's character, or do they mean to stop me from ever having a relationship so I can live at home forever?"

Bennett leaned around me to close the car door then stayed like that, loosely trapping me between his body and the door.

"Do you like him?"

The question was laced with an angry growl and delivered close to my ear.

"I don't like anyone, Bennett. I know better. Liking people gets me sent away. I was asking because I was curious, and I thought after our little breakthrough, you might give me a real answer. Guess I was wrong. Now, can we go inside and eat?"

He stepped closer.

I ducked under his arm and fled to the house before he completely lost it.

Why did it always feel like one step forward and two steps back with him?

Once I was safely in my room with the door closed, I let out a long breath, relieved that I had averted another crisis, and went to change into my pajamas. I wasn't ready for bed yet but wanted to change the bandages and apply more ointment.

My phone buzzed with messages while I worked, and I wondered which parts of today Bennett had shared with Mom. The tripping incident this morning? Unlikely. If he'd wanted to share that, he would have done so right away. And I knew he hadn't because she hadn't called.

I paused with a frown.

Wait...he'd said *they* were worried after what happened and had touched my scrapes. Did that mean Mom knew and *hadn't* called to check on me? What the hell?

My phone buzzed again.

If it wasn't the tripping, it probably wasn't my meet-up with Sophia either. After all, he'd found me there, and they hadn't reached out after that, which meant he'd let them know where I was and who I was with.

And if it'd been the talk before my nap, there would have been texts waiting for me when I woke. The only messages had been from before he'd found me.

That meant they were messaging me because of my conversation with Walt in the elevator or my question to Bennett just now when we'd gotten home.

My bet was the latter.

I closed my eyes and coached myself.

You've been through much worse, Wren. Sure, it was because of their smothering love, but that's in the past. Keep your cool in the present so you can have an amazing future—a future with no mean girls, no injuries, and no restrictions.

Letting out a calming breath, I opened my eyes, smiled at myself in the mirror until it felt real, then finished redressing my scrapes before grabbing my phone.

Mom: Bennett mentioned your frustration today, and I'm sorry.
Mom: I talked to Dad. You're right. We should have a family conversation about your future. Are you free tomorrow night?

Bennett: I'm sorry. Can we have dinner together and talk?
Bennett: I have more chocolate.

My inner peace had an eye twitch as I read through all of that a second time. Am I free? I didn't have a life. Of course I was free.

And Bennett could shove his chocolate up his chocolate factory.

"No mean girls, no injuries, and no restrictions," I mumbled to myself as I typed out a response to Mom.

Me: Of course I'm free for dinner tomorrow. Where, when, and how am I getting there?
Mom: I'll let Bennett know the details. He can drive so your hands can heal.

"Pfft. Right." I left my phone on my vanity and went downstairs instead of messaging Bennett.

He was pacing in the kitchen while the bag of food sat on the counter. He stopped when I entered and watched as I grabbed the bag and turned around.

"I told you it wouldn't take long," I said as I marched out of the kitchen.

I closed myself in his bedroom, sat on his bed, and proceeded to gorge myself on *all* the fast food. Was I starving? No. I was petty, and eating Bennett's food was a form of revenge for being a pain in my ass.

When I was full, I mashed what was left of his burger with my forearm, rewrapped the flattened disc, and put it back in the bag by the door. Then I sat on his bed and planned.

A lot of bad things had happened to me in the few days I'd been home. The face bruise from Miranda, being pinned to a wall by Milena, and then tripped by Storm. Mom's concession to talk about the future didn't give me any warm, hopeful feelings. No, I knew better. It was an appeasement talk. A "be patient" talk. We'd had plenty of those in the past, usually after something happened and I expressed a desire for something—like leaving that seventh-ring-of-hell school—that didn't align with what they wanted. I would be coaxed and managed until I conceded to whatever they wanted.

Which was why I needed Bennett on my side.

Aiden and Karter would have been preferable, but the assholes weren't here.

And now I was stuck with moody Bennett.

I sighed.

A second later, he knocked on the door.

"Can I come in?"

"No. Go away, Bennett. I'm thinking and don't need you to add to my headache."

The door didn't open, and after a few minutes, I relaxed and went back to contemplating the problem that was Bennett. He was volatile, and that unpredictability was messing with my plans.

If he would just claim his mate already, I'd have my bed, and he'd stop doing weird things like pinning my hands above my head and trying to taste what I drank.

"You said you would stop running away from me," he said suddenly on the other side of the door.

Annoyed, I got off the bed, grabbed the food bag, and yanked open the door. He caught the bag when it hit his chest.

"I didn't run; I walked. And I'm avoiding you so I don't say mean things until I've calmed down." Rather than shutting the door in his face, I kept going.

"Why do you always treat me like that when you're in a mood? I'm a person with feelings, too, Bennett. How would you like it if someone bigger and stronger tried to physically intimidate you every time you annoyed them?

"And for the record, my choice would be to *not* annoy you at all... by not being here. So don't even try to say it's my fault for being annoying."

One second, I was standing in the doorway, verbally slapping some sense into him; the next, my back was against the wall, and he was holding my hands to my sides as he met my gaze.

His pupils were spasming between fully blown and pinpoints, making him look like the lunatic I knew he was.

"I know you're a person, Wrenly. I wasn't trying to intimidate you."

"Right, because holding someone down during a conversation is normal."

His lips pulled back in a snarl, but he didn't let me go.

"Are you sure you're not annoying me on purpose?" he asked.

"Nope. It just comes naturally. Why are you here?"

"It's my room."

"Give me my bed back, and I'll get out of it."

He closed his eyes, and I knew from the way he took a slow breath that he was struggling to keep calm. A wise person would have been afraid. But I wanted to laugh.

Served him right!

His eyes snapped open. His pupils weren't spasming anymore but had completely swallowed his irises.

And there was the fear...filling me quite quickly.

"Remember, I break easily," I said faintly.

Frustration crept into his expression a second before he leaned in. His lips brushed my ear as he said, "I'm not your enemy, Wrenly. I would never hurt you."

Then he was gone, along with his mashed food.

Alone, I hurried to close the door, then stared at it as the feel of his breath on my ear haunted me. It hadn't felt brotherly.

The things he'd said to me over the last several days—things I'd been desperately not overthinking—ran through my head.

I don't hate you.
I will never see you as my sister, Wrenly.
I am not your brother, Wrenly.
What do you see me as, Wrenly?

No...it wasn't...he couldn't.

Don't fear me. I won't hurt you.
I would never hurt you.
I'm trying to understand you, Wrenly.
This time, she's home for good.

Like a marionette on loose strings, I stumbled back to the bed and sat hard. Mom's voice filled my head.

He's more patient than most. He'll give her the time she needs, even if it drives him crazy.
He's deeply afraid she'll reject him.
She's never shown any interest in him as a mate.
If he looks like he's going to lose his temper, hug him, Wrenly.
I think you're the only person he needs to see.

I shook my head. No, I was wrong. There was no way that *I* was the mate that Bennett was waiting for. But I thought back, and so many things were aligning with this new and very unsettling suspicion.

The kiss at the museum. Pinning me to the wall after I stomped on his foot and saying maybe I'd want to play later.

Grandma suggesting flattery.

The way he'd reacted when he found me sitting next to Walt in the park, which I'd blamed on Mom and Dad's "No Boys" rule.

How he'd freaked out about the other woman's scent in his office, but was fine with me napping on his couch.

All the ways he'd messed with me after my panic episode.

What if what he'd done hadn't been a test but an actual kiss on my neck?

The fact that he'd thrown Aiden and Karter into a wall when they mentioned his mate but never did anything to me...they were shifters, though, and could withstand his version of a spanking.

His horrified tone when he'd asked if I liked girls.

I covered my ears as if it could stop my thoughts.

I was wrong. The idea was completely and absolutely ridiculous.

I *had* to be wrong.

CHAPTER THIRTEEN

I GROANED at the sound of my alarm. It'd taken hours to fall asleep after my stupid brain spun its stress-induced theory about Bennett's mate being me, which wasn't true. I'd known him since he was nearly fourteen. Sure, he denied any sibling relationship with me, but he'd also never, not once, shown any interest in me. All his weirdness now stemmed from not claiming his mate.

Grandma had once told me a story about a guy who went insane waiting for his mate to accept him. Obviously, that guy was Bennett's current role model.

"Are you going to turn the alarm off or sleep through it?" Bennett asked.

"I'm thinking about feeding it to you."

"Hmm. It is almost as flat as last night's burger."

I opened my eyes to glare at him. He was leaning against the doorjamb, watching me.

"And you've learned nothing."

"Not true. I didn't try waking you up with a different alarm, and I'm staying a healthy distance away. See? Baby steps."

The smile he flashed at me highlighted how devastatingly good-looking he was, which was completely unacceptable.

Rather than telling him to get out, I flipped back the covers and marched to my room to get ready for the day, ignoring his soft chuckle.

It would have been great if he'd left me alone while I showered and got ready, but he didn't. He talked to me through the door as soon as I turned off the water.

"How are your hands? Do you need help with the ointment?"

"No. I'm fine."

"Do you want me to brush your hair?"

"Nope, I can manage it today."

Only by sheer will, though. My palms felt raw and bruised, and it hurt to use them.

I looked down at them, knowing I could use them as an excuse not to go to work. Would I be stuck home alone with Bennett, though? Better not to risk it.

Since I had the foresight to bring clothes into the bathroom with me this time, I was dressed when I opened the door and found him standing by my vanity, looking at all the things Mom had purchased for me.

He held up a mascara box.

"You haven't used any of this?"

"No. Makeup isn't my thing."

Confusion flashed in his expression as he looked at the mascara.

"I thought you asked for this brand while you were at school."

All the expensive makeup I'd asked for over the years had been used as currency: bribes for information or silence. But I wasn't about to admit that to him.

"Put it down, Bennett, or I'm going to smash your lunch too."

His lips twitched, but he set the makeup down and followed me out the door without asking any more questions.

Sandy was putting our plates on the table when we walked into the dining room. Eggs, hash browns, ham, sausages, tomatoes, and mushrooms...a full breakfast.

She caught my look and smiled.

"Bennett mentioned you were extra hungry last night and asked me to make something hearty."

I shot Bennett a look. We both knew that eating his food had nothing to do with my appetite.

He pulled out my chair for me. I didn't make any move to sit. The way he was watching me was making me nervous, and the thoughts from last night resurfaced.

What if you're right?

"I know how to sit, Bennett. Go away."

Frustration flashed in his expression.

"It's called courtesy."

"Courtesy is just another bar in the cage of obedience."

His mask slipped into place, and he straightened away from the chair to take his seat right next to the chair he'd held out. I walked around the table to sit across from him and pulled the plate and silverware toward me.

"Is there a reason you don't want to sit next to me?" he asked.

"It's easy to see you this way."

His gaze studied mine.

"What? No sniff to see if I'm telling the truth?"

"You seem…" He shook his head.

"Go ahead. Finish that thought."

"You seem more confrontational today. Why?"

He was right. I was being confrontational and needed to stop. I needed him on my side for tonight's conversation with Mom and Dad. But anger was safer than the other emotions I was trying to suppress—emotions tied to questions I was too afraid to ask.

"Talk to me, Wrenly. Please. I'm sorry for losing control yesterday. I want to promise it won't happen again, but I won't lie to you. My patience is—"

"Not my problem," I said. "You said you're not my enemy. Well, I'm not yours either. So, stop taking your frustrations out on me, and we'll get along fine. Now, less talking and more eating, or we'll be late."

Focusing on my food, I ignored him and followed my own advice. As soon as I finished, I stood with my plate. He stood too, his food mostly untouched, and took my plate from me.

"I'll meet you by the car."

His words were more subdued, and I pushed the guilt that wanted to rise off a mental cliff. Any hint of weakness and he'd revert to his bad behavior. Polite distance was better. Safer.

I ran upstairs to get my things. When I reached the garage, he was standing by the passenger door of his car. He watched my approach like he was waiting for another, "Go away, Bennett."

"Thank you for driving," I said instead.

Confusion and surprise broke through his mask.

"You're welcome."

He opened the car door for me and watched me get in, but instead of closing it, he reached in and had the seatbelt around me before I knew what he meant to do. It was the same thing he'd done the day before, but my thoughts were different now. Panic hit me hard when he turned his head and our faces were only inches apart.

His gaze swept over me as he inhaled and retreated.

While he walked around the car, I fought to take a calming breath and slow my racing heart.

"Don't do that again," I said when he opened the door.

"Why?"

"Because I didn't like it."

"Why?"

I turned my head to look at him. "You don't need to figure me out, Bennett. You just need to get along with me until September."

"September?" he asked, starting the car.

"The end of August, technically. That's move-in day for the dorms, which you'll hear about tonight. Mom said she was going to send you the address for our college-talk dinner."

He pulled out of the garage and didn't say anything until we reached the parking garage at work.

"What do you want to go to school for?"

The question shocked me so much that I turned to stare at him for a second. No one had ever asked what I wanted to do in the future.

"Interspecies social worker," I said.

"Really? I would have thought finance. Your math grades qualify."

"Being good at something doesn't mean it's your passion."

"And interspecies social worker is your passion?"

"There are a lot of kids out there struggling to fit into families of different species. Helping them adapt and not feel so alone, different, or maybe even unwanted, calls to me a lot more than sitting in an office, searching expense lists for overspending."

He got out, and I was quick to unbuckle before he opened the door for me. Instead of stepping back so I could get out, he leaned down to look into the car at me.

"Is that how you felt? Alone? Unwanted?"

"Seven years, Bennett. I was sent away for seven years. Who wouldn't feel alone and unwanted?"

I wished I could smell what he was feeling because his expression gave nothing away as he looked down. But he was so still, like a predator hiding from its prey so that the prey wouldn't startle and run away. I was afraid to move.

No more running away from me.

Before the panic could set in, he stepped back and let me out. We didn't talk on our way up to the main lobby.

Walt was waiting at the elevator bank, along with two dozen other people waiting for their turn.

"Good morning," he said when he saw me. He gestured to my neck. "Looks a little better today."

"Ten hours of sleep works like magic."

"Impressive."

I smiled. "It was."

Ten was unheard of for me. But since coming home, I'd been sleeping more deeply—obviously, since Bennett managed to move me—and longer. Even though I'd been displaced and ignored, I still felt safer there at the big house than I had at school. Hopefully, the change in my sleep meant I was putting everything that happened at school behind me. The idea of swinging at Sophia for waking me up, just as I had done for Bennett, was worrying.

Bennett's fingers brushed mine, interrupting my thoughts. I lifted my hand and smoothed my hair back to avoid his touch.

The elevator doors in front of Walt opened.

"Hope you have a good day," I said.

He nodded, and I dropped my friendly smile the second the doors closed. Bennett didn't try to touch me again.

When we reached the administrative floor, almost everyone was already at their desks, and I felt the stares of the women as Bennett walked beside me.

Whatever was going on in their minds really needed to stay there. I had enough bruises, thanks to the she-bitches circling him, and didn't need to add to the collection.

Thankfully, Bennett shut himself in his office and closed the blinds as soon as we got there, so I didn't have to worry about him. Unfortunately, the first woman approached a minute later.

"Is Bennett in?" she asked.

"You just saw him walk past. Unless he can teleport, he's in. And if you're asking because you're looking for permission to interrupt him, I don't get paid enough to be his abused gatekeeper. So do what you want. Just don't hold me accountable for his shitty mood swings." I said all of it while booting up my laptop and opening the spreadsheet I'd worked on the day before. "Oh, and if you can pass the word that I lost the *privilege* of eating unsupervised this week, I'd appreciate it. I'd really like to go back to how things were."

I lifted my gaze to meet hers. She studied me for a long, silent moment.

"If there's nothing that I can do for you, I'm going to get to work."

When she still didn't say anything, I ignored her and focused on the mind-numbing task of judging other people's expenses. The expenses for the original companies I'd looked at had been easy to spot the financial bleed. However, it was becoming increasingly harder with each new company, mostly because I didn't know what some of the companies did, which meant I spent time searching the internet. Could I knock on the door and ask? Sure. But I didn't want to.

A few minutes later, one of the office women walked by me, knocked on the door, and went in. She left almost immediately. In what mood, I didn't know because I didn't look up from what I was doing. Not even when I felt the weight of Bennett's stare.

The soft snick of the door was surprising.

No tantrum?

The blinds suddenly opened. Had I been looking at them, I probably would have jumped. Instead, I pretended he hadn't startled me and didn't exist.

The next woman hesitated when she saw the blinds were open, and I could feel her looking at me.

"Not my monkey; not my circus," I said without looking up.

She walked away without trying the door.

It didn't end. The stream of women was non-stop. Why they kept wanting to talk to me made no sense when I *knew* the message I'd given the first girl had been passed around.

Just before ten, I picked up my phone and walked away from my desk.

Me: Do you have any headphones I can use?
Mom: Ask Bennett. He can get you whatever you want.

I paused outside the bathroom and stared at the message with growing anger, which got the better of me because I typed out a fast reply and hit send without cooling off.

Me: Is Bennett my parent, or are you? I can't tell anymore. If

I'm a burden, just say so, and stop passing me off like the unwanted charity case they all say I am.

Something banged loudly on the other side of the floor as Miranda came out of the bathroom. We both looked in that direction before looking at each other.

"Heard your lunch times in Bennett's office are a punishment," she said.

"If I had even an ounce of interest in Bennett, maybe I would see them as an opportunity like you do, but I don't. I've been here less than a week and am ready to sacrifice a small goat to whatever species deity is willing to listen to get me out of here as fast as it can. Now, can you do me a favor and tell my mom I went out to get my own stuff when she comes looking for me?"

I turned on my heel before Miranda could respond and went to catch the elevator down to the lobby.

My phone started to ring. I looked at it and saw it was Mom. Ignoring it, I sent her another text.

Me: I'll see you at dinner. We'll talk then.
Mom: You are my daughter. Always. From the first moment I saw you, I've loved you. You aren't a burden. You are wanted more than you know.

My eyes started to water in anger and hurt as I read her text. Then why had I grown up a foster and not adopted? Why did they send me away?

I made it to the street before I started to cry. Rather than taking a ride-share to buy some headphones like I intended, I walked to the park and sat down on a bench to watch the geese swim in the sun.

The wind dried my tears, and the fresh air helped lift my mood. When I felt like I could, I opened my text messages with Mom and re-read them. Passing me off to Bennett again and again hurt, obviously. But it had also nudged that little box of worries in the back of my mind that I'd thought I'd put away last night.

Why did they keep pushing me toward Bennett? If I were wanted, then it meant...

I let out a long, slow breath.

"Where are you, Wren?" I said softly. "You're sitting on a bench. You're in a park. Get out of your head. Ground yourself in the present. You can't control what *might* happen. You can only make choices now. Here."

And my choices right now were simple ones. Stay in the park and soak up the peace a little longer, or head back and face the fallout from my anger?

I leaned back into the bench, closed my eyes, and tipped my face to the sun.

Avoidance as a coping mechanism wasn't healthy. Avoidance to regroup and calm down wasn't bad, though. Neither was avoidance as a way to stay safe. Mom's hug was probably going to be bone-crushing when she got her hands on me.

When I opened my eyes, Bennett was squatting down in front of me, his expression a little lost and sad. The stark, red handprint that stood out on the side of his face stopped me from being angry that he'd followed me. Again.

"Who slapped you?" I asked.

"Mom."

The answer shocked me. Mom didn't slap. Ever.

"Why?"

"She knew you weren't happy living and working with me. I told her I had it under control. Today proved that I didn't."

"Today had nothing to do with you," I said.

He tilted his head at me. "Doesn't it?"

I looked away, choosing to watch the geese swim freely in their pond rather than face his intense gaze.

"I haven't been happy for a very long time, Bennett. It has nothing to do with you and everything to do with the lack of freedom in my life to make my own choices. It's not your fault. I don't blame Mom and Dad either. But I'm tired of doing what they want, Bennett. I want to do what I want."

He moved fast, sitting next to me and hugging me before I knew what he was going to do. Although he'd been careful not to pin my arms, he was too close, cradling the back of my head as he dipped his to breathe in my scent from my neck.

Panic exploded inside of me, and I pushed at him.

"Get off me, Bennett."

He released me and stood fluidly. My heartbeat thundered in my chest as I stared at him with wide eyes. Then, I looked at the hand he was holding out like he was offering me a hot poker.

He wanted me to touch him after that? Hell, no.

I stood without taking his hand. He tried to snatch my fingers, and I batted him away.

"I know you don't need to hold someone's hand," he said, "but I do. I don't want a matching handprint."

"Then dodge. I'm not holding your hand."

Speed walking away from him, I heard his soft chuckle.

Mom was waiting for us outside the building's main doors. When she saw me, she burst into tears. Guilt speared through me, and I hurried to hug her.

"I'm sorry, Mom. What I said was purposely hurtful, and you didn't deserve it."

She held me tight until her tears slowed, then pulled back to look at me.

"It may have been purposely hurtful, but I think I needed to hear it, whether I deserved it or not. Is that really how you feel? That I don't want you as my daughter?"

"No, Mom. I know you want me. I promise."

She breathed deeply then kissed my cheek. I didn't miss the angry scowl she shot at Bennett as she pulled back.

"It's not his fault either," I said.

She made a noncommittal sound and led me into the building.

We didn't talk about anything on the ride up; she just held my arm like she was afraid I'd vanish. Once we reached our floor, she walked me to my desk, where new earbuds waited next to my computer.

"Thank you, Mom," I said.

"For you, I'll do anything, Wrenly. Always."

I hugged her again and nudged her toward the door.

Her loving gaze swept over me, but hardened when it shifted to Bennett. A low, warning growl emanated from her before she pivoted and left.

"Told you I needed protection," he said, his fingers brushing mine.

I batted his hand away and pointed toward his office.

"Go work."

He went after a particularly hard shove, but kept his office door open.

For some reason, though, no one showed up. Not even for the lunch I'd ordered. The receptionist called to say that the food was there, but I had to pick it up myself. I didn't mind the break. However, when I returned to my desk, my laptop was missing. I wanted to groan. Instead, I went into Bennett's office.

He was working and didn't look up as I unpacked our lunch. Grateful he was too busy to join me, I ate quickly and grabbed my laptop. Although I was tempted to leave, I remembered his warning that lunch meant an hour in his office. So, I made myself comfortable by kicking off my sneakers and settling sideways on the couch to work.

When he sat next to me to eat his lunch, I barely noticed.

The distance, silence, and open door gave me a sense of security that I realized was false when his fingers circled my ankle and tugged my foot onto his lap. I jerked my leg back so forcefully, the laptop fell off my lap—thankfully landing on my sneakers—and it felt like I might have lost some skin.

Pulse racing, I pressed back against the couch arm and stared at him, waiting for his next move.

He frowned at me, concern clearly visible.

"Why did you panic?"

"Why do you keep touching me? I don't like being touched."

"I thought you didn't like your face covered. The arm pinning is still debatable. Sometimes you're okay with it, and sometimes you're not."

"I'm never okay with it." Yet, I remembered the times he'd pinned them above my head, and I hadn't panicked. That had been before he'd started acting weird with me, though.

"The face thing, too, maybe. Mom hugged you, and you were fine."

"Mom is Mom," I said. "She has different rules."

"True."

I continued to wait. When he didn't try anything else, I glanced at the clock in his office and saw lunch was over.

"What time are we meeting Mom and Dad for dinner?" I asked.

"They made reservations at six at the Seventeen-Twenty-One."

"If you think I know what that is, I don't."

"It's a place downtown. Fancy. The dressy kind."

I scowled at him. "Why didn't you say something this morning?"

"You were already mad, and I know you don't like wearing those kinds of clothes."

"I also don't like standing out." I swung my legs over the couch, officially out of his reach, and picked up the laptop.

"If you give Mom another chance and ask her, she would love to take you shopping," he said, watching me.

"Or..." I held out my hand. He took it in his so fast I missed the transition. I tried pulling it away like I had my leg, but he held fast.

"I'll take you shopping. Anything you want."

"Let go, Bennett. I don't want *you*; I want your *credit card*." When he frowned but still didn't let go, I added, "You're hurting me."

He released me, and I gently rubbed my healing palm.

"Why don't you want me?"

"Because I'm not going shopping either." I held out my hand again. "Card, please."

He pulled out his wallet and handed over a black one.

"Thank you. I'll be right back."

After putting on my shoes, I left his office and hurried out to where the other women sat. Ignoring the rest of them, I went to Miranda. Milena and Olivia were the most determined she-bitches after Bennett, but both had burned bridges. And although Miranda pushed me into the door—I took partial blame for that—she hadn't been aggressive since then. A little bitchy, but not mean, and she'd also clued me in on why Aiden and Karter had been sent away. I owed her for that.

"Possible opportunity for you," I said, holding out the card. "I was just told I have to go to dinner somewhere dressy tonight, and I'm wearing this. I could go shopping for a dress, or you could shop for me."

"Why would I do that?"

"To show Bennett your helpfulness and impress my mom."

She considered me for a moment, then took the card.

"You already know my mom well enough to know what she'd like," I said. "Please don't make it too loud or too tight. I need to eat. I'll let Bennett know you're doing this favor for me. Be back before five."

She glanced down at my sneakers.

"Shoes too?"

"Yeah. Flats, please."

"You'd look better in heels."

"Maybe, but I run better in flats."

"Are you planning on running?"

"Only if I make someone angry."

"She'll be running," one of the other women said under her breath.

Miranda smirked and grabbed her purse.

"If I end up regretting doing this, you will too, Wrenly."

"Noted."

I returned to Bennett's office and found him where I left him. He looked at my empty hands then met my gaze expectantly.

"Miranda is willing to get a dress for me. I hope you don't dock her pay for it."

"Why Miranda and not you?"

"I don't like that kind of shopping, and she does."

"How do you know?"

"Because I have eyes and see how she dresses. She'll pick out something nice and have fun doing it. I won't. It's a win-win for both of us."

"What about for me?"

"For you too, because I won't be angry from shopping and take it out on you."

Something close to amusement flickered in his gaze, and I hurried to grab my laptop.

"See you after work." I fled.

CHAPTER FOURTEEN

A HAND WAVED in front of my face, breaking my focus from the numbers on my screen. Startled, I looked up at Miranda as I pulled out an earbud.

"Sorry," I said.

"Dress and shoes," she said, lifting both bags.

"I really appreciate you shopping for me. Would you mind hanging them up in Bennett's bathroom when you give him back his card?"

Her gaze slid to Bennett's open office door as I put my earbud back in and looked down at my screen. Could I have done both of those things? Yes, but I didn't want to. She did.

She moved away, and as tempted as I was to remove an earbud and listen, I didn't. The blinds were open, and I'd caught Bennett watching me several times already this afternoon. So I focused on my spreadsheet and waited for some kind of explosion.

Miranda passed my desk several minutes later. Although I didn't look up to gauge her mood, it seemed like a relatively peaceful exit.

My phone pinged with a new message. I glanced at it.

Bennett: Don't you want to check what she bought?

Me: I'll check after five.
Bennett: What if it doesn't fit?
Me: Then I'll ask Mom to pick a different restaurant.

Had I not already upset her, I would have made that suggestion first, but I was playing nice. I really wanted tonight's conversation to go well. It was no longer about permission but about acceptance. I *was* going to attend the university I chose.

At five on the dot, Bennett came out and knocked on my desk to gain my attention.

"Go change," he said as soon as I pulled my earbuds out. "Let me know if you need help with anything."

Miranda came around the corner just then.

"Miranda can help me," I said quickly. "Right?"

She looked from me to Bennett

"That's why I came back here," she said, offering him a sweet smile he didn't even notice.

"Thanks. I'll call if I need anything."

I darted around Bennett and claimed his bathroom for the next ten minutes. My hands weren't in the best shape for the dress that Miranda picked out. The apron neckline had a tiny button at the back of my neck that I couldn't quite manage, and the snug mini skirt required a little tugging to get it into place, but the dress itself wasn't awful.

With the exposed shoulders and the entire back cut out, it required me to ditch my bra, which I didn't mind. Thankfully, the sheer front slit overskirt helped me feel less exposed.

"I need help with the button," I called.

Instead of Miranda, Bennett opened the door.

"Where's Miranda?"

"Not here. It's me or nothing."

Play nice, I reminded myself.

With a sigh, I lifted my hair and turned away from him. His

fingers skimmed my back, dragging up toward the neckline at the same time as something brushed my neck above the button.

Panic exploded inside of me.

Pivoting, I raised my hands, ready to push him away, but he was just standing there, hands at his sides like nothing happened. I knew something *had* happened, though. My neck was still tingling from the ghosted brush of his lips.

I wasn't crazy. I knew what I'd felt.

"I'll figure out the button on my own."

He spun me around and had my wrists pinned against the wall a second later. This time, I was facing away from him. My breath whooshed out of me.

The only thing stopping me from freaking out was the fact that he wasn't pressing me against the wall. Just carefully holding my hands there.

"This is why I don't trust you," I said, my voice shaking.

His other hand brushed my hair over my shoulder and expertly fished the button through the tiny hole.

"This isn't why you don't trust me, Wrenly," he said close to my ear. "You haven't trusted me since you came home. Why?"

His fingers trailed over my shoulder, and my panic spiked. I tore a hand free from his hold and drove my elbow into his ribs without thinking. Pain exploded.

"Dammit!" I yelled, immediately cradling it.

He spun me around and tried extending my arm.

"Stop manhandling me."

"I just want to make sure it's—"

"Not your problem. Back off, Bennett, or I'm going to have a lot worse than a bruised elbow."

He inhaled deeply. "Why are you afraid, Wrenly? Do you think I'm going to hurt you?"

I closed my eyes, willing myself not to give away more than I had.

Be angry, Wren. Angry is safe.

Focusing on the pain, I let anger take control.

"Why is my elbow bruised, Bennett?"

"Because you elbowed me instead of using your words."

My eyes snapped open, and I glared at him. "Take me to dinner before I try strangling you and hurt my hands more than they already are."

His gaze swept over my face, and I saw a hint of his frustration, but he moved aside instead of getting angry.

"Thank you," I said.

Miranda was sitting at my desk when I strode out. I glared at her, knowing she'd heard it all and hadn't done anything. Although it may have been a little ridiculous of me to expect her to. Likely, it would have gone against whatever Bennett had told her to do.

Her gaze bounced between me and Bennett as I passed her.

"Thank you for your help, Miranda," Bennett said behind me. "The dress looks good. Mom will be happy."

"Glad to help," I heard her say.

Him, but not me, obviously.

But what did I expect? We both knew that was why she'd gotten the dress—to impress him.

Bennett followed me to the elevator and didn't say anything until we were inside alone.

"You look really pretty," he said.

"Gee, thanks. I've now achieved my purpose in life, looking pretty," I said.

In the reflection of the polished metal, I saw him close his eyes and tip his head back. Why did seeing his exposed throat make me want to karate chop it so badly?

The doors opened, and more people got on. I was forced to move closer to Bennett as it grew more crowded. My pulse jumped each time his fingers brushed my skin, and I was ready to push my way out the doors the second it reached the lobby.

He held me back by snagging my collar. I glared at him. He scowled in return, and I realized I needed to calm down.

It's just a casual touch. You're overreacting. Allies, not enemies, Wrenly. You need allies.

I relaxed my jaw, then my tongue, setting it lightly against my teeth, and focused on each inhale and exhale as we made our way to the next elevator.

He touched you while buttoning your dress. It happens. That brush you felt was probably a stray piece of hair, not his lips. Your imagination is overactive because of last night's paranoia.

Bennett watched me closely as we rode the elevator down to the parking garage with a few other employees. Those few minutes were what I needed, though.

By the time we reached our car, I'd talked myself into a more positive mood.

"Thank you," I said as he opened the door for me.

"You're welcome."

His mask was back in place, probably because I'd given him whiplash with my fast mood swing.

"Did Mom talk to you about dinner tonight?" I asked once he was on the road.

"She did."

"What are the chances they're going to hear what I have to say?"

"I'd say very good."

"Good."

"Mom said you applied to several colleges already. Any in the city?"

"No."

"Why not? Hildcrask is one of the best in the country. It has a Social Science degree and the best graduating employment rate for the program."

"It does," I said calmly, glad I could practice my counter-argument on Bennett first. "However, Hildcrask is too connected to the power players in the city, including the Wulf family. Even though my last name is Belak, I'm still tied to the Wulf family and want to go somewhere where the Wulf name isn't well-known. That way, I know without a doubt that my association with a powerful family doesn't influence the people around me.

"I want to know I can stand on my own."

"Is it really that bad to be associated with the Wulf name?" Bennett asked.

"It's not about being good or bad. It's about having the freedom to choose my own path in life."

The steering wheel crackled, and I looked over at his white-knuckled grip.

He knows I'm going to upset Mom again by wanting to leave. That's all that means. Don't panic. You need to coax him to your side, or you will never leave this place.

I slowly let out a breath and smiled, attempting to evoke a calm, happy state of mind.

"Do you know what I'm looking forward to? Walking to a gas station and buying junk food. I like the idea of stockpiling some chips, chocolate, and cola and then studying for hours." I turned toward him. "If you had to pick three items from a gas station to help you study, what would you pick?"

His hold on the steering wheel didn't relax as he frowned at the road ahead.

"I don't think anything there would help me focus," he said. "I need my mate, Wrenly. That's it."

My stomach dropped, and I faced forward again, losing my smile.

"How long until we get there?" I asked.

"Soon."

The rest of the ride passed in silence. When he pulled in front of one of the grand buildings on the other side of downtown, I wished the night were already over.

A valet jogged around to Bennett's side of the car as soon as he parked in front.

Bennett got out and handed the keys to the guy as another valet moved to open my door.

"She's mine," Bennett said with a growl in his voice.

My stunned gaze met the man's through the window before he quickly backed away.

Bennett didn't mean it like that. He's just protective because I kept getting hurt.

I loosely fisted my trembling hands in my lap and focused on my breathing while staring at the door handle and debating opening my own damn door. Bennett walked faster than I could decide, though.

He opened it and held out his hand. I moved to get out on my own, but he stepped in front of me, blocking my way.

"Take it, Wrenly," he said.

Play nice. Just get through tonight.

I reluctantly placed my hand into his and pretended like it wasn't shaking like crazy. His warm fingers closed over mine, steadying me as he backed up a step so I could stand.

Then he leaned in until his mouth was close to my ear.

"This didn't scare you before," he said. "Why do you smell like you're two seconds from running?"

"Because I am. How are you going to explain that to Mom?"

He pulled back and studied me. His jaw clenched, and his hand started shaking more than mine.

"I'm already nervous enough, wearing clothes I hate, walking into a conversation that they've been avoiding for months. Please don't make tonight worse," I said softly.

He breathed in deeply as he closed his eyes, and this time, I knew he wasn't testing the truth of what I said but trying to control himself.

When he opened his eyes again, he wrapped my hand around his arm and walked me to the entrance.

He hadn't exaggerated when he'd said the place was fancy.

The lobby had marble floors. Gold and crystal fixtures. Decor in dusky reds and twilight blues accented by primarily cream walls. It was pretty and screamed designer money.

"Good evening, Mr. Wulf," the hostess said. "Would you like me to walk you to your room? The rest of your party is already seated."

"No need," Bennett said.

Keeping a firm hold on my hand, he led me past what looked like a reception desk and down one of the hallways leading off the lobby. The restaurant had a strong hotel feel with its numbered doors.

He stopped at room 112 and opened the door for me.

Mom and Dad's whispered conversation immediately stopped as they watched us enter.

"That dress is stunning, Wrenly," Mom said.

"Thank you."

Bennett led me to the seat next to hers. I could feel his tension as he held it out for me, and I swore to the moon god I would unman him if he touched me in front of Mom. He didn't, though. He just pushed the chair in like a rational, normal person.

"Is there anything you want to drink?" Mom asked. "We have wine and some mineral water."

"Water, please."

Bennett poured it for me while Mom took my hands in hers.

"I am so sorry for this morning."

"So am I. I was frustrated and let it out. It won't happen again. I promise."

"Of course it should happen again. If we're doing something that upsets you, tell us. Don't keep it in."

I wanted to laugh. How many times over the years had I tried to do that? So many that I lost count. I'd learned it didn't do any good. Well, not true. Usually, gifts would show up after a complaint.

You're sad at school and miss home? Here's a gold watch, Wrenly.

You don't like your classmates? Here's a pair of diamond earrings.

Gifts meant to placate me into silence.

"Well, not talking about what university I want to attend has been a little upsetting."

"I know. And we'll talk about that. Let's order first." She patted my hand and passed me a menu.

The deflection was expected, so it didn't upset me. Opening the menu, I glanced at the selection, then closed it again.

"You can order whatever you want for me," I said, passing the menu back.

"I thought you wanted the freedom to make your own choices," Bennett said.

My gaze drifted to the fork on the table, and I remembered the last time I'd had to use one as a weapon. It worked decently against humans, but wouldn't do shit to a shifter. I was still a little tempted to give it a try.

"Exactly," I said, choosing words over violence. "That's why we're here tonight. To talk about reclaiming a tiny bit of freedom.

"I've applied to Coalwell University and received my acceptance."

Mom looked down at her menu, and I saw how it trembled in her hold.

Dad pressed the button on the table to summon the server, and the other door in the room opened. I focused on relaxing and mentally resetting as Dad ordered steaks for everyone.

"Can you add a grilled cheese to that? A regular one. Nothing fancy," Bennett said.

I glanced at him in surprise. He held my gaze as he said, "French fries too. Salted. That's it."

He handed the menus to the server without looking away from me.

"You didn't want steak, did you?" he asked once the guy was gone.

"No."

"What about the grilled cheese?"

The way he was looking at me made me nervous. I knew that if I said I didn't want it, he'd be pressing that button. Why, though? Why did he care if I was getting what I wanted? Did he think giving me a grilled cheese sandwich would stop me from wanting to go to Coalwell? If so, he was insane.

Without answering him, I looked at Mom.

"My grades were good enough that I was awarded a decent scholarship."

"Your grades weren't just good, sweetheart," Dad said. "They were exceptional and can open better doors than Coalwell's. Did you apply to Hildcrask or Wellborn? They're both highly acclaimed schools with diverse programs. Bennett even owns an apartment almost between the two, so you wouldn't need to commute."

Why couldn't they just stop pushing me off on Bennett?

I fisted my hands, despite the ache, determined not to give in to the fear threatening to consume me as I repeated my reason for not wanting either of those schools.

"I thought you hated being away from us." Mom said.

"I did. Then, I got used to it," I said.

Mom flinched and looked down at the table. Dad wrapped his arms around her shoulders.

"What if we compromise?" Dad asked. "Attend Hildcrask for the first year; then transfer to Coalwell. You can spend more time with us before you leave again."

He made it sound so reasonable, but it wasn't. Not really. It was a way to pull me into their plans and make me forget my own.

"I'd rather not deal with transferring and just go to the school I want from the start."

Mom and Dad exchanged worried looks. Then Mom glanced at Bennett. I didn't look.

"I'm going to use the restroom," I said, standing.

Dad and Bennett both politely stood when I did, but I saw Bennett move to follow me.

"I think I can manage this on my own, don't you?"

A slow flush crawled up his neck, and his eye twitched. I didn't know what that meant, but it couldn't be anything good. I left quickly before I found out.

While I took my time in the posh restroom to regroup, an older woman walked in on the phone.

"Darling, tonight is your night. Bennett Wulf is having dinner at

Seventeen-Twenty-one right now. Go change into that lavender sleeve dress, and wear your diamond waterfall necklace. Hurry. His group just placed their order." She paused to look at herself in the mirror and pulled a tube of lipstick from her purse. "If we time it right, you can bump into him as he's leaving his room."

I finished washing my hands and wished luck to whomever the woman was talking to. Charming Bennett was like trying to sweet-talk a volcano into not erupting.

When I returned to our private room, the conversation between Mom, Dad, and Bennett abruptly ended. Bennett looked like he was two seconds from flipping the table, and Mom looked like she was ready to bury her firstborn. Not the best mood to resume our conversation, but I was tired of waiting for what I wanted.

I gave Mom's shoulder a comforting squeeze on my way to my chair. Bennett stood and pushed it in for me as I sat again.

"My choice of school shouldn't be the cause of an argument," I said.

"We just feel it would be better for you to attend Hildcrask or Wellborn," Dad said.

"I understand. They're good schools. I'm sure I would have a bright, carefully arranged future by attending them. But that's not what I want. And this conversation wasn't to ask for permission. It's to inform you of my choice so you can make peace with it and spend whatever time with me you want before I leave."

"How are you going to pay for it?" Bennett asked.

Mom's growl was so faint that I almost missed it.

I glanced at her, unsure if she was mad at my insistence or at Bennett for bringing up exactly what I'd known they would try to use to get me to attend the school of their choice.

"Whatever the scholarships and my wages from this summer don't cover, I'll earn. If I need to take out a loan, I'll do that." I didn't say anything about my savings, wanting to keep it a secret just in case.

"You've given me enough already. I can do this on my own. And if I can't...if I run into any trouble, I know who to call."

The glasses on the table started to rattle. No one's hands were on the surface, though, so I wasn't sure who was doing it.

"We know how much you want this and understand you're not asking for permission," Mom said. "But please don't shut us out. We want to be a part of your life, Wrenly. You've been gone for so long. We finally got you back. I thought you'd stay." Her voice broke at the end, and she began to cry.

The table shaking stopped as Dad hugged Mom.

I fisted my hands under the table, willing myself not to feel guilt, not to react.

"We've heard what you've had to say," Dad said. "And I guess there isn't much we can say to change your mind. I'm sorry."

"Me too," I said, although I wasn't sure what he was apologizing for.

Our food arrived. Mom barely ate any of her meal before she and Dad excused themselves.

"How is the food?" Bennett asked.

I looked down at my plate and realized I'd eaten most of it without tasting a thing.

"Fine."

"Do you want to go somewhere else?"

"No. This was—"

"Don't say fine."

I told myself his voice didn't sound desperate and tortured. That I was projecting what I felt—desperate for understanding and tortured that no one did.

"I think I'm done."

He stood and pulled out my chair for me, leaving his plate mostly untouched. If his fingers brushed my arm, it was just an accident. The way his hand briefly settled on my lower back was just a courtesy. Aiden and Karter would have done the same.

When we reached the hall, my stomach almost dropped to my toes at the sight of the woman from the bathroom and...

Lindi.

I fought to keep all my emotions in check as she stumbled into me. Bennett released me to catch her and prevent me from falling.

"I'm so sorry," she said. "I wasn't watching where I was going."

Bennett made a noncommittal sound as he extracted himself from her tentacle hold. When he reached for me again, I sidestepped.

Lindi's light brown gaze swung to me, not showing a hint of the maliciousness I knew she possessed. Her perfectly styled brunette hair was swept off her neck to showcase the necklace she wore.

"Lindi," I said. "I didn't expect to see you here. Nice necklace."

She smiled prettily and touched the diamond strands.

"Thank you, Wrenly. I never thought I'd see you here either."

"You know her?" Bennett asked me.

"I do," I said neutrally. "From school."

She held out her hand. "Lindi Shane. And you are?"

He looked from her to her hand and reluctantly shook it. "Bennett Wulf."

"It's a pleasure to meet you, Mr. Wulf. I would love to meet for coffee sometime, if you're interested."

She plucked a business card from her tiny clutch and passed it to him when he released her hand. Again, he hesitated for several seconds before accepting it.

"I hope I hear from you," she said.

With a polite nod, she walked away with her mom.

CHAPTER FIFTEEN

THE AIR OUTSIDE helped cool my overheated skin as I focused on remaining calm. I could feel Bennett's gaze on me as we waited for the valet and hoped he wasn't smelling my fear and anxiety.

"How well do you know her?" Bennett asked.

"Well enough to know she'd pick up on the third ring if you called her."

"You don't sound happy about that."

"Your love life and who you choose to spend your time with is your business, not mine. If you're interested in her, I wouldn't stop you."

I'd push you with both hands, I silently added.

"I'm not interested in her. Just curious."

The car pulled up, and Bennett opened my door for me. I got in and glanced at the restaurant's entrance, half-expecting to see Lindi there. She wasn't. She was too smart to be spotted. But she was somewhere watching, probably trying to figure out how I knew Bennett.

While at school, I'd been very careful to disassociate myself from the Wulfs. Every time Mom and Dad had visited, I'd ensured it was on a weekend when most of the students were gone. I'd even switched out Mom and Dad's contact information with Grandma's on my registration form when some of the girls started to ask questions.

I was so lost in thoughts of school hell that I didn't realize Bennett had taken a different exit until we left the neighborhoods and entered fields and trees.

"Where are we going?"

"I need to go for a run."

"Why out here?" I asked, getting nervous.

"Because I don't think I could handle any of the pack joining me right now."

I glanced at him, but his expressionless mask was in place again, making his mood hard to read.

"Wouldn't it have been better to take me home first?" I asked.

"No."

He pulled over suddenly. "Get out."

"What?"

"You want to run away from everyone and everything so badly? Get out."

Was I afraid of being out in the middle of nowhere? No. I had a phone and was used to being on my own and making it work. Was I afraid of being out in the middle of nowhere alone with Bennett when his jaw was ticcing like a bomb counting down? Yep.

If he looks like he's going to lose his temper, hug him, Wrenly.

I reached for the handle and opened the door myself.

His door slammed as I stood, and he was in front of me a second later, pinning me against the car.

"Do you want to go for a run, Wrenly?"

"In this dress? It was almost five thousand dollars, Bennett."

His gaze dipped to my neck, where my pulse fluttered.

"You hate the dress."

"The dress is pretty. I'm not going to wreck it just because I don't like it." Before the end of the summer, I planned to add it to the name-brand resale site I used to trade high-end items for cash.

"Then take it off."

"I'm not wearing a—" I took a breath and tried again. "Bennett, I don't care what happens at pack runs; I'm not taking off the dress to run down the road in broad daylight."

His gaze skimmed lower, and I pushed at his chest. He caught my wrists and held them against him.

"Your insanity is showing, and I want to go home."

His mask shattered, and the look in his eyes wasn't healthy… for me.

"What home? You mean the place you want to leave?"

My panic skyrocketed when he started leaning into me. I closed my eyes and let myself feel all the anger, frustration, and *fear* I'd been suppressing.

He growled and dropped his forehead to mine.

"Get back in the car. I'll be back in an hour. Don't even think of driving with those hands."

He released me.

Trembling, I stayed right where I was.

After several minutes, I slowly opened my eyes and found myself alone with a pile of clothes folded neatly on the hood.

I didn't even hesitate. Scooping up his clothes, I found his keys and phone. The phone I left on the side of the road. The clothes and keys stayed with me as I executed a smoother Y turn than my last attempt and headed back the way we'd come.

When I reached a stop sign, I used my phone to send him a text.

Me: I'd rather high-five a cactus than wait around for your moody ass. You deserve this! Enjoy the run home.

Were my hands shaking as I used my GPS to figure out my way home? Absolutely. But not because of the drive.

I had no doubt Bennett would retaliate. I just hoped I was safely locked in my closet before he found his phone.

Forty minutes later, I pulled into the garage and almost crashed into Dad's meticulously restored pride and joy, vintage Ford Model A when I saw what waited for me.

Slamming on the brakes, I gripped the steering wheel and stared at my harbinger of doom.

Bennett, fully nude, leaned on the hood of my grey sedan. His chest heaved with each breath. Sweat glistened on his skin, proof that he'd pushed himself hard to beat me home since wolves didn't break a sweat easily.

My gaze traveled over his length, taking in the tension in his faux-relaxed pose, along with the impressively chiseled ridges he possessed. My heart skipped a beat. He was so...*nice* to look at. Why couldn't he be nice to be around, too?

He pushed away from the hood, muscles rippling hypnotically, as he stalked closer to the car.

I slammed my eyes closed before I looked where I shouldn't.

He's your brother, Wren. He is not *good-looking. Not even a little.*

He knocked on my window, and I shook my head, grateful the car was still running and the doors were locked.

"I've enjoyed my run home and want my clothes, Wrenly," he said, sounding surprisingly calm through the glass.

"No. I don't trust you," I said without opening my eyes.

"What would it take for you to unlock the doors for me?" he asked.

Dammit. I couldn't pass up this chance. But it had to be something big.

"I want my bed back and five thousand dollars," I said.

"Done. Now, unlock the doors."

"And you need to go into the house first," I added.

His chuckle sent a shiver down my spine. A second later, the car's horn honked twice as the door unlocked.

My eyes flew open, and I looked at Bennett through the glass as he held the spare fob.

"Put it in Park."

Damn him for knowing I was thinking about slamming it into reverse. Too bad my Y-turn skills wouldn't allow me to whip the car around fast enough to escape. So, I parked the car and turned off the engine.

Maybe it was my imagination, but I thought I heard, "Good girl," through the window as he retreated a step and opened my door.

I knew nudity wasn't a big deal to them, but it still was to me, and I was extremely uncomfortable with the potential view at eye-level, so I quickly got out.

"Clothes are in the passenger seat," I said, bolting.

He caught me around the waist, and a second later, I was up in his arms.

"Why are you carrying me? Put me down!"

"Look at your hands, Wrenly."

"Who cares about my hands. You're naked."

"You noticed?"

"I'm not blind." As soon as those words were out, my face flamed with embarrassment, which was good. Safe.

He shifted my weight to one arm and carried me into the house. Not stopping at the stairs, he marched right up them and into my room.

"You have two minutes to change; then I'm dealing with your hands. You'll get your bed back after." He put me down, turned around, and left.

I looked. Bennett had a really nice ass. And noticing that was not okay. I released a freaked-out breath, hurried to my closet for my pajamas, then closed myself in my bathroom.

When I opened the door almost fifteen minutes later, my bed was back, fully made, and Bennett was on sitting on it, wearing a loose pair of shorts and nothing else. Seeing his bare chest bothered me more than it should have.

"Let me see your hands," he said.

I made a face, cautiously moved a little closer, and held up my newly bandaged hands.

"Not good enough," he said. "Closer."

He stayed right where he was as I inched toward him until I could almost touch him. This time, when I held out my hands, he captured one, turning it and running a finger lightly over the bandage.

"You can get mad at me. You can leave me in the middle of nowhere without clothes—thank you, for leaving me the phone, by the way—but you can't hurt yourself. Ever. When you want to get away from me, tell me. Do you understand?"

"I want to get away from you," I said.

A hint of a smile tugged at his lips. "I know. Why are you so nervous around me, Wrenly? You weren't like this yesterday. What changed?"

"Your unpredictability leveled up."

He looked down at my hand and smoothed his thumb over my bandage again.

"It has. But I promise I'm trying."

I wasn't sure what, exactly, he was trying to do. Not to kill anyone or break anything? Those were good things. Not to use me as a substitute for his missing mate? Also good, but very concerning.

He's more patient than most. He'll give her the time she needs, even if it drives him crazy.

"I really want to get away from you," I said, my voice a stressed whisper.

His gaze snapped to mine, searching.

"Please." It was almost a whine.

I was so close to breaking down under the intensity of his stare, and I didn't like what that meant. The delusion I was clinging to was a fragile, thin shard that would take nothing to shatter.

"Okay."

He released me, and I stumbled back several steps, my hands

tingling and trembling. I hid them behind my back so he wouldn't see as he stood.

"Get some sleep." He paused at the door on his way out. "What do you want for breakfast? Pancakes with chocolate chips?"

I nodded, not caring about breakfast but wanting him to leave. Once he did, I hurried to the door and locked it.

You made it through seven years of hell. Ten more weeks will be nothing.

My shaking grew more pronounced, and I hurried to my bed.

THE SOFT SNICK of a door closing brought me fully awake. I opened my eyes and saw that it was daylight, and my bedroom door was closed. Gazing around the room, I saw that both my bathroom and closet doors were open.

My gaze returned to my bedroom door. I'd locked it. I knew I had.

Slowly turning my head, I looked at the space beside me. The blankets were in place, but there was a slight indent in the pillow. Sliding my hand under the covers, I touched the bedding.

It radiated heat.

I struggled to come up with a reasonable explanation. Maybe Mom had come home and slept beside me.

You know she didn't, Wren.

Maybe I moved in my sleep.

You never have before, Wren.

Maybe I…

I scrambled for something, anything other than what I'd been trying to dismiss since the welcoming party. But I'd run out of excuses. My hand was touching the truth.

Bennett had slept next to me last night. And not because I was in his bed or there were no other beds in the house. But because I was his mate. The mate he was patiently waiting for. The mate slowly driving him insane.

The carefully crafted shard of delusion that had protected me from the truth shattered. With a whimper of denial, I desperately sought to recreate it.

I had to be wrong. I couldn't be his mate.

My chest grew tighter, and breathing became harder.

Mates never parted. I would never be able to leave.

It can't be me. I have plans. I wanted to go to University. Why me?

How long had he known?

That thought speared through me, and I remembered how, for as far back as I could remember, he'd always denied me as his sister.

And Mom and Dad had never scolded him for it. They'd always tried smoothing it over, telling me he still loved me.

He'd known since the beginning. They all had.

A pained sob broke through as I understood what that meant.

They'd only fostered me because I was Bennett's mate.

The door banged open suddenly, and Bennett rushed in. He was still wearing the shorts from last night, and his hair was partially flattened on one side. Worry reflected in his gaze as he crossed the room.

"Wrenly, what's wrong?"

When he tried reaching for me, I lost it.

"Don't touch me!" I scrambled out of the bed, wheezing for air I couldn't quite take in.

But he was faster, catching me by my arms.

"Wrenly, baby. You're safe."

With a scream that sounded more like a wounded animal than human, I covered my ears and slowly crumbled into a ball on the floor.

He kept talking to me, but I didn't hear any of it. My panic was too loud.

It was all a lie.

They didn't fall in love with me the first time they saw me. Bennett had.

I was a child bride. They'd raised me for Bennett.

They'd locked me away for Bennett.

I screamed, all my anger and hurt that I'd endured burning through me, ripping me apart.

Bennett stopped touching me. A second later, something stung my arm, snapping me out of my downward spiral.

"I've got you, baby," Bennett said. "You're safe. You'll be okay. I won't let anything hurt you. I promise."

The pain and fear melted away, and I started feeling unnaturally tired.

"What did you do?" I asked, my words slurring.

"Just gave you something to help you calm down."

"Asshole."

And then I was out.

WHEN I CAME TO AGAIN, I was in bed, and Grandma was sitting in a chair beside me, holding my hand.

She smiled at me when I looked at her.

"How are you feeling, my little Wren?"

My blink took a little too long as I considered her question.

"Tired." Yet, even as I said it, I felt more alert.

"Are you still feeling upset?" she asked.

"Why would I—"

The pain returned as the fogginess in my mind cleared, but it was less intense in the face of her compassionate focus.

It was all a lie.

Both her hands cradled mine.

"My sweet girl, no more tears. Tell Grandma what's wrong. We'll fix it together, okay?"

Grandma. She'd never treated me as anything other than the most precious person in her life. She'd scolded Aiden and Karter countless times for me. Bennett, too, though not as often because he hadn't been around.

Maybe she was the one person who'd been real in my life. But that didn't mean I could admit what I knew. Once I did that, they would make it impossible for me to leave.

"I remember a story you told me," I said. "About a wolf who waited too long to claim his mate. He went insane. I think Bennett is going insane."

Her worried expression turned to compassion and almost started me crying again.

"Is that why you were upset? He did something to upset you?"

He had. He'd picked me as his future mate. But I couldn't tell her that. I withdrew my hand from hers.

"I think I want to sleep some more."

"Sleep isn't going to help whatever is provoking that intelligent mind of yours, is it?"

"No."

"When you hide from the things bothering you, they always find a way to haunt you. Don't hide, my little Wren. You're too courageous for that."

"I'm not hiding. I'm processing."

She smiled and nodded. "Then, process. I'll wake you again later."

I accepted her forehead kiss and waited for the door to close before I quietly cried for the lie my childhood had been. My feelings fluctuated between anger and self-pity.

The reason why Mom and Dad had never let me come home, even when I said how much I hated school, was clearer now. A hurt part of me whispered that they'd safely locked me away until I was old enough to be Bennett's mate. But I knew them better than that. By sending me away, they'd given me a measure of freedom from his possessiveness while I grew up. Unfortunately, I hadn't been safe where they'd sent me.

I'd kept silent, stupidly believing I wasn't wanted. If I'd been honest with them about what had been happening instead of thinking they'd kicked me out because Bennett and I couldn't get along, maybe things would have gone a lot differently.

I didn't hate them. But I wasn't sure I could forgive them either.

As I lay there, I realized I was at one of those pivotal moments in life where I had a choice to make, and what I chose would irrevocably impact the path my life would take. I could choose to hold onto my anger and hurt indefinitely, or I could accept that the choices they'd made up until now had hurt me and move on. Accepting didn't mean forgiving. It just meant I wouldn't let their decisions continue to define my life.

Closing my eyes, I got to work on accepting all the bits of my past with the new understanding that their concern for me had been as Bennett's future mate and not their daughter. I also began to come to terms with how hurt they would be when I rejected him and walked away from them all.

Grandma returned a few hours later with a light knock on the door and a bowl of ice cream in her hands.

"Double-chocolate with bits of other things that looked good," she said. "Want a bite?"

I sat up in bed and accepted the bowl.

"Aiden and Karter are worried. Your parents, too. You should answer them."

I glanced at my phone on the nightstand but didn't reach for it. Grandma did. She had no problem unlocking it and opening my messages. She frowned, and I quickly ate a spoonful of ice cream.

"Their messages are missing. I see your mom and dad, but not Aiden and Karter."

She looked at me, and I shrugged.

I watched her inhale, gauging my mood. She wouldn't find much. I'd tucked away everything I could. A bit of sadness lingered, but that would fade in time, too, as I regrouped.

Did finding out why the Wulfs had taken me in change my

perception of everything? Yes. Did it hurt? Immeasurably. But it hadn't changed my goals; it solidified them.

"What time is it?" I asked when she said nothing.

"Almost dinner. Are you hungry for something more than ice cream?"

"Not really."

"How about taking my old bones for a walk around the neighborhood then? I've been sitting too long, I think. We can walk past Duneklin's place and bend the mailbox flag."

I shook my head at her, amused despite myself.

"He'll know it was you."

"That's what makes it even better. He won't be able to do a damn thing about it."

Her antagonistic attitude toward the elder Duneklin had something to do with a pack run incident when Grandpa was still alive. She never gave the details, but always said he deserved it.

"Fine, I'll take you to terrorize the neighbors, but you take all the blame."

"That's a given," she said, grinning.

I didn't bother changing since my pajamas were just a pair of shorts and a tank top. Everything that needed covering was covered. So I followed her out of the room and down the stairs.

Bennett waited at the bottom, watching me with an intensity that had me sidestepping partially behind Grandma. He frowned at me.

Grandma turned to look at me questioningly, too.

"Don't ever give me anything again without my permission," I said.

He didn't respond, just stared at me.

"Wren, he did what he thought was best for you. You were scratching at yourself. He was worried you'd hurt yourself."

She took my hand and led me to the mirror hanging in the entry.

"Look."

There were minor scratches near my ears. I hadn't realized I'd done it.

"When Bennett was out of control and throwing people into walls, did anyone think to give him a shot to control him? No. Don't hold me to a different standard."

Grandma shot Bennett a long look then took my hand with a kind smile and led me out the door.

We walked around the neighborhood for hours, during which time Grandma was a complete menace to everyone but me. She bent mailbox flags. She clipped flowers to make a bouquet that would irritate Bennett's nose—she sneezed a lot, too. House numbers were rearranged on mailboxes. Mail was hidden around the neighborhood like a toddler-aged easter egg hunt.

She wasn't sneaky about anything, and whenever she was caught, her answer was, "Go tell Bennett," while I stood behind her, shrugging and shaking my head.

Several people stormed off to do just that.

She laughed each time, and I had to admit I found it a little funny, too, as I imagined them all telling on her. Bennett wouldn't be able to control her any more than her son-in-law and current pack leader could control her.

"Well, this was a good walk, Wrenly. Did you learn anything?"

"Yes. You're a menace to society."

She hummed thoughtfully. "But just the right amount of menace. Not bad enough to call the police or your father. Just bad enough to get under their skin. Do you understand what I'm saying?"

I looked at Grandma with new understanding and felt my eyes start to water. She knew I was upset about something, and she was showing a way to vent my frustration without getting into trouble.

"Thank you," I said softly.

"Anytime."

"Can I ask you a question?" I asked as we started back.

"Of course."

"Why didn't you ever mate again?"

Her expression turned bittersweet and wistful. "Because no man could ever replace the mate I had. Even in death, we're still bound. I can still feel him."

She placed her hand over her heart, and I saw pain flash in her gaze.

"How did you survive Grandpa leaving you?"

She'd told me a long time ago that the stronger the mating bond, the more dangerous it was for the surviving mate when the other died.

"The bond is a complicated thing. Stronger for some, almost non-existent for others. Regardless of the strength, the bond between mates changes when we have children. It expands just enough to allow a connection to our young. It's my connection to my daughter and Bennett and Aiden and Karter...and most especially you...that keeps me here."

"How do you know if the bond is strong or not?"

"You feel it the moment it's made."

"What would have happened if you'd rejected Grandpa's bond?"

She glanced at me, and suspicion lit her gaze. I tried to push my panic away but knew I wasn't fully able to when she sighed and pulled me into a hug.

"If I'd rejected him, I would have missed out on the best thing that ever happened in my life. But that's me, Wrenly. Not all mate bonds are like mine."

When she withdrew, she cupped my face. "I hope you find someone who lights up your life like my mate lit mine. I hope *all* my grandkids find that level of completion. It's not an easy road, though, searching for that person. That's why so many of my kind settle for good enough. Don't settle, Wrenly."

She kissed my cheek then patted it before releasing me.

We walked back to the house, holding hands like when I'd been little and too afraid to venture out on my own because of the neighborhood girls. It felt good to be protected, and it made me realize how exhausted I was from having to watch my own back for so long.

Bennett was in the kitchen making something that smelled good when we walked in. My stomach growled, and Grandma winked at me.

"Did you make enough for three?" Grandma asked.

"Enough for five. Mom and Dad will be here in about fifteen minutes."

"Why?" The question popped out before I could stop it.

Both Grandma and Bennett glanced at me.

"They're worried," he said.

Tired of only seeing them on their terms and not ready to face them, I said, "I'll pass on the family dinner and turn in early."

Neither of them said anything to stop my retreat.

CHAPTER SIXTEEN

THE MATTRESS DIPPED NEXT to me, not quite waking me but disturbing me enough to bring me closer to awake than asleep.

"She's fine, Christine," I heard Grandma say.

"She doesn't look fine." Fingers lightly touched my cheek. "Did she say what upset her?"

"No. But...I think she *knows*."

The bed shifted as Mom stood.

"Do you think that's why she hurt herself?" she asked, her voice fading as they left.

I willed myself to sink back into a deeper sleep. It was safer than thinking about what I'd just overheard.

However, Grandma was right about hiding from problems.

Bennett haunted my dreams. He stalked me in the office, watching everything I did, and he waited. For what, I didn't know. But I felt it. His impatience. His need to hold me. To breathe me in.

When I woke to my alarm, I didn't feel rested but restless.

My hand slid under the covers to touch the warm space beside me. The panic I felt wasn't as consuming as it had been the day before, but it was still there, spurring me to come up with a solution.

I could move out, but then I'd be dipping into the money I'd already saved. While I would still have enough to cover the first tuition, I'd need to keep working. What was the point of moving out if I still had to see Bennett at the office until I found another job?

Sitting up, I pressed my hands to my face and tried rubbing away my frustration.

"Are you hungry?"

I screamed at the sound of Bennett's voice and tumbled off the other side of the bed, only to spring to my feet and stare at him with wild eyes.

He wasn't fast enough to hide his shock.

"Are you okay?"

Slowly, lowering my arms, which had come up defensively, I tried to act as normally as possible, given the circumstances.

"Please stop coming into my room without permission."

He tilted his head as he studied me.

"Chocolate chip pancakes?" he asked.

"Are Mom and Dad here?"

"No. Grandma told them you needed some time to yourself."

"Is Grandma still here?"

"No, but she said you can call her and she'll be a menace with you whenever you need."

My nose started to tingle, and I nodded to hide how much her understanding meant to me.

"Pancakes are fine," I said after a moment.

"If you're not hungry for pancakes, I can make something else."

He sounded…off.

I really looked at Bennett, noting the darker circles under his eyes, the way his hands were tucked into the pockets of his pants, the stubble coating his jaw.

An odd calm settled over me the longer I looked at him. I stepped around the bed. Without moving, he watched me slowly close the distance between us. When I stood in front of him, his mask slipped back into place as I met his gaze.

He was hiding. From me. Why?

I looked down at his hands. He'd fisted them in his pockets.

"Show me your hands," I said.

He hesitated a second then held them out, palms up. They trembled.

I met his gaze again. "Today's a bad day." It was both a statement and a question.

After a moment, he said, "Yes, today's a bad day."

There were so many things I wanted to say. That holding me at night wasn't going to help because I was never going to accept him. That the sooner he let go, the better off he'd be. But I'd lived with shifters long enough to understand they didn't give up when they thought they'd found a potential mate. They aggressively, obsessively pursued their mate until they said yes to them or someone else.

If I wanted to leave, either Bennett or I needed to hook up with someone else. Since I didn't want to end up with some guy I barely knew, that meant getting Bennett to focus on a different potential mate.

"Let's grab something on the way into the office," I said.

Surprise flickered in his gaze. "We don't have to go in today."

"I want to."

He tucked his hands back into his pockets.

"Is there any chance you'll talk to me about what happened? That's the second time you—"

"No."

I turned away from him, and his arms wrapped around me from behind. I froze, heart hammering and panic surging through me.

"This isn't normal, Wrenly. Someone touching you like this shouldn't make you panic this badly."

"Let go now, or I'll hurt myself again," I said hoarsely.

He spun me around to face him, his hands anchoring my shoulders.

"Talk to me. Let me help you."

"If you want to help me, let me go. Please."

His gaze searched mine. His worry disappeared behind his mask, but not before I glimpsed his desperation and hurt.

"I'll meet you in the garage in twenty minutes," he said, releasing my shoulders.

We arrived on time and rode the elevator up to the twelfth floor in silence. The women greeted him as they always did, ignoring me. Except for Miranda. She was watching me. I looked away and walked faster to my desk.

Bennett left me alone but kept his door open.

No one bothered either of us until ten, when I took a break to get something to drink from the break area.

Miranda found me there.

"Interesting choice of office attire." she said.

I glanced down at my shorts and printed T-shirt that said "Warning: Rage Volcano. Anticipate seismic safety releases and maintain a safe distance." It seemed fitting. Too bad I'd just grabbed it without thinking. It was a shirt I'd worn at school after Lindi and her crew had wrecked my last clean uniform.

"How'd the dress work?" she asked.

"Mom said the dress was pretty." I started adding enough sugar to my coffee to send me into a diabetic coma.

"Bennett seemed to like it too," she said.

I turned to look at her as she leaned against the counter, studying me. I openly returned the favor. She was pretty and radiated confidence and strength. A lot of guys would find that appealing. But did Bennett? What he preferred wasn't something I could ask him. But maybe I could ask her. It was sad that Miranda, the girl who'd pinned me to the bathroom door, was my best option for help.

Unfortunately for me—and maybe for her too—I'd been surrounded by mean girls for what felt like my entire life, so collaborating with one didn't bother me. What bothered me was that she might figure out what was going on with me if I asked too many questions, and acknowledging my status would make my life infinitely harder.

How could I get her to help me without her figuring out who Bennett's mate was?

"I'm not interested in dressing pretty to make boys happy," I said, responding to her comment.

"Bennett's not a boy, though, is he?"

"No, he's a pain in my ass. But I'm pretty sure I already made my thoughts on him clear."

She shrugged. "Things can change."

"You're right. We could be friends and help each other."

A brief smile tugged her lips as she considered me. "Maybe."

She left me alone to sip my sugared-up coffee and contemplate my life.

When I returned to my desk, the blinds to Bennett's office were open, and a piece of chocolate waited for me. The sight of it made my chest ache, and I wanted to think about why, but I knew I couldn't afford to with his door still open.

Ignoring his watchful stare, I sat at my desk and tried to find something to order for lunch, even though the thought of sitting in the office with him for an hour killed any appetite I had.

I ordered two salads for us, no dressing and extra onions. Then I ate his dumb chocolate.

That, on top of the sugar in my coffee, helped improve my patience as the first office girl approached. I put in my earbuds without looking at her.

She hesitated in front of my desk.

From the corner of my eye, I saw Bennett move.

Bless her heart, she's not running, I thought.

I turned up the volume on my music and focused on the lyrics until the people in the office faded, allowing me to concentrate on expenses. Whenever she left or he sat down again never registered in my mind. If someone else approached, I didn't notice. I worked until another piece of chocolate landed on my keyboard.

Staring at it, I very briefly wondered what would happen if I flicked it away and kept working.

You knew escaping their plans for you would take time, Wren. The reason why they had plans for you doesn't change that. Play the long game that you started playing two years ago.

I closed my eyes briefly, resisting the memory from two years ago that wanted to surface.

You're smarter than they are. Play them all, and watch them stumble and fall.

When I opened my eyes and looked up at Bennett, I only showed the part of myself I wanted him to see. The slightly annoyed part that plucked the earbud from my ear.

"What?"

"I grabbed lunch from reception. Hungry?"

"Not really," I said, removing the other earbud and putting it away.

"We don't have to eat takeout. If you'd rather go out and grab something, we can eat in the park."

"Yes," I said, standing.

Spending time outside was much better than being stuck in his office with the blinds and door closed.

I power walked my way out of the office, well aware of the attention I was drawing. Would they think I was as crazy as Bennett? Probably more so. As a human, I didn't have an erratic behavior excuse.

"We don't need to stay a full day," Bennett said when we were in the elevator, just the two of us.

"Why not?"

He ran a hand through his less-than-meticulously combed hair. Actually, he didn't look as neatly put together as he normally did. His tie was loose and a little crooked, like he'd been tugging on it.

And he'd ditched his jacket. The sleeves of his white shirt were wrinkled, like he'd rolled them up for a while.

What did it mean that he was falling apart because I'd fallen apart? I didn't know enough about bonds to understand what it meant that he cared this much, but it couldn't be good.

"Can I have dinner with Grandma tonight? Alone?" I asked as the elevator reached the ground floor.

"You don't need to ask permission, Wrenly."

"Don't I?" I asked, turning my head to meet his gaze, letting him see my anger.

He ran his hand through his hair again.

"No. Just...just let us know where you're going so we don't worry."

"Right." I now understood that "us" and "we" only meant Bennett, and it hurt more than it should have.

Getting off the elevator, I walked through the lobby and out into the sunlight, ignoring my unwanted companion as I focused on relaxing. I passed by all the sandwich shops and fancy bistros without stopping. His offer to eat somewhere else hadn't interested me as much as time in the park had.

When we reached the park entrance, Bennett pointed to a food truck.

"How about trying that?"

I had to admit, it tempted me. But so did a run in the midday sun.

"Maybe after I'm done exorcising my mood. You can sit on a bench and watch me lap the pond...unless that's too dangerous?"

He looked like he wanted to break something. "You need fuel to run like you do."

"That's what this morning's coffee and my rage are for."

Without waiting for his answer, I took off running. It felt so good.

Tension slowly melted away as I warmed up, and I realized I felt more relaxed than I had in a while. When I pinpointed why, I frowned.

With Bennett watching, I knew no one would be able to trip me.

At least, not like Storm had. And no one would try to chase me, not like the group of guys someone at school had paid.

Having someone who actually had my back was new, and I didn't hate it. In fact, I wanted that more than anything. Just...not with Bennett. His level of protection came with stifling restrictions, and I'd already had enough of that.

Don't hate your life, Wrenly. Fight to make it what you want until you love it.

I sped up, letting myself run all out, not caring about sweat or anything else as I lost myself in the one freedom I had. Before it felt like I'd pass out, I slowed to a jog and focused on breathing.

All the endorphins were doing their job when I finally slowed to a walk. I felt good. Really good.

When I finished my lap and approached Bennett, he held out a bottle of water, which he'd already opened for me. Had it been anyone else, I wouldn't have trusted it.

"Thanks." I tipped it back, taking two long gulps, and sat next to him to let the breeze finish drying my sweat.

"Why do you run like that?" he asked.

"What do you mean?"

"You push yourself to go as fast as you can. Are you training for a race?"

I grinned at the thought. "No. I just like knowing I can outrun anyone chasing me. Anyone human, anyway." I glanced at him, still riding my high and not thinking clearly. "I know I can't outrun non-humans. That'd come in handy if I could, though."

"Do you have a lot of humans and non-humans chasing you?"

"Even one is too many, but it's enough to learn to run."

"Who chased you, Wrenly?"

The smooth rumble of his voice set off all my internal warnings, and I choked on the water I was sipping. He patted my back gently, and I coughed longer than necessary to collect my thoughts.

There was no recovering from that slip, and I wasn't about to admit any past abuse to Bennett. Not in his current state. I didn't trust his reaction.

"Do you think they have hot dogs?" I asked when I stopped coughing. "I could really go for a hot dog."

"Do you know how frustrating you are?"

"Yep."

He removed the hand from my back to run it down his face.

"This is one of those moments when, if you let it go, our afternoon will be much happier," I said.

He sighed. "Okay."

Maybe Bennett wasn't completely impossible to deal with after all.

He got up and ordered from the food truck, and we ate on the way back to the office. No one commented on our late return, but I heard some whispers about my clothes and sweat stains. Bennett silenced those with a warning glare, but they weren't wrong. I wasn't upholding any kind of corporate image, and I definitely wasn't up to the wealthy Wulf family's standards.

When I got back to my desk, I sent Grandma a text asking her to meet me in the city for dinner; then I started working. Bennett brought me a water not long after and one of the salads I'd ordered. Since I was still hungry, I munched while I worked and waited for the afternoon to pass.

Before quitting time, Miranda showed up at my desk with a retail clothing bag. She glanced at Bennett's open door and blinds before meeting my gaze.

"Pretty quiet afternoon," she said.

"Yeah. Is that why you went shopping?"

"This is for you. Heard you're having dinner with your grandma and thought you might not want to go smelling like anger, frustration, and…" She leaned in and sniffed. "Grief? Did you drop your ice cream cone while at the park?"

I grinned at her, finding her question more funny than antagonistic. She surprised me by almost smiling back.

"How much do I owe you?" I asked.

"You don't."

She held up Bennett's credit card and arched a brow at me.

I shrugged. "Mom said he owes me for being an ass and to think of him as a wallet with legs."

"Well, that's a picture I won't forget," she said, glancing at Bennett, who was now standing in the doorway to his office.

"Mom didn't say I was being an ass."

"It was inferred."

He let out a long breath that screamed barely checked patience, then said, "You can use my bathroom to shower and change. I can drop you off at the restaurant after."

"Restaurant?" I asked even as I picked up my phone to check for a message.

Grandma: You know I hate texting. I'll meet you at Rexbies Pub at 6.

"What's Rexbies?" I asked, looking up at Bennett.

"A bar that serves burgers and sandwiches."

"It's better than the hot dog you ate for lunch, but only barely," Miranda said.

I took the bag of clothes and peeked at what she'd bought. Jean shorts and a T-shirt. Even underwear and a bra. I didn't see a single tag on anything, though. I wasn't above borrowed clothes, but I did find it odd that Miranda would be willing to lend something to me, especially jean shorts. Those didn't seem to be her style.

Confused, I looked up at her.

"Don't worry, it's all clean. I dropped it at an express wash after buying it."

"Ah. Got it. Thanks."

"I'm getting paid to shop. It's not a hardship." She passed Bennett's card to him without a hint of flirting, nodded to me, and walked away.

I glanced at Bennett and found him watching me. The look in his eyes wasn't frustrated or desperate. It looked almost tender. My stomach did a weird dip that made my heart skip a beat. It felt like panic...but not.

He inhaled slowly, and that odd feeling grew.

"I'll hurry," I said, darting past him.

I locked the bathroom door and breathed a little easier as I turned to the glass-paneled shower. The first time I'd noted it, while searching for cleaning supplies, I'd rolled my eyes. Now, I appreciated being able to wash away the smell of my lunch run and change into something soft and clean.

Tying up my hair, I took a quick shower then changed into the new clothes. The waterlogged bandages on my hands were falling off by the time I finished. I removed them and frowned at the scrapes, knowing I couldn't leave them uncovered.

A quick search through the cabinets for replacement bandages yielded nothing.

Bennett knocked on the door.

"I have the first aid kit out here."

Making a face, I debated what to do. I did not want Bennett playing doctor again. That was too much touching.

"I was looking for a tampon."

"You don't have your period."

"It's for you."

Something thumped against the door.

"Eventually, counting to ten is going to stop working," he said. "Then what are you going to do?"

"Run faster? Buy a taser?"

"Open the door, Wrenly."

"Open the door, Wrenly. Come here, Wrenly. Sit down and shut up, Wrenly."

"I never said that."

"But each time you order me around, that's what I hear!"

"Will you please open the door? Please?"

I knew I couldn't stay in the bathroom forever. I just hated that he was waiting on the other side. Then I realized he'd given me the golden ticket.

"What'll you give me?"

"What do you want?"

"Nope, that's not how it's going to work this time. You need to offer something up. Be creative."

I heard another thump on the other side of the door and grinned.

"I'll make you breakfast tomorrow," he said. "Anything you want."

"No, thanks."

"We can go for another run at lunch tomorrow."

"I don't need permission, remember?"

Another thump.

"What do you want?"

"I want you to understand that there's nothing you can give me that I want."

In the silence that followed, I heard my heart beating in my ears. Was I playing with fire? Yep. But I'd lived in survival mode for too long not to recognize the trap the Wulf family had quietly set for me, and I needed Bennett to know I wasn't going to cooperate. The sooner he realized that, the faster he could let go.

"I'll be waiting for you by the elevators."

I gave it five minutes before I opened the door and walked out.

He had me against the wall and my hands pinned over my head the second I cleared the door. The look in his fully dilated eyes was a little unhinged as he stared at me.

"How were you not in constant trouble at school?" he said.

"Who said I wasn't? You already know the teachers and cameras were wrong."

"Are you purposely provoking me?"

"Wouldn't dream of it."

His gaze dipped to my mouth, and all my bravado vanished under a waterfall of fear.

He inhaled and immediately released me.

"Will you please sit on the couch and let me look at your scrapes?"

"Asking it as a question instead of stating what you want doesn't actually mean I have a choice, does it?" I said, marching to the couch and sitting down.

He followed, knelt in front of me, and took my hands. The only thing that stopped me from going on the offensive was his brief touches. He only did what was necessary to apply more ointment and new adhesive bandages.

Once he was done, he turned his back on me and started putting everything away. I slipped out of the office, shut down my laptop, and waited by the elevators.

He drove me to Rexbies in silence and pulled over at the curb to drop me off, which still involved him getting out to open the door for me. Grandma was waiting for me by the entrance.

"That felt like I was back in grade school being dropped off," I said to her.

She chuckled and patted my hand.

"A good man worries about you. A bad one doesn't even think about what happens once you're off on your own."

She led me into the pub, which was an eclectic mash-up of bar, diner, and lounge that played music at a reasonable volume for conversation and smelled like deep-fried nirvana.

"I got us a private room in back," Grandma said, tugging me along.

The private room was about the size of my closet, which was decent, and had a table big enough for six but set for two.

As soon as she shut the door behind us, all the sound disappeared.

"There, now we can talk without anyone hearing." She motioned for me to sit. "Heard you were late because you were giving Bennett a tough time."

"Just enough for him not to call the cops, but apparently enough to tattle to you."

She laughed. "We both know I'm not the enforcer in the family."

"Pfft. That's like saying Mom's not the life manager."

Grandma smirked at me but didn't comment on that. Instead, she said, "So tell me why we're really having dinner together."

"Because you're the only one I trust to answer me honestly. I hope you don't break that trust today."

She got really serious. "Never. Speak your mind, and ask your questions."

"Am I Bennett's mate?"

"Yes."

My heart tripped over itself, and my chest grew painfully tight with the panic I refused to give in to

"What does that mean? For him, not for me. Aren't there any other options?"

CHAPTER SEVENTEEN

GRANDMA'S GAZE was filled with compassion and sorrow as she sighed and folded her hands on the tabletop.

"If there are other potential mates for Bennett, he's never noticed them in the last thirteen years. Once he saw you on TV, that was it."

"Saw me on TV?" I had no idea what she was talking about.

"The fire that killed your family was on the news. You were in the background. I think a firefighter was holding you. Bennett saw you and, without even smelling you, said you were his mate. We tried to tell him that wasn't possible, but he was so insistent that we relented and arranged for Christine and Aaron to see you in person.

"Christine fell in love with you at first sight. Whether you were Bennett's mate or not, she thought you were precious and wanted to adopt you then. But they were worried about what would happen if Bennett was right. You were human and didn't know anything about our kind. He was too young for...well, everything. And most importantly, mates don't find each other that young. Ever.

"It always happens after maturity. The youngest we know of was fifteen, and that was back when most females that age were getting married."

"Why didn't anyone ever tell me this?"

"We were afraid you would think you were only fostered because of Bennett."

"Well, that's what I do think."

Grandma shook her head. "Christine was decided, but she needed to know for certain if Bennett was right, to protect you both. So she brought something of yours home for him. He reacted to your scent immediately, but not the way a mature mate would. He held your hair tie, looked at Christine, and said you needed their protection or you would disappear and he'd never find his mate again.

"You know Bennett well enough, I think, to know he isn't overly emotional or dramatic. His firm certainty convinced us. So we made arrangements and brought you home soon after."

The light above the door blinked rapidly.

"That'll be our dinner," Grandma said.

We waited for the server to enter, carrying a tray with burgers and soft drinks on it. Once he handed everything over and left again, I looked at Grandma.

"I don't understand. If I'm Bennett's mate, why did they send him away within a year of bringing me home? I thought he hated me." I nibbled on a fry.

"Not at all. Just the opposite. He was…entranced by you. When you played with Aiden and Karter, Bennett hovered close by, worried you'd get hurt. He was very aware of your human fragility while Aiden and Karter were less mindful of it. His concerned attention along with his insistence that you weren't his sister any time you tried to claim him as your brother, like you did with Aiden and Karter, began to upset you.

"Although not intentional, he was hurting you, and it was frustrating him. All he wanted to do was to protect you. His focus on school dwindled, and he began to snap at Aiden and Karter for being too rough with you, even though you were clearly enjoying their play.

"We sent him away so you could both continue to thrive

separately. It didn't work like we'd planned. You were slow to thrive, and Bennett struggled, often calling for updates or asking for pictures as if he needed proof that you were safe. The instructors at his school said he wasn't sleeping well and would pace at night while the others were resting. We implemented more physical training, which helped for a time, but the only thing that truly helped him focus was clothes."

I choked on the bite of burger I'd taken.

"Excuse me?" I knew he liked his suits, but they actually calmed him?

"Only the clothing you outgrew," Grandma said.

"*My clothes*?"

"What clothes did you think I meant?"

"His suits!"

She laughed so hard she cried. When she was done wiping her tears, she shook her head at me as I kept eating.

"Your scent calmed him."

"I want to say that's disturbing, but I know that's the judgy human in me not empathizing with your wolfy obsessions. So is that why I was sent away when he came home? Because he was still smotheringly annoying?"

"In part."

"And the other part?"

"There were several, but the most important one was so you could experience life a bit more."

I snorted. "By locking me away in an all-girl boarding school? Right. Is there a chance he'll find someone else once I reject him?"

"Are you sure you want to?"

"Why wouldn't I want to? I haven't been free for the last twelve years. Why would I commit to a lifetime of that?"

"Oh, Wren, that's not what it's like."

"Really? Because that's exactly what it's been like since I got home. I can't breathe, Grandma. It's suffocating. So, just give me a straight answer. Is there a chance he'll find someone else once I officially reject him?"

"That he found you and bonded with you so young is very rare. It indicates a bond stronger than any I've ever seen or heard of. If you reject him, I doubt he'd find someone else." She held my gaze. "Do you want all of the truth or only what you're asking?"

The way she said it made me nervous. Whatever she had to say probably wouldn't be good. Yet, I'd rather know everything than be ignorant.

"I want all of it."

"In order to reject the bond, you first need to complete it."

My stomach gave a nervous lurch, and I set my burger down.

"How do you complete it?"

"Remember watching the pack run?"

"Unfortunately, yes." Most girls got a lesson on how to use pads and tampons during their first period. I got a bonus lesson in shifter mating. Seeing pairs rutting in the woods in their fur had been both traumatically embarrassing and fascinating for tween me.

"Remember the biting?"

"Yeah, that's the part I've been trying to forget."

"That's the mating bond. Without the bite, you won't be Bennett's mate, only his potential mate. And if you're not his mate, you can't truly reject him. Everything you're doing now, you're just refusing to admit he's a potential mate, which is understandable. Humans don't have the same instincts we do."

"So what you're saying is that there's no way for me to get rid of Bennett unless he bites me?"

"Unless you mate *and* he bites you. But I have to warn you, the stronger the attraction, the stronger the mate bond will be once it's completed. You might not want to reject him once the bond is made."

"Okay, so sex with Bennett to get rid of him is out. What about setting him up with other women?"

"I doubt it would work. He's been working in that office for years with different women throwing themselves at him. If there had been even a hint of interest, I'd tell you, but there wasn't."

"What am I supposed to do, then? I don't want to keep living like I'm in a cage."

"Then don't. Be yourself. Be a menace. Live your life the way you want to."

"I want to leave for school."

She nodded. "I heard. Coalwell. Sounds like it'll be fun. Bennett missed out on fun. He needs it."

My frustration vanished, and I looked at Grandma suspiciously.

"What do you mean?"

"Oh, he's already buying an apartment for you near campus. It'll have enough room for a home office for him."

And just like that, the frustration was back. I didn't talk much after that. Too many thoughts were filling my head. Mostly not nice ones. I appreciated knowing that Mom and Dad hadn't fostered me solely because of my potential mate status with Bennett. It didn't make me less bitter about the time I'd spent fighting for my life at school, though. Or make me less determined to leave.

Bennett's interest in me was his problem.

Hadn't he pretty much said the same thing Grandma had? Live my life the way I wanted to so I could love it?

"Are you ready to go home?" Grandma asked when we were both finished.

I wasn't, but I also knew that avoiding Bennett forever wasn't an option. Grandma messaged her driver that we were ready then settled the bill at the bar. The owner was a good-looking man with a flame tattoo running up his arm. His brown gaze met mine, and he smiled. I quickly turned away before realizing what I'd done.

Because of how I'd been sent away, I was afraid to show any interest in a guy, and now I was just supposed to be okay with the fact that Bennett was interested in me? It just felt so hypocritical.

"Is it going to get worse once he knows I know?" I asked once we were in her car.

"I don't think so. It might get easier once you acknowledge what you are to him."

"Might," I said. "That's not a guarantee."

"Very little in life is a guarantee."

I still hadn't decided what to do by the time Grandma dropped me off at home with a kiss on my cheek.

Bennett opened the door for me as I approached and inhaled deeply. I knew he was trying to gauge my mood. Did he already know why I'd wanted to meet with Grandma? I thought of what I'd overheard Grandma say to Mom last night, and thought he probably did. If so, there was no use trying to pretend I was still ignorant. Both of us would be able to move forward better once everything was in the open.

"We need to talk," I said as he shut the door behind me.

"Okay."

When I faced him, I saw his mask slip into place even as his pupils expanded.

"I don't want to be your potential mate, and I don't want to have sex with you just to officially reject you."

He shoved his hands into his dress pants pockets so hard I heard seams rip. When he looked down at the floor, nothing about it said guilt or submission. It screamed barely contained anger.

"I also don't want to live in an apartment with you at Coalwell. So, where does that leave us?"

"Can I ask why?"

"Why what?"

"Why are you refusing to see me as a potential mate?"

"Because I see you as my brother."

His gaze flew to mine, and I knew the moment he smelled the lie. His slow smile sent a thread of panic through me.

"If you take one step—"

He had my hands pinned to the wall above my head before I could finish. My pulse slammed into overdrive.

"I hate when you do this."

He didn't let go, so I stomped on his foot. He grunted but didn't release me. Instead, he bent down so his face was level with mine.

"Do you know how much I want to headbutt you right now?" I said.

"Do you know how much I want to kiss you?"

Heart pounding, I turned my head away and closed my eyes. Did I want Bennett to kiss me? No, I knew where it would lead. But I wasn't afraid of it, which made the reason for my racing pulse confusing.

"Why me? Haven't I been tortured enough?"

"How have you been tortured, Wrenly?"

I kept my mouth shut.

His lips brushed the skin just below my ear. My eyes popped open, and fear finally bloomed.

He trailed his nose along my skin, inhaling deeply.

"I think I'm the one being tortured, Wrenly. When you smell like fear...because of me..." A shuddering exhale escaped him. "Let's make a deal. One I think you'll like."

"Doubt it," I said, fighting not to give in to the need to try to tug my hands free.

"If you can overcome your fear of me by the end of the summer, I won't move to Coalwell with you."

"What does overcoming my fear mean? Let you have sex with me?" I asked, unable to keep my scorn from my tone.

"No, not sex. It's as simple as it sounds. Be around me without being afraid. Any other emotion is fine except fear."

"Why?"

"Because I'm the one person you'll never need to fear."

My heart gave an unsteady thump, and I finally turned my head to meet his gaze. "You're the person I need to fear most."

That smile ghosted his lips again. "Looks like we're going to be roommates for a long time."

"It's an unfair deal. What if you threaten to hit me? Of course, I'm going to be afraid."

He shook his head. "I would never do that. But you're right. We should be specific. You need to do three things without being afraid. Hold my hand. Hug me. Kiss me."

"I'm not kissing you."

"Okay. Let me know what day we're moving."

"I hate you."

"No, you don't. That's the fear talking. If you don't see me as a potential mate, the three conditions we set won't be a big deal. But I think you're afraid I might be right, which is why this bet scares you."

"No deal. I'm the one taking all the risk."

"I promise you I'm taking a bigger risk. What do you think watching you leave again will do to me?"

I studied his blown-out pupils and felt the trembling in his hands. Everything Grandma said ran through my head again.

"The entire time I'm at Coalwell, you'll stay away?"

His mask slipped, and I saw the desperation in his gaze even as he nodded.

"How do I know you'll keep your word?"

"That's the whole point of this deal, isn't it? Let me show you that you can trust me, Wrenly."

"You can start by letting go of my hands."

"Figure out a way to make me." He didn't say it like a threat, but as a plea.

I lightly twisted my hand in his hold and was able to move it, but when I tried to tug it free, he wouldn't let go. His mask slipped back into place as I studied him, trying to figure out what he wanted from me. Then I realized he'd already said it.

My gaze dipped to his mouth. A rush of panic zipped through me, and I looked away. He didn't move or say anything as I continued to test his hold carefully.

"I'm afraid you'll take anything I do as a yes," I admitted.

"I'll only take a yes as a yes, Wrenly. Anything else is still a no." He dipped his head to my neck, breathing in my scent, then added,

"I'm not a fool. I know exactly what you'll do if I mark you before you're willing to accept me."

His words teased my ears and made my pulse race faster. I twisted my hands again. This time, I turned them so our hands were palm to palm, and I threaded my fingers through his.

He made a pained sound and dropped his forehead to my shoulder.

It felt like my heart was going to beat right out of my chest. I was so afraid that if I could have, I would have pushed him and run.

He straightened away from me and brought one of my hands to his mouth. His lips brushed my knuckles as he watched me.

"You're brave, baby, but you're not fearless. Not yet. Go. You can try again tomorrow."

The second he released me, I bolted for the stairs, taking them two at a time. I heard him behind me, keeping up step for step, which spurred me to run faster. Reaching my room, I slammed the door in his face and slowly backed away from it.

"Next time, don't run up the stairs," he said roughly. "I don't want you to hurt yourself trying to get away from me."

THEIR QUIET LAUGHTER and whispers filled the room. The weight of the blanket pinned me to the bed as they put their weight into it. My nose was being crushed, and I couldn't breathe through my mouth.

"Know your place, Wrenly," one of them whispered.

Then they poured the water. I thrashed against the weight holding me as the wet blanket blocked what little air I'd been wheezing in.

A corner lifted. I struck out with my fist.

"Wrenly! It's me!"

Bennett's hoarse rasp brought me out of the dream, and I immediately stopped fighting against him. He released his hold on my wrists.

The bed moved, and a light clicked on.

His hair was wild, and he was holding his throat. Again. The shorts he wore rode low on his hips, showing the long, muscled line of his torso.

He'd been sleeping next to me? Like that?

"Get out, Bennett."

Ignoring me, he sat on the edge of the bed, facing me and rubbing his throat.

"That's the second time," he said.

I could tell it hurt him to talk.

"You're pretty accurate."

"Why are you in here?" I demanded.

He swallowed with difficulty and tried to clear his throat.

"You sleep better when I'm with you."

"Oh, really? Your throat says otherwise."

"You don't usually do that unless I startle you."

"Get out, Bennett."

"I will if you tell me what the dream was about."

"Let me throat punch you again, and I'll think about it."

The crazy fool lifted his chin, exposing his throat to me. Instead of answering his challenge, which would probably end with me pinned to a wall, I threw back my blanket and got out of bed.

"Where are you going?" he asked.

"The bathroom. Do you want to come with?"

He wasn't stupid and stayed where he was.

I closed the door and ran water to splash on my face as the memory faded. Why had I dreamed that tonight? Probably because Bennett's stupid bet was making me feel trapped and helpless again.

I splashed more water on my face, used the toilet, then returned to bed, where he was blatantly reclining, waiting for me.

"Get out, or I'm not going to try anything tomorrow," I said.

"Try something now, and I'll leave."

"Another throat punch?"

He smiled, my threats clearly amusing him. "I was thinking an apology hug."

"If you want to apologize for sleeping in my bed without permission, a hug isn't the way to go."

"What would work?"

"Leaving."

He laughed. A real chuckle with his disarming smile, and I almost smiled back. Instead, I got into bed and lay facing away from him.

"Does this mean I can stay?" he asked.

"Do I have a choice?"

"You do. You can kick me out with one small hug."

"Stay on your side of the bed, or I'll throat punch you again."

I closed my eyes and willed myself to fall asleep.

It took a long time.

THE NEXT TIME I opened my eyes, it was light out, and I was using Bennett as a body pillow. I'd never woken up more comfortably in my life, and it took a few seconds to realize why it was so wrong. Once I did, I scrambled out of bed like I'd just discovered a spider in it.

"That counts as a hug," I said, staring at him wide-eyed as he calmly watched me with his hands behind his head.

"Sorry, baby, but that doesn't count. The second you were conscious, fear took over."

"Whatever."

"Do you want to go for a run before or after breakfast?"

Damn him. I'd planned on escaping for the day and meeting up with Sophia, but he just had to dangle a carrot I knew I couldn't refuse.

"Before, but I need an apple or something."

"All right. I'll get dressed and meet you by the door in ten minutes."

He started to get out of bed, and I hurriedly shut myself in my closet to get ready.

Ten minutes later, I jogged downstairs and found him waiting by the door with an apple and a water bottle for me.

"Thanks," I said, reaching for the apple.

His fingers brushed mine as he handed it over. A jolt ran through me, and I quickly reached for the door with my free hand.

He placed his hand on the surface, shutting it and using his body to cage me in, facing the door.

"I can hear the way your pulse races when you touch me. I can smell your confusion and panic. Help me understand why."

"As soon as I figure it out, I'll let you know," I said.

His exhale teased the back of my neck.

"Are we going to go for a run, or would you like to spend the rest of the day asking yourself 'What went wrong?' while holding an ice pack on your big boy parts?"

His chuckle sent a shiver down my spine.

"I think you need a run." He had me out of the way and the door open a second later. "After you."

I munched on my apple as I did my warm-up walk down the driveway.

"Do you mind if we run in the community today?" Bennett asked. "I need to fix some mailboxes."

I couldn't stop my grin and nodded, loving Grandma even more just then because Bennett was having to do clean-up for her.

Despite having to stop frequently to right Grandma's wrongs, Bennett didn't slow me down. Occasionally, I would run ahead, but never out of sight. It was enjoyable. .until I spotted Storm running toward us in her shorts and sports bra.

"This is a new twist on a pack run, but I'll take it," she said, turning so she ran alongside Bennett.

"Are you here to trip Wrenly again?" Bennett asked. The low

rumble that accompanied those words would have been funny before, but it wasn't now that I knew why he was defending me.

"I told you, I thought she saw me and would dodge. Like your brothers have never tried tripping each other."

She wasn't wrong. I'd watched them mess around with each other like that on countless occasions.

"Wrenly isn't my brothers. She's human and doesn't dodge like us. You know that."

"Which is why I'm here." She looked at me around Bennett. "I'm sorry I tripped you, Wrenly. I promise not to do it again. Maybe we could go running together sometime?"

"That's about as tempting as waiting in line at the 'We Care, We Share' needle recycling center."

Bennett tripped. Storm stopped to comfort him. I kept running.

They both caught up to me again while Storm was still making little soothing sounds as if Bennett's stumble had somehow hurt him —it hadn't.

"What kind of school did you go to?" she asked, scowling at me.

"A shitty one."

"Obviously. Your attitude is worse than when you left."

I stopped running. Bennett did the same.

"I'm heading back. There are still three more mailboxes down this way that need fixing."

"They can wait." He looked at Storm. "You should go home."

Instead of getting rid of them, they both followed me, and I had to listen to her attempts to reel Bennett into a date.

"What are your plans for the rest of the day?" Storm asked. "Maybe I could come over."

"I'm busy."

"What about next weekend? I heard you're representing the Wulf family at the annual charity auction. I could be your date."

"Wrenly's my date."

"Wrenly has plans," I said.

"Furniture shopping for the apartment?" he asked.

I glared at him, and his pupils dilated. Was he angry, or was he thinking about living with me? My pulse tripped, and I lost my glare.

Storm witnessed our little exchange and silently snarled at me behind Bennett's back.

"You're both annoying," I said, speeding up to a jog. "Go away."

"See?" Storm said. "Wrenly doesn't want to go. I do."

"Wrenly made a bet with me. If she wants to win, she'll need to go," Bennett said.

I wished Storm would trip *him*.

CHAPTER EIGHTEEN

AFTER FIVE MORE MINUTES OF nagging, Storm left in a pout.

"A needle recycling center, huh?" Bennett said, jogging beside me. "Where do you come up with this stuff?"

"Years of pent-up bitterness and frustration," I said.

"Was the school we're not allowed to talk about really that bad?"

I shot him a look and didn't say anything else until we reached the front door.

"I want to meet up with Sophia again today. Am I allowed to take the car, oh smothering potential mate dictator?"

His whole face twitched.

"I think that's a precursor to an aneurysm."

"You might be right. Yes, you can take the car into the city. Or if you'd like to catch a ride with me, I can drop you off downtown, and we can meet up after you're done."

"Why? So you can stare at me through windows again?"

"No. I'm hoping to meet up with someone too."

My stomach twisted weirdly.

"Oh. That sounds nice."

But it didn't, and I knew he'd scented the lie when his lips curved. Rather than waiting for him to call me out on it, I retreated to my room to shower and get ready. By the time I finished, Sophia confirmed she could meet up with me downtown.

Cautiously excited for my first friend outing ever, I jogged down the stairs. Bennett was waiting at the bottom, watching me with his stoic mask in place.

My pace slowed as I neared him.

"Don't," he said.

"Don't what?"

"Don't stop being happy."

Unsure of his mood, I simply nodded and walked around him. He followed me out to the garage and opened the door to one of the fancier cars.

I waited until he was sitting to poke the brushed leather seats.

"Whoever you're meeting must be important," I said.

"Not as important as you are."

I made a face and focused on the drive.

When we reached downtown, he dropped me off in front of the high-end clothing shops where I'd agreed to meet Sophia. His hands settled on my shoulders, trapping me on the curb before I could escape.

"Call me when you're done or if you run into any trouble." He leaned down until we were eye level and ran a finger over my cheek where the bruise had almost faded to nothing. "Don't run into any trouble."

It wasn't a command as much as it was a plea.

"I'll do my best to avoid doors, the pavement, and she-bitches."

He sighed and shook his head.

"I'll be fine. Go meet up with your important person."

I twisted out of his hold, but he caught my arm.

"Wait. Take this."

I looked down at the credit card he was holding out.

"Why?"

"So you can buy whatever you want."

"I'd rather have the five grand and the bank account I'm owed."

His expression shifted, showing his frustration.

"Wrenly?"

We both glanced at Sophia, who was watching us with a hint of concern.

"Everything all right?" she asked.

"Yep. It's fine." Ignoring the card Bennett was offering, I stepped out of his hold and hurried over to her.

"You sure?"

The sound of the car's engine as he left drained the tension from my shoulders.

"Absolutely. Ready to window shop?"

"Window shop? Not a chance. Come on."

She towed me into the closest store, where display cases of luxury fashion jewelry dotted the area along with uniformed jewelers who spoke to a few of the shoppers. The back of one shopper in particular was unmistakably familiar.

"Don't bother wrapping it," Lindi said, turning her head right and left as she studied herself in the mirror. "I'll wear them out."

Seeing her the second time outside of school wasn't as startling as the first time. I still knew to watch her closely though.

She handed over her card then turned to watch the other shoppers.

The second her gaze locked with mine, she smiled. The fake-friendly one she always used just before she did something truly evil. I knew her choices for torture would be limited, though. There were cameras everywhere, and I wasn't alone.

Verbal sparring was my bet. She never came out a winner whenever she tried. At least, not in my opinion. Hers, too, or she wouldn't have spent so much effort retaliating against me.

I glanced at Sophia, who'd wandered closer to a display case, as Lindi strolled toward me.

"Wrenly, I bet you thought you'd never see me again after graduation."

"It was definitely a wish that hasn't come true yet. But there's a lot of traffic out there, so I'm still holding out hope it won't happen again."

"How cute. You still think you're witty. Can you even afford to be in here?"

She said the last part loudly enough that Sophia heard. When she looked back at Lindi, her face was starting to flush. Whether in embarrassment or anger, I couldn't be sure.

"Oh look at you flexing with your parents' money," I said with a "bless her heart" tone. "I'm sure the people here who have to work for their income are super impressed with your rich-girl entitlement attitude."

Lindi's smile grew. "Probably more impressed than with your poor-girl grudgitude."

The jeweler approached with Lindi's receipt and a bag that presumably had the earrings she'd worn into the store.

"Well, this has been entertaining, but I have a date with someone actually worth my time. I believe you know him."

She walked out of the store without a backward glance, putting on her sunglasses with a toss of her hair.

"Who was that?" Sophia asked, coming to stand next to me.

"The queen of mean girls," I said. "Do you like anything in here?"

"Nah. Let's keep shopping."

I nodded and followed her out of the store. Lindi was walking ahead of us on the sidewalk, her stride purposeful and steady.

My phone buzzed.

Bennett: Did you see anything you liked? If you'd like my card, I'm happy to hand it over. Just say the word, and I can be there in five minutes.

Why did my stomach somersault when I read that?

Me: Don't be a stalker.

"Was it from the guy who dropped you off?" Sophia asked.

"Yeah."

"Can I ask who he was? He was pretty hot."

"He's...complicated."

"Aren't they all?"

I grinned and watched Lindi get into the backseat of a Maybach parked in a loading zone.

"Is she for real?" Sophia asked.

"Yep. And if you meet up with her in a dark alley, run the other way."

"You know some interesting people."

"Not by choice. Where should we go next?"

Shopping with Sophia was more enjoyable than I thought it would be. We walked down the line of shops on the main street, browsing from the windows for some and going into others. We laughed and talked, and it just felt so normal.

She bought a skirt that looked cute, even if it was insanely overpriced, while I simply looked. I didn't want to spend the money I'd set aside for clothes. A tiny part of me thought of Bennett's offer, though.

Close to lunchtime, my stomach started to growl. Sophia laughed and promised that our next stop would be a popular French restaurant with amazing food.

We were halfway through crossing an intersection at a light when I noticed Bennett sitting near the window of the place we were headed. He looked up from his phone, and his gaze locked with mine.

My attention shifted from him to his companion.

Lindi sat across from him, a practiced smile on her face as she spoke.

When I glanced at him again, he was texting. My phone buzzed a second later.

Bennett: How angry are you?

"Hold up, Sophia," I said when we reached the sidewalk. She paused so I could answer.

Me: Why should I be angry?

After he read the reply, his gaze found mine again. The longer he stared at me, the more I wondered what was going on in his head. Did he honestly think I would be jealous? I was trying to get rid of him.

Lindi glanced over her shoulder to find what had his attention and saw me. Her smile grew, and she started talking faster.

Understanding hit me like a bolt of lightning. Anger and humor clashed.

He was trying to find out more about my time in hell from the queen herself. That was laughable, but also...how dare he?

Me: Use your nose. She's a habitual liar.
Bennett: Evasive too. My life would be easier if you would just talk to me.
Me: My purpose in life isn't to make yours easier.

"Hot guy again?" Sophia asked.

"Yep. He's sitting in the restaurant you want to go to."

She looked around and spotted him as he sent another message.

Bennett: So I've gathered. Did you find anything you want to buy?

"Want to change locations?" she asked.

A brilliant idea made me smile.

"Yes. But first, I want to annoy 'I have money and you don't.' Can you wait out here? I don't want her to target you because of me."

Sophia shrugged. "Sure. It'll give me time to look for somewhere else to eat."

"Thanks."

I went inside, trying not to salivate over the delicious smells. When the waiter asked if I had a reservation, I said I was grabbing something from my brother and pointed to Bennett, who was watching me.

He didn't take his eyes off of me as I weaved my way through the tables to reach theirs.

Lindi, realizing she'd lost his attention, turned to watch my approach. Her fake smile was fully in place.

"Hi, Wrenly."

I ignored her, encircled Bennett's impressive bicep with both hands, and stuck out my bottom lip.

"Can I pretty please have your card, Bennett? I want some earrings."

His pupils exploded wide, and he reached into the inner pocket of his jacket with a trembling hand.

I was playing with fire in so many ways but didn't care. Lindi had made my life a living hell for too long not to find some way—no matter how minor—to get revenge.

He pulled out a card and handed it to me as his gaze dipped to my mouth.

"Thank you," I said, plucking it from his fingers. "I'll buy you a tie and leave it on your bed with the card."

Without another word, I left.

My phone buzzed before I reached the door.

Bennett: Three ties for the restraint I just exercised.
Me: Color or pattern preferences?
Bennett: The only preference I have is that they're picked
by you.

"Did he really just hand you his credit card?" Sophia asked as she joined me, walking away.

"Yep. I have to buy him three ties with it, but lunch is on him today."

She grinned with me.

I WAVED goodbye to Sophia and shifted the bag I carried to the other hand so I could send Bennett a text. Three messages I hadn't heard come in waited for me.

Bennett: Please use the card.
Bennett: What did you eat?
Bennett: Can we grab takeout before we head home?

I looked at the time and realized we were close to dinner already.

Me: I had a roast beef sandwich for lunch and used the card to pay for it. Ready to see your ties?
Bennett: You promised to leave them on my bed.

My stomach did a crazy flip at the thought of going into his room, which was weird since I'd been sleeping in it. But that had been before I knew how he saw me.

Me: I'm fine with takeout. Tell me where you are and I can start walking toward you.
Bennett: I'm almost there.

I looked around and spotted him a block down. His long stride was eating the distance between us at a rapid pace that he somehow managed to make look unhurried. When he reached me, he took the bag and stole my hand, threading his fingers through mine.

He started walking, and I moved on autopilot as that simple contact fried my brain.

"You didn't buy anything other than ties," he said. "Does your friend know that you hate shopping in the downtown stores?"

Heat radiated from his palm, warming mine and making my heart beat faster.

"Wrenly?"

"Nope," I said, tugging my hand free. "She doesn't know. And I didn't hate it."

He tried stealing my hand back, and I quickly tucked both of my hands under my arms. His slow smile didn't help calm my racing pulse.

"What were you doing?" I asked. "Just walking around, waiting for me, or stalking?"

"I was at Rexbies, having a drink with some friends."

"You have friends? Since when? How? Did you have to drug them?"

"Even in the middle of your panic, you're funny."

"I'm not panicking."

"Are your hands cold, then?"

"Nope, I'm getting ready to drive us home since you've been drinking."

He chuckled. "All right."

The easy way he gave in to me made me nervous. Especially when we reached the car in the parking garage and he opened the driver's side door for me.

"The traffic headed out of town should be light enough at this time of day. Don't worry. You can pull over at any time."

He didn't talk again until we were out of the city.

"Any time I asked a question about how you were in school, she deflected. At first, I thought she simply liked talking about herself. She seemed the type. But then I realized, like you, she didn't want to talk about what happened at school."

A surge of old panic and fear twisted my stomach, and I focused on my breathing.

"What happened there, Wrenly?"

"Nothing worth remembering or talking about," I said. "What are we having for dinner?"

He took the hint and let me change the subject.

"Take the next right. There's a fast food place."

For the first time in my life, I drove through a drive-thru. It was a lot harder than Bennett had made it look, and I hit the curb with his fancy car. After the tire thumped back down, I cringed and glanced at him. He was grinning but didn't comment.

"Not everyone can be born perfect at everything," I grumbled.

"Is that how you see me? Perfect at everything?"

I snorted. "I'm not feeding your already inflated ego."

"You think my ego is inflated? More like beaten down and on life support."

"Yeah, right. 'Is Mr. Wulf in?'" I mimicked.

"Why do you think the unwanted attention of a few would inflate my ego, when the one person I've waited twelve years to see doesn't want me?"

"I think it's supposed to rain tomorrow," I said, leaning forward to look through the windshield. "Crazy how things can go from sunny and beautiful to dark and gloomy."

He chuckled. "Deflecting isn't going to help you, Wrenly. Unless you really do want to live with me for the next four years. If that's the case, deflect away. Keep the distance between us."

I didn't say anything as I drove the rest of the way home.

He carried in the food, while I took his ties upstairs and set them out on his bed.

Curious whether I'd picked out anything he already had, I went to check his closet.

The row of my school uniforms stunned me and drew me forward. I touched the ripped skirt of one, remembering how the rip had happened. It'd been the day of a power outage. Without the cameras, I'd known Lindi and her group would come for me and had run for the wall. I almost hadn't made it. My mad scramble had wrecked the skirt, but I hadn't thought of it once I'd returned after the power had been restored. A new uniform had been delivered with the clean laundry.

My fingers found the dirt still clinging to the hem. When Grandma had said my old clothes helped him, I'd thought he was keeping them until the scent faded and then getting rid of them. However, the number of uniforms indicated that he was keeping them even after my scent had faded, as if he were collecting them. I wasn't sure how I felt about it. I should have been scared, but I wasn't.

"Wrenly..."

I glanced back at Bennett, who was standing in the doorway.

"Why?"

"I was struggling being apart from you. The staff sent me the damaged uniforms. Your scent helped calm me."

He looked afraid. Of me. Of my reaction to knowing that he'd been hoarding my dirty uniforms for my scent.

I faced the uniforms again, counting them.

"Fifteen. I know I didn't wreck that many this year. How long have you been collecting these?"

"Since your sophomore year. Mom made me get rid of the ones before that. She said you were too young and people would think I was—" he cleared his throat. "Being creepy."

It felt like the floor dipped beneath my feet, and I reached out to steady myself on the wall. He'd been collecting my clothes since the beginning?

Before I completely freaked out, I realized what was happening was bigger than his collecting. He was being honest with me. Completely and totally, unfiltered.

"Are you going to keep your word, Bennett, or are you trying to trick me into accepting you with the handholding, hugs, and a kiss?"

"Both. I hope you'll accept me if you can do those three things, but if you still want to leave after doing them, I'll let you go."

Hearing what I'd already suspected, I turned, wanting to escape the closet, but he didn't move out of my way.

"Move."

"No."

"Please."

"Not this time, Wrenly. Talk to me."

What could I say? Anything close to the truth—that I didn't know how to do the things he wanted without feeling something—would doom me and elate him.

No matter how I tried to fight it, I was attracted to Bennett. I had been since I first saw him standing on the stairs when I'd come home. But I'd known then that I couldn't acknowledge it. He was supposed to be a brother. At least, that's what I'd thought. Now that I knew better, my attraction to him was even more dangerous.

I wanted my freedom. I'd *earned* it by surviving seven years of hell.

"You're frustrated. Why?"

"Because I've suffered enough, dammit!"

His arms closed around me.

"How? Talk to me. That was supposed to be the best school in the country. I researched for months before deciding. What went wrong, Wrenly?"

I froze in his arms, not believing I'd heard him correctly, and slowly pulled back to look up at him.

"*You* sent me there?"

The worry on his face disappeared behind his mask.

"It was *you*?" My voice shook along with my limbs, and I pushed at his chest.

"Wrenly, please, baby, talk to me. What happened?"

My breathing started coming faster and faster until I was hyperventilating.

It was Bennett. Bennett sent me there. Bennett was the reason for all my abuse. School. Office. Pack. The one person who was supposed to love me above all reason had condemned me to seven years of hell. Why? Because he was in hell, he wanted me to suffer with him?

"You get one chance to let go of me," I said, barely keeping my head above a complete panic attack.

He seemed to sense it, too, because he immediately released me.

"Please don't do this, Wrenly."

"Do what? Hate you? It's too late for that."

I left his room on shaky legs and closed myself in my bathroom, where I turned on the shower, sat on the floor, and cried my heart out. After the pain faded, a numbness crept in along with exhaustion. I sat there, listening to the shower and thinking of nothing.

A knock on the door, and Mom's voice penetrated my mental haze a while later. My legs had lost feeling. It took two tries to stand and unlock the door.

Mom immediately pulled me into a hug. I didn't hug her back. I couldn't. Something inside of me knew that welcoming her concern would open the floodgates to my own emotions, and I wasn't ready to deal with that yet.

"What's wrong?" she asked.

"What's right?" I asked with no inflection.

She pulled back to look at me, her hands framing my face and her thumb wiping at the tears trailing down my cheeks. I thought I'd stopped crying. Maybe they weren't tears but liquid pain leaking out because I just couldn't contain it anymore.

"Sweetheart, you're scaring me. Please tell me what's wrong."

I focused on her face, seeing her concern. Her love.

"You want me to say something reassuring. Something to make you feel better, but I won't. He sent me to hell. Four years of being chased. Cut. Burned. Held down. Suffocated."

Tremors rocked through me, and Mom's pupils exploded wide. She stumbled back a step and held her hand to her mouth.

"What?" she gasped.

I was done trying to protect the people who loved me like they'd failed to protect me.

"I *hated* school. I asked you to let me come home, but you told me to hang in there. That it was the best school for me. People put their kids on waitlists before they were even born. I was supposed to be grateful."

Something crashed somewhere in the house.

"I'm done being grateful, Mom. I'm done cooperating with your plans for my future. I'm done."

I closed the door and returned to my spot on the floor.

Another crash shook the floorboards. I leaned my head against the wall and stared at the water raining down from the shower.

I WOKE up with a headache in a dark room. The reason for the heaviness in my chest slowly resurfaced. I didn't cry. Sleep had helped me move past the pain-filled tears.

"They don't know what to do," Grandma said from the darkness. "I told them to stop trying to do anything. That's what caused the problem in the first place."

The pain leaked out again, and she wiped it away.

"Life is hard, my little Wren. Sometimes it's harder than it needs to be. I'm sorry for everything you've suffered."

Her hand closed over mine.

"It's so easy to want to protect you. Your smile and laughter light up a room. You shine so bright, no one wants you broken. But sometimes, when we hold too tightly, we break what we're trying to protect.

"Now, tell me what you need from me."

"Keep them away for now."

"Done. Anything else? Do you want Karter or Aiden to come home?"

More pieces fell into place. The pictures of their partying. Their Bennett-centric replies. Aiden and Karter weren't actually seeking their mates. They hadn't been sent away because they'd asked about Bennett's mate. They'd been sent away because of me. Or rather because of Bennett's jealousy.

A flat laugh escaped on an exhale. "Why bother? I've been isolated for years. Why change things now?"

"Because we've realized how badly we've managed things."

"We? Were you part of the decision-making?"

"By keeping silent, by not speaking up for you, wasn't I?"

Another drop of pain trailed down my cheek.

"I don't want to think yet."

She patted my hand. "Then don't. I'll be here when you need me."

I nodded and closed my eyes. It took forever to fall asleep again.

When I woke, the room was still dark, but I could tell it was daytime from the faint glow coming from around the curtains. A soft rumble of thunder and the steady patter of rain against the windows soothed me.

"Thirsty?" Grandma asked.

I accepted the cup she held out and sat up to drink.

"You were crying in your sleep," she said.

"Did I say anything?"

"No. Do you talk in your sleep now?"

"Sometimes I scream myself awake. I don't know if I actually talk."

"Were any of the years you were gone okay?"

I reached out to turn on the light so I could see her. She looked tired. I scooted over on the bed and patted the spot next to me. She smiled and switched from the chair to the bed.

"School was hard," I said. "Some years were harder than they needed to be."

She made a noncommittal sound and wrapped an arm around me. I rested my head on her shoulder.

"I'm always here for you, my little Wren. Whenever. However."

CHAPTER NINETEEN

I SPENT the day in my room. Grandma delivered meals and spent time with me when I wanted it but otherwise left me alone. It gave me time to think. And the more I thought, the angrier I got.

Bennett had manipulated every aspect of my life. It didn't matter how well-intended his actions were; he'd still exercised a control that wasn't his to exercise. Potential mate or not, my life was my own.

After I'd eaten dinner, Grandma knocked on my door and said that Mom wanted to talk to me. I wasn't ready to face her yet, though, so I shook my head and lay facing away from the door.

The soft murmur of their conversation in the hallway reached me, but I couldn't make out what they were saying. It didn't matter. Like I'd already told her, I was done.

I WOKE with a gasp and struggled to sit up. The arms caging me from behind didn't relent, though. They held me against Bennett's hot chest. His breaths were coming as fast as mine.

"Tell me who hurt you," he pleaded. "Give me names."

I knew why he wanted them and what he'd do. But it wasn't his place to right the wrongs done to me by others. Especially not when he'd put me there in the first place.

"There's only one name."

"Tell me."

"Bennett Wulf."

He growled and ducked his head so his exhales warmed my neck. "Please, Wrenly."

He had no right to think he could make up for what had happened by going after the women in that school. First, he needed to deal with the source of the problem. Himself.

"Bennett Wulf," I repeated. "Now get out of my room."

"Why are you protecting them?"

"I'm not. I'm just choosing which of the people who hurt me should pay first. Now, are you leaving or am I?"

He released me and got out of bed. "Tomorrow, I want names."

"And I want memories of a better childhood than what I got and a family that actually treated me like a human and not a ready-made mate for their son. Looks like neither of us can have what we want."

The soft snick of the door closing answered me.

BENNETT WAS WAITING in the hallway when I opened the door the next morning, which wasn't a surprise. Not after what he'd said last night. His gaze traveled the length of me, noting I was showered and dressed for the day.

The bandages were no longer necessary, and I was finally free of bruises. At least, outside ones. I felt battered on the inside.

"Did Grandma leave?" I asked.

"She's waiting for you at the table. There's a breakfast burrito for you."

I'd started walking when he said she was downstairs, but I

hurried my pace when he said what was waiting for breakfast. At school, we'd had all sorts of made-to-order options. Yogurt parfaits, fruit plates, oatmeal with a dozen different add-ins, toast with cream cheese and smoked salmon, and an occasional culinary special. Never anything fried or anything you'd eat with your hands like a burrito.

My thoughts were on food and not people, which is why I skidded to a stop when I saw Mom and Dad at the table with Grandma.

While I hadn't anticipated their presence, it wasn't entirely unwelcome. I'd done a lot of thinking after Bennett left last night and acknowledged a few things to myself.

Yes, my life at school had been hell. However, some of that hell had been self-inflicted. I'd been angry and had purposely provoked the wrong people. But most importantly, I hadn't spoken up about what was happening. Not to them, and not to the staff. Had I done so, things wouldn't have gotten out of hand.

Was I taking on all the blame? No. But it was a bit ridiculous for me to think Mom and Dad should know things they hadn't been told. Their fault in all of this was not *listening* when I'd said I hated school and *telling* me to keep trying instead of asking why.

Rather than turning around and walking away from a confrontation I wasn't yet ready to have, I just stood there and waited.

Mom stood, her eyes watering.

"Wrenly. Please."

"Please what?" I asked.

"We're so sorry we didn't listen. We should have—" Her composure crumpled. Inside, mine wanted to do the same.

Mom finally understood.

And she was giving me space. She didn't rush at me in her tears but stayed where she was, crying. Dad moved to hug her, watching me with sad eyes.

"We never wanted to hurt you," he said. "We didn't realize you felt alone and unwanted. If we thought for even a moment you were being hurt, we never would have left you there. All the reports we received were that you were quiet, but excelling."

"Do you know why I was excelling?" I asked. "At first, I just wanted to make you happy. Then I realized it was the fastest way to prove to you that I could manage my own life.

"I forgave you for leaving me there a long time ago. My anger now stems from the things you've kept from me and the fact that, up until now, you still haven't been listening to what I want."

"We understand," Dad said. "We promise we won't interfere anymore. Tell us what you need, and we'll do our best to provide it."

"Right now, what I need most is the space and freedom to make my own plans for the future."

Mom nodded, but Dad glanced at Bennett behind me. The significance of that look wasn't lost on me. Neither was Bennett's silence. He didn't need to say anything, though.

I already knew Mom and Dad weren't the ones attempting to control my life now. They hadn't been for a long while. Bennett was the one I needed to put in his place. I just needed them to stop taking his side so that I could do what needed to be done.

I looked at Grandma. She gave me a sad smile, stood, and started for the garage door. Mom and Dad followed her.

Once they were gone, I sat at the table and reached for the burrito.

"I want my bankbook," I said, knowing Bennett was somewhere behind me.

"I want names."

Taking a bite, I focused on the food and how I wanted to respond to him. He patiently waited.

"What are you going to do when I give them to you?"

"Make them pay."

"How?"

"Depends on what they did."

"What about someone who locks me up for seven years in a place where other people abuse me?"

The back of my chair crackled ominously, and a thread of fear wormed its way down my spine as I imagined him gripping it and leaning over me.

"Tell me what punishment I deserve. Tell me how to make this right."

Setting down my food, I spun in my chair and met his uncomfortably close gaze.

"Let me go. Forever. Find someone else."

He closed his eyes. "I can't do that."

"Can't or won't? There's a difference."

"Can't, Wrenly. I'm barely hanging on. Please give me—"

"Go to hell, Bennett. I've given enough."

I turned back around and picked up my burrito.

The chair crackled again, but I ignored it and finished my breakfast. He reached around me and took my plate to the kitchen. Once he was gone, I went upstairs to get my things. I didn't know he'd followed me until I turned around with my wallet in hand.

"What are you doing?" he asked.

"Going to work."

"I think we should—"

"If you don't want me to hate my life, you need to stop trying to control it."

"I'm not trying to control it, Wrenly. I'm trying to understand you. To talk to you."

"You can't understand me by talking to me, Bennett. To understand me, you need to listen. Now, are you getting out of the way, or is our day going to go downhill really fast?"

He ran his hand through his hair. "I'll be ready in ten minutes."

"For what?"

He had the grace to look confused. "Aren't you going into work?"

"I am, but I don't need you to take me. I have a car of my own, right?"

He closed his eyes for a second, and I watched the tremors rack his body. My satisfaction that I'd won was short-lived because I was against the wall less than a beat later, my hands pinned above my head, and his lips skimming my neck.

"You need time. I know that. But I'm not sure how much more I can give you. I gave you twelve years of what I thought was freedom. It was a mistake. Maybe marking you when you were younger would have been better for both of us."

Although he wasn't pressing against me, my breath left in a whoosh, and my eyes went wide in panic. I tugged at his hold.

"I am listening, Wrenly. My mate is miserable. She cries in her sleep but calms when I hold her. She feels alone and abandoned. I can give her the connection she needs. But she's saying no to all of it. So I'm waiting and watching her misery and dying inside because of it. I'm coming undone, baby, and I don't know how much longer the rational side of me will hold out against the instinct to make you mine. Do you understand?"

And then he was gone, leaving me sagging against the wall and panting in relief that he hadn't tried anything.

Because a little part of me had wanted him to.

I blamed it on his hands-to-the-wall move. It was both dominating and tender. It made me captive, but I never felt controlled when he did it. Only held still. Protected, which was completely insane.

Dropping my head back against the wall, I waited for my pulse to slow then went downstairs.

He was already there, wearing a suit with one of the ties I'd purchased. My heart skipped a beat.

"We're not driving together," I said.

"I know."

In the garage, he held my door open for me, but he didn't get into the passenger seat. Instead, he took the car next to mine.

He followed me all the way to the office, which made me feel both nervous and comforted. I parked in his spot in the underground garage and felt a little bit of satisfaction when my phone started ringing.

"What?" I answered.

"Wait for me."

I rolled my eyes, waited until his car pulled away, and got out. Was I playing with fire again? Yes. But if I didn't establish some boundaries now, how would things change? Plus, I needed a little alone time to regroup.

Unfortunately, when I reached the main lobby, there was a line for the elevators going up. A few of the office girls were already waiting, including Milena. Her pupils dilated as she stared at me.

"Are you above the company dress code?" she asked.

"I'm not above anything, Milena. I'm rebelling to get fired. Make sure to complain to management for me, okay?"

"Too good to work for your money? You just want it handed to you?"

I shook my head and ignored her. If her level of stupidity were fixable, it would have already been corrected by someone else. She wasn't my problem to solve.

"She really is a charity princess," one of them muttered.

The elevator from the garage arrived then, and Bennett exited, looking pretty annoyed. Either Milena didn't know how to read a mood, or she chose to ignore it as she rushed over to his side and attempted to grab his arm. He dodged and strode toward me.

I studied the closed elevator doors in front of me, willing them to open.

"Bennett, my six-month review is overdue," I heard her say. "Do you have time for a one-on-one meeting today?"

"No."

"Actually, he does," I said, without looking at them. "His calendar is wide open, starting at noon."

"I can do a lunch meeting," she said as the doors opened.

The rest of her group got on, but she didn't.

"I can't," he said. "Wrenly's eating in my office."

"No, she's not," I said. "Wrenly fulfilled her end of the deal and is now free to enjoy her lunch hour however she pleases."

The second elevator opened, and I got on with the remaining people in front of us. Unfortunately, so did Bennett and Milena.

"Great," Milena said. "I'll order something, and we can have lunch while we review my performance."

Bennett stepped closer to me, and his fingers brushed mine. I quickly reached up to push back my hair. His frustrated sigh was audible to everyone in the elevator, including Milena.

In the reflection of the elevator's wall, I saw her expression crumble a little until her gaze caught mine. It wasn't like I had any pity for her just then—the bruises on my neck had finally faded, but the memory of her chokehold hadn't. And that non-pity solidified as her expression twisted with anger.

Bennett turned to look at her, and his warning growl filled the elevator. The other passengers moved nervously, and I elbowed him.

Once they got off the elevator, Milena tried to engage Bennett in conversation by asking what foods he liked to eat and which restaurants were his favorites. His answers were terse, but she kept trying. And when the doors finally opened to our floor, he was right on my heels as I bailed.

"I'll see you at noon," Milena called after him.

He waited until we reached my desk to say, "My office. Now."

"No, thank you."

I moved around my desk to sit down, but he caught my arm.

"Wrenly…"

The low warning in his voice made my knees weak, but I'd never been one to cower in fear. I was too feral for that.

So I met his angry gaze with one of my own.

"I don't need this job badly enough to put up with your shit, and I don't get paid enough to act like your shield. Let go of my arm." When he didn't, I stepped closer. "Ask yourself if you'll survive Mom's anger if I walk out of here and vow never to see the Wulf family again."

His jaw muscles jumped and twitched as he stared at me.

"Um, is this a bad time?" Miranda drawled.

I didn't look away from Bennett but waited for him to decide.

He released my arm and walked into his office, slamming the door hard enough that I heard something crack.

"So that was interesting," Miranda said. "Boy troubles?"

I glanced at her, trying to gauge what she meant by that. She held up her hands a second before the blinds snapped open. I flipped the bird in the general direction of the windows without looking.

"I heard you're no longer on a lunch timeout. Thought maybe you and I can grab a bite."

Stay here and endure Bennett, or risk my safety with Miranda. The choice was easy to make.

"Just to be clear, they haven't forgotten about me yet," I said, referring to the threat she'd made after she'd introduced my face to the bathroom door. "They track where I am at all times. If the tracking suddenly stops, they go to the last known location."

Her mouth dropped open a little. "Are you serious?"

I nodded.

"Now we definitely need to have lunch. Meet me at the elevators a few minutes before noon."

MILENA ARRIVED at my desk ten minutes before lunch, and I couldn't have been happier.

"Is he in?" she asked.

I gestured to the blinds, which had remained open all morning despite the closed door. Through them, I knew she could see Bennett sitting at his desk.

In the last few hours, he hadn't moved much. The calls he'd taken had been brief, and he'd scowled at me the entire time. Not that I'd paid much attention to it. I'd finished another spreadsheet and sent it to him, Mom, and Dad about thirty minutes ago before starting on the next one.

"You know that's not what I meant, right?" Milena said. "What kind of mood is he in?"

Clasping my hands under my chin, I looked up at her.

"Use your eyes. Does he look happy to you?" Some of the joy bled out of her expression. "Careful, he's watching. He's been glaring at me all morning, and I'm about to leave for lunch. Who do you think he's going to transfer his anger to?"

I locked my laptop and stood.

"Enjoy your meeting. I hope, for your sake, your performance meets his expectations."

I made it two steps toward the exit when his office door opened behind me.

"Where are you going, Wrenly?"

"To get something to eat."

"Order in."

I flipped him off over my shoulder as I kept walking.

"You should fire her," Milena said. "Anyone would be a better assistant than her."

"She's reviewed a dozen subsidiaries and found more than a million dollars in unnecessary expenses in the nine days she's been here. I doubt you could do the same in two months."

Internally cringing on Milena's behalf because her review wasn't going to go as she hoped, I left them to their co-misery and waited for Miranda by the elevators.

"You're early," she said.

"So was Milena. I bailed while I could."

We rode the elevators down without talking until we reached the street out front.

"Why are we having lunch together?" I asked. "If it's revenge for trying to hit you, you might want to wait until the end of summer."

She chuckled. "It's not revenge. After I cooled off, I realized your response had been in defense. Automatic, not confrontational. And I've also been paying attention."

"To what?"

"To you. To Bennett."

I glanced at her.

"I have a nose, too. We all do, but I think the rest of the office is still in denial...like you seem to be."

My stomach sank to my toes even as I asked, "Denial about what?"

"You know that most of us would kill for him to look at us as a potential mate, right?"

"Is this where you lead me to a dark alley?"

"No, this is where I offer my help."

"Why?" I didn't quite manage to keep the shock I felt out of that question.

"That's simple. Either I help you reject him, which gives me another chance at him. Or I help you accept him, which puts me in close with one of the city's ruling Alpha families."

Bluntly stating how each option benefited her actually helped me believe she was being honest, which I appreciated.

"So a win-win for you, no matter which option I choose," I said.

"Exactly."

"What if I don't want your help?"

"Oh, I know you don't, and I understand why. We had a bad start. But I'd like to start again."

I stopped walking and faced her. "Every single person in my life that I've trusted has betrayed me."

She slowly inhaled, and I watched her expression change to confusion. "But the Wulfs..."

"*Every* person."

She frowned slightly and indicated we should keep walking. "So you really want to reject him then?"

"I do."

"Your scent's...not even a little conflicted."

I sighed. "Maybe Bennett would be the ideal mate for another shifter, but I'm human. I don't want to be smothered. Or locked away under some misconceived attempt to protect me. I've already let them know I've enrolled at Coalwell and will start this fall. They weren't happy."

"Do they know you plan to reject him?"

"Yes, which is why Bennett hasn't done anything. He's being cautious and hoping I'll change my mind."

We went into the sandwich place I'd visited before and got in line to order.

"Well, if you're sure you want to reject him, it should be pretty easy. Just strip in front of him and get down on all fours. You'll be mated and claimed before you can say 'ow.'"

The imagery was a bit too vivid for me and made my pulse trip.

"I'd prefer to keep that as the last contingency plan."

"Really? Why? It'd be the quickest and most effective way."

I glanced at Miranda, weighing how much to tell her. The pure truth—that a small part of me feared I wouldn't reject him like I wanted to—was out. I didn't know her and didn't trust that it wouldn't make its way back to Bennett. So I settled for a piece of the truth.

"I was sent to an all-girls boarding school when I was twelve. Before that, I hung out with Aiden and Karter, whom I completely view as my brothers. I saw Bennett briefly in the months between when he graduated and I left. Beyond that, I've had very little contact with men."

Miranda's stare went from disbelief to amusement. "So you're a virgin?"

"Worse. I've never even held hands—at least romantically."

"By the moon…"

"Yeah. So you can probably see why the prospect of going to that extreme would be my last resort, right?"

"Wow. Okay."

She remained thoughtfully quiet for several minutes. When our order was called, I grabbed it, and we headed out to the sidewalk again.

"Still want to help me?" I asked.

"I'm not sure I know how now."

"By answering any question I have as honestly and as accurately as you're able."

"All right. What questions do you have?"

"Is there any way to switch his interest to another woman?"

She snorted. "Do you think we wouldn't have already done that if there was a way?"

"Is there any way to make him disinterested in me?"

Her gaze swept over my clothes and hair. "I feel like you've already given that one your best effort."

Other people might have found her rude, but I could see the humor in her eyes, and it matched my own.

"Don't forget you bought me clothes just like this."

"I shopped to match your fashion sense, not mine."

I made a dismissive sound. "So we can't switch his interest or turn it off. I'm down to two options, then, excluding the failsafe."

"Don't leave me in suspense," she said as we neared the park.

"Until I know I can trust you, I'm going to have to. I don't want to ruin my chances."

"Okay. I guess just let me know when you need something then."

"Any chance you'd be willing to risk an ongoing lunch date with me this week?"

"Sure."

She sat on a park bench and started opening her sandwich. I did the same.

"What do you want me to tell him when he asks me what we're talking about?"

That she was smart enough to realize that he'd do that and asked what answer to give ahead of time gave me some hope. But I knew not to trust it.

"Tell him I've asked about all the different ways to kill a shifter without them seeing it coming."

She slowly smiled as she bit into her sandwich.

CHAPTER TWENTY

BENNETT'S WILLINGNESS TO give me space dwindled rapidly. He watched me through the office window the remainder of the afternoon and followed me to the parking garage at the end of the day. Again, it was both a comfort and an annoyance to see his car in the rearview mirror on the drive home.

Sandy had a homemade macaroni and cheese bake waiting on the table for us. As soon as we sat at the table together, he seemed to relax. He asked questions about the expenses I'd reviewed and very casually asked about my lunch with Miranda.

"I didn't think I'd be able to make any friends at Wulf Enterprises. She might be an exception. It's still too soon to tell, though."

He didn't say much after that, and I went up to my room to check in with my online class, which kept me busy for the rest of the night.

Tuesday started rough since Bennett was still in bed with me when I woke up.

I threw my pillow at him and locked myself in the bathroom until I knew he was gone. He didn't complain that I wanted to drive separately again. However, he tried to claim my lunch hour with a required meeting.

"Am I really not allowed to make friends? I thought the whole point was to get me to like working here so that I stay."

His face grew dangerously red. "Will you be eating lunch with her all week?"

"Unless someone tries to stop me, yes."

He nodded and returned to his office, closing the door nicely instead of slamming it like I'd thought he would.

By the end of the day, though, he was pacing in front of his desk. Each of the women who approached me turned around and left without asking whether he was busy. Miranda stopped by to drop off an expense form for me and saw him. She shook her head and left without comment.

At five, he seemed to calm down a little and walked out of his office with a hint of his calmer self. We rode the elevator down together without incident, and he followed me home again.

When we walked in through the kitchen door together, Sandy had another dinner on the table, waiting for us. I realized then that her schedule—when she cooked for us versus when Bennett cooked for me—was solely dictated by Bennett's agenda. Dinners were usually sit-down, and whether I sat depended on my mood and what was being offered.

Given my current avoidance of him, he'd known I would reject going out somewhere after work for a sit-down meal. And if we had picked something up, I would have eaten it in my room. Did he honestly think more manipulation would tempt me to spend more time with him?

"I have a lot of homework," I said, picking up my plate. "I'm going to eat this as I read."

The soft growl that echoed behind me made me want to run up the stairs, but I resisted the urge.

Wednesday morning, I woke up lying on him and dug my elbow into his diaphragm to get off instead of pummeling him with the pillow. He grunted but didn't move to protect himself as I got out of bed. It made me wish I'd used my knee. Although considering his current mood, he might have taken that as affection.

He left me alone to get ready and opened my car door for me in the garage, seeming to be in a better mood than when he went to bed. Maybe he *had* taken that elbow as something affectionate. However, the reason for his good mood became clearer when we arrived at work and the parking space next to his was empty. He parked beside my car and opened my door for me.

I didn't comment as we rode the elevator up together.

He went straight to his office and kept the door open. Since he wasn't staring at me angrily through the window and wasn't pacing, everyone took that as a sign that he was approachable. They quickly drained what little patience and humor he'd started the day with, and a few minutes before noon, I fled to meet Miranda at her desk.

Several of the women turned to look at me as I sped past like I'd lost my mind, including Milena.

"Rough morning?" Miranda asked with a grin.

"You have no idea."

"Oh, I might. We could all hear him that last time when he yelled, 'Get out.'"

"I think the third floor heard him," Milena said. "You're clearly not helping the situation. If you're not willing to do your job, step aside so someone else can take your place."

She stood with her purse and left.

I waited until Miranda and I were outside to ask, "Does she know?"

"Probably. She'd have to be nose blind not to know. He smelled like repressed sex and frustration before you came home, which was driving us all crazy. However, it's slowly changed, especially after you both took the day off last Thursday. It's less frustration and more anticipation now."

"Less frustration? He got so red in the face yesterday that I thought he'd have a stroke. And today, he threw Olivia's folder so hard that the corner of it embedded in the drywall."

"Impressive. Bet he couldn't do that again if he tried."

"Not the point. He seems way more frustrated, not less."

She shrugged. "I'm just telling you what I smell and why Milena probably knows. That subtle change is what tipped me off. That and the scent of your desperation."

"I'm still not sure if this is a budding friendship or the origin story of mortal enemies."

She laughed. "How do you feel about Mexican food for lunch?"

"Friendship it is."

We didn't just order food; she ordered us drinks too. The strawberry margarita was amazing, and I felt so relaxed as we walked back to work.

"How bad are your periods, usually?"

Her random question broke through my little bubble of happiness.

"What?"

"I bought you the drink to help you make it through the day, but that was before I realized you were getting your period. Since you're underage and he's overprotective, if we call the margarita medicinal, I might not get yelled at for it."

It took a few extra seconds for my mind to catch up to what she was saying. Even knowing that Bennett would smell alcohol on me and scold her, she'd bought me a drink anyway. And she—and everyone else in the office—would smell I was getting my period.

"Pain-wise, my periods are survivable. The first day is always the worst. But I think the emotional trauma of knowing that everyone will know when I have my period should win the 'why Wrenly drank at lunch' award."

She laughed. "It's not a big deal. We're used to it."

"Well, I'm not."

"You will be. There are supplies in the bathroom closet. Take what you need."

When we returned to work, she not only walked me to my desk

but also went into Bennett's office without knocking and closed the door behind her.

I watched him look up from his computer. His gaze shifted from me to the door where she stood. His frown slowly faded the longer she was in there. He glanced at me once more, nodded, and looked down at his computer again.

Miranda let herself out of his office, closing the door behind her.

"We're both good," she said.

About an hour later, as I was nodding off at my desk, my phone buzzed.

Bennett: Can I talk to you for a second?

As soon as I stood, I felt the first stabbing cramp and pressed my hand to my abdomen. He was starting to stand when I glanced at him through the window and gave him the "I need a second" finger. Seeing that one instead of the one he was used to seemed to surprise him.

He nodded and sat back down. I made my way to the bathroom and raided the supply closet.

A chocolate and a blanket were waiting for me on his napping couch when I returned.

"Thanks," I said, taking both and making myself comfortable.

He watched me eat the chocolate and lie down.

"Is this what you wanted to talk about?" I asked.

"No, but I was going to offer it. You looked like you were going to pass out at your desk."

I closed my eyes, already giving in to the call of sleep.

The nap didn't last long. I woke an hour later, cramping lightly, and rolled over. The blanket, which had slid down, was tugged up over my shoulder again.

I opened my eyes and looked up at Bennett, who was leaning over me.

"Are you all right?" he asked, moving so I could sit up.

"Fine. Just some twinges."

"I called Milo to pick up your car and made reservations for dinner after work. Pizza, but we can change it to anything."

"What? Why?"

"You drank at lunch. Underage drinking means you'd lose your license. Do you want to risk that?"

Everything he was saying sounded reasonable. But it still felt off.

"Did you make the reservation and arrange for Milo to pick up the car before or after I came back from lunch?"

Frustration flashed in his eyes, and I wanted to strangle him for trying to manipulate me. *Again.*

"Don't pretend this is about protecting my interests when it's about protecting yours. Ass." I threw my blanket aside and left. My attempt to slam the door was thwarted by his hand stopping it.

"Keep it open," he said.

I went to the bathroom and didn't return for an hour. He kept his distance for the rest of the afternoon and didn't say a word when he left his office and waited by my desk for me to shut down.

He tried talking to me once we were in the car, but I ignored him. At the restaurant, he asked me to order, which I did, then attempted a conversation again. My responding silence wasn't simply anger. It was a boundary.

I knew that if I gave him what he wanted—my attention—he would continue manipulating my life with increasing frequency until he got what he wanted, regardless of what I wanted.

His frustration grew as we sat at the table, waiting for the pizza. When it arrived, I took a piece and started eating. He asked how it was. I said nothing.

By the time the meal was over, his frustration had disappeared behind his mask. He paid the bill and walked me to the car.

He offered ice cream on the way home. I was so tempted but didn't say anything.

Once we were home, I went to my room and focused on studying, grateful I'd signed up for the class.

Thursday morning, I woke to Bennett spooning me. His open hand heated my lower belly, where I had cramps, and it felt so good that I didn't move right away.

"Good morning," he said after several minutes had passed.

I felt like a raging bitch when I got out of bed without answering him. His hand on my stomach had been nice, but I knew I couldn't admit that or thank him.

Nine more weeks after this, Wrenly. Stay strong.

He made it easy to stay mad at him after that, though, when I discovered the keys to my car and every other car in the garage missing from the key box.

I turned and held out my hand.

"Give me my keys."

Instead of surrendering them, he took my hand and threaded his fingers through mine.

"If you can stay like this for five minutes, I will."

"No." I pulled my hand free. "That's part of another deal. Give me the keys because you said the car was mine and no one would take it from me. Plus, I didn't hit you this morning for sleeping next to me."

"Why does everything from you need to be part of a deal?"

"Why do you need to take what I'm not willing to give? Why can't you wait to see if I give it?" I was yelling, and it wasn't helping the storm brewing in his eyes. He stepped closer to me, his hand capturing the back of my neck.

"I *have* been waiting. For *years*."

"For you, it's been twelve years, but for me, it's been seven days. Stop trying to force me, Bennett."

He exhaled heavily, closed his eyes, and touched his forehead to mine.

"I'm trying not to."

He released me and withdrew a set of keys from his pocket.

"Are you driving, or am I?" he asked.

"You should, or I'll murder us both."

I was still simmering when we reached the office. Miranda took one look at me and followed us to my desk.

"Do we need an early lunch? Or a shopping excursion, maybe?"

Bennett paused on his way to the office.

"She needs something for the charity auction dinner this weekend."

"She *what*?" Miranda turned on me. "Do not tell me you were planning to purchase something off the rack for that."

"I'm not going."

Bennett made a call on speaker.

"How is the progress on the apartment?" he asked as soon as someone answered.

"The soundproofing is almost finished. After that, drywall will go up. I sent a few ideas to your email that I'll need an answer to by the end of the day tomorrow. After that, it's finishing work. I'll have another email about that on Monday."

"Thanks."

Bennett hung up and smiled at me. There was nothing funny about it, though. It screamed "man on the edge."

"I think Miranda and I will take an early lunch to shop for a dress."

"Do you honestly think we're going to find what you need in an hour?"

I saw an opportunity and ran with it. "How much time do we need? All day?"

She looked at Bennett. "How much time can we take off?"

His gaze never left mine. "If I give you today, I want your word we'll stay for the entire auction."

"How long is the auction?"

"Four hours. Plus the drive there and back. Together, not separate."

"Plus two drinks."

"Deal."

"Deal."

I grabbed my purse and would have walked away, but Miranda stopped me.

"I think you're forgetting something."

She nodded her head toward Bennett, and I looked at her in panic. Did she want me to kiss him goodbye? My pulse started to race as I remembered the last time he'd kissed me, and I shook my head slightly.

She rolled her eyes at me and physically turned me toward him.

He was holding up his credit card.

His gaze swept over my face.

"I'd give anything to know why you're flushing and panicked."

"Cancel the apartment, and I'll tell you."

A slow smile curved his lips. "I don't think I will."

He moved closer with the card, and I couldn't back away because Miranda was still holding me.

"Send me a lot of pictures, Miranda, and your bonus will match the price of the dress you talk her into buying."

MY FEET HURT. So did my brain. The amount of money Miranda had convinced me to spend was insane.

But you can sell it all when you're done using it, Wren.

That was the only saving grace for a day of shopping with Miranda. I had a dress, shoes, earrings, a bracelet, and a necklace. And Miranda was giddy knowing her bonus would equal the total of all of it.

"I feel like you're my personal shopper with you carrying everything," I said as the elevator pinged for our floor.

"Today, I am. Plus, I don't trust you not to drop your shoes purposely. I saw the way you looked at them."

"No one will know if I wear sneakers."

"*I* will know, and I will hunt you down if you try it."

I laughed, which drew Milena's attention. She stood as we approached her section.

"Must be nice to be the owner's daughter and take off to shop whenever you want. Does it feel good to fuck over your coworkers?"

"Wrenly isn't the only one who got to go shopping today," Miranda said. "Your jealousy is holding you back."

We continued past her desk to Bennett's office suite.

His door was closed, and he was on the phone when we arrived, but as soon as he saw us, he waved for us to come in.

I groaned, not wanting to deal with him.

"Don't be a baby. He just spent a fortune on you."

"Not by my choice," I said.

She nudged me toward the door, which I opened for her, and proceeded to hang up my garment bag on a hook near the bathroom door. After she carefully set the shoe bag down, she went to his desk with the jewelry. She honestly was like a shopping assistant because while she did all of that, I went to his napping couch and collapsed horizontally.

Bennett hung up the phone.

"I'm never shopping with her again. She can go by herself."

"What happened?" Bennett asked.

I could hear the warning in his voice and glanced over to see him staring down at Miranda.

"Wrenly has no stamina or patience. That's what happened. You saw the dress options and her expressions. She wasn't into it at all, which is a shame. We could have bought so much more."

I snorted. "You're just thinking about your bonus."

"There's no shame in earning a fair wage for services rendered. I put up with your complaining for seven hours straight."

"Not straight. I couldn't talk when you gave me that granola bar, which doesn't count as a meal, by the way."

She looked at Bennett.

"She's hormonal and needs some sugar. Good luck with her tonight." Then she turned to me. "That dress had better be in perfect condition when you arrive at the auction on Saturday. I want pictures, Bennett."

She exited the office, and I closed my eyes. "How did you survive her on your own?"

His chuckle teased my ears.

"Are you regretting your choice of a maybe-friend?"

"Not really. She had the patience I lacked. And the dress isn't awful."

"What about the shoes?"

"I hate those. There's no way I'll be able to run in them."

"If you need to run, just tell me. I'll carry you."

"Or...I could take them off and run barefoot. If my feet recover by then."

His hands suddenly clasped my ankles and lifted my legs. My eyes flew open as he sat down and plucked off a shoe.

"Stop that. What are you—?"

A groan escaped me at the first press of his thumb into the arch of my foot.

I closed my eyes and let him have his way with my dying appendage until he touched my toes. With a squeal, I jerked my foot away from him and lifted my head to glare.

"I didn't know," he said, trying and failing to hide his smile. "It won't happen again."

When he reached for my foot, I reluctantly let him have it. He went back to the kind of rubbing I liked. With one last warning look, I relaxed again.

The second shoe came off, and I melted into the couch. When he started kneading my calves, I didn't even think to stop him. It felt too good. Until he accidentally brushed the skin behind one of my knees. Something happened—a bolt of electric awareness of him...his hands...his heat...shot straight through me.

I scrambled off the couch.

He closed his eyes and tipped his head back on the couch.

I stood there, debating whether to grab my shoes or just run barefoot like I'd threatened.

"Give me five minutes," he said roughly. "We'll stop for ice cream on the way home."

His stillness gave me enough confidence to creep closer.

Just as I was bending to pick up my shoes, his arm hooked around my waist, and he pulled me onto his lap.

"No lunch with me next week if you let me hold you ten minutes."

My pulse leapt, and I started pushing at his shoulders. My gaze darted to the open window as he dipped his head to the side of my neck.

"Five minutes," he begged.

His exhale warmed my skin a second before I felt his lips there.

"I've waited so long to smell you like this, Wrenly. Imagine the best thing you've ever smelled in your life times ten." His nose brushed my skin as he inhaled again. "That's what your scent was like just now. Not addictive, but irresistible on a level you can't begin to understand." His lips brushed my skin again, sending a shiver racing through me. "But I am resisting so that you don't have to."

His hands captured mine, which had stopped pushing at his shoulders.

"Let yourself feel what comes naturally."

He nuzzled closer, kissing my neck tenderly as I sat on his lap, locked in an internal battle that I was losing.

I *liked* the way he made me feel. It was new and exciting and insanely potent. His touch had my head spinning, and I struggled to remember why it was a bad idea. Why was I trying to leave?

"Sorry to interrupt, but I need Wrenly for a second," Miranda said, jerking me from my daze.

I scrambled off his lap and bolted out the door.

"You're fired," I heard Bennett say.

"No, I'm not. You're going to give me a raise before the end of next week."

She closed the door on him and turned to raise an eyebrow as she grinned and held out my shoes.

"Let's go for a walk."

I groaned and took my shoes from her. From the corner of my eye, I saw Bennett stand from the couch to watch me put them on.

"Is he really going to fire you?" I asked.

"He can try, but I think if I weren't here, you'd stop coming to work."

Her self-satisfied smile was contagious because she wasn't wrong. We walked out of the office suite together and took the elevators down to the lobby.

"What work aren't you getting done by hanging out with me?" I asked as we left again, this time to stroll along the sidewalk.

"Nothing important. All that stuff was delegated to the other girls so I could be your emotional support shopper today, which is why Milena is so mad. Who wouldn't want to get paid to go shopping?"

"Me."

She chuckled. "You're the exception, not the norm. So what happened back there? Are you changing your mind about accepting him?"

"No! That was...an accident. He was rubbing my feet, and one thing led to another when my guard was down."

"I thought that might have been the case, which is why I'd interrupted. But are you sure you want to keep fighting it? I could smell your attraction. You liked it. A lot."

If she knew it, then so did Bennett.

My stomach dipped at the thought.

CHAPTER TWENTY-ONE

I ONCE AGAIN DEBATED HOW much to tell Miranda and decided that, with her nose, I wouldn't be giving much away by being honest.

"The problem has never been my attraction to Bennett. It's about leaving the cage they put me in and finding my freedom."

"That sounds a bit dramatic."

I paused and looked at her. "Do you remember how I reacted when you pinned me to the door?"

She frowned a little. "You didn't really react at all. No fear. Just… you. Are you trying to make me feel guilty about that? Because it's working."

"Don't feel guilty. Your response was the reminder I needed. The people around me now aren't human, and I can't protect myself in the same way I'd been protecting myself. It was a reminder not to be complacent. If you'd been human, that move would have given me the upper hand.

"Now, start asking yourself the right questions. How did the very human Wulf Princess, who'd been pampered her whole life and sent to one of the best all-girl boarding schools in the country, know that move? Or better yet, why did she know that move? Why hadn't she been afraid when pinned to the door?"

Miranda's frown had grown deeper with each question. "What did the little Wulf Princess endure at that school?"

"Hell. Pure and simple. The people who tormented me knew exactly when to let up so I wouldn't be marked in an unexplainable way or, worse, die. So I got smarter, stronger, and faster to fight back. Obviously, not strong or fast enough to fight one of you."

"Do the Wulfs know?"

"They know as much as you do now. And they know my time at school is why I want to leave. That's all, though. I haven't given specifics or names."

"Why not?"

"Because revenge won't absolve them of their role in my hell. It won't absolve Bennett for putting me there and never once listening to my pleas to come home."

"Damn." She looked back at the Wulf building. "What are you going to do then?"

"Leave for college this fall. Bennett plans on forcing me to live in an apartment with him unless I can do three things. Hold his hand. Hug him. Kiss him. Without a hint of fear. And apparently, I have to initiate while awake."

"He's smart. Look at how you let your guard down for a foot rub."

"Not as smart as he thinks. Like I said, rejecting the mate bond is my last resort. I'd rather walk away without sleeping with him. But if that's what ends up happening…" I shrugged.

"Are you sure you'd be able to?"

"Why wouldn't I? I know exactly what it's like to be under his thumb. Why would I want a life like that?"

She started walking again, but slower.

"So you think mated life would be another cage?"

"One with less abuse…unless the sex is rough; then maybe just a different kind of abuse."

She breathed out another curse and looked off in the distance.

"Have you talked to Bennett about this?"

"Yep. He got me a car to prove I was free. Then he found reasonable explanations for driving me everywhere until he finally just took away the keys. He's either blind, stupid, or manipulative. I'm going with the latter because I've been pretty vocal about how I feel."

"You might be right, but I think it's out of desperation to be close to you."

"His need for me is his problem, not mine."

"True, I guess." She sighed and shook her head. "His life would be a lot easier if he'd just fall for one of us."

"Exactly. One of you would never resist him like I am. You'd smell his lust and be doing a bareback lap dance in his office five times a day. From me, he gets throat punches, nose bleeds, yelling, and 'Go away, Bennett.' I'm starting to think he's got a rejection fetish or something."

"Maybe. Did you actually give him a bloody nose?"

"Accidentally. Don't startle me. Some things can't be unprogrammed. At least, not in a few weeks. And I almost broke my hand hitting him, which just makes me more mad at him. He could have dodged."

She chuckled.

When we reached the end of the block, we turned around and headed back.

"So what are you going to do?" she asked.

"I don't know."

"Yes, you do. You already know what he's trying to do, so turn the tables. Hold his hand on the way home, then give him a hug and a kiss goodnight. There's no point in avoiding him anymore, now that he's already smelled that he physically turns you on. Meet all three of his requirements then tell him he doesn't need to move with you this fall."

"Shouldn't I wait until the last minute to do that?"

"No. Waiting will give him hope. Doing it now, especially after what happened, will be more of a reality slap. Yes, you're attracted, but not enough to give up your dreams."

I thought about what she was saying all the way back to the building.

Bennett was waiting for me by the parking garage elevator. He had my dress draped over one arm and my shopping bag in the other. I glanced at the time. He wanted to leave forty minutes early? Fine by me.

"Thanks for the walk and the talk," I said to Miranda.

"Anytime. Good luck."

I walked over to Bennett.

"How can I hold your hand when both of them are full?"

His surprise and the way he quickly switched the bag to the other hand were almost comical. I took his hand, holding it and hating the way my racing heart gave away just how much I liked it.

When we got into the elevator, I pushed the button without releasing him. His thumb began to move against my skin. Little circles that felt good and made my heart skip a beat.

At the car, I checked the time.

"If I let go of your hand now, does that restart the timer, or can we pause while you put that stuff away and continue in the car until the time is up? Did we establish a goal time?"

The circling thumb stilled, and his mask slipped into place as I stared up at him.

"Why are you holding my hand, Wrenly?"

"It's the first condition to leave for college without you following me. Why else would I be holding your hand?"

He let out a slow, measured breath. "Five minutes and it starts over when you let go. No matter the reason."

"Okay." I checked the time. "We're not in a rush, right? We can wait two minutes."

He let go of my hand and opened the door for me.

"Get in, Wrenly."

I'd hurt him. On purpose. And I refused to let myself feel bad about it, even when I wanted to, because then he'd know, and I'd never be free.

Harden your heart, Wren. Life is mean. And you'll only survive if you're meaner.

After laying my dress in the back, he got in and kept his hands firmly on the steering wheel all the way home. I tried holding his hand again once we were in the house, but he said he had work to do and wouldn't eat dinner with me.

His retreat didn't surprise me. He'd regroup and be back.

However, he left me alone the remainder of the night. I ate dinner by myself and finished all my schoolwork. Bored, I messaged Sophia.

Me: Want to meet up for lunch again next week?
Sophia: How about this Saturday at my uncle's club? You need to get out and have some fun.
Me: Saturday won't work. I'm already committed to a charity dinner.
Sophia: That sounds...boring?
Me: It probably will be. But I promised.
Sophia: Okay. Lunch next week it is. Does Tuesday work for you?
Me: Yep!
Sophia: I'll find somewhere nice and let you know.

I liked her last message and got ready for bed. Bennett still hadn't shown up by the time I'd started dozing off.

In the morning, I woke up alone, but the spot next to me was warm.

What a chicken.

Breakfast was waiting for me on the table, along with a note saying that I didn't need to head into the office. Milo would take me into the city in an hour to meet up with Miranda for a spa day.

Me: Why did you leave without me? Don't I get a say in what I do? What if I don't want a spa day?
Bennett: Message Miranda to cancel. It was her idea.

I didn't text her, I called.

"Hey, friend," she answered. "I'm so excited for today."

"He's avoiding me."

"What?"

"Bennett. He knows that I'm trying to meet his criteria, so he's avoiding me. Did you instigate this spa day, or did he?"

"He messaged me last night, asking if you needed anything else for Saturday. I said your hair could use a trim and that you might benefit from a makeup tutorial since you never wear any. He told me to make it happen and that we could go during our work hours. I said you seemed stressed and might like a massage. Honestly, I was trying to get away with as much as we could. You seemed like you didn't mind skipping out of work."

"I don't. But now that I'm committed, I just want to get this part over with."

She chuckled.

"He's taking you to the charity auction on Saturday. Let him run while he can. You'll have four hours with him."

"I don't want to hold his hand in a public setting."

"What about the kissing and hugging?"

"What do you think?"

She laughed again. "Get ready for some relaxation. You need it."

I OPENED THE ENTRY DOOR, grateful that the second day with Miranda hadn't been anything like the first one. A full spa day had been as relaxing as she'd promised. First, she'd insisted that I needed a makeup education session beforehand due to my lack of skills. So, I'd impressed both the cosmetologist and Miranda by artfully transforming my face with an artistically sickly-looking contouring.

The memory of Miranda's words, "If you go to that auction in that dress, looking like a shipwreck survivor, Bennett won't be able to save you from me," made me smile as I closed the entry door behind me.

After promising that I understood how to use makeup, I'd let them pick out what they wanted me to apply tomorrow, and we'd moved on to the facial phase of the treatment. It had felt a little weird to have someone laying hands on my face, and I'd almost tapped out when she tried to put a hot cloth over me, but she'd been very nice when I'd said I was too claustrophobic to have my face covered like that and had switched up her method. The scalp massage had helped calm me down again.

The beautician had worked wonders on my hair after. I had highlights that made me look even more sun-kissed than my naturally light brown hair, and the beautician had put something in it that made it feel incredibly soft.

Through it all, we'd been given restorative drinks and snacks.

The finale of the day had been the most amazing massage. So amazing that I'd already booked another appointment to repeat. The masseur's hands had found and eliminated all tension in my body. Why hadn't I been getting those all along? Oh, right…locked up in an all-girl school.

Stupid, Bennett.

At least I was a complete puddle of well-fed relaxation, now. I climbed the stairs with only one thought on my mind—my bed.

I wasn't paying attention to the top of the stairs as I plodded upward. My eyes were on my feet, and my brain had a flickering vacancy sign in it. How else could I have missed the presence of a fully grown man standing in my path?

My forehead connected with his chest at a slow speed, so I only bounced back a little. But at the top of the stairs. My eyes went wide.

As I tipped back, I grabbed his suit jacket. His arm wrapped around my waist, and his lips curved into a sexy smile that melted my insides as our torsos connected.

Adrenaline from the almost fall cleared the post-massage brain fog, and I saw the opportunity for what it was. With a little hop, I jumped up and wrapped my legs around his waist.

His humor vanished.

"Wrenly."

I darted in for a kiss and found myself on my feet, listening to the thunder of his steps down the stairs.

"Chicken!" I yelled after him.

Amused rather than annoyed, I shook my head and continued to my room. My phone buzzed as I closed the door.

Bennett: Take a shower before bed. I can smell another man on you.

Me: I'll do what I want.

Me: And of course you can smell him. He touched me ALL over.

Something crashed downstairs.

Keeping my man-scented clothes on, I hurried to get under the covers and was grinning as I passed out.

"Why can't you see I'm going crazy?"

The soft murmur of Bennett's voice floated into my semi-sleep awareness as he held me from behind.

"I thought I could give you everything you wanted, but everything I gave you only hurt you. You don't want me to make up for it. You just want me to leave." His hold tightened. "If that were an option, I'd give it to you, Wrenly. I'd give you anything. But I'm too far gone for that." He growled. "I hate that you smell like another male."

Still mostly asleep and needing to reposition, I rolled over, facing him, and wrapped my arm around his waist.

"Why can't you do this while you're awake?" His fingers carefully brushed back the hair from my forehead. "You own me, Wrenly. Every thought. Every action. It all revolves around you. Please give me a chance to prove I can be a good mate."

Tiredly shifting my hand up his chest, I covered his mouth.

"Shhh. Sleep."

He removed my hand, hugged me closer, and kissed the top of my head.

"I will."

I woke up alone, but the spot next to me was still warm, so he hadn't been gone long. Lounging in bed, I thought about what Bennett had said last night. He'd acknowledged what I'd wanted but said leaving me wasn't an option. Did that mean he wasn't going to honor the deal he'd made if I met his conditions or that he would do whatever he needed to do to ensure I didn't meet them?

You own me, Wrenly.

My guess was that it was the latter. So I'd need to trick him into helping me meet those conditions. How?

Lost in thought, I reached for my phone and checked the messages.

Miranda: Let me know if you want me to come over and help you get ready.
Me: Do you still doubt my makeup skills?

Bennett: Aiden and Karter haven't heard from you in a while and are worried. Did they do something to upset you?

Me: Yes, tell them they should keep enjoying their best lives and that I hope they mistake a Rottweiler for their mates when they're drunk.

Bennett: I have breakfast ready if you're hungry.

Me: I want to go for a run first. Alone.

Bennett: Okay.

Miranda: Yes.

Me: I'll send a picture before I leave and pack my makeup bag. If you don't like it, you can crash the party to fix it.

Miranda: Interrupt your evening with Bennett and risk my raise? We're both smart enough to know how that will end. Still send me a pic!

Shaking my head at her, I got out of bed and changed into something more comfortable for running.

Bennett was waiting for me in the kitchen with a piece of toast slathered with peanut butter. He looked...twitchy. His hair was neatly styled. He wore what he considered leisure clothes—dress pants and a T-shirt. But something about the look in his eyes was off as I accepted the toast and took a bite.

"What are the chances you'll return hurt again if you run?" he asked as I turned around to leave.

I paused, considering the question as I tried to swallow the peanut butter.

Once I could speak, I glanced back at him. "If?"

"I know you never actually promised not to run alone after Storm tripped you, so I was hoping you'd consider making a deal with me."

"What kind of deal?" I asked, curious what he thought he could offer me.

"I pay for your school. No other strings attached to this deal. Let me watch over you on every run in exchange for your tuition fully paid."

"At the school of my choice?" I asked.

"The school of your choice."

He'd actually found something I might have wanted…if I had any trust in him to keep his word, which I didn't.

"Counteroffer. You give me my bankbook and deposit fifty dollars each time we run together."

He looked down at the floor, something he seemed to do when he didn't like what I said and needed a moment to think instead of react. I saw his distraction as an opportunity.

You own me, Wrenly.

Closing the distance between us, I held my toast to the side with one hand and set my other hand on his chest. He froze, and his gaze flew to mine as I looked up at him with my saddest, most pleading, innocent expression. I'd spent hours practicing expressions and knew it was a good one. But I hadn't thought I'd ever use it on Bennett or that it would actually work on him.

I watched him crumble.

His hands came up to cup my face as desperation filled his gaze.

"I'll pay," he said hoarsely. "Anything you want."

"The bankbook too?"

His expression shifted, looking more tortured.

"Why do you want the bankbook if I'm willing to pay your tuition?"

Frustration got the better of me, and I pushed away from him. He caught my hand and pulled it back to his chest.

"Keep playing your game with me, Wrenly," he said.

I was about to say something aggressively rude when he added, "I'll give you another five grand."

"Why?"

"You've never shown me the softer, coaxing Wrenly before. I want to see where this goes."

I set aside my toast and debated my next move while he studied me.

"Do you know how hard it is to control my temper around you?" I asked finally. "I've told you so many times what I want. Freedom. Yet, it's what you keep denying me. Why can't I access the money I'm earning? What do you think I'm going to do with it? Is it that bad for me to want to be in control of paying my own tuition?"

He groaned, closed his eyes, and set his forehead against mine. He breathed in deeply, and his fingers teased my hairline. Then he was holding my face firmly and bringing his lips toward mine.

My heart slammed into overdrive. I gripped his wrists as I tried to pull free from his hold.

He stopped advancing and opened his eyes. We were too close for me to focus properly, and I was too panicked.

"When are you going to stop fearing me?"

I kicked his shin. It hurt like a bitch, but at least he grunted and released me. I grabbed my toast, turned on my heel, and started for the front door.

"Five hundred dollars cash for letting me follow you today."

His words stopped me.

"You give me the cash before the dinner, or I don't go tonight."

"Deal."

Taking another bite of my toast, I continued toward the front door. Bennett followed.

I didn't hate that he was with me. But there were plenty of other things that I did hate. That he was even needed. That I still lived in the big house. That I couldn't escape yet.

As far as runs went, it was a decent one once we left Alpine Run. I set an aggressive pace—for me, not for Bennett—and I didn't turn around until we hit five miles. When I saw the gate ahead, I slowed to a jog then walked back to the house.

"Do you usually run ten miles?" Bennett asked.

"I try to get a longer run in at least once a week," I said, stretching as I removed my shoes. "Usually, three to five miles is enough. Depends on how much time I have."

"What do you usually eat after a long run?"

"Anything works."

"Over-easy eggs, hash browns, and bacon sound good?"

As I straightened, I nodded. "Really good."

"It'll be ready by the time you're done with your shower."

The endorphins from the run that kept me mellow lasted through the shower and to the dining table, where breakfast and Bennett waited. He hadn't showered or changed, but he hadn't been sweaty like I had.

Five one-hundred-dollar bills were fanned out next to my plate as he held out my chair for me.

CHAPTER TWENTY-TWO

THIS TIME, I sat without comment, letting him push my chair in as I pocketed the cash. He took the seat across from me.

"Do you have any other plans before we need to leave?" Bennett asked.

"Not really. Just working on the latest assignment for the summer class I'm taking."

"Miranda mentioned that she offered to help you get ready. If you'd like her help, she's welcome here."

I opened my mouth, ready to say that Storm would be willing to come over too, but stopped myself in time. Today, I needed to switch up my game so he wouldn't avoid me. At least, not yet. As he'd pointed out this morning, I'd never exposed him to the coaxing side of me. If I played my hand right now, he'd be more willing to cut the night short later, and I'd be in bed before my feet hurt.

"I can manage putting on a dress and makeup on my own," I said. "It won't take me long to get ready. Once I'm done with my assignment, I'll still have a few hours if you want to do something."

He paused with his fork partway to his mouth, and when he looked at me, his pupils were spasming like crazy.

"Or not," I said quickly. "Not a big deal."

"I want to do something."

"Okay." I kept eating my food as if indifferent to the idea while he stared at me.

Several minutes passed before he resumed eating.

I waited until I finished to say, "There's a movie I've been wanting to watch if you're interested later." I picked up my plate. "I'll let you know at lunch how much more time I'll need."

He left me alone in my room until noon. I'd drafted, edited, and completed a plagiarism check on my paper before he knocked on the door.

"Come in."

He opened the door.

I was on my stomach on my bed with the laptop in front of me. Fully clothed. Nothing hanging out. But he was staring at me like I was naked as I idly swung my feet in the air behind me.

You own me, Wrenly.

I decided to lean into that ownership a little. Although I'd never flirted with a guy, I knew what to do and what not to do...for the most part. Openly flirting with Bennett was out. It would tip him off that I was up to something and really wasn't necessary. With him, all I needed to do was be non-confrontational and...feminine.

Ridiculous. But easy enough to manage.

Softening my expression with a hint of concern, I sat up.

"You all right? Is lunch done?"

He swallowed hard as I stood and walked toward him. His pupils were blown so wide that I couldn't see any brown left, and I hadn't even really done anything yet.

Putting a little pout on, I said, "I hope you made me something good. I'm starving."

He started to shake. Not just his hands this time but his whole body.

I froze. Sudden movements around stressed-out shifters were a bad idea. Always.

He closed his eyes and breathed deeply.

"Your scent. It's…" Another round of tremors coursed through him. "There's no fear."

"There's about to be."

His eyes snapped open. "Come here, Wrenly."

"I don't think that's a good idea."

"You can try whatever you want. Hold my hand. Hug me. Kiss me."

"I'm going to take a rain check on all of the above. My self-preservation has kicked in."

His slow smile made my insides feel like they were doing back flips, and my pulse skyrocketed.

"Do you want to run, Wrenly?"

He shifted his weight, crouching ever so slightly like he was getting ready to spring.

"No. I won't run. I'll keep my word. On all of it, Bennett. Do you know what that means? I'll do exactly what I said I would do. Are you sure you're ready to be rejected?"

The smile left his expression.

"I thought you wanted to win me over," I said, pressing my point. "This isn't winning me over. This makes me want to disappear from your world forever."

He jerked like I'd hit him, and the tension left his body. Straightening, his gaze swept over me, assessing and carrying a hint of sadness.

"I'll go for a run. Wait a few minutes; then come down for lunch."

I nodded and watched him leave. Once he was gone, I let my knees give out and sat on the floor. As I stared at the vacant doorway, I reconsidered my plan.

Perhaps meeting his conditions wasn't the best option. I wasn't sure he would be able to let go once I did what he wanted. I didn't think he was trying to trick me, but rather that he was overestimating his control.

With a shaking hand, I reached for my phone and sent a text to Grandma.

Me: Why am I living alone with Bennett? Is it so he can spend more time with me or because he's not safe to be around?

Grandma: Mostly to spend time with you. Did something happen?

Me: Depends. Do you think Bennett would ever rape me?

Grandma: Never. He would try to persuade you so you're willing. He wouldn't do anything to cause you to reject him. Do you need me to come over?

Me: No. He went for a run. I should be fine.

Grandma: Can I tell him that he scared you enough to ask about this?

I thought about it for a second before replying that she could, grateful that she'd asked permission before just doing it.

Feeling reassured and steadier, I went downstairs. The sandwich he'd made for me was waiting on a plate across the table from his. Staring at it and thinking about how he'd reacted to me, I continued to debate the wisdom of attempting to meet his criteria.

My time at school had taught me a lot about when to hold my ground, when to advance, and when to retreat. Even though I knew the more often a person retreated, the more they tended to lose, I hesitated to advance.

With Bennett, the rules didn't seem to be the same. Sometimes the more I retreated, the more I got. But retreating now wouldn't prove that I was able to take care of myself...that I didn't need him. And I definitely needed to prove I was self-sufficient, stable, and able to survive on my own. After all my panic attacks and meltdowns, he was already questioning my sanity.

Maybe that was the key. I needed to push Bennett until he questioned his own sanity. Could I walk the line and survive? There was only one way to find out.

Be a menace, Wrenly. Keep them guessing, I silently told myself as I picked up his sandwich.

I licked the top of it, turned it over, and licked the bottom. Licking bread was a textural horror, but I endured. Lifting the bread, I licked the sliced chicken for good measure. Then, I put his sandwich back on his plate and took mine to my room.

While eating and proofreading my paper with my door open, I listened for his return. It didn't take long. Fifteen minutes later, I heard a thump downstairs. I closed my laptop and sat up to watch the door.

He appeared a few seconds later, looking just as wild as when he'd left.

"Thank you for the sandwich," I said.

His gaze searched mine as he inhaled deeply.

"Do you feel better?" he asked.

"What do you mean?"

"Why did I taste you on my sandwich?"

"Because you're too unstable to try to kiss directly."

His hands gripped the doorframe, and I heard the wood crackle under the pressure.

"It was a kiss? You weren't angry?"

I neither confirmed nor denied it, but I watched him weigh the possibility of both. I could almost hear his mind working.

Was the lick revenge for how he'd pressed me? I had threatened to spit in his lunch, after all.

I saw the moment he decided it wasn't me being petty.

A second later, I was on my back on the bed with Bennett on top of me. His hands threaded through mine over my head as he nuzzled my neck, nipping and licking.

I'd been prepared for this kind of reaction from him, but not my response to it. He was short-circuiting rational thought with just his mouth. Danger signals fired as fast as the pleasure ones, and in the storm, I could only feel it all. Each swipe of his tongue. Each brush of his lips. Each groan and growl.

I knew I was in trouble. I needed to stop him. But his grip had no give. Or maybe I had no strength. Why did his mouth on my skin feel so good?

"Bennett…"

He groaned and lightly bit the side of my neck. A sound escaped me. He growled and lifted his head to meet my gaze.

His tremors shook the whole bed as he inhaled deeply.

"Finally."

His gaze dipped to my mouth, and he started closing the distance. How much I craved to feel his lips against me worried me enough to think rationally. If I didn't control the situation, I would never be able to leave.

Swallowing hard, I said, "Start the timer, Bennett."

He jerked back, and I watched the blind lust dissipate from his gaze.

"What?"

"I'm holding your hands without fear, and we're about to kiss. Set a timer. We should probably talk about what defines a hug, too. I feel like this should count since our bodies are—"

He got off of me like I was a hot coal and ran his hand through his hair in agitation.

"Do you know how frustrating you are?"

I sat up. "Yeah. It's a skill I've worked hard to hone."

He turned his head to glare at me, and I shrugged.

"Keep in mind who started this and who set the rules. I'm just going with the flow. Now, do you still want to watch a movie, or should we forget it?"

He held out a hand with a surly expression, but showed no aggression.

Smiling, I took it and stood, believing I'd won the round.

That was a mistake.

He pulled me into his arms and hugged me close, dipping his head to the same side of my neck that he'd been kissing. A zing of… something snapped through me, putting me right back into the same place as where he'd left me.

Pulse racing, barely able to breathe, I gripped his forearms for support as his hands caged my sides, keeping me upright.

He growled and licked my skin like I'd licked his sandwich.

I shivered.

"Why are you fighting this? Me?"

Sanity returned.

"I can smell how much you—"

"Is the timer running? Does this count as a hug?"

He growled in frustration and pulled back to glare at me.

"I'm not the problem, Bennett. You are. You're not following the rules *you* set for the deal we made."

"Why does everything have to be a deal?"

"Because that's the only way for me to fight for the life I want to live," I said, throwing his words back at him. "And next time you do anything without starting a timer, I'm going to be rude. Probably with a knee. Definitely with a fist. Are we clear?"

He pulled his lips back in a silent snarl that I didn't think was entirely directed at me, but more at the situation and my stubbornness.

"I think I need Miranda's help getting ready after all."

He took a deep breath and slowly let it out. "No. I'm okay. We're okay. Let's watch a movie."

He reached for my hand and started threading his fingers through mine. He immediately let go with another scowl. I wanted to grin at the fact that he was listening for a change.

"I won't take what you aren't willing to give," he said, catching the look on my face. "Ever, Wrenly."

"Thank you."

We settled in on the couch downstairs and started the movie. He didn't try to hold my hand or hug me, but he did tug my feet into his lap. Since the last foot rub had been nice and I knew I'd torture my feet later with heels, I allowed it as I focused on the movie.

His fingers melted the tension I didn't know I carried, and I found myself relaxing in a way I'd never managed before, not even while running. My heart gave an odd skipped-beat thump, and I lifted my hand to rub my chest.

"Are you all right?" Bennett asked.

"Yeah. Just a weird heartbeat."

His hand drifted up to my calf, rubbing the muscle there. It felt so damn good. He slowly worked his way up to my knee, then returned to my Achilles to work the path up a second time. His fingers feathered over the skin behind my knee when he reached the top.

My heart gave another odd skipped-beat thump.

Without looking away from the movie, I said, "Don't make me break a toe trying to kick you in the face."

He didn't say anything as he removed his touch and switched to my other foot.

By the time the movie ended, my legs were pudding, and Bennett's fingers had teased every inch of skin behind both knees. Complete relaxation in exchange for some roaming fingers felt like a fair trade.

I knew Bennett didn't mind. I could feel the tremble in his fingers as they skated over my skin.

"Thank you for watching a movie with me," I said. "And for the foot massage."

"You're welcome."

I attempted to lift my legs from his lap, but he caught my ankles and tugged so hard that I slid down from my reclined position to lying flat. He was on top of me a second later, his pupils completely dilated and a wild look in his eyes.

"Are you taking, or are you timing?" I asked.

"Why are those my only two options? Why can't you just give in, Wrenly?"

"Because I've given enough, remember? Would you like to see the grease burn on my inner thigh?"

He jerked again. "Yes."

Suddenly, he was kneeling between my legs and grabbing the waistband of my shorts.

"It wasn't an invitation to be pervy, Bennett," I said, grabbing the material to keep it in place.

"Show me, Wrenly."

"No!" I planted a foot in his chest and pushed hard. He didn't budge, but my shorts were starting to. Lifting my foot, I kicked him in the face with my heel.

He grunted, and his head moved. More than that, I heard a crunch. The second his hands left my shorts, I barrel rolled off the couch, sprang to my feet, and turned to face him with my hands up and fisted.

He stared at me, blood dripping from his nose onto the couch. He didn't make any move to come at me.

"'I won't take what you aren't willing to give, Wrenly. Ever.' Remember? You said it two hours ago, you ass."

His shoulders moved with the depth of his sigh.

"I wasn't trying to take anything, Wrenly. You asked if I wanted to see the burn, and I said yes. If you don't want to show me the burn, then at least tell me how it happened."

I lowered my fists. "In the school kitchen during a power outage. They chased me in there before I knew...anything. They were good at what they did. Perfectly planned and perfectly arranged. It's a small burn. A lesson and a promise to know my place, nothing worth reporting, mostly because I knew the staff wouldn't believe me, and reporting it wouldn't change anything. I still wouldn't be allowed to come home because I had a brother who hated me and parents who were trying to play both sides."

He closed his eyes, and I could see him struggling.

"Do you understand yet, Bennett? I've earned my freedom already. I survived. Whatever conditions you put on me now, I'll either meet them or fight you until my last breath because I'm done. Done giving. Done being afraid. Just done."

He nodded and opened his eyes. I saw his anguish and hated that I felt even a hint of compassion.

"What if you don't have to do anything but be happy? That's all I want for you, Wrenly."

"Then set me free."

His gaze swept over me as he slowly stood.

"I can't. Not without trying to show you how I can make your life better."

"Like sending me away to school."

He ran his hands through his hair again, showing his frustration.

"Shifters are just like humans. We make mistakes too. But I'm learning, Wrenly. I promise I am. Give me names, and we can take hugging off the list."

"Ha! No deal."

"Kissing then."

"No way. I already gave the only name I'm willing to give."

He snarled, spun on his heel, and strode away from me.

"We leave in an hour," he called over his shoulder.

I checked the time. An hour was too early, but I didn't care. I planned to be a pain in his ass the whole time.

BENNETT GLANCED at me again as he pulled up to the event entrance.

"Wait for me to open the door," he said as he put the car in Park.

"You got it, boss."

He growled softly and got out as the valet jogged over.

"I've got her. Just park the car." He threw the keys at the guy and was at my door a second later.

His eyes locked on me as he offered his hand to help me out. I needed it. The dress Miranda picked out for me had a long skirt with a thigh slit so my shoes would be visible as I walked. It almost posed a potential trip hazard when transitioning from a sitting to a standing position. But I was pretty. Miranda had taste.

Gripping his fingers with one hand and holding the skirt out of the way with the other, I stood with well-practiced grace. Bennett's gaze raked over me hungrily as I moved out of the way so he could close the door.

When he tucked my hand into the crock of his arm, his hands were shaking again. I glanced at him and found his gaze had dipped to my bare shoulders and the thin, one-inch scar often hidden by my sports bras.

"If you do anything inappropriate here, the deal we made to stay 'til the end is off," I said.

"Tell me how you got that."

"A knife fight."

His gaze flew to mine, and I grinned as he inhaled slowly to see if I was lying. I wasn't, but it wasn't as scary as it sounded. The knife had been my own when I'd been practicing throwing it. It'd slipped from my fingers, and that'd been an important lesson in my quest to learn to throw a knife accurately. A skill that had come in handy to turn the tables a few times.

I started walking, dragging him toward the entrance of the well-lit venue as his shaking continued.

"Wrenly, I need—"

"Therapy? A one-way ticket to Antarctica? A rabies vaccine?"

His shaking stopped, and he shot me an annoyed glance. I practiced my polite yet bored smile. His annoyance turned to a scowl.

"Don't be a baby. Let's get this magical night over with so I can take off these heels. How long is this torture session again?"

"Four hours once it starts. We're a little early."

"Oh, joy."

At the entrance, he handed over his invitation. The woman welcomed us and passed the invitation to a waiting server, who led us through the carpeted welcome area and into a large room filled with round tables set with crystal stemware and gold flatware. Near the front of the room, additional tables and jacketed individuals waited next to easels displaying pictures of various items, including jewelry and paintings.

"This is your table, Mr. Wulf," the man said, showing us to one of the round ones near the front. "You're welcome to view the auction items and mingle before the dinner starts."

"Thank you," Bennett said.

I waited until the man went away to say, "Mingling? Does he want you to scare everyone away?"

Bennett frowned at me.

"Yep. That right there. Your business smile needs work. Like this." I smiled warmly. "It's so good to see you, Bennett. What have you been up to lately? Please tell me not just work. You need to visit the Maldives soon. It was magical. I discovered this little place that served the best drinks. Speaking of, be a dear and fetch me some champagne."

While I spoke, his shaking disappeared, and his stoic mask slipped into place.

"One glass," he said.

"Two. We agreed. Or you keep them coming and let me get tipsy so my guard is down."

I saw a glimmer of concern in his gaze. "If you lower your guard to let me in, I don't want it to be because of alcohol."

I shrugged indifferently. "The result will be the same either way."

He sighed, and I tucked my arm in his.

"Let's get my drink."

We returned to the welcome entry, and Bennett snagged a flute from a server and handed it to me. More people were being led inside by the servers, and others were gathering. One of the incoming guests caught sight of Bennett, clapped the server on the back, and left the man standing there as he strode over to us.

"Bennett, I'm glad you made it tonight." The man's gaze slipped to me. "And you, little one, have been the center of this man's stories since I met him. It's nice to finally meet you, Wrenly. You're more stunning in person than the pictures he carries around."

He didn't offer a hand in greeting but tucked both into his pockets as he grinned at me.

I glanced at Bennett. "A friend?"

"This is Drokonnen Steele. We met when I was away at school. And, yes, he's a friend on most days."

The man snorted. "People who don't know me call me Drokonnen. The ones who think they do call me Drake. Friends call me Konni, with a K."

"Are you suggesting I call you Konni?" I asked.

"No," Bennett said at the same time Konni nodded.

"Still moody, I see. I thought bringing your moonlight mate home would fix that." He winked at me.

"What's a moonlight mate?" I asked.

"A mate he's loved since he was old enough to love. His first and only crush."

My heart did that odd skip beat again.

"Potential mate," I said, handing my drink to Bennett. "I'm going to the bathroom. Don't follow me."

Konni's laughter sounded behind me, along with Bennett's answering growl as I walked away.

CHAPTER TWENTY-THREE

W<small>EAVING MY WAY THROUGH PEOPLE</small>, I found the restroom. Another woman was in there applying lipstick. I closed myself into a stall while replaying the conversation in my head.

Bennett had pictures of me? As in plural? And what stories did he have to tell? He'd spent maybe six months around me before he left.

When I left the stall, the woman was putting away her lipstick. How much lipstick did a person need? She smiled at me in the mirror.

"Zellon's, right? The earrings?"

I thought back to my day of shopping torture with Miranda and nodded.

"Beautiful pieces. I love their work. I believe they have several in the auction tonight. Will you be bidding?"

I flashed my practiced smile. "Anything to help raise the charity funds, right?"

Her smile turned a little chillier even as she agreed.

I watched her leave, then turned to face the sink to wash my hands. My reflection caught my eye. I didn't look like myself with my makeup done. Covering my freckles and contouring my features to look as high-end as I'd known this place would be was a mistake, especially with the dress and jewelry Miranda picked out. The woman obviously thought I was competition for whatever jewelry she had her eye on here.

When I emerged from the bathroom, the size of the crowd in the welcome area had almost doubled. Bennett and his friend stood in the same place, but they'd turned to watch the restroom doors.

I was so focused on Bennett's overprotective ridiculousness that I didn't notice Lindi until she stepped in front of me. Another woman I didn't recognize was with her.

"Wrenly? Are you sure you're in the right place?" Lindi's gaze swept down my length. "And in the right clothes?"

The gown Miranda selected might have been "off the rack," but it was exquisite with beaded embellishments and outshone what Lindi was wearing.

"Did you need something, Lindi? Makeup tips, maybe? You have a little lipstick on your teeth."

Her fake humor vanished, and her stare hardened.

"Do you even know who you're talking to?" the woman next to her asked with a condemning tone.

"A friend. Right, Lindi? Isn't that why Bennett invited you to lunch?"

Lindi's brittle expression softened It always amazed me how she could slide into the "sweet girl" role so quickly.

"I meant to ask how you're acquainted with Bennett Wulf. Are you one of the scholarship recipients the Wulf Foundation for the Underprivileged supports?"

I knew for a fact there wasn't such a foundation, thanks to all the expenses and reports I'd reviewed since coming home.

"A charity recipient?" *If only I were so lucky,* I thought. "My connection to the Wulfs is much closer than that. Why else would Bennett hand over his credit card to me? By the way, do you like my earrings? They're from Zellon's. One of a kind. Spent a fortune on them. Where did you get yours again?"

Did I enjoy pulling a rich person flex on Lindi? Absolutely. I didn't hate money. Money was nice. It made things easier. What I hated was pretentiousness and fakeness. The boarding school had been filled with people like that, people who'd all followed Lindi. Once I'd known Mom and Dad would never let me come home, I'd understood any flex I made at school would be pointless and only make me a bigger target as the unwanted and abandoned foster kid—the charity case.

But that wasn't the case anymore.

"One word from me and you'll be kicked out of here," Lindi said.

"Doubtful. We both know the Shane name doesn't carry nearly as much weight as the Wulfs, the Steeles, and the Zellons here. But, by all means, give it a try."

"Is there a problem?" Bennett asked from behind her.

Lindi turned to smile at him. "Nothing that can't be resolved later. It's nice to see you again, Mr. Wulf. I saw we're assigned to a nearby table. I look forward to talking to you some more later." She nodded at me, then left with her friend.

I snagged the champagne Bennett was still holding and drained it. He frowned at me. Konni, who'd tagged along with him, grinned as he looked between us.

"I think I'll need to change my seat. Tonight is looking to be very entertaining."

"How do you know I'm already planning on a second glass to numb the pain of enduring a four-hour charity dinner?"

Konni laughed and clapped Bennett on the back. "She's everything you said she was."

"I'll tell you what I think about Bennett, too, if you get me another glass," I said, holding out my empty one.

"As you wish, princess." He took my glass and left.

"He won't be back, will he?" I said, looking at Bennett.

"He will. What were you saying to Lindi? I caught the last bit about whose name carries more weight, but not what led to it."

"She was questioning my relationship with the Wulfs. I deliberately provoked her. It was a good distraction."

"Tonight I'll prove to you that being associated with the Wulf name isn't all bad. I promise."

He took my hand and wrapped it around his arm.

"Why does it feel like you just cursed me?"

His fingers stroked over mine. "Because I made the wrong choices in the past that hurt you and lost your trust. I'll show you I can do better."

I didn't try contradicting him.

He pulled out my chair for me when we reached the table, and his fingers grazed my neck. I looked up at him.

"That's not better; that's worse."

He sighed and sat to my right, moving his chair closer to mine.

Konni approached with another glass of champagne. Bennett said something under his breath as he handed it to me.

"Relax," Konni said, taking the seat to my left. "She's smart enough to understand the risk of getting drunk around you." Konni looked at me. "One giggle, and you'd be his, am I right?"

I lifted my glass in a silent toast. "Here's to never laughing again."

"Ouch. She's a tough one."

"You have no idea," Bennett said moodily. "I look forward to the day you find yours so that I can ply her with drinks for you."

Konni grinned as I sipped my second glass. It helped take the edge off, and I was able to people-watch as the room slowly filled. Konni gave a quiet commentary, which was entertaining, while Bennett's moody scowl deepened.

"I thought we were here to mingle," I said when I finished the second glass. "People are avoiding you because of your face."

Konni belted out a laugh. "His face usually draws unwanted attention, not repels it."

As if his words summoned her, Lindi appeared next to Bennett and set her hand on his shoulder. He reached up, likely to push her hand away, but her words stopped him.

"I remembered something, if you have a moment to speak privately."

He glanced at me, his mask fully in place now. I just grinned at him, knowing full well that she wouldn't tell him anything important, which would only push his temper. When I gave no other reaction, he briefly scowled at me, then stood, dislodging Lindi's touch.

"After you," he said, motioning to the bar.

I watched them walk away with a smirk.

"I'd offer to get you another drink to know what you're thinking right now, but he'd try to kill me," Konni said.

"Try?" I asked, glancing at him. "Are you an alpha too? Visiting the Wulf territory in search of a mate?"

"Not visiting. Motan is my home. And like all of my kind, I'm always searching for the keeper of my heart."

I studied Konni. "You're not a wolf shifter, are you?"

"No."

"Ah."

"Just ah?"

I shrugged. "What other reaction should I give?"

"Fear? Curiosity?"

"Bennett trusts you enough to leave me alone with you, so I have nothing to fear. And curiosity is for those who are interested. I'm not."

He clapped a hand to his chest even as he grinned at me.

"I'm wounded."

"Doubtful."

"Will you tell me what you were thinking anyway? Think of it as a favor owed. Within reason. I won't cosh your mate on the head when he's annoying, but anyone else is acceptable."

I decided Konni might just be a friend, like Miranda.

"Lindi and I went to school together. Bennett knows things happened to me at the school, so he's trying to find out from Lindi. It won't work, though. She'll evade direct answers, and he'll walk away from her, frustrated and on edge. He and I have a deal that I have to stay until the end of the night. I'm banking on leaving early because of him."

"There's a lot in here to unpack."

"Oh?"

"What happened to you at school?"

"Abuse. Mental and physical."

"Who abused you?"

"That's the question, isn't it? I believe it's the one who put me in that place. And the ones who didn't listen to me when I pleaded to come home."

Konni's expression lost its humor.

"You blame Bennett."

"Shouldn't I? I was perfectly happy living with the Wulf's, but because of his jealousy after he got home, they sent me to hell."

"So you want him to suffer like you did?"

"No. I just want him to let me go. I want to be free to make my own choices for a change. I can't do any worse than they did."

Konni looked across the room at Bennett, where he was talking to Lindi.

"I don't think you realize how dangerous what you're doing is, Wrenly."

"What do you mean?"

"Not knowing who hurt you will drive him mad. He's already holding onto his sanity by a thread Before you came home, we were meeting almost every night to spar. It was the only thing that was keeping him in check during the day. That and your—"

I studied his guilty expression. "My what?"

"Nothing. Forget I mentioned it."

"I don't think I can. What keeps him in check, Konni?"

He glanced at Bennett. I did the same and saw he was watching us.

"Tell him to tell me," I said, meeting Bennett's gaze from across the room.

Bennett nodded, which drew Lindi's attention. She glanced back at me with a smile that some people might think was kind. I knew better. It held a hidden malice.

"Your scent," Konni said.

"Ah. Yeah, I already found my old uniforms in his closet. He's lucky it wasn't my underwear. I would have killed him."

Konni choked on his laughter.

"Pretty sure your mom would have killed him first."

I hummed an indecisive response, no longer sure who had more of Mom's loyalty.

Over the speakers, someone asked everyone to find their seats for dinner. I glanced at Bennett and Lindi again. She didn't look like she was letting up on her conversation. She even had her phone out and was showing it to him. Whatever it was, it couldn't be good, based on his fisted hands in his pockets and slowly reddening face.

"Are you a betting person, Konni?" I asked softly, not looking away.

"Depends on the odds."

"I'm betting Bennett's considering wrapping his hands around Lindi's neck right now, and she's completely clueless about it. Sucks being human. We don't have the noses you shifters do to smell other people's emotions. If we did, I bet she wouldn't still be talking to him."

"You're probably right on all of it, so I'll pass on betting."

"That wasn't the bet. This is—something bad will happen to me before the end of the night."

I faced Konni and caught his shocked expression.

"Do you think Bennett's going to hurt you?"

Flashing my most innocent smile, I shook my head. "I already know he'd never intentionally hurt me."

"But you think he'll do something that'll unintentionally hurt you?"

I shrugged. "It's happened before. So do you want to take the bet?"

"What are we betting?"

"A bigger favor."

"What's the favor?"

"I think that'll depend on how badly I'm hurt."

He glanced at Bennett again.

"Are you going to hurt yourself, Wrenly?" he asked. "Bennett said you've already threatened it."

"No, I said I hated my life and didn't want to live it anymore. That wasn't a threat, and I don't intend to hurt myself. Ever."

He leaned back in his chair, considering me in silence as other people joined our table.

"You have a deal," he said finally.

The woman on his left leaned forward, curiosity in her gaze.

"Deal? What deals are we making?"

Konni artfully deflected the question and steered the conversation.

Bennett joined us again. I glanced at Lindi, who was smirking at me from her table, like she'd gotten one over on me. But there was no win for her when it came to Bennett. If she admitted she'd been the ringleader of my abuse, she was as good as dead. And no matter what she'd said, it would never distract him from learning more about me, like she wanted.

With a smirk of my own, I looked at Bennett. Whatever she'd told him hadn't been good. He was struggling hard, hiding his tremors with quick, angry movements.

As he sat, I leaned toward him.

"What do you need from me to stay calm?"

His surprised gaze flew to mine.

"You."

I smiled for everyone who might be watching, like Lindi, and stood. With a hand on his shoulder, I turned around and perched on his knee to whisper in his ear. The position meant I was facing Lindi as I spoke.

"Please note my exceptionally cooperative behavior despite the embarrassment I'm feeling by drawing attention to myself." And I was drawing attention. Lindi's gaze narrowed. Nearby, men were chuckling and nudging one another, and women were glancing at me with distaste.

"If we have to leave because you lose control, that's not me breaking our deal. That's on you."

He captured my face when I pulled back from his ear. The brush of his lips against mine was there and gone before I even realized his intent, then he kissed my forehead.

"Thank you," he said loudly enough to be heard by anyone close enough. "You're wise to remind me."

I rose to return to my chair, which he stood to push in for me.

Konni watched everything closely with a question in his gaze, but he didn't ask. He continued to steer the conversation as course after course was served.

Bennett was calmer, but not calm. He didn't talk much and barely ate his food. I stared longingly at the servers who passed with fluted drinks, but knew better than to take one. I was already feeling tipsy, which was why I'd willingly sat on Bennett's knee.

Once everyone finished their meals, the servers set dessert tiers on the tables and moved the picture of the items to the side. The auctioneer walked to the front of the room along with several suited men and a well-dressed woman. She was holding a velvet bust with a necklace that had more precious gems than gold.

The auctioneer explained that it was a necklace from the Zellon collection and stated the opening bid.

Bennett glanced at me. I realized why and wanted to kick him under the table. Instead, I leaned toward him. He obliged by leaning toward me.

"If you think buying something here will help your cause, you're a delusional idiot."

Konni started choking behind me as I pretended to straighten Bennett's tie.

He glowered at me but didn't pull away until I was done. The necklace sold for almost five million. The auctioneer announced the next item while the first one was escorted out. I was bored to tears until a pair of gemmed high heels was brought to the front. The women were staring at them rabidly. Even Lindi.

The corner of my mouth tilted. Bennett caught it and looked confused. I took out my phone rather than whisper.

Me: Rich people are masochists. Heels are bad enough. Why add to it?
Bennett: A show of wealth, I guess. Is there really nothing here that interests you?
Me: The bathroom. Is there an intermission to this thing, or do I just sneak out?

Bennett was still reading my message when the auctioneer announced a short break. The servers converged on the tables, refilling wine glasses as event goers stood.

"Be right back," I said.

I knew what this mass exodus would mean—a long line. So I tried to hustle, but there was no hustle with the number of people present. Out in the welcome area, a line had already formed. Women chatted with the people they knew as they waited. I took my place in line.

Several minutes passed with barely any movement.

"There's another restroom down the east hallway," one of the staff said to the people behind me.

I watched them mass-exodus that way and debated staying or going.

A man with a serving tray caught me staring after them and approached.

"Would you care for—"

I snagged the champagne. "Thanks."

He smiled then leaned in to quietly say, "There's a staff restroom farther down this hallway if you need it."

MELISSA HAAG

"Thanks."

I headed in the direction he'd indicated as I downed the champagne. It was sweeter than the kind Bennett had gotten me and had an odd aftertaste.

Swearing under my breath, I let myself into the staff bathroom and quickly checked the stalls. After verifying they were empty, I sent Bennett a quick text to find me and placed the garbage can in front of the door so I could hear when someone entered.

A wave of dizziness washed over me as I fumbled with my dress and sat.

Fucking Lindi. I was going to kill her.

The garbage can clattered to its side just as I finished.

"No scolding me," I said, sounding slurred to my own ears.

I struggled with the door lock and almost knocked myself over when it finally swung open.

Bennett wasn't waiting for me on the other side. Some random guy dressed in street clothes was.

"Did she pay for rape or murder?" I asked, stumbling toward him.

He grinned, catching me. "It's not rape if you're willing."

"Not willing."

"You will be. Give it a few minutes."

I laughed. "He'll be here before that."

"But you won't."

The guy slapped me hard, bent low, and threw me over his shoulder as my world spun and my cheek throbbed.

I laughed. He spanked my ass hard.

"Shut up."

I did, but not because he told me to. The sting from his hand on my ass wasn't right. It was heating. Spreading. Starting to throb, but not just my butt where he hit me. Everywhere, especially between my legs.

What in the hell was in that drink?

The guy left the bathroom and turned down the hall away from the main welcome area. I lifted my head to look behind him. The dizziness was getting worse as I struggled to see the empty hall.

"I win," I slurred.

"Quiet." He slapped my ass again, turned down another hallway, and opened a door.

When he righted me, I stumbled back against a table. He followed, pushing me so I lost my balance. I fell hard onto the surface, knocking the wind from myself and hitting my head.

"I don't know what you did to piss her off, but you should learn your lesson after this," he said, his hand pushing my slit skirt to the side.

"Pain is a good teacher," I slurred, not fighting him.

He smiled and leaned back to reach for his pants. My shoes were pointed—I'd thank Miranda for that later—and the target was perfect. I kicked hard. He grunted and grabbed himself as he folded forward. I kicked his face. My foot throbbed, but not as badly as other places.

The man fell to the ground, and I pushed myself upright, wobbled on my feet, and stepped over him to get to the door.

He caught my ankle. I fell hard, clipping my chin on the floor.

"Wrenly!"

I laughed at the sound of Bennett's voice. Blood dribbled from my mouth.

The man pulled me toward him and rolled us so that he could pin me underneath him.

"Bitch," he breathed as he gripped my jaw forcefully.

His mouth crashed against mine painfully as the door opened.

"Maybe we shouldn't—"

Bennett's snarl drowned out the rest of what Lindi said. He pulled the man off of me and planted his fist in the guy's face three times in rapid succession.

"Bennett, stop," Lindi said. "You saw the pictures. People like different things."

Pictures? What pictures?

Lifting my head, I saw Konni standing next to Lindi in the hallway. Konni looked worried. Lindi's expression was calculating as she watched Bennett.

What is she trying to do? What did she give me? My skin felt too hot, but from the inside out.

I sat up with a grimace. "Bennett."

At the sound of my voice, Bennett dropped the man and crouched next to me. His hand drifted to my face like he wanted to touch me, but he hesitated.

"Wrenly," Lindi said from behind him. "Is there someone we can call for your boyfriend? It looks like he might need to go to the hospital."

My gaze didn't waver from Bennett's anguished expression as I understood what she was trying to do.

"My chin hurts," I said to him. Tipping my head back, I pointed to the spot that felt both wet and bruised. "Will you kiss it?"

His gaze locked with mine for several seconds before he gently did as I asked.

"My tongue hurts, too. I think I bit it." I gave him my best sad face.

He swore under his breath, and his mouth was on mine a second later.

The heat flared inside of me, and the rush of need I didn't understand had me parting my lips to taste him. His tongue touched mine, and if I hadn't been sitting already, my knees would have given out.

With a whimper, I gripped his shoulders.

He jerked back and swore under his breath.

"Wrenly, have some decorum," Lindi said. "You were just making out with someone else."

If I weren't so busy trying to pull Bennett back to me, I would have flipped her off.

"Will it hurt if I pick you up?" Bennett asked, ignoring her.

I shook my head and was in his arms and crushed to his chest a second later. I pressed closer, feeling relief in his nearness.

"Wrenly's been drugged," Bennett said.

"Drugged or took drugs?" Lindi asked.

Bennett looked down at me for a second then at Konni.

"Take him. We're going to the hospital and getting answers."

"On it," Konni said, already bending down to pick the guy up.

CHAPTER TWENTY-FOUR

BENNETT TURNED TOWARD THE DOOR, and I met Lindi's gaze. Anyone who didn't know her would see concern. I saw her silent panic. Could Bennett smell it?

"If you want, I can take him there," she said.

"It'll be easier to bring him with us, but thank you for the offer," Bennett said, walking toward her. She had no choice but to step aside.

"Please call me when you get there so I know Wrenly's all right."

I laughed against Bennett's chest as he walked away. His hold on me tightened, and my humor vanished. The throbbing in my ass, chin, and various other points was echoing between my legs.

A small sound escaped me.

"I know it hurts," Bennett said. "Hold on, baby. It'll be better soon."

He weaved through the people still lingering in the welcome area and called out to the valet as soon as we were outside.

The cool air made my skin prickle, and I pressed closer to Bennett. The throbbing increased.

"Bennett." My hand hooked around the back of his neck, pulling him close.

He groaned as I tipped my head back, offering my lips.

"I'll drive you," Konni said a second before Bennett's mouth settled on mine.

His tongue stroked over my mouth briefly, and he pulled back enough to set his forehead against mine.

"Wrenly, baby, I can't keep kissing you. When the drug wears off, you're going to blame me."

"No, I know who to blame."

"You say that now, but—"

This time, I started the kiss. His growl sent a shiver through me, and the throbbing between my legs started to match the rhythm of my heartbeat.

"Please, Bennett," I said against his lips as I pressed myself closer to his chest.

"Car's here," Konni said.

Bennett swore under his breath and lifted his head to look at Konni. He was stuffing the unconscious man into the front passenger seat. When he finished, he opened the door for Bennett, who tried to deposit me into my seat, but I wasn't having any of that.

My skin hurt whenever Bennett tried to let go of me. So I held on as best I could, clinging to him. He said things that didn't fully register as he tried to untangle himself. Promises. But I knew better than to trust his words. I needed actions. I needed his hands on me, on my skin.

Letting go of him, I reached behind me to pull the zipper of my dress down as he withdrew and closed my door. The other door opened, and Bennett slid in next to me. His fingers caught mine, stopping me. He pulled me to his side, pinning my arms so I couldn't move.

It didn't bother me. His neck was right there.

"Go, Konni."

My lips skimmed the skin right above his starched collar.

"Speed," he added as I kissed him.

"Bennett. I need you."

"I need you too, baby, but not like this. I don't want you to hate me any more than you already do."

"Shh," I said, trying to stretch to reach his jaw. "I don't hate you. I just want to taste you again."

He made a pained sound.

"Konni."

"I'm doing what I can, Bennett. Hang in there. Don't wolf out, or you'll hurt her."

"You can hurt me a little," I said. "It feels good."

He swore, grabbed my chin, and kissed me hard. The fire under my skin grew. I freed an arm and ran my hand over his hard chest.

"Wrenly, what's your phone number?"

Konni repeated the question several times before it pierced the fog clouding my mind. Bennett wasn't kissing me anymore. He was holding me and shaking hard. I liked the shaking. It felt so good.

"Wrenly, what's your phone number?"

I frowned, trying to remember all of it as I said the first three numbers.

"What's Grandma's phone number?" he asked when I finished.

That came more easily.

"Say it again," he said as a phone started to ring, distracting me.

"Bennett?" a man asked. "Aren't you supposed to be wining and dining your mate at the charity banquet?" a man said.

I turned my head to look at Bennett and the phone he was holding.

"She's been drugged with shifter-grade pheromones. Who's at the hospital?"

"I just started my shift. How far away are you?"

"Two minutes," Konni said from the front.

"I'll meet you by the door. Hang in there."

Bennett's gaze locked with mine, and I tipped my head back to offer him my mouth as he ended the call.

"Wrenly, remember you started this," he said.

A second later, he had me pinned under him. His hand gripped my hip as his mouth devoured mine. It felt like heaven.

I couldn't move my hands to touch him as his hand stroked the skin of my exposed thigh. I whimpered my need into his mouth.

"Here!" Konni said.

The car jolted underneath me. I heard the door open but didn't stop kissing Bennett and arching my body into his.

A sharp pain stung my arm. Ripping my mouth from Bennett's, I cried out as the pain started to spread. He snarled above me.

"Pull him out," I heard someone say a second before his weight disappeared.

I heard snarls and thuds as someone grabbed my inflamed arm and pulled me from the car and into a strong set of arms. Bricks and lights swam in my vision as he turned and started to run.

"Hang in there," a man said.

I was getting tired of that phrase. Hadn't I hung "in there" for twelve years?

"Bennett…"

A hand covered my mouth.

"Now's not the best time to call him back. Give him a few minutes to work off the steam."

The brightness of the light increased along with the pain slowly crawling through my body.

"Is the room ready?" I heard the man ask.

A minute later, he set me on a bed, and it ignited a full-body burn that had me arching off the mattress.

I screamed.

Hard.

Loud.

And I didn't stop until I lost my voice.

People were yelling. I didn't know what.

Something else pierced my skin, and darkness swallowed me whole.

Beep.

Beep.

Beep.

I struggled to open my eyes and look for the source of the sound. The monitor next to my bed showed my pulse. Confused, I looked around the room.

Mom sat next to my bed, sleeping in her chair.

"Mom?" The sound was barely a rasp, but she woke with a jolt.

"Wrenly. Sweetie. Thank the moon. Here." She grabbed a white cup with a straw and handed it to me. "Sip it slowly."

The ice water felt amazing on my throat.

Slowly, pieces of what happened slipped into place. The drugged champagne. Thinking that Bennett had entered the bathroom. Getting tossed over some guy's shoulder and almost raped. Bennett's arrival. Lindi's shitty attempt to deflect. Making out with Bennett in the back of his car.

I cringed and glanced down at my hospital clothes, then around the room. When I looked at Mom, she handed me my phone.

"Try not to talk. You strained your vocal cords."

Setting my water aside, I sent her a text.

Me: How long was I out?

"Almost twelve hours."

Me: Where's Bennett?

"With Konni. They questioned the guy who drugged you, but he's not talking. Yet."

Me: He didn't drug me. He just got paid to make me look bad.

"Do you know who drugged you?" Mom asked, leaning toward me.

Me: Yeah, I have a good idea. No proof though.

"Will you tell us who it was?"

I thought about it. What benefit would there be? Lindi's family wasn't as powerful as the Wulf's or Steele's, but they still had sway in the city. Was I worried about what they would pull? Not really. I was more concerned about whether or not Bennett would let me go once he knew how many people I'd pissed off who would like to see me disappear for good.

"Wrenly, is there a reason you don't want to tell us?"

Me: Yes. It will create an endless cycle of concern and confinement. I don't want to be caged anymore because the people who love me are worried.

I watched her read the message. When she looked up at me, I saw her compassion and sorrow.

"We broke your trust in us with the decisions we made. We understand that. What if we decide together how to handle who drugged you and every decision that follows?"

Me: You might be willing, but will Bennett? I kissed him last night.

Her smile was sad and slightly pained. "I know, Sweetie. That's why he's not here. He thinks you'll hate him more now. Do you?"

Again, I thought it over for a minute before shaking my head.

Me: I don't hate him for giving me what I wanted at the time, but I'll hate him if he reads into it or thinks it gives him power over me.

Mom smiled and got up to hug me. "You are so beautiful inside and out, Wrenly. Even after everything you've suffered, you've held onto that piece of yourself. I don't know how, but you have. And I'm so grateful for your strength that allowed it. But I don't want you to have to be that strong all the time. I want you to be able to lean on someone. To trust someone to support you unconditionally. Okay? I'm not saying it has to be Bennett. I hope it will be, but it doesn't have to be. Just don't close yourself off. Don't lose that piece of yourself."

I hugged her back and whispered, "I love you, Mom."

She sniffled, pulled back, and quickly wiped at her eyes as she turned away.

"I'm going to tell the doctor you're awake."

As soon as she left, I got out of bed. My joints hurt with each hobbling step toward the bathroom. But by the time I finished using the toilet and brushing my teeth, things hurt less. Except my chin—I'd hit that floor hard—and I had some faint bruising on my ass.

I hope Bennett broke his nose.

When I left the bathroom, I saw a man in a white doctor's coat standing next to my hospital bed.

"You're moving better than most do after the shot I gave you last night."

"Yeah, I'm not thanking you for that," I rasped. "That shit hurt."

"Sorry about that. It would have hurt more to leave the drug in your system."

I gave him a questioning look.

"The drug only had fifteen minutes to take hold. The heat you felt after the shot I gave you was the sped-up version of what you would have felt after an hour. Each hour after that, the pain intensifies until you're successfully impregnated."

I paused my trip to the bed, turned, and grabbed his hands.

"Thank you for the soul-burning shot. May I have another, please?" Talking hurt less than it had but was still tender.

He chuckled and helped me back into bed.

"Bennett hadn't exaggerated your sense of humor."

I frowned at the doctor. "He talked to you about me?"

He smiled. It was a nice smile, but it didn't quite meet his eyes. He looked tired. Not sleepy tired, but life tired.

"We went to school together. Bennett, Konni, and me. My name's Giovanni. You can call me Gio. Now, let's get your vitals so I can report back to your mate."

"Potential mate."

He made a noncommittal sound as he used a light to check my eyes. He checked my throat, told me to try to rest it for the next few days, confirmed I'd bruised my jawbone, and was feeling my back when Bennett rushed into the room.

He stopped in his tracks and stared at Gio.

"Doctoring, Bennett. That's all," Gio said.

Bennett's gaze shifted to mine. I saw worry and raw fear there and wanted to look away, but I knew that'd only make things worse. His hands were shaking, and his hair looked messily styled, which I knew meant he'd been running his hands through it. Blood dotted the collar of his shirt.

"Is that my blood or the other guy's?" I asked.

"The other guy's," Bennett said roughly.

Gio pulled the back of my shirt down.

"She said her back hurt. The bruises aren't deep, and nothing seems broken. If you want, we can do some X-rays."

Bennett's gaze stayed on me.

"Your choice," he said.

I shook my head. "Not much can be done for a fractured rib anyway."

"Odd thing for someone your age to know," Gio said.

I glanced at him. "The school I went to, though, is known for its great education."

"They offer medical courses now?"

"No."

He frowned and glanced at Bennett.

"I'll leave you two to talk and get the discharge papers ready."

"Thank you, Gio," Bennett said as the doctor left.

Alone, we stared at one another.

"I'll go first," I said when the silence stretched. "I don't blame you for anything that happened last night. If you try continuing anything that I started when I wasn't in my right mind, I will, though."

He tucked his hands into his pockets and nodded once.

"Mom said you know who drugged you and paid the man to attack you."

"I do. Don't you want to ask if I know the guy?"

Surprise shifted over his expression before his mask slipped into place.

"I'm sorry. I assumed you didn't. Do you know him?"

"No. I just wanted to know if Lindi's comments made you doubt me. What took you so long?"

He briefly closed his eyes, his expression pained, before he hid that away.

"Lindi."

He didn't say anything else. He didn't need to. I knew how she worked. Yet, he hadn't stayed with her. He hadn't believed a word she'd said. He'd believed me. He'd stayed with me.

I'd always heard that mates were protective of each other, but it was the first time I'd felt it.

"What would you do if I gave you the name of the person who drugged me?"

He opened his eyes, and the intensity of his gaze made me hopeful for the revenge I might finally get.

"Anything you want me to do," he said.

I smiled and drew my knees up to my chest under the hospital gown. "I like that answer."

He slowly approached the bed and sat in Mom's chair.

"Will you tell me?"

"Will you promise not to do anything, no matter how small, without my approval first?"

He leaned forward, leaning his arms on his knees.

"I promise."

"What pictures did Lindi show you?"

He got out his phone, tapped the screen a few times, and handed it to me.

I saw the texts from her. Simpering. Flirtatious. Finally, the pictures that the guys she'd paid to beat me up had taken with me. Their faces were cut off in each one. But not the rest of them.

The sight of the dick too close to my bloody face repulsed me, and I gave the phone back to Bennett.

"What was the story she gave?"

"Are the pictures real?" he asked.

"They are."

Bennett looked down at the floor as his chair started to make clicking sounds due to the tremors running through his body.

"His dick didn't stay there for long," I said. "I was winded from running, fell, and pretended to be unconscious while they took the pictures. When I knew what they meant to do, I stopped pretending. I grabbed that bottle next to me on the ground—you can see it in the picture—broke it, and made them bleed before running again."

I grabbed my cup to take a drink to soothe my throat.

"When did that happen?"

"End of sophmore year."

"No one said you were hurt."

"No one knew. The makeup Mom gave me that month went to good use."

He scrubbed a hand over his face.

"*I* sent the makeup, Wrenly. Me. And the purses. And the clothes. I was so…oblivious. I thought you were thriving. Happy. What really happened? Where did all the things I sent go? Who hurt you enough that you know about broken ribs?"

"One thing at a time," I said. "Let's deal with last night first, okay?"

His shaking only got worse, though. I took another drink.

"The internet told me about the ribs. I thought one was broken at one point after a bad fall. It wasn't, but I learned things. I learned a lot there, Bennett. Stuff that's made me who I am. Now, if you want to know who's responsible for what happened last night, you need to take a few breaths."

Once he stopped shaking, I said, "Lindi arranged it. I don't have the proof. But I think we can get it. She's probably already wiped the surveillance footage and paid off the waiter who gave me the champagne. But you have more money and can smell a lie. Talk to the waiter."

"What do you plan to do with the proof?" Bennett asked. "Drugging you probably won't get her more than a year of jail time."

"Even two days in jail are enough to ruin her reputation. That's good enough for me."

"Will it stop her from coming after you again?" he asked.

I considered what he was saying and shook my head.

"Did she hurt you in school?"

"Yes, Bennett," I said in frustration. "She hurt me. Again and again and again. Directly and indirectly. Do you feel better having a name? I hope you sleep like an angel tonight."

He closed his eyes.

"I won't sleep until she's completely destroyed. Since drugging isn't enough, is there anything else we can get her for...legally?"

My annoyance evaporated. "Legally? Are there illegal ways to get her?"

"I'm not sure how to feel about the excitement in your scent at the prospect of doing illegal things."

"Go with gratitude. What are the illegal options?"

He opened his eyes and looked at me.

"I meant, if there aren't things that might put her away for the rest of her life, then we can do things that don't involve the police, like putting pressure on her family's business until they cut her off. Until she's in a position to suffer some of the hardships you've suffered."

My mind went to all of the things she'd done to me over the years. Things Bennett would go to jail for if he did them. He was a pain in my ass, but I didn't want him to go to jail.

"She doesn't need to suffer all of them," I said after a moment. "She just needs to lose all the power and influence she loves abusing so that it's harder for her to make anyone else suffer in the future."

"I'll make it happen. Will you trust me with the details? I'd rather you didn't know everything. Plausible deniability."

"As long as everything you do is within the law, you don't have to tell me how you take away her power, influence, and money. Just tell me when it's done."

"Deal."

His expression shifted, filling with guilt.

"Will forgiving me ever be possible?"

The question surprised me because he wasn't asking for forgiveness or how to make up for what happened. Did he finally realize the depth in which he'd hurt me? Why did that make my heart hurt?

"I don't know. Maybe."

"Even if you don't, will you tell me everything someday? When you're ready?"

"Telling you would only hurt you. Why should we both suffer?"

"That's what mates do. They shoulder life's burdens together. Always."

"But I'm not your mate."

"Since I'm the cause of your burden, shouldn't I be responsible for sharing it with you?"

This less demanding version of Bennett was nice. And dangerous.

"Maybe. I'll think about it."

He glanced down at his clasped hands.

"I want to hold you and comfort you so badly, Wrenly, and it kills me that you don't find comfort in being held."

"I do find comfort in hugs and being held, just not every hug or hold. Especially when I don't trust the meaning behind them."

His gaze flew to mine. "Comfort only. Nothing else."

My heart skipped a beat as I saw the need and hope in his gaze as he waited for my answer.

"Since you made my chin feel better, I'll allow a brief hug," I said.

He had me on his lap and wrapped in his embrace a second later, somehow not tugging on the I.V. in my hand. His slow inhale while his face was buried in the crook of my neck and the slight shiver oddly relaxed me.

"Better?" I asked.

"I should be asking you that."

"We both know this hug is more for you than me. I'm fine."

"You're not. Konni said you knew you were going to get hurt last night. And I don't think it was premonition but experience that gave you that level of insight." His hold tightened. "Why didn't you tell me?"

"You would have focused on the wrong thing, like you always do. 'Give me a name, Wrenly.' You're desperate to cast blame and right the wrongs."

"What should I do instead?"

"Ask why. Why does someone hate me enough to hurt me?"

"Okay. Why does someone hate you enough to hurt you?"

"Because everyone thinks I'm not worthy to be a part of the Wulf family. Everyone except you and the other family members. You have no idea what kind of target has been on my back since the day Mom brought me home…because of you. You want to beat everyone down for their jealousy and hate, but you're not addressing the real issue."

"What's the real issue?"

"Their perception of the Wulf family and their perception of me in it. You're not blind, Bennett. You saw how often the pack girls bullied me when I was growing up. All the scrapes and scratches that were written off as shifters learning not to be too rough with a human. Instead of claws that leave marks, I got hair pulling and tripping. I get pinned against a bathroom door or held to the wall by the throat. I will never measure up to you in the pack's eyes or elite society's eyes. Ever. Why do you think I want to attend a school where the Wulf name isn't known? I'm tired of fighting, Bennett. I want to be able to let my guard down and not wake up with my heart racing and my fists ready anymore."

Pulling back, I met his frustrated gaze.

"I know my worth. I'm amazing. My resilience and grades prove it. What I'm saying isn't self-pity. It's just reality. And I know you want to deny it. But before you do, use your eyes. Pay attention to how people look at me when they think no one is watching. Listen to the whispers. Put your view of me aside and see me through an outsider's eyes, not to change your opinion but to open your understanding of what I've been facing. Okay?"

He nodded, kissed my forehead, and pulled me back into his hug. I melted into it, letting him comfort me like he wanted.

A few minutes later, I heard the door open.

"Please tell me she wasn't drugged again." Konni said.

I rolled my eyes at him without lifting my head.

"Your timing is perfect," Bennett said. "There's something I'm going to need your help with."

CHAPTER TWENTY-FIVE

THE HOUSES GREW INCREASINGLY LARGER the deeper Milo drove into The District until they couldn't be called houses anymore. The ostentatious mansions that The District was known for were interesting to see in a spectator kind of way, but were not something I'd ever want to live in.

"There are a few places for sale if you're interested," Bennett said, watching me stare.

"I was just thinking the opposite of that. I'd hate living in places like these. They look cold and unwelcoming."

"Konni lives here. I'll let him know it's a mark against him."

I shot Bennett a look, and he grinned. His teasing smile made my pulse skip and my thoughts drift to last night's kisses. Ignoring him, I continued to look out the window.

Milo slowed the car and turned into the next driveway, where he pushed a call button. I listened to him give our names and watched the gates slowly open in response.

"What are you going to do if they don't care?" I asked as Milo drove down the long driveway.

"They'll care," Bennett said. "Maybe not today, but they'll figure it out quickly."

Bennett's plan for revenge had started while he still held me earlier today. After telling Konni that it had been Lindi who'd drugged me, he'd called Lindi and asked if she and her family would be home in a few hours. He'd said he wanted to speak to her parents about her help the night before and how he wanted to repay her. She'd quickly confirmed that they would be home and looked forward to welcoming him.

Milo stopped in front of Shane Manor and opened Bennett's door. "Ready?" Bennett asked.

I nodded. He got out and held out his hand to me. Accepting his help, I stood, enjoying the feel of the pantsuit I wore. The shoes were sensible in that they were flat, not in what they'd cost.

After being discharged, Bennett had taken me shopping. I dripped with money from the earrings in my ears to the silk blouse I wore. Every piece had been carefully selected with the sole purpose of showing my place at his side. And without understanding his plan, I would have never agreed.

Today, we blatantly show her that you can take what she wants. That you have more power than she does. It'll make her fall more bitter.

I met Bennett's gaze and smiled as he dropped my hand.

"You make my knees weak when you do that," he said quietly.

"You're ridiculous. Stay focused."

He sighed and turned his back on me. I followed with my head tipped down in subjection...or remorse. It depended on what anyone watching wanted to believe.

Someone opened the door as we approached and invited Bennett in. I trailed behind him until we reached the sitting room, and he stopped.

"Mr. Wulf, welcome," a man said. "Please, take a seat."

"Thank you."

Bennett sat in a chair. I stood beside him. Close, like I'd promised.

Lindi's parents sat on the sofa, and Lindi took the chair nearest Bennett's, on the other side of me.

"Lindi filled us in a little about what happened last night. If you're here to discuss confidentiality, I assure you that we have no intention of speaking publicly about what transpired. This is the girl, I presume."

I lifted my head and met Lindi's father's judgmental gaze as Bennett introduced me.

"This is Wrenly Belak, my fiancée."

Lindi and her parents looked equally shocked.

"You mean ex-fiancée?" Lindi asked.

"Fiancée. And I'm not here to suppress what happened last night. I'd prefer to expose it, but Wrenly suggested I speak to you about your daughter's part in drugging her last night first.

"The waiter who delivered the wine and the rapist your daughter hired already confessed. We have the transfer records from her decoy company's account to theirs as well as a recording of your daughter's instructions. Her intent to harm my fiancée is inarguably clear. However, we both know your lawyers will have her sentence reduced to a large fine and minimal jail time, at most. Rather than add to the workload of our lawyers, I thought we could settle this outside of court."

Her father's face had gone from pale to slowly red. Her mother kept glancing at Lindi. Lindi was the perfect model of innocent shock.

"Transfer records? Recording? Why would I want to harm Wrenly?"

I stopped my docile act and set my hand on Bennett's shoulder.

"Because I have what you want. Power. Money. Respect."

Lindi scoffed. "Respect? After the way you've thrown yourself at men? Please, we both know what you are."

"My fiancée," Bennett said again. "And my future *wife* has told me all about her time at school with you, Lindi—years of being chased, cut, burned, held down...*suffocated*."

Shock rippled through me, hearing my own words.

"Tell me you had nothing to do with any of that," he said.

"Of course I didn't."

He leaned forward suddenly.

"Do you even know who I am?" he asked.

She looked genuinely confused for a second. "You're Bennett Wulf, president and heir to Wulf Enterprises."

"You forgot the next Alpha to the local pack," he said.

Lindi looked surprised, but no less interested in Bennett due to his revelation. Her parents didn't seem upset by the news either. None of them had realized the issue yet, but Bennett quickly clarified for them.

"I can smell a lie better than you can spend your father's money. You had avocado toast with an over-easy egg for breakfast, an almond milk latte, and used whitening gel on your teeth before we arrived. And you have *everything* to do with what happened to my future wife while she was at that school."

Bennett's gaze pinned Lindi's father. "Do you need any other proof?"

Mr. Shane was quick to placate Bennett. "No. Thank you for bringing Lindi's behavior to our attention. We'll ensure it never happens again."

Bennett leaned back in his chair.

"It's escalated past that. Wrenly might not be willing to demand compensation, but I am."

"Name your price."

"Your daughter."

Her father looked shocked. Her mother and Lindi looked elated, though.

"B-but you already said you have a fiancée," the father said, his gaze flicking to me. "Are you suggesting Lindi become your mistress?"

"Wolves never cheat on their mates," Bennett said, patting my hand. "I want you to disown your daughter."

"What?" her mother gasped.

"She's just a child," her father said.

"She's a monster," I said. "She's done things that would be considered war crimes in some countries."

"You have a choice," Bennett said. "Disown your daughter, cut her out of your lives completely, or watch everything you've built slowly crumble."

Bennett stood and wrapped my hand around his arm.

"Lindi has my number. If I don't hear from you within twenty-four hours, I'll assume you're willing to give up everything for a child no one will touch once they know the truth about her."

Lindi's father got scarily red and grabbed his chest.

"No need to see us out," Bennett said as both Lindi and her mother rushed to Mr. Shane's side.

Bennett led me out to the car, where Milo was waiting. Once we were inside, he called Konni.

"As of today, I'm blacklisting the Shanes. Call in favors. Whatever you need to do to get investors to start withdrawing."

"You got it. How's your princess?"

"Elated," I said, since he was on speaker phone. "Lindi's finally going to get a taste of the suffering she deserves. I do feel a little bad for her parents, though."

"Kids don't just go bad. They choose to be that way. Either her parents were oblivious or supportive. Bennett's given them the chance to save themselves. It's their choice now."

I glanced at Bennett.

"If you want me to stop, I will," he said. "But I hope you don't ask me to."

"I won't. I'll trust you only to punish the people who deserve it and not to take it too far."

"Good," Konni said. "Stay elated. I've got some calls to make."

"Thank you for your help," I said. "With this, the bank records, and convincing the men to talk."

"Anytime. I owe you, remember?"

I grinned, and Bennett ended the call with a scowl to make another one to Mom and Dad.

"How did it go?" Mom asked.

"As expected," Bennett said. "I could smell their refusal and don't expect they'll abandon her willingly. I've already made the call to Konni. We'll focus on investments first. Once they're worrying about how to replace their cash flow, I plan to go after their talents."

"I've already let our recruitment officers know," Mom said. "They're ready to make offers that will be hard to refuse."

"Mom, I don't want to cause Wulf Enterprises any problems," I said.

"Sweetheart, recruiting top talent is good for the company, not bad. Our offers will reflect their worth, I promise. Now, hurry home. Grandma and I are making dinner for you."

I woke up with a sense of anticipation for the day, despite it being a Monday and my chin still hurting like a bitch.

Rolling over, I looked at the empty space beside me and slid my hand across the mattress under the covers. It was still warm. Slowly, I inched my way over to that warmth and lay in his spot, wondering what in the hell was wrong with me. I should be telling him to leave me alone...to leave the situation alone, but I didn't want to. And I knew what that meant. He was pulling me in.

"You're so stupid, Wrenly," I said softly before throwing back the covers and getting into the shower.

When I emerged, the bed was made, and a new outfit was waiting on it. My heart skipped a beat at the sight of it and the note waiting on the cute halter top blouse.

I think Cindi or her parents might show up today. Wear whatever you think works best for listening to pleading. Mom liked this one, but there are more options in the closet.
Bennett

Wrapped in a towel, I walked to the closet and stared at the new clothes he'd snuck in. I recognized a few as options I'd looked at with Miranda and shook my head, knowing very well she'd sent Bennett pictures of what I'd liked.

"You're not mad."

I looked over my shoulder at Bennett.

"No."

"Good."

My chest tightened with regret and something I couldn't name but felt a lot like panic...but not.

"I sold them. All the other clothes you gave me. I'll do the same with these. So don't buy me anything else, okay?"

His mask was in place as he studied me and slowly nodded.

"Okay. I'm sorry I didn't ask first."

"No, it's fine that you bought these. You're right about dressing the part for a while. I just...I wanted you to know nothing's changed. I still want to leave for school."

His gaze swept over my clothes.

"I understand."

"Good. Then can you leave so I can get dressed?"

My back was against the wall, and my hands were pinned over my head a second later. I scowled up at Bennett and tried to stomp on his foot. He was ready and faster than me.

"I thought we'd moved past this," I said.

He dipped his head, his lips brushing my ear, which sent a jolt of hyper-awareness through my nervous system.

"I thought you didn't want to live in an apartment with me at school.

Weren't you trying to kiss me last week? I'm ready to start the timer." His lips skimmed my neck, and heat burst inside my chest at the contact. My eyes started to close as the warmth spread outward, stealing my breath.

He growled and trailed a path of light kisses along my jaw, getting closer to my mouth. The heat increased along with my confusion and a growing panic.

"Wait," I breathed.

His lips immediately left my skin.

Panting, I opened my eyes and found him watching me.

"The timer doesn't start until my lips are on yours, Wrenly." His gaze dipped to my mouth.

"No. No timer."

His slow smile sent another pulse of heat through me.

"I mean, no kissing." I pushed at his chest with mine since he had my hands, but he didn't budge.

"Your towel's loose again. Close your eyes."

I listened.

He stepped away, and the towel fell.

Why did I listen?

His lips skimmed my collarbone, then the top of my breast.

My next inhale was more of a wheeze than a breath.

"Shh. It's okay. You're safe with me, Wrenly. Always."

His lips moved to my forehead.

"I can smell your nervousness. Then your desire. Do you know what's missing?"

"My fucking towel!"

He chuckled. "Fear, baby. You weren't afraid."

"You're going to be if you don't let go of my hands now."

His hold disappeared. The door to my room clicked shut, and I opened my eyes. He'd actually left. On trembling limbs, I bent and grabbed my towel.

It took three tries to get my underwear on, and my bra tried to strangle me, but I managed to dress myself in what Bennett had set out. I even applied some makeup again and styled my hair in a loose yet artful bun.

He was waiting in the hallway when I opened the door. His gaze swept the length of me. The intensity of his gaze stirred the memory of his mouth on my skin, and I felt my face start to flush.

"Would it upset you if I said you look beautiful?" he asked.

"No. Why do you think it would?"

"Because I know you don't like those clothes."

"I guess then my reaction depends on if you're complimenting me only because of the clothes and the makeup I put on."

He took a step toward me, and I quickly retreated. Rather than backing away, he moved super fast and had me against the wall with my hands over my head again.

My pulse spiked, but not with annoyance. Why was I liking this? Was I that twisted? I hated being held down. But he wasn't really holding me down. He was holding me still so he could dip his head toward my neck and breathe in my scent.

I shivered.

He groaned.

"I wish you were bribable," he said. "I would give anything for you to say yes to a kiss right now."

My thoughts scrambled as he breathed in deeply again, lightly brushing his nose against my skin, then his lips.

"Bennett…"

"Tell me what you want," he said.

I wanted him to touch me, which didn't make sense because he already was.

"I don't know…"

He swore under his breath, and his lips covered mine a second later. Gentle. Testing. Teasing. Kiss by tender kiss, he coaxed me until I opened my mouth and let him in.

He growled a second before his tongue swept against mine. My head swam with how it felt to be kissed by Bennett. It felt like I was falling but being caught at the same time. My senses were in chaos, but centered, too. On him. On the sweep of his tongue. On the heat building inside of me, and the gentle way he was holding my hands and my cheek.

When he pulled away a few minutes later, I was breathing heavily and dazed.

He looked into my eyes, searching for something. Whatever he saw there had his mask slipping back into place.

I frowned at him.

"I hate when you do that."

"You'd hate it even more if you knew how desperate that kiss made me."

His hold on my wrists loosened, and he brought my hands between us, rubbing his way up my arms from wrists to shoulders. It evaporated any annoyance that had risen.

"Can we try again?" he asked.

Confused, all I could say was, "Huh?"

"We were short of the five minutes."

My pulse stumbled a beat at the thought of kissing like that again.

"We're going to be late," I said.

"We can work from home today."

"What? No way. You said—"

He sighed and kissed my forehead.

"Then we should leave now before I change my mind and try to convince you that a day in bed with me would be more pleasurable than what's waiting at work."

He threaded his fingers through mine and led me from the room.

The touching didn't stop there. He brushed my hair back from my face once I was in the car. He buckled me in, too, and kissed the side of my neck before he retreated. Every touch left a subtle tingle in its wake.

"That kiss wasn't an invitation to do what you wanted," I said as he drove us to work. "Please keep your hands to yourself once we reach the office."

He parked in his parking spot and, instead of getting out, turned toward me. I saw his intent as he reached for me, but he was too fast to avoid. One hand cradled the back of my head while his mouth devoured mine. His free hand kneaded my side, adding to the heat of his kiss.

The contact overwhelmed me and fried any logical thoughts. Clutching his shoulders, I held on for dear life, sinking into the desire he was coaxing from me with each swipe of his tongue.

When he pulled away this time, he was breathing just as hard. He set his forehead against mine. I felt the fine tremors running through him.

"If you shift in here, I'll be hurt," I said.

He nodded but didn't let go. I held still as he took a few deep breaths and worked to bring himself under control again.

With a final kiss to my brow, he released me and got out to open my door.

I was quick to step away from him when his gaze dipped to my mouth.

"If you kiss me again, you sleep in your own bed tonight," I said.

He chuckled and held up his hands.

"I'll try to restrain myself."

I gave him a doubtful look before heading toward the elevator.

The main elevator banks were still crowded when we reached them. A few women from the office were present, including Olivia. Her pupils dilated when our gazes locked. She looked away first.

Bennett kept me close in the elevator. He trailed a finger down my bare arm. I brushed his touch away and shot him a warning glare. He smiled, and his hand settled on my lower back. I elbowed him.

He grunted as if I'd hurt him, but I knew better.

"So Wrenly is your mate?" Olivia asked when the elevator emptied of everyone but the three of us.

"Yes," Bennett said at the same time I said, "No."

Olivia's gaze shifted to me. "I thought you were supposed to be smart. Say the word, and I'll willingly take your place."

I opened my mouth to tell her to go for it, but Bennett's hand covered it.

"We're still negotiating terms," Bennett said. "For your safety, please refrain from interfering."

"When you're ready to consider more cooperative options, let me know."

The doors opened, and she got out. Bennett waited for the doors to close before pinning me to the elevator wall and leaning over me.

"No sending other women to me, Wrenly. It'll be dangerous for everyone involved now. Do you understand?"

I snorted. "More dangerous than before? I doubt that."

His free hand settled on my side, gently kneading a path upward toward my breast.

My lips parted. From shock or sensation, I couldn't be sure.

He ducked down and kissed me swiftly before releasing me and walking out the now open doors. He paused, waiting for me to follow. The fog his kiss had started disappeared when we reached the cubicles, and every woman there was staring at us.

Internally sighing, I kept my head up and walked past without a backward glance. Bennett had no idea what kind of target he'd painted on me by declaring me his mate. If I were lucky, the worst I'd face is a bucket of water thrown over the bathroom stall. If I weren't, I would likely wear another scar before I headed off to university.

Walking past my desk, I went straight into his office and closed the door behind me.

He stopped and watched me warily, sensing the shift in my mood.

"Why did you tell Olivia I was your mate?" I asked.

"She could smell me on you. It's safer for you if she understands that I see you as a mate rather than her thinking that you're trying to seduce me." He tucked his hands into his pockets. "But you're welcome to seduce me if you'd like."

Even though the first part made sense to a degree, I rolled my eyes at him for the second part.

"No thank you. And I'm not sure potential mate is any safer than seductress. They'll see me as competition either way. Calling me your sister would be safer."

"You're not my sister, Wrenly," he said without heat. "You'll never be my sister."

"Still noted. Keep your blinds open from now on."

I opened the door and found Miranda on the other side. She looked from me to Bennett and back again.

"I'm here for charity details and to find out why Olivia is telling everyone you're on your way out."

"Big mouth said I'm his mate."

Bennett let out an aggrieved sigh. "I kissed Wrenly in the car and knew Olivia could smell it."

Miranda's brows shot up. "You've progressed to making out in vehicles since Friday? I'm not sure I can wait until lunch for details."

"No skipping out of work today," Bennett said. "I need Wrenly close by."

Miranda smirked. "I bet you do."

I turned her around and pushed her toward my desk with me. His chuckle followed.

"Close your door, Bennett."

He did, and I faced Miranda.

"Did you change your mind?" she asked.

"No."

"Ah. Then you're meeting his—"

The blinds snapped open. She grinned and waved at Bennett.

"Why does he need you to stick around today?"

I turned on my laptop and put my purse away.

"Because the charity auction was a disaster. The main villain from my origin story arranged for people to drug and rape me. Bennett stopped the rape but not the drugging."

"Sweet moon goddess...how is he so calm?"

I shrugged. "Probably because he's already paying back the

person responsible, which is why he wants me here. He thinks she or her parents will show up today."

"Okay, I don't know the backstory, but I'm already invested in the outcome."

She strode to the door and opened it without knocking. I saw Bennett look up in surprise.

"You okay with me moving my stuff next to Wrenly for a few days?"

"Yes."

She closed the door. "Make some room. I'm sticking to you like glue. This is going to be better than the dramas I watch after work."

CHAPTER TWENTY-SIX

THE PHONE on my desk rang. Miranda beat me to answering it and put it on speaker.

"You have guests, Wrenly. Mr. and Mrs. Shane and their daughter. Do the Wulfs know you're socializing during business hours?"

"Check your tone, Paisley," Miranda said. "And put them in the conference room for the big spenders. Tell them Mr. Wulf will be with them soon."

"I already put them there. I have eyes and can see they're in the Wulfs' circle. They wanted to speak to Wrenly alone, though."

"Do you want to give them what they want or what Bennett wants?"

"Whatever. I delivered the message." She hung up on Miranda.

"She's lucky she doesn't drive," Miranda said.

"Why?" I asked.

"I'd key her car if she did."

I shook my head at her and started to stand.

"Wait. Where are you going?" she asked, catching my arm.

"I'm going to tell Bennett that they're here."

Miranda shot me a pleading expression.

"But don't you want to find out what threats they're going to deliver that they think they can get away with drugging you? Tell Bennett they're here, but ask to talk to them alone first."

"No thanks. I like breathing."

"Alone as in without Bennett. Your personal assistant, Miranda, will be with you."

"He'll never say yes," I said.

"He doesn't have to."

If I were honest with myself, I was curious about what tricks Lindi and her parents had that they thought would work after the ultimatum Bennett gave them.

"Can I trust you, Miranda?" I asked, watching her.

"To overspend on Bennett's credit card every time he hands it over? Yes. To betray you in any way that would cause you physical harm? Never. I like breathing."

I sighed, and she gave me a sad smile. "You might not want it, but you have my pity, Wrenly. I can't imagine what kind of life you've lived that you have no one you can depend on. If you take me into that conference room with you, I promise to prove you can depend on me."

"What's your plan to circumvent Bennett?"

She popped out of her chair and opened his door without knocking...again. He was on the phone.

"I'm taking Wrenly to a conference room. I can't wait 'til lunch. Be back in five."

He nodded without pausing in his conversation, and she closed the door.

"Come on."

"You're an ace at telling the truth-not-truth," I said, following her.

"We all are." She winked and towed me out of the office suite while I wondered what truths-not-truths Bennett might have told me.

I already knew he was going to make it impossible for me to meet the criteria he set to leave without him, just like he knew I would reject him the moment we mated...*if* we mated. We were stuck where neither of us was willing to give any more ground than we already had—a silent war of wills.

How was he going to try to win an "us"?

When Miranda and I reached the conference room, she opened the door for me.

I walked in confidently, noting that Mr. Shane had taken the seat at the head of the table. Mrs. Shane and Lindi stood behind him on each side. Miranda kept up with me as I went to the opposite end of the table and took a seat. Lindi didn't look like she was worried about being disowned, which made me wonder what ace they thought they had up their sleeve.

Mr. Shane stared at me.

I stared back.

Lindi should have warned him that I wasn't the type to play games with. I played to win, no matter the cost. It was easy to do when I had little to lose. So after a full minute of silence had passed, I stood and started for the door.

"Don't you want to hear what I have to say?" Mr. Shane drawled.

"Not really." I kept walking.

"One word from me and your pictures will be plastered on every corner of the internet."

I paused and looked over my shoulder. My slow smile unnerved him. I didn't need a nose to see that.

"I look forward to the fallout from that, Mr. Shane. Lindi isn't the only one who took pictures."

"Liar," Lindi said softly.

"You're right. It wasn't a picture. It was a video. History class. March Seventeenth. You were bent over the desk while the substitute instructor satisfied your itch. You were making noises like a cat in heat. The window caught your o-face reflection perfectly.

"I believe his farewell gift for your years of service was a finger in your ass, wasn't it?"

Lindi paled as Mr. Shane bolted to his feet, his face red. He turned on his daughter.

"Is it possible she has a video?"

She hesitated. He slapped her hard across the cheek. Her mom tried to stop him from delivering another on the backswing. It didn't work.

The door opened.

Bennett looked from me to the Shanes. "Am I interrupting?"

"I believe the Shanes are close to deciding between their livelihood and Lindi," I said. "If I'm not needed for anything else, I have work to do."

Miranda stuck with me as I left the room. Bennett stayed behind and closed the door. I briefly wondered what new threat he would deliver, then decided I didn't care. The slap Lindi received from her father replayed in my mind all the way back to my desk. I couldn't stop grinning. When I would have sat, Miranda caught my arm and dragged me into Bennett's office.

As soon as the door was closed, she had her hands out pleadingly.

"Please, please tell me the video is real. I want to see it."

I rolled my eyes at her. "I thought you could smell a lie."

"Your emotions were all over, and you gave specific details of the events, but didn't say what the video was." She made grabby hands. "Let me see what you have."

I pulled out my phone, unlocked it, and handed it over to her.

While she scrolled through my pictures, I went to stand in front of the blinds to watch for Bennett. I wasn't so sure how he'd feel about using his office to watch Lindi porn. He turned the corner at the same time Miranda started cackling.

"You absolutely need to release this to the public," she said.

I held out my hand. "Bennett's coming."

She snorted. "If that were true, he wouldn't still be so moody."

I shot her a look, which she didn't see. She was too busy flipping through my camera roll. I watched her humor fade and knew what she was seeing—evidence of my past abuse. My trashed room. Wrecked clothes. Bruises. Cuts. Burns.

"If you're my friend, you'll hand that phone to me now and leave," I said.

She looked up, anger flashing in her eyes on my behalf, and handed over the phone just as the door opened.

"We'll talk more about this at lunch," she said, stepping around Bennett to leave.

He watched her for a moment, then focused on me.

"What happened?"

"The Shanes threatened to release the photos Lindi already sent you. I'm guessing they wanted to get me to talk you into leaving them alone, but they never finished their threat when I said I looked forward to the fallout of posting the video I have of Lindi having sex at school."

"Sex?" Bennett said with a frown. "With a female instructor?"

I snorted. "Someone fed you a big lie. The majority of the instructors were female. A few were men, mostly the subs who covered maternity leaves."

Bennett's expression grew darker, and I knew I needed to distract him.

"Why did you show up so quickly?" I asked. "Who tipped you off?"

"Paisley said you were socializing during business hours. I was curious who you'd want to talk to. Why did you go alone?"

"I wasn't alone. I had Miranda with me."

He glanced out at Miranda, where she was typing away on her laptop, which was two feet from mine.

"Do you mind sharing your desk with her?" he asked.

I tried to read more into why he was asking, but his expression was a carefully neutral mask again.

"It's a little tight, but no one's bothered me. That makes the coziness a positive trade-off in my book."

"You could have more space if you worked in here with me and let her have the desk out there." His pupils pulsed larger briefly.

"Would you get any work done with me in here?"

"Yes."

"Want me to call Miranda in here to sniff-test that lie?"

He smiled and tucked his hands into his pockets. Was it really the relaxed pose he was trying to convey, or was it a way to stop himself from reaching for me? My guess was the latter.

"I plan on having lunch with Miranda today. Do you need a hug or something to hold you over?"

"Yes." The drawn-out word was punctuated by more eye dilation, but he didn't move to hug me. Instead, he watched me hungrily as I closed the distance between us.

I was playing with fire as I slipped my arms around his waist. The more contact I gave him, the more he seemed to want. Would he let me reach the time limit this time?

My heart gave an odd skipped beat again as I rested my head against his chest and pressed close. He didn't take his hands from his pockets to hug me back. Instead, a tremor ran through him.

"What did Mr. Shane say after I left?" I asked, hoping to distract him.

"He tried to appeal to my sense of family. He said Lindi is their only child and just as important to them as you were to me. He said he would send her abroad for five years to mature and develop, and we wouldn't see her again during that time. I told him that wasn't good enough and left."

I rubbed my hand over his back in the soothing way Mom did when she hugged me.

"What do you think they'll do next?" I asked.

"If you have the sex video you said you do, I think they're going to get more desperate as their investors start withdrawing, but I don't think they'll abandon her yet. They'll try to talk to their connections and pull in investments from other resources."

"Will anyone help them?"

He finally removed his hands from his pocket and wrapped his arms around me as he kissed the top of my head.

"No. With the Steeles and the Wulfs blacklisting them, no one will take that risk. Not even the small players. They might attract some foreign investors, but it will ultimately be a loss for the Shanes. I'll make sure of it."

I reached up to feather my fingers through the hair at the back of his neck. Another tremor ran through him. Tipping my head back, I looked up at his tortured expression and closed eyes.

Then I quickly glanced at the clock.

"I know what you're doing, Wrenly," he said roughly.

"Is trying to comfort you a bad thing? You're making it sound like it is."

His eyes snapped open, and he searched my gaze.

"We both know this isn't about comfort. At least, not mine. Is living with me that bad?"

I didn't pull away and kept touching his hair.

"It's not about bad or good, Bennett. This is about what I want. And I want to go to school like a normal person, not as a mate who has no freedom."

He frowned. "Haven't I been better?"

"Yes, you've been very careful about giving me choices and explaining what you're doing. But is that what you want, Bennett? A mate you need to tiptoe around?"

"It wouldn't be like this forever. We're learning more about each other. Adapting is normal."

I set my head on his chest again, which gave me a view of the clock. Four minutes had passed.

"Is it? Don't people with the same interests and backgrounds have it easier? Less adapting?"

He started pulling away with ten seconds left. I let him go and watched him walk around to his desk. His hands were fisted, and tremors were running through his body.

"You want me to want you like you want me. That won't happen, Bennett. The faster you adapt to that, the sooner we can both move on."

I walked out and closed the door behind me.

Miranda looked up at me.

"Well? What happened after we left?"

"They tried begging. It didn't work." I sat next to her as her gaze shifted to Bennett's office window.

"Yeah, begging Bennett for anything would be a waste of time, considering his current mood."

I turned to look at him with her and caught him with his elbows on his desk and his head in his hands.

"What did you say to him when you were hugging him?" she asked.

"That I won't ever want him as much as he wants me, and the sooner he accepts that, the sooner we can both move on."

"Really?" Olivia said, coming around the corner. "I'm happy to help him move on."

"You're an idiot," Miranda said. "We both have noses and know he'll never—" She cringed and cleared her throat. "Is there a reason you're here other than to tempt fate and the drywall?"

"I just thought I'd join in the gossip session and say that those people you all talked to left smelling like rage and revenge."

"It's their signature scent," I said, focusing on my laptop.

"You seem pretty indifferent to it. The girl was quietly promising her parents she'd deal with you."

"I'd like to see her try. Bennett rarely let me out of his sight *before* this weekend. Pretty sure he's going to be worse now." As I spoke, I realized the truth of my words. He wouldn't let me out of his sight at all now. I could feel a familiar tightness build in my chest. "I think I'll go to the bathroom on my own while I'm still allowed."

I fled before either could say anything.

In the bathroom, I splashed water on my face and focused on my breathing. Then, I used the toilet. Of course, the door opened when I was mid-stream.

"If you have a pail of mop water, don't do it. Bennett's already mad."

"How many times have you been doused while peeing that that's what you say when you hear the door open?" Miranda asked.

"A few." I finished and left the stall. She was leaning against the counter and watched me wash my hands.

"You weren't wrong about him not giving you space now. He saw you leave and was about to follow. I volunteered as tribute after suggesting space was what you needed the most from him. Hope you don't mind the switch."

I shook my head.

"Why did you start to panic?" she asked.

"I think it was the idea that I'm going to be even more caged now." Sighing, I smoothed my hands over my hair and met Miranda's gaze. "I've stayed awake for three days before. Straight. No naps. I remember how exhausted I felt. Exhausted and not really with it, you know?

"I'm getting to that level of tired again...and I'm sleeping at night. I keep telling myself to hang in there, that things will get better once I leave for school, but I think that's a lie. Nothing is going to go my way as long as I—" I shook my head. "Someone told me that sometimes life is harder than it needs to be. I lost my family to a fire when I was six. I was fostered by a family that accepted me on the surface but left me feeling rejected for the next twelve years. Life isn't *sometimes* harder for me. Struggling is the only way I know how to live, and I'm so fucking tired of it, Miranda."

She hugged me so hard I could feel her cup size.

"Um..."

"No, keep feeling sad. Rub against me a little too. This is going to get us a longer lunch break and a few margaritas."

I snorted but set my head on her shoulder and let my self-pity free for a few seconds. Then I pulled myself together and walked out of the bathroom with Miranda.

She marched right into Bennett's office, and from the corner of my eye, I watched her waft the air from her body toward Bennett.

Miranda wasn't the friend I'd expected. I'd been looking forward to a normal friendship with Sophia, but I didn't hate the support Miranda was giving me. It felt more real than anything I'd ever had in my life. Even more real than Aiden and Karter.

When she emerged, she gave me a subdued thumbs-up and grabbed her purse.

"Let's go."

THE FISH BOWL margarita wasn't equally shared, but I still had enough that I was feeling pretty mellow when we returned to the office past the normal lunch hour. If anyone gave us looks and said anything under their breath, I didn't notice.

"Nope, not the desk," Miranda said, steering me toward Bennett's office. "You won a free nap with your lunch."

A nap didn't sound like a bad idea.

I quietly let myself into Bennett's office so that I didn't disturb the call he was on, then kicked off my shoes and settled onto the couch.

Sleep claimed me quickly...the brush of fingers against my cheek brought me out of it a while later.

Opening my eyes, I looked at Bennett, who was crouched beside me.

"You're beautiful when you sleep. When you're awake, too. When you run. When you laugh. When you scowl... I can't think of a single instance when I've looked at you and didn't think you were beautiful."

"Are you trying to give me a new goal?"

He smiled.

"No. I'm trying to tell you, nothing you do will change how I feel. I would apologize for it, for not giving you what you want, but I think I'm giving you what you need after feeling abandoned and unwanted for so long. Unconditional love, Wrenly. Whether we stay together or not, you will always hold my heart."

He leaned in and kissed my forehead.

"Now, are you ready to tell Mom why you drank so much that you needed a nap on my couch?"

I sat up quickly. "You told her?"

He shook his head. "You staggered past her on your way back. She has a nose."

I groaned.

"You can use my bathroom if you want to freshen up first."

Knowing I couldn't avoid her, I nodded and left the napping couch behind. He'd set out a new toothbrush for me, which I used before finger-combing my hair back into its artistically relaxed bun.

When I emerged, Bennett was waiting for me.

"Want backup?"

"Nah, I think I'll be okay. Do Mom and Dad know everything about the Shanes?"

He nodded once, showing his wariness.

"It's okay. I'm not mad about it. I'll blame that." I winked at him and turned toward the door.

My back was pinned against it a second later with my hands caged over my head again. I arched to tip my head and meet Bennett's gaze. His pupils were going insane.

"How would you feel about rules?" he asked, his voice rough.

"It depends on the purpose of the rule," I said, unsure of his mood.

"For safety."

"Safety rules are good."

"No winking."

"What? Really? Why?"

He ducked his head to set his forehead against mine. I could feel him shaking.

"Playful Wrenly is the most dangerous version you have. Please...please don't let her out. I can't..." He tilted his head, and his lips found mine. His need devoured me. My head spun as he poured his desperation for me into that kiss. And when he pulled away, the hunger in his expression had only increased.

I managed a few shaky breaths as he remained locked in place, visibly struggling for control.

"Are you going to let me go, or is this going to turn into something that won't end well for either of us?" I asked carefully.

He immediately released my wrists. He didn't back up, though, which made squeezing through the narrow door opening a little difficult.

"I'm surprised he let you leave smelling like that," Miranda said as I closed the door behind me.

"Like what?"

"Unfulfilled lust." She sniffed visibly. "Although I think most of it is his."

"Nose your own business," I said. "Unless you want to come with me to explain to Mom why I was tipsy and needed a nap."

"No thank you. And remember how many times I helped you as you consider shifting the blame to me."

"Don't worry, I won't throw you under the bus tires. The Shanes deserve some tread marks."

With a wave, I left her to go find Mom. She was in her office, talking on the phone but hung up when she saw me coming.

I let myself into her office and took a seat on one of the chairs in front of her desk.

Her sternness melted a little as she inhaled.

"Did Bennett wake you?"

"Why do you ask when you already know?"

"I only know that he kissed you, not whether or not he interrupted your sleep."

I glanced at the clock and internally cringed at the time. "He woke me, but considering the time, I think it was warranted."

"After what happened this weekend, I think you needed the sleep. More than you did the alcohol. Why did you drink, Wrenly? Is it for coping? I have the name of a doctor that you could—"

"Mom, stop. Please. I drank because I wanted to. I could list a million reasons why...stress, the Shanes, Bennett, you and Dad, this job, all the people who hate that I'm Bennett's mate, all the shit that happened to me in the past, but I mostly drank because I wanted to feel like I was in control of what I can and can't do."

She nodded and didn't say anything as she studied me for a moment.

"I don't want to make any more mistakes," she said finally.

"Isn't that what life is, though? Are you even living if you're not making mistakes?"

She gave me a sad smile. "I'd like to make fewer mistakes with you than doing the right thing."

"You're doing the right thing now. Talking to me instead of getting mad. Asking why instead of assuming."

"It doesn't feel right. It feels like I might be ignoring a potentially dangerous situation because I'm terrified I'll lose you for good."

CHAPTER TWENTY-SEVEN

MOM'S WORDS broke my heart for both of us. She was the only Mom I remembered, and I didn't want to lose her either.

"No matter what, I promise you won't lose me for good," I said. "Not if I have any say in it."

She sniffled, and we both stood to hug.

"I love you, Mom."

"I love you, too, Sweetheart. So much. Can I ask how things are going with Bennett, or is that a closed topic for us?"

"It's not closed. But I don't think you'll like the answer."

"Say it anyway," she said, leading me to her office couch.

"He wants me to stay with him, and I want to leave. We're at an impasse."

"But I can smell—"

"Attraction doesn't mean I'm willing to give up more of my life for him. I've given up enough."

"Will you tell me if he does something you don't like?"

"If you want."

"I do."

"Okay. Then I will." I considered her for a second. "I don't hate him. Not for any of it. I'm mad, but I can understand too. None of it was intentional, but intent doesn't undo the damage or my need to make my own choices. If something bad happens, I want it to be because of the decisions I made, not because of what someone else arranged for me."

"I understand. What are your plans for dinner tonight?"

"I don't think we have any."

"Could we try a family dinner again?"

"Sure."

She smiled and patted my hand.

THE SPOT beside me was still warm when I checked. Five days had passed since I woke up in the hospital, and for the first time in what felt like forever, I was bruise-free.

While I appreciated the reprieve, it also showed the level of boredom the last five days had been. Eat, sleep, and work—that was it—all under Bennett's very protective presence. Except for the few times he let Miranda take over. Like when I went to the bathroom at work and a very brief lunch meetup with Sophia.

Restlessness was a real problem with me when life got too quiet. It always felt like the lull before the storm, and I hated it.

I glanced at my open bedroom door.

"What's your schedule like this morning?" I called.

He appeared in my doorway a second later, wearing loose shorts as he towel-dried his wet hair.

"An acquisition call at eight and a partner meeting at eleven. Why?"

"I think I'll drive in later on my own."

He stopped towel-drying his hair and sat on the edge of the bed, facing me.

"We've been cutting off the Shanes each time they grab a lifeline. Their desperation makes me nervous that they'll try something. I'd prefer you stay close to me, Mom and Dad, or Miranda."

While I appreciated that he didn't just say no, I wasn't a fan of his non-no either.

"I want to go for a run."

"What if you bring your running clothes to work and run with Miranda while I'm at the partner meeting?"

"At what point in my slacking off do you think the rest of the office will mutiny? I took a three-hour nap on Monday, and now I'm going to go for a run during work hours. The week before that, I was out too."

"If they haven't mutinied yet over my behavior, they shouldn't over yours either."

"Completely different standards, but okay. I'll take a work-run with Miranda."

"Thank you." He didn't leave.

"Is there something else?"

"There's a pack run tomorrow right. I'd like you to go. With me."

"So you can say I'm your mate in front of everyone? No thanks."

"The news has already spread. I'd like you to go so everyone understands you're under our protection even more now."

"I don't think it's going to work like you think it will, but okay. I'll go under one condition."

"What's that?"

"If I'm maliciously hurt at the pack run, you stop sabotaging my attempts to meet your conditions to stay at school on my own this fall."

He frowned, looking uncomfortable. "You won't be hurt."

"Then it's an easy deal for you to make, isn't it?"

"And if you're not maliciously hurt? Are you willing to kiss me? No timer, and you initiate it."

"Sure. It's a deal. Now get out so I can get ready for work, or you'll be late for your call."

He darted in and kissed my lips then left me alone to get ready.

His touching was becoming more frequent, and while I didn't hate it, I knew it wouldn't make anything easier for either of us.

I texted Miranda to pack some running clothes for an extended lunch then hurried through my morning routine. Bennett was in the kitchen, plating a piece of avocado toast topped with an over-hard egg when I entered.

"What days does Sandy work?" I asked. "You seem to be in the kitchen more than she is, not that I'm complaining that she doesn't work. I'm just curious."

"She cleans while we're gone, does the grocery shopping, and is willing to make meals when I ask. I usually don't ask."

He motioned for me to sit at the counter and set the plate in front of me.

"Do you like cooking?"

A hint of a smile ghosted his lips.

"For you, yes."

"Why? I'm not very grateful about it."

"I think that will change when I find the foods you like."

I shook my head and took a bite of his breakfast. "If you're trying to find my favorites, avocado toast is probably at the bottom of my list. Most of the food the school served would be at the bottom."

"Because you didn't like how they tasted or because you didn't like what they represented?"

His question hit home, and I stared down at the toast for a second before taking another bite. This time, I set aside my bias and focused on the taste.

"Maybe there's something else you don't like because of what it represents rather than how it actually is?"

"No, I'm pretty sure my reason for not liking a mate is accurate. Even Mom says mates are unbearably clingy until the first child is born. No thanks."

He let out an annoyed huff.

"But you're right about the avocado toast. My problems with it have nothing to do with the taste."

"Stubborn," he said under his breath.

"Which means you'll need to be the flexible one if you want us to be mates, right?"

"Eat your toast, Wrenly."

I grinned as I wolfed it down.

"Look at your cute little human legs go," Miranda said, keeping pace beside me.

"I think I like running with Bennett better. He's quiet."

She snorted. "Maybe outwardly, but not inwardly. I'm betting he watches the way your boobs bounce in that sports bra, and he's probably hoping he doesn't trip over his hard-on. Have you noticed it?"

I almost tripped.

"What? No! What is wrong with you?"

She laughed until tears streamed down her face, but she never lagged behind. Not even a little.

"What's the point of this run, by the way? Are you worried about your weight or something? I hear humans obsess like that."

"I'm rethinking our friendship."

"That's a lie. Seriously, though, you're running all out. Humans usually do that when they're training. Are you training?"

"Sort of. Bennett asked me to go to the pack run with him."

"Oh." She said it with all the tone of *bless your heart*. "You're not going to try to actually keep up with the run, are you?"

"Don't be ridiculous. I just want to be fast enough to reach a tree to climb."

"You do know that we can climb trees, too, right?"

"Yep. In human form. Shifting takes time, which I'd use to my advantage by screaming my head off for Bennett."

I felt her glance at me.

"You think something is going to happen, don't you?"

"I've been home for three weeks. In that time, I've been thrown to the ground, tripped, held by the throat against the wall, bruised against the bathroom door—not holding any grudges about that one, by the way—drugged, and almost raped. And that was all while under the Wulfs' considerable protection. You're as crazy as Bennett if you think something *won't* happen."

We completed the first lap around the park, but neither of us slowed.

"Did you tell him?"

"I did better than tell him. I made a deal. If I'm hurt maliciously, he has to stop sabotaging my attempts to meet his terms for the other deal we made."

"The one for living alone at University?"

"Yeah."

"And he agreed?"

"Of course he did. He's positive that he's all the protection I need. If that were true, I wouldn't still wake up screaming once a month."

Her gait faltered.

"Does screaming yourself awake have to do with the villain in your origin story?"

I hesitated for only a second before nodding.

"Are you ever going to tell me the full story?"

"Maybe."

"Can I get a little hint today?"

"She knows how to hurt people without leaving a physical mark. Suffocation using a wet blanket. No hands to struggle against that might leave bruises."

Miranda didn't say anything for the rest of that lap.

"Does Bennett know?"

"The specifics? No. There's no point in telling him or my parents. Why make anyone else live with the hell that happened to me?"

"What about me?"

"You're not emotionally invested in me enough to be fully traumatized by it. You'll only be a little traumatized."

She snorted. "So that's why you know how to defend yourself and why you reacted like you did when I reached for you."

"Yeah."

"How long ago did that happen?"

"Three years? Four maybe? The pictures she has of me were from about two years ago. I got a lot smarter after that. Meaner too. I wasn't afraid of leaving marks."

Miranda was quiet for a few minutes.

"Lindi Shane won't be at the pack run, though. So who do you think will hurt you?"

I laughed.

"Every single female who thinks she has a chance at Bennett if I stop breathing. That's at least what? Fifty maybe? Maybe more if the older ones are thinking of rejecting their mates for him."

"Hmm. You're not wrong. But I don't think they'd do something right under his nose."

"They won't. Something will happen to separate us, and they'll get me to the river where a group will be waiting. No one will chase me directly. Scent trails and all that."

"Bennett said you predicted what would happen at the charity auction."

I glanced at her again. "You talk to Bennett?"

She sniffed and grinned. "Careful, I think there's a hint of jealousy in there."

Scowling, I focused on the path.

"You have nothing to be jealous about. He only calls when he wants help keeping an eye on you, like this run. He's worried. He mentioned that you told his friend something would happen before it did and that I should pay attention to what you say. How many times are you right about that kind of stuff?"

"I'd say about ninety percent of the time."

"Okay. I don't normally go to pack runs, but I think I'll make this one an exception. Just to see what happens."

"Is that your way of saying you won't step in if there's trouble?"

"Depends. Do you still want to go to school without Bennett?"

"Yes."

"Then I won't intervene until it looks like you'll be seriously hurt."

"Thanks. I'll owe you a shopping trip."

She grinned. "So will Bennett."

We finished our run, grabbed some hot dogs from the street food cart, then walked back to the office. Miranda went to the ladies' room to change into the clothes she'd stashed there since she hadn't broken a sweat. I hadn't been as lucky. I walked past the other women in my shorts and sports bra, hearing their muttered grumbles.

"Flaunting your scent won't help you get rid of him," Olivia said as I passed her desk.

Ignoring her, I kept walking.

"See you at the run, charity bitch."

Some of the other women laughed.

How did they know I'd be there?

Rounding the corner to enter the office suite, I saw Bennett on the phone through the blinds. He waved for me to enter, so I quietly let myself in.

"She just walked in. Yes. I'll tell her."

He hung up the phone and inhaled deeply.

"You're annoyed. Wasn't it a good run?"

"It was. How does Olivia know I'm going to the pack run?"

"I told Mom. Olivia overheard."

"Who was on the phone just now?"

"Karter. He wants to know how long the silent treatment is going to last."

I shrugged and started for the bathroom. "If they really wanted to talk to me, they'd come home."

Bennett's arms wrapped around me from behind, hugging me to his chest as he kissed the top of my head, then breathed in my scent.

"Sending them away hurt you. I'm sorry I did that."

"They could have said no and stayed."

He turned me to face him. "No, they couldn't have. I was—I *still* am jealous of the way you can laugh and be happy with them, but not me. They're my brothers. I love them. But I would have put them through a wall if you'd hugged them like I want you to hug me."

"That sounds like a you problem, not a me problem."

He huffed out an impatient breath. "I don't want you to hate them for something I made them do."

"I don't hate them. However, that doesn't mean I'm ready to forgive them for abandoning me when I needed my brothers. But I get it. I don't really have any brothers. They were just loaned out to me."

Bennett's grip on my arms twitched.

"You are exceptionally good at provoking me."

"And you're getting better at not reacting to it."

"Is there a reason you need to provoke me?"

"Yeah, to remind you why I don't like you."

"I've smelled your desire and know that's a lie."

"Desire is attraction; it's not affection."

His jaw clenched, and I patted his chest before extracting myself from his hold.

"I'd better shower and get to work."

Closing myself in his bathroom, I studied myself in the mirror. My light brown hair was damp around my temples. My face was flushed from the run, making my grey eyes more vibrant. It didn't mask the hint of sadness in them or the determination.

Playing dirty wasn't nice, but it was necessary. An angry Bennett today would provoke Olivia to try harder to come after me tomorrow at the pack run. Did I want to be hurt? Hell no. Pain sucked. But a little pain now was more likely to ensure minimal pain in the future. And that was all I wanted.

A pain-free future that I shaped with my own choices.

Something slammed outside the door, and I started the shower, hurrying through the process so Bennett wouldn't storm in. However, he wasn't in his office when I emerged again clean and fully dressed. Miranda was, though.

She was sitting in his office chair.

"Pretty sure he's not going to like that," I said.

She shrugged. "Pretty sure he can't get any madder. What did you do to him?"

"Same old, same old. Said stuff he didn't like hearing."

She lifted my phone from the surface of his desk.

"It's been making a lot of noise."

I checked and found ten missed calls from Grandma and Mom.

"This family is suffocating me," I said without any feeling.

"Maybe it only feels like that because you're used to thinking no one cares."

I looked up from my ringing phone and stared at Miranda for a few seconds before answering Grandma's call.

"Jorge's whore house," I said. "If you've got the bank, we've got the spank. Who are you calling for?"

Miranda lost it so bad that I could barely hear Grandma's snort.

"You don't seem to be in a bad mood," she said as I moved away from Miranda.

"I'm not. Bennett is, though. Is he why you called?"

"He's in with your Mom. He said you're acting like you don't have a family again."

"He's not wrong."

"Why?"

I sighed and sat on the couch. "Because loving someone can't be forced. Because I'm so tired of being emotionally manipulated. Because…I'm angry. All the time. I guess I'm just being a menace."

She chuckled.

"Okay. Then carry on. I love you, my little Wren."

"Love you too, Grandma."

"Grandma?" Miranda asked as I hung up. "You answered like that for your Grandma?"

"Bennett's Grandma, technically, but yes."

"What was her reaction?"

"She was amused."

"I know you don't feel this way, but you are so lucky. I'd kill for in-laws that loved me like that."

"Thanks for the warning. I'll watch my back."

She laughed and followed me out of the office.

Bennett came back after an hour. He scowled at me as he stalked past and kept his door open. Miranda and I didn't talk, but I could sense she was bursting with silent commentary.

Five minutes before it was time to shut down, Bennett knocked on my desk to gain my attention. When I pulled my gaze away from my spreadsheet to look up at him, I regretted it. He didn't look well. His pupils were blown wide, his jaw was twitching, and his hair was sticking out in a few places.

"Mom and Dad want to have dinner with us tonight. What would you like to eat?"

"A bacon cheeseburger?" I said it like a question since I didn't want to set him off.

His expression slipped behind his mask again.

"You smell nervous," Miranda said. "It's making him smell nervous."

His gaze flicked to her. She shrugged and closed her laptop.

"I'll see you tomorrow," she said to me. "Maybe less attitude at dinner."

Then she left me alone with Bennett, who still looked like a bomb that was one sneeze away from exploding.

"What time are we meeting them?" I asked.

"Do you still consider Miranda your friend?"

"Yeah. Why? Shouldn't I?"

He sighed and ran his hand through his hair. "No. She's fine. Can we talk in my office?"

"Sure."

He followed me inside and closed the door.

"Are you still mad about what I said?" I asked.

"I'm not mad. I wasn't mad when you said it. I'm...lost." He closed the distance between us but didn't reach for me. The mask slipped, and I saw his need and desperation. "Do I matter to you at all? Even a little?"

His words speared me.

"No," he said, hugging me desperately to his chest. "Don't feel guilty. I don't want your guilt, Wrenly."

I pushed at his chest. "I can't breathe."

He released me as quickly as he'd grabbed me and ran his hand through his hair again.

Understanding that I'd pushed him too far, I caught his free hand by his fingertips. He froze then slowly lowered his other hand to his side.

"I'm sorry."

His expression turned pained. "No, Wrenly. You have nothing—"

I covered his mouth.

"I'm sorry for being mean on purpose. Can I hug you to make it up to you? No timer."

He nodded, and I dropped my hand to his waist, leaning into him.

"You do matter, Bennett. You always have."

A tremor shook its way through him, and I felt his lips brush the top of my head. I held him until his shaking stopped, then pulled back to study his calmer expression.

"Do you think you can make it through dinner now?" I asked.

"Do you still want to go?"

"Do you?"

His gaze swept over my face and landed on my mouth.

"Don't kiss me if you're going to cut it off shy of five minutes again," I said.

He caught my face between his hands. My heart started to beat faster in anticipation as he closed the distance between us. His lips gently met mine in a fleeting, sweet kiss. Then he touched his forehead to mine.

"I'm starting to understand how you feel. I hate my life, Wrenly."

"No you don't. You just hate the mistakes you've made that are keeping you from what you want."

He groaned and kissed my nose, my cheek, my eyelid. Tipping my head back, I let him pepper my face with little kisses, even while knowing I shouldn't encourage it. But I didn't want to stop him either. It felt nice, each one softening my resistance just a bit more.

His thumbs stroked over my cheeks as his mouth hovered over mine for two heartbeats. His lips met mine again, but the gentleness was gone. Hunger had consumed it and attempted to do the same to me as he nipped my bottom lip and stroked his tongue against mine.

My head swam with need for him.

When one hand left my face and settled on my side, just below my breast, I tore my mouth from his. I only managed a brief gasp for air before his mouth was on me again. He swallowed the sound I made as his hand covered my breast. He kneaded it, sparking something dangerous inside of me. Something that had me gripping his shoulders for balance.

He ended the kiss, breathing heavily against my temple as he wrapped me in his arms. His shaking was so pronounced that it felt like a never-ending shiver.

"I need...don't move...give me a minute."

His desk phone started to ring. I looked at it, and he growled, which earned him a poke to his side.

"I think it's Mom. You should answer it."

Untangling myself from his hold wasn't easy. It took so long that the phone stopped ringing.

"Bennett, cut it out. Let go."

"I can't."

"I'm going to stomp on your foot again."

"Okay."

I pulled his hair instead. He grunted and finally let go.

"You're annoying me."

"Same," he said with a scowl.

Rather than turning my back on him, I pointed to the door.

"Out. I'll follow."

"No."

"Afraid I'll watch your butt and like it?"

He blinked at me. His stunned expression was so comical that I couldn't help but grin.

"You won't know unless you try it," I said.

He turned and walked out the door. Feeling a little victorious and relieved that I didn't have to watch my back, I followed him, stopping briefly at my desk to shut down and grab my things.

Mom and Dad were headed our way as we turned the corner.

"Oh good," Mom said. "I was worried we missed you. I thought maybe we could drive together."

"No," Bennett said at the same time as I said, "Sure."

Mom's smile faded as her gaze bounced between us, and Dad put his arm around her.

"Maybe we should drive separately," he said.

"Why? Because Bennett's in a mood?" I asked. "If he'd rather drive by himself, let him. I'd actually like to spend some time with both of you...If I'm *allowed* to."

The sound of Bennett's defeated exhale was like the end of the round bell in boxing. I smiled at Mom and moved to hook my arm through hers.

"Where were you thinking of eating?" I asked, leading her away.

CHAPTER TWENTY-EIGHT

When I opened my eyes the next morning, I was alone. My hand drifted to Bennett's spot before I realized what I was doing. The lack of warmth dissipated my lingering grogginess.

Frowning, I sat up and wondered if Bennett was still in a mood. He hadn't shaken it by the time we'd gotten home the night before, and hadn't said anything to me when I'd gone to bed, either. I'd assumed he would sneak in and sleep next to me like he'd been doing pretty much every night since stealing my bed. That he hadn't made me a little nervous.

I glanced at the door and caught sight of the breakfast tray table waiting beside my bed. The mini waffles and fried eggs were still steaming, but that didn't catch my attention as much as the small vase with a blooming peony in it.

I plucked it from the vase and smelled it, hating how much I liked that he'd picked a flower for me.

A note was pinned under the vase. Pulling it free, I read it.

This is your first clue.
When you're done eating, go to your closet and find
something blue.
Bennett

I read it twice, surprised. What was he up to now? Curious and a little excited, I grabbed a waffle and ate it as I went to the closet to look for something blue.

Another note was hidden in a pair of my blue underwear.

"Pervert," I said under my breath.

Clue number two.
Finish your breakfast. You'll find clue three when you're done
with your shower.

Eager for the next clue, I quickly finished my breakfast like it said then closed myself in the bathroom with the blue underwear.

The bed was made and the dishes were gone when I emerged again.

Another note waited next to a set of clothes I didn't recognize.

Clue number three.
The fourth clue is waiting downstairs. Follow the arrows.

After dressing, I left my bedroom and saw a Post-it on the hallway wall, pointing toward the stairs. Pulling it off, I followed the arrows all the way to Bennett's office.

A bouquet of peonies waited on his desk with a note. I inhaled their fragrance before reading the next clue he'd tucked between the blooms.

Clue number four.

The flowers are yours. Peonies symbolize prosperity. I hope your life is rich with love, laughter, and family every day. Thank you for being you, Wrenly. You're perfect the way you are, even if it drives me crazy at times.

The next clue is your choice. You can find your running shoes, or you can check the swing outside.

Choice? What did he mean by that? Was he acknowledging I still wanted to leave? No, the tone of the notes had been playful. This choice wasn't about anything big then.

Since the door to the swing was closer, I went that direction.

The swing swayed gently in the early morning breeze as I walked to it. There was nothing on or under the seat. Unsure what to do, I sat on it and started to swing, knowing that Bennett would show up eventually.

He did.

From behind, he started to push the swing for me.

"I thought you'd choose to run," he said.

"The swing was closer."

He was silent for a second. "I wanted to do this for you for so many years."

"You should have."

"It's not too late, is it?"

I glanced back at him. He was dressed for running.

"Are you going to tell me what this game was about?"

"I wanted to show you that, while I might not be good at it, I can learn to be fun too."

My heart tried to trip over itself, and I didn't know how to deal with what I was feeling because of him. Anger was safe. Denial was safer. But I couldn't do either of those anymore. We were so past that.

"Thank you for the flowers," I said instead. "What would have happened if I'd picked the running shoes? We would have gone for a run?"

"Why don't you go check them?"

He stopped the swing for me and followed me through the house to the garage door, where we kept the shoes. I took the note from mine.

If you'd rather skip tonight's pack run, we can go for one now instead. The choice is yours.

"It's still your choice," he said.

"Is this your way of backing out of our deal?" I asked.

"No. Miranda mentioned that you didn't feel safe going. She said it was her duty as your friend to promise me bodily harm if anything does happen to you."

I snorted, not doubting that was exactly how the threat had been delivered.

"If you don't feel safe, you don't have to go."

"Whether I'm there or not, your words will have the same impact. I'd rather go."

"Because of the deal?"

I nodded, seeing no reason to try to lie at this point.

He brushed back my hair.

"I won't let anything happen to you, Wrenly."

"It's not fun eating your own words, Bennett. Be careful of the promises you make."

We ended up going for a run anyway because I was restless and he could smell it. Homework helped the time pass once we were back home.

Around dinner, Grandma stopped in to check on me. The whole family knew that I thought something bad was going to happen at the pack run. That everyone knew reduced the chances of something actually happening, but only marginally. After all, Bennett was rich, handsome, and a shifter, and he and I weren't from the same world. We were a shitty match in everyone's eyes, outside of the Wulf family. And the Wulfs were outnumbered, even if they were the ruling pack family.

Grandma reassured me that nothing would happen and that Bennett wouldn't take his eyes off me. I nodded, pretending to go along with it, but she could smell my disbelief. Just before dusk, she kissed my cheek and reminded me to be a menace.

"I always am," I said.

The meetup location was about twenty minutes away from Alpine Run. Bennett drove us since he was familiar with where we needed to go. It gave me time to overthink everything.

The pack ran on a swath of land that covered over twenty square miles. Trees covered the majority of the land, with a few meadows along the river that meandered through the north side. I'd need to avoid the meadows and stick to the trees. Climbing was my only hope.

I was so lost in thought that I didn't realize we were close until Bennett pulled into a gravel parking lot already partially filled with cars.

His hand covered mine when I reached to unbuckle myself.

"I can smell your nervousness," he said softly. "No one will hurt you."

I studied him in the dim light, seeing his concern but also his tension. The way his gaze dipped to my mouth showed the direction of his thoughts, though. It brought back memories of my last visit here and the unbridled matings that had occurred.

"You're thinking about everyone else, but what about you?" I asked.

His shock was pretty clear in the fading light.

"Never."

"I've been to one of these before, you know. Mating during the rush of the run is a common occurrence. What are the chances we're going to mate tonight?"

His mask slipped into place.

"Have you changed your mind about accepting your place as my mate?"

"No."

"We won't mate until you do."

"Are you sure? Because then I'll never be your mate."

I reached for my door and got out without waiting for him. His answering growl and knowing what waited for me in the trees kept me by my door until he joined me.

"Ready?" I asked, holding out my hand.

He glanced at it, his conflict visible in his expression, before he motioned for me to follow without taking my hand. I internally sighed. By not holding my hand, he was essentially declaring he didn't care about me, which would incite the females to act against me. While that worked for me in terms of gaining my freedom, it was counterproductive for leaving this run without serious injury.

Several more cars pulled in as we walked the path to the small clearing just inside the trees. People were already talking and undressing, preparing for the run. The moon was bright in the twilight, its light hiding nothing.

I didn't look, and I didn't let myself feel any embarrassment. The people here already had enough fuel to reject me as their future Alpha's mate. I didn't need to humble myself more.

Mom and Dad stood near the front of the clearing, talking with another couple. Thankfully, they were both still dressed. When Mom saw us, she smiled and motioned us forward.

"I'm so glad you're here," she said.

My nod of acknowledgment was the best I could do because I wasn't glad. I would have preferred a quiet night at home—alone— eating a pizza and watching a show.

"You probably don't remember the Duneklins…"

Mom slipped into her hostess role and began reintroducing me to the pack members. She didn't say I was Bennett's mate, but rather, I was the daughter her heart always yearned for. She kept me close to her side with an arm around my shoulders.

Her presence made the introductions more tolerable and less awkward since the number of people without clothes was increasing.

Bennett stayed next to Dad, chatting with anyone who approached them as Mom and I moved around the clearing. It was fully dark when Mom excused us, and we made our way back to Bennett and Dad.

Bennett's gaze searched mine as we approached. I couldn't tell what he was looking for, though. Nerves? Fear? He wouldn't find those anymore. I'd already made peace with both and accepted the outcome of the night as soon as I got out of the car. And each stilted greeting and long look from the females Mom had introduced was enough to confirm what I'd suspected the moment Bennett told Olivia I was his mate: I wouldn't hold the position of potential mate for long if they had anything to say about it.

"Before we begin, we have some welcome news to share," Dad said.

He looked at Bennett.

"The mate I found twelve years ago has finally acknowledged me." Bennett intertwined his fingers with mine before lifting our joined hands high. Shocked murmurs rippled through the crowd.

Mom and Dad beamed, either pretending or oblivious.

"On that happy note, let the pack run begin!" Dad said, unbuttoning his shirt.

Those already undressed started shifting.

Bennett turned me toward him.

"We'll stay here while the others run," he said.

"Why bother coming if you're not going to run?" I asked.

"Baby steps. We'll run next time."

We?

The clearing slowly emptied. I looked around, grateful for the moonlight but not the location.

"What's the point of staying?" I asked.

"Staying proves you have a place here."

I snorted. "You're as blind as Mom and Dad. If you had used your eyes, you would have seen that no one was happy about your announcement just now. Staying isn't going to prove anything."

But staying *would* give people the opportunity they needed.

"I did use my eyes. And you're right. People weren't happy. That doesn't mean they want to hurt you, though, Wrenly."

"Not the people here, maybe," I said under my breath.

When going around with Mom, I'd noticed a few key people missing. Olivia and the office girls, along with Storm and her crew. The numbers weren't in my favor. Having Miranda nearby would have helped, but I hadn't seen her either.

Bennett caught my arms and gave them what he probably thought was a reassuring squeeze.

"We're staying just in case Dad needs—"

Harsh snarling broke out deeper in the trees. A yip followed.

Bennett's attention immediately shifted in that direction. The way he tensed wasn't reassuring.

I reached for his hand. He glanced at me. I could see his concern and hesitation as his gaze swept over my face. Whatever was happening wasn't good. I opened my mouth to tell him I could run to the car, but I was up in his arms a second later.

He ran through the trees, and the sounds of snarls grew louder as we approached a pair of fighting wolves. It'd been so long since I'd seen Dad in his fur that I almost didn't recognize him. His opponent darted in for a nip to his flank, but Dad spun around with a snarl and went for him instead. The other wolf pivoted, rolled, and sprang to his feet, dodging the attack fluidly.

Before I could worry that Dad was outmatched, one of the three wolves watching the pair shifted to his human form.

"No interfering in a challenge," the man said.

I glanced at Bennett. His smile was chilling as he set me down.

"I was about to remind you of the same," he said. "Let's both act as witnesses."

"Are you sure you want to witness this challenge and not your mother's?"

I knew from Grandma that anyone in the pack could challenge the Alpha to take his position as Alpha. The only reason to challenge a pack member who wasn't the alpha was to take their position in the pack. In Mom's case, it would be her position as the Alpha's mate.

My heart skipped a beat, and the men smirked knowingly at me.

Don't let them smell your fear, Wrenly. That's what they want.

Bennett's hand settled on my shoulder.

"Who is dumb enough to challenge my mother? Everyone knows my parents are devoted to each other," Bennett said.

"As the Luna, your mom is responsible for guiding the next Alpha in his or her choice of a mate, a mate who will strengthen our pack, not weaken it."

Bennett's laugh wasn't filled with humor.

"Then you're challenging the wrong people. Who I choose as a mate is up to me, not my parents," Bennett said.

"Fine. Then I challenge you for the right to ascend."

The man shifted back into his wolf form and sprang toward Bennett. Bennett stepped in front of me, knocking the wolf aside. I retreated a step, then another as Bennett shifted to his fur, too.

The other two wolves watched me, rather than either of the fighting pairs.

"Let the chase begin," I said under my breath before I pivoted and ran.

Running on paths was fine. Running over obstacles was a lot harder. Almost four weeks of paved runs hadn't softened me, though. The muscle memory from my days of being chased down alleys and parkouring off trash was still there.

I cleared fallen tree trunks, hurdled over brush, and ran like my life depended on it. Because it did.

Spotting a large pine ahead with dead lower branches, I adjusted my path and, without slowing, caught a lower limb. I climbed hard and fast through the branches, scraping my palms and legs in my scramble. The pain didn't slow me down. Neither did the blood. The sap kept my grip from slipping.

When I heard a sharp crack below me, followed by a thud and cursing, I knew I'd climbed as high as I dared and stopped. I looked down and saw a man on the ground, lying on his back and dazedly staring up at me as he tried to draw in a breath. His partner was still on the tree limbs, trying to reach me.

"I'm lighter than you by at least fifty pounds," I said.

The rest of my warning died as the branch he grabbed broke. He lost his balance and fell, taking out several branches on the way down to join his friend.

I grimaced as he landed.

The first man to fall shifted to his fur and howled. An answering howl came from nearby. I looked off in that direction then up at the sky, trying to determine what direction it'd come from. Bennett's or the river?

"What's the point of climbing up there?" the second man who'd fallen asked.

I looked down at him.

"What's the point of chasing me?"

"You don't belong here."

"Yeah, I'm more of a pizza and movie streaming person than a run through the woods and climb a tree person, but I guess that's life. It's full of surprises."

"You're as mouthy as Storm said."

"Oh, I'm mouthier. I just don't know you well enough to give it any real effort."

He slowly got to his feet as something approached.

Please be Bennett.

The wolf didn't look like anyone in my family and stopped a healthy distance from me before shifting. It was Milena.

"You were supposed to chase her to the river."

"Yeah, well, she climbed a tree."

"And they're too heavy. Are you willing to risk everything to climb up here and get me, Milena?"

Her gaze flicked to me, showing all her hate.

"Listen, you're all barking up the wrong tree here. Literally. I wasn't given any choice about being Bennett's potential mate. If you don't like it, convince him to let me go. Going after me isn't going to fix the problem. It'll make it worse. He likes throwing things when he's mad. And you killing me is going to make him mad, not horny and desperate for a new mate."

"We won't know until we try," Milena said.

"By all means." I gestured to the branches below me.

She didn't move, though. By attacking me now, she'd leave her scent on the tree and me, which would ensure Bennett's hate, and she knew it.

Another howl rang out.

Both men swore. Milena looked from me to the direction from which she'd appeared.

"Plan B," she said. "Regroup in the clearing."

She shifted and sprinted back in the direction she'd come.

The men grumbled but shifted and ran off in the opposite direction.

Like any smart human, I kept my ass in the tree and my eyes on the ground, watching for a sneak attack. It didn't happen, though.

After several muscle-cramping minutes balanced in the tree, I watched Bennett approach in his fur. He sniffed where the two men had fallen, then looked up at me.

"Don't shift," I called. "I'll climb down to you. They're regrouping in the clearing, so I suggest that we avoid that and head for the car."

As I spoke, I started the arduous trip back to Earth.

"After they realized they couldn't get me down, Milena showed up. They were supposed to drive me to the river so whoever was waiting there could take care of me without leaving their scents all over."

Bennett growled below me.

"Hey, don't blame the messenger. Blame yourself for all of this. I told you this was going to happen. You could have claimed any of them as your potential mate and made everyone's lives easier. Did you honestly think that a pack of shifters would openly welcome a human as their *future alpha's* mate?"

During my tirade, I focused on where to place my feet and carefully lowered my weight each time. My hands were aching, and my arms were shaking by the time I reached the last branch.

The hands that gripped my waist were both a blessing and a curse.

"I told you not to shift," I said, knowing he was now completely naked behind me. I squeezed my eyes closed just before he spun me around.

"Look at me, Wrenly."

"No thank you."

He growled again, grabbed my chin, and kissed me. The gentleness of it made my heart race faster than his demanding kisses. I tried to fight the need to melt...to soften my mouth and welcome his touch, but it was impossible.

Heart thundering and chest aching, I parted my lips and kissed him back.

He cupped my face, keeping the kiss light and gentle, as he explored. It was so perfect that I didn't realize my arms had circled around his neck until he broke away to look down at me.

"No one can ever take your place, Wrenly. It's been you for over a decade. It'll be you for the rest of my life."

I closed my eyes again.

"I like you better when you don't talk."

"Liar," he said tenderly.

He took my hands, flipping them over to look at the sap-covered scrapes, which made him sigh and kiss my forehead before he threaded his fingers through mine.

"I'm walking back like this. You can peek if you want."

"Shut up, Bennett," I said, opening my eyes to avoid tripping as he led me through the trees.

My gaze didn't stay on the ground, though. It kept traveling the length of him, admiring the width of his shoulders, his lean back, and his ass. Was I a pervert? If I wasn't yet, I would be by the time we reached the car.

I was so busy being distracted that I didn't realize where he was leading us until I heard the faint echo of raised voices. Tearing my gaze from Bennett's backside, I focused on the trees and spied the clearing ahead.

I tried tugging my hand free of Bennett's, but he didn't ease up.

With absolutely no willingness, I entered the clearing a step behind Bennett to see a divided crowd. More than half stood behind Mom and Dad, who were facing off with the remaining pack members.

"Wrenly has been a Wulf for the last thirteen years. She has always had our love and our protection. As the future Luna of this pack, she also deserves your respect," Mom said.

"She's unworthy," Olivia said.

"It's our right to challenge," Milena said.

Mom's face was scratched, but she otherwise looked okay. By okay, I meant uninjured. Her mood was another story. She looked two heartbeats away from murder.

"She's human," Mom said. "It's against our laws to harm humans unless in the preservation of another life. Wrenly isn't harming anyone."

"She's harming our pack," a man said. "How can a human lead our pack?"

"A human won't. Bennett will," Dad said.

"Our laws state we can challenge for a position," Milena said. "I challenge Wrenly for her position as Bennett's mate. The law is there to preserve the strength of the pack. If you can't uphold our laws, you and your mate aren't fit to lead."

"Fine," I called. "But I get a knife since I don't have claws."

Everyone's attention shifted to me. The half who were arguing for their right to challenge looked stunned.

Bennett and Mom both shot me a look of frustration.

"What? This is the path you set us on the moment you decided I was your mate." I shrugged. "We reap what we sow."

I looked at the pack members. "Who has a knife?"

"This is a pack run. Why would we have knives?" Olivia asked.

"I have a few in my truck. Hold on," a man from Mom and Dad's side said. He shifted and bolted for the parking lot.

"I invoke position preservation," Mom said.

"You can't. You're related."

"Not by blood," Mom said.

"What's position preservation?" I asked Bennett as they argued about relationships by choice.

"It's where another unrelated pack member accepts a challenge on behalf of an injured or sick pack member. It's meant to keep challenges fair and show strength through support when physical strength doesn't exist."

"Even though she's not blood related or legally your daughter, you've always treated her like one. And as Bennett just pointed out, she's not injured or sick. She's *human*," Milena said.

"This is how you show your loyalty?" Dad said. "The Wulfs have helped each family here over the years. We've prospered together. If you think you can do better without us, so be it. I won't just step down... We'll leave the pack."

Leaving the pack meant all the financial support would go too. The people supporting my parents started to argue again with the people trying to evict me.

The man returned while everyone was still yelling at each other.

I accepted the knives from him, briefly testing the grips and weights before handing back all but one.

"Wrenly, I'm not going to let—"

Bennett's words were cut off when Miranda appeared beside me.

"It's for your own good, Wrenly," she said, stealing the knife from my hand.

Pain bloomed across my forearm before I even saw her move.

CHAPTER TWENTY-NINE

"FUCK!" The word didn't alleviate the burning sting as I slapped my other hand over my forearm. While it wasn't my first cut, it was definitely the deepest.

"Get something to stop the bleeding," Bennett snarled.

"I invoke position preservation," Miranda called over the sound of my harsh breathing. "I'm not related, and Wrenly's too injured to fight."

Someone passed a shirt to Bennett. The pressure helped ease some of the pain as I watched Miranda stride to the center of the clearing.

"What the fuck, Miranda?" Olivia seethed. "You're siding with the normie?"

"I'm team Wrenly all the way," she said.

She sure had a funny way of showing it.

"Now, who exactly am I fighting in Wrenly's place for the position of Bennett's mate? Or is the female who issued it going to try to slink away with her tail tucked now that it's a fair fight?"

Milena snarled and stepped forward.

"Five of us issued the challenge."

Miranda smirked. "Oh, I think I'm going to like this."

I glanced at Bennett, who wasn't looking at the females who were joining Milena, but at me.

"Is she going to be okay?" I asked.

"We need to get you to a hospital. She cut too deep."

"She cut just deep enough," Mom said calmly, coming to stand beside me. She was wearing clothes again, and the scratch on her face was healed to the point that it looked like a fading scar.

"The rules for a challenge are clear," Dad said. "One on one. No interference from anyone. Interfere and you're banished from the pack."

"What?" one of the women cried. "Why?"

"To preserve the strength of the pack," Dad said. "I won't tolerate members who can't obey pack laws."

They didn't like having their argument thrown back at them.

"You shouldn't have accepted the challenge," Mom said from beside me.

"Do you honestly think they were going to stop if I'd said no?" I panted, desperate for the lingering sting and throb in my arm to stop.

"No. We knew they wouldn't, which was why we were willing to leave the pack. Wulf Enterprises has a global reach. We can move our headquarters and start a new pack anywhere." She spoke loudly enough for everyone to hear.

Clever woman. She was giving them all a choice. Fight fair, or the Wulf's will leave.

"Well?" Miranda demanded. "Who's first?"

Milena spread her arms wide in acceptance.

"Skin or fur?" she asked Milena.

Milena answered by shifting. Miranda was a second behind her, which Milena tried to use to her advantage. It didn't work. Miranda twisted out of the way as her claws formed, and she raked them across Milena's face.

Milena yipped and snarled as she tried again. It took seconds for me to realize that Miranda was toying with her. But why? She had four more to fight. She couldn't afford to—I glanced at them and realized the four women were starting to look worried.

Understanding hit me like lightning. I knew from my own experience that body strength and speed were only part of the fight. The rest was mental.

"If Miranda takes one of Milena's eyes out, can I have your card for another shopping spree day?" I asked Bennett.

One of the four women paled.

I glanced at Bennett, who was still staring at my arm, or rather, the bloody shirt covering my arm, and stuck out my bottom lip in a pout. He glanced up, and I watched him have a full facial twitch, like he couldn't decide how to feel about what I was doing.

"Please?" I said softly.

His gaze met mine again, and he looked drunk.

"Anything you want."

I grinned and looked at Miranda just as she snarled and dove for Milena in a direct attack.

Milena squealed and immediately rolled to her belly before Miranda even touched her.

The chuffing snort that came out of Miranda conveyed her contempt quite well.

"Milena, you've forfeited your right to challenge for Wrenly's position as Bennett's mate," Dad said. "Yours is the only forfeit I'll accept tonight."

"Why?" someone called out.

"A challenge isn't a game. Each challenge questions the strength of our hierarchy and destabilizes the pack. We fight until we cannot stand. Now, who's next?"

The other four exchanged glances. The most nervous of them stepped forward.

"I withdraw my challenge." She faced me, got to her knees, and bowed until her forehead touched the ground. "I recognize Wrenly as Bennett's future mate."

The other two quickly followed suit, with Olivia reluctantly kneeling last.

"This ends tonight," Dad said. "All challenges to Wrenly's position as your future Alpha's mate are open for the next three days. After that, if her position in this pack is ever again questioned solely based on her race, the Wulfs will leave the pack. We want nothing to do with a pack that discriminates based on race rather than looking at an individual's contribution to the pack."

I watched the group opposing my position exchange glances.

"An Alpha who prevents challenges isn't fit to lead," one of them said.

"I'm not preventing all challenges—just the ones issued because of her race. If you don't believe she has a place as the future Luna of our pack, know that Wrenly has saved Wulf Enterprises over three billion dollars since returning home. I used the money *she* found to invest in Bill's garage, Emily's middle school, Carly's catering, and Winter's farm. Cars were purchased for the families who needed new ones. Your pups' tuitions were paid. And all of it was because Wrenly found the extra money.

"She's sitting in the same chair that dozens of other people have sat in and has done more in the few weeks she's been home than all of them combined, and you're still saying she's not worthy? Why? Just because she doesn't have fur? What good is fur at the bank? What good is it when your mortgage needs to be paid? Only a small portion of our lives is lived in the woods. Get with the times."

Dad looked angry until his gaze met mine, and he sighed.

"You're more tolerant than everyone here, and I'm sorry for everything you've had to suffer, Sweetheart."

His sincerity made my chest ache more than the cut on my arm.

"I think I need to go to the hospital now," I said, looking at Bennett's bloody hands.

"I'll drive," Mom said.

"I call shotgun," Miranda said, surprising me.

Mom nodded, and Bennett scooped me up into his arms. I hissed at the renewed sting and throbbing in my cut and leaned into him as he ran.

A LAYER of taped gauze covered the seventeen stitches in my forearm. I made a face at it, knowing all the future trouble it would bring me. My bandaged palms were nothing in comparison.

"Hey, a little pain now saves you from a lot of pain later," Miranda said.

I shot her a glare, and she shrugged before turning to watch Mom and Bennett talk to the doctor.

"How exactly are seventeen stitches going to help my long-term goals?" I asked under my breath. It wasn't soft enough, though. Bennett's gaze briefly flicked to me.

"My goal was to keep you from long-term hospitalization or death. I achieved it. You can thank me later with a shopping trip. That was a nice touch, by the way, asking for her eye. If she hadn't rolled over so fast, I would have gone for it. There's a designer bag I've had my eye on forever but can't afford."

"Are you forgetting that you still have to face any challenges for my position that are issued over the next three days?"

"Pfft. Do you honestly think any of them have the backbone to face me?"

I considered her question. "Maybe not the women from the office but…" I thought of Storm, weighing what I knew of her now, which was very little, against what I remembered of her when we were younger.

Before I could say anything else, Mom and Bennett came back to where I was sitting.

"You look exhausted, Sweetheart. Bennett has all the care instructions and can take you home now. Dad and I will come tomorrow to check in." She leaned in to kiss my forehead, then faced Miranda. "I'll give you a ride back."

"Thanks, Mrs. Wulf. See you Monday, Wrenly."

I watched the pair of them walk away and then looked up at Bennett. His jaw was tight. Again. Sensing he was a wolf on the edge, I gave him my best sad face.

"I'm hungry."

He inhaled slowly, and his anger and frustration evaporated.

"What are you hungry for?"

"A greasy breakfast that we have to stop somewhere to eat."

"Okay."

He held out his hand, and I placed my good—well, better—one in it to stand. He didn't let it go. We walked to the car like that, definitely reaching the five-minute time limit. But I didn't say anything. I just let him open the door for me and got in.

The twenty-four-hour diner he found wasn't exactly the cleanest and smelled like old fryer grease when we walked in, but I didn't care. I hadn't lied when I said I was hungry. It was close to three in the morning.

I ordered the "Big Man Breakfast" and smiled when Bennett did the same.

"What?" he asked when the waitress walked away.

"I thought you wouldn't eat anything here."

"Why?"

"It's not your level."

"I didn't know I had a level."

I snorted. "You wear tailored suits, Bennett, and I'm guessing you make seven figures a year, easily."

"Wrong on the second part," he said with a smile tugging his lips. "High income is the way to pay high taxes, so I'm paid in stocks instead."

I rolled my eyes at him.

"Either way, your net worth does not equate to dive-dining."

"But it equates to you, and you like dive-dining, so that's what I like."

"What are you going to do about Miranda?" I asked, preferring to change the subject so I could watch him eat his words once the food was served.

"Give her a raise and hand you my card so you can take her shopping."

I lifted my arm. "Nothing for this?"

He raised a brow. "Should I give her more?"

"Seventeen stitches, Bennett! Is she even my friend?"

He started to lean back in his seat in his borrowed clothes, thought better of it, and leaned in toward me.

"She did what I couldn't, what Mom was afraid to do, and what Dad would have had to do if Miranda hadn't stepped up. None of us wanted to see you hurt, Wrenly, but Miranda was right. How she hurt you is better than what would have happened."

My thoughts veered to what Grandma had told me about Bennett seeing me on TV and saying I would disappear forever if they didn't bring me home.

"Maybe you're right. Maybe the hell-school you sent me to saved me from something worse, too. I still hate you for sending me there, though," I said before I could stop myself.

He flinched, and his mask slipped into place.

"That is a mistake I'll regret for the rest of my life."

I shrugged and looked down at my arm.

"I have a lot I'm regretting too." *Like coming home*, I thought silently. "It's not going to be fun trying to type with this."

"You can take off as much time as you need."

"From work, maybe, but I have my summer course I need to keep up with."

"I'll help you turn pages, type, anything you need."

I glanced up at him and saw the yearning in his gaze. For what, though? To make up for the cut? To be with me? For my acceptance?

Rather than figuring out the answer, I realized just then that

Bennett probably understood some of my suffering. At least, more than anyone else. He knew exactly what it felt like to be unwanted. Why did that make me hurt for him?

I looked away again, watching as the waitress grabbed our plates from the cook.

"I wish I could hear your thoughts," Bennett said.

"It's mostly a confused jumble that would land you in a padded room within four hours."

He sighed and didn't say anything until the waitress delivered our food and left.

"It's frustrating when you deflect. I don't know if you're doing it because it's a closed subject or if you're doing it to keep us from getting closer."

"Closer implies we're close," I said, picking up my fork.

"We sleep together."

"Not by choice. Eat your food, Bennett."

I awkwardly forked a mix of eggs and hash browns into my mouth with my non-dominant hand and fought to keep my face straight. Years of eating posh food had either ruined me, or the cook was using a griddle that hadn't been properly cleaned since the turn of the century.

Without looking up, I continued chewing and got my next bite ready as I waited for Bennett to take his first bite. It was comical. He froze for two seconds then reached for his napkin. I moved fast, reaching across the table to steal it from him.

"Seventeen stitches. Swallow it, Bennett."

He did. Without chewing.

"I will have the exact same food waiting for you at home if you promise me we can leave without finishing this," he said, his revulsion still on his face.

"No deal. There's no reason to wake Sandy up in the middle of the night. We go home, and *you* make the food while I shower. And when I go back to work, I get absolute freedom during my lunch hour to do what I want without interference from you."

"I agree to cooking while you shower, but not absolute lunch freedom. Not while you're hurt. You don't have to be with me, but you have to be with someone I trust to keep you safe, like Miranda, Mom, or Grandma."

"How is Miranda first on your list when she cut me?"

"You know why."

Because she'd done what everyone else would have hesitated to do. I sighed.

"Fine. Cook for me while I shower, and I'll do what I want with my lunch hours with an approved escort for as long as I have stitches."

"Deal."

"Deal." I laid my napkin over the food and stood.

Bennett tossed a one-hundred-dollar bill on the table and walked out behind me.

The numbness in my arm was starting to wear off by the time Bennett pulled into the garage. Even though I didn't say or do anything, he knew I was hurting. I could tell by how frequently he glanced at me.

"Food, Bennett."

He got out and came around to open the door for me.

"How fresh should the oil be for your hash browns? Is a week too fresh?" he asked.

I snorted and followed him into the kitchen.

"Just make them greasy and good."

He stopped me when I would have left.

"Wait. Let me wrap your arm."

He had it plastic-wrapped and taped off before he sent me on my way.

It took some time before I reemerged from my shower.

Bennett was sitting on my bed, holding a steaming plate of food. His gaze swept over me from head to toe, lingering on the towel I had pinned to my chest with my non-stitched arm.

"I can eat downstairs."

"You could, but I know you're tired. Did the stitches stay dry?"

"They did. Are you going to leave?"

"No."

He was right about the tired part because I didn't care enough to tell him to get out. Ignoring him, I walked into my closet and turned to close the door. A second later, I was pinned to the wall, his hands on my shoulders.

"This is new," I said. "Guess the hands above the head thing is in a timeout until the stitches are removed."

His pupils expanded. "I guess I'll just need to find out another way to sweeten your scent."

"Is that what you were doing?"

"Do you have any idea how desperate you make me when you respond like this? Calm. Slightly challenging. Unafraid. Kiss me, Wrenly."

I snorted. "No, thank you. I'll risk tearing stitches when I try to hit you."

"You won't need to hit me. Just one kiss like you promised."

"When did I promise to kiss you?" I asked, more amused than annoyed.

"You said that you'd willingly kiss me with no timer, and you would initiate it if you weren't maliciously hurt tonight."

A laugh escaped me, and I lifted my arm.

He slowly shook his head. "That wasn't malicious. Miranda was preventing you from being maliciously hurt. And you weren't hurt before that."

I lifted my hands to show the scrapes that the doctor hadn't been too concerned about.

"Those don't count. They were self-inflicted."

"And I'm only unhurt otherwise because I ran and climbed fast."

"A deal is a deal." He leaned in closer. "Kiss me, Wrenly."

I considered him and my options. If I refused, he'd never make a deal with me again. We'd lose the trust we'd gained. But I also saw his current state. Would he be content with just a kiss, or would his desperation only increase? I trusted him not to take what I wasn't willing to give, but I also knew he would try anything and everything to get me to say yes. And my attraction to him and what he could do to my scent would push him to push me.

He was already a wolf on the edge. I didn't want to tempt him more.

Or maybe I did.

"You're right. A deal is a deal, and I won't go back on my word. Would you consider delaying payment until my stitches are out so I don't hurt myself if it evolves into more than a kiss?"

He made a choked sound and started to shake violently.

Seismic-level tremors.

I only had a half a second to think, "Oh shit," before he pushed away and let out a strangled sound. His clothes ripped as he suddenly shifted from skin to fur.

Pivoting, I ran from the closet and slammed the door behind me. The solid thunk of his body hitting it was followed by his claws scrabbling for the knob as I bolted for my phone. Shaking hard, I speed dialed Grandma and locked myself in the bathroom.

She picked up with a serious, "What's wrong?"

"Bennett shifted. I shut him in the closet."

"Do you want me to come over or talk to you until he calms down?"

"Will he?" I could hear his clawing through the doors.

"He'll have to if he wants to come out of the closet."

Despite everything, I snorted.

"There's my Wren," she said softly. "Do you want to tell me what happened?"

"We made a bet that I lost. He wanted to collect on the kiss that I owe him, but I asked for an extension until the stitches are out." I hesitated for a second. "I said it was in case the kiss turned into something more on purpose so he'd agree to wait."

Grandma chuckled. The soft sound helped deescalate some of the fear running through me.

"I imagine it will be a while before he can use his hands. Do you want company?"

I looked down at myself, realizing my only covering was the plastic wrap.

"No, I don't think so. Will he be all right with me once he's out?"

"Yep. What you need to do is sit outside that door and tell him how much he scared you, and ask if he's going to shift and risk your safety every time you try to get close to him. That'll set him on his heels for a good while. The last thing he'll want to do is risk your safety. And he certainly doesn't want you to be afraid of getting closer to him."

"If he hurts me, you have to promise to be his executioner on my behalf."

"Without hesitation," Grandma said. "I love you, my sweet little Wren, and that has nothing to do with who you might be to Bennett. Now go make him regret his frayed control."

"I will. Thank you, Grandma. And I love you too."

As soon as I hung up, I eased the bathroom door open, hoping that he wouldn't hear me. Based on the continued scratching and growling, he didn't. I streaked out of my room and into his. Then I raided his closet for a shirt that covered my ass.

Less exposed, I returned to my room. I didn't approach my closet, though. I stayed right by my door.

"Bennett? Can you hear me?"

All sound from inside the closet stopped.

"You told me not to be afraid of you...that you'd never hurt me. But what just happened scared the hell out of me. And the way you're clawing that door isn't giving me any safe vibes. Are you going to shift and risk my safety every time I try to get close to you?"

A soft thud came from the door.

"I'm going to take my plate to the kitchen and eat there to give you some time to calm down. When you're back to yourself and dressed, come find me. Okay?"

I heard a quiet chuff, which I took as a sign of agreement.

Watching the door, I crept around the bed for the plate of food he'd left there. Then I bolted.

Everything had happened so fast that the food was still warm when I sat down at the island. I ate a few bites, then removed the plastic wrap from my arm.

After I finished my food, I put the plate in the sink and debated what to do next. I was tired and just wanted to go to bed, but I wasn't sure it would be a good idea to fall asleep before I knew Bennett's state of mind.

I wandered out of the kitchen.

My phone buzzed with a text before I reached the bottom of the stairs, and my stomach dipped when I saw Bennett's name.

Bennett: I left a pain reliever and a glass of water on your nightstand. If you're willing, we can talk in the morning.

CHAPTER THIRTY

I STARED at the hallway at the top of the stairs, debating what to do.

It didn't bode well for me that Bennett was keeping his distance this time, not after that big of a control slip. I shouldn't have insinuated that I was willing to do more than kiss him because I wasn't. I hadn't changed my mind. After everything I'd been through, I deserved a life of my own, on my own terms.

Me: Thank you. I'll see you in the morning.

He didn't answer. I looked up the stairs again, feeling nervous. Was he waiting for me? Would he pounce? Would I survive if he did?

I glanced at my bandaged arm and made a face at the white gauze, my only protection against the big, horny shifter who wanted me to be his mate.

Me: He's still upstairs, and I'm tired. Will he leave me alone if I go to bed, or will I wake up pregnant?
Grandma: He'll leave you alone, but I'm happy to come over and sit outside your door if you have any doubts.

I bit my lip and debated between my fears and my guilt over interrupting Grandma's sleep. Guilt won.

Me: No need. I'll stop being a baby and go to bed.
Grandma: You're not a baby, and I understand why you
don't trust him. My phone is right next to me. Call or text
anytime. I love you, my little Wren.

Her unwavering support helped bolster my courage. If I hadn't been wearing just a T-shirt, I would have felt less nervous. Not that underwear would have been much protection in his current mood.

I quietly crept up the stairs and saw his door was closed when I turned down the hall—a good sign, since I hadn't closed it. My bedroom door was open, but my closet door wasn't. What did that mean? Was he still in the closet, or his room?

Unsure how safe I was, I quickly got under the covers and turned off the bedside light. With my stitched forearm prominently displayed on top of the covers, over my chest, I closed my eyes. I thought it would take me forever to fall asleep. It should have with my suspicion that Bennett was still in my closet. But between the two runs and the trauma, I was out before I even knew I was going under.

THE RHYTHMIC SENSATION of someone petting my hair roused me out of sleep at some point before dawn.

"I'm not going to survive," Bennett said softly.

His mouth brushed my forehead, and I realized I was using him as a body pillow with my stitched arm on his chest.

"I'm losing my mind thinking about you possibly wanting me like I want you. I should leave, but I can't."

His words brought me further out of sleep.

"Shh. Sleep," I murmured.

"Sorry, baby. I'll go to sleep."

I nodded against his chest and sank right back under.

THE SPACE beside me was empty when I woke up. I started to reach out to feel his spot and winced at the feel of my heartbeat in my arm.

"I have an ice pack if you want it," Bennett said.

Turning my head, I saw him standing next to the bed.

I flushed and nodded, wondering if he knew what I'd been reaching for.

Instead of handing over the ice pack, he carefully placed it on my arm as he sat beside me. He looked tired, his hair wasn't styled like he usually did, and he was wearing a long-sleeved shirt and pants that didn't match.

"I'm sorry about last night. The cut. The stitches. Losing control. All of it."

He kept his gaze on my arm instead of looking at me like he usually did as he continued speaking.

"Grandma says true mates rarely wait. Like humans, we sometimes date first—but the deeper the bond, the faster we claim each other. If we delay, it's usually because we're unsure or hoping for someone better.

"For me, it's always been you. From the moment I saw you, I knew. My certainty has never wavered.

"Every day we were apart cut deeper than the last. I could barely think straight some days.

"You said I was perfect, but I'm not. I mastered everything I set my mind to because I had to. It was the only way to survive wanting you. I pushed myself to become the mate who could protect you in both our worlds. I could run Wulf Enterprises or challenge for Alpha without hesitation. But when it comes to you...I've never known how to stop needing you.

"I'm good at everything I've set my mind to, except you. I promised I would do better, but every time I try, I fail. I thought I was listening, but I wasn't."

He finally looked up and met my gaze. "I won't stop you from going to Coalwell. No strings. No conditions. I'll stay in the apartment—not to watch you, just to be close, in case you need me."

I should have been elated, jumping with joy. Instead, it felt like a hollow victory. Maybe that was just the stitches and my throbbing arm talking, though.

He continued to watch me, waiting for a response, but I wasn't sure what one to give. I could tell him I'd be safer without him around, but my time at school proved that was a lie. I could thank him for finally listening, but he wasn't actually letting me go. At least, not fully. He would still be close by.

The words he'd whispered last night rose in my mind.

I'm not going to survive.

My heart gave an uncomfortable lurch.

No matter what, I couldn't say the truth—that the thought of him living alone after he admitted each day without me hurt him left me feeling empty and selfish. Hating that feeling, I looked down at my arm.

Don't go soft now, Wrenly. Tell him you're safer without him. You earned your freedom.

When I lifted my gaze again, he was a little too slow masking his anguish.

Dammit.

"Can we agree to stop worrying about tomorrow and focus on each day as it comes? At least until the stitches are out?" I asked.

He nodded as his mask slipped back into place.

"Good. I need some food, a pain reliever, and my laptop at the dining table for some study time."

I didn't ask him what he needed because I already knew. Me. He just needed me.

He handed me the medicine he had left for me the night before, along with the glass of water.

"Do you want to shower again? I can wrap your arm."

"No, I think I'll skip that for now. Would you mind carrying my laptop downstairs while I get dressed?"

He hesitated, his gaze flicking to my closet.

"Would you mind if I picked out some clothes for you again? I'd rather you not go into your closet until I fix the door."

"Okay."

While he went to the closet, I got out of bed and used the bathroom. My laptop was gone, and the bed was made by the time I walked out again. The set of clothes he'd selected was comfortably loose and easy enough to pull on left-handed. Worming my way into a sports bra was a little more difficult and took some time.

The scent of something mouthwatering drew me downstairs to the dining room.

"What is that?" I asked, looking at the pool of whitish-grey gravy on the plate next to my waiting laptop.

"Biscuits and gravy. It wasn't something the school ever served, so I thought you might—"

My ass was in the chair before he could finish, and I could feel him watching me messily scooping up a bite with my left hand. Half of it fell back onto the plate before I could get it to my mouth, but what did make it in was divine.

I moaned in appreciation and wiggled in my chair as I chewed. How long had it been since I'd tasted anything like this? I scooped up another bite, losing another portion of it, and shoved it into my mouth.

Bennett held out his hand, interrupting my bliss.

My gaze shifted from his hand to his face. His pupils were fully dilated, and the intensity of his gaze spelled trouble. For me.

"What?" I asked.

"Give me your fork."

I made a sad face and pulled my fork close to my chest.

"I'm not taking it away, Wrenly. Let me help you."

Understanding that he wanted to feed me, I shook my head.

"If you want to help me, get me a spoon. Please?"

He hesitated. I could see in his gaze that he was waging a silent war with himself. One side wanted to feed me because he was desperate to be the one to make his mate happy. Yet, I'd asked for something different. By not listening to me, he'd make me unhappy.

Listening to me won. Withdrawing his hand, he stood and went to the kitchen. I continued to use my fork until he handed over a spoon.

By the time my plate was messily scraped clean, I sat back with a full belly and a sense of relief since the ice pack and pain relievers were finally doing their job.

"That was the best breakfast I've had in years," I said.

"Would you like it again tomorrow, or should I find something else you might like?"

I thought about it for a second.

"Surprise me."

The corner of his mouth lifted with a hint of a smile that made my heart trip over itself.

"Can I surprise you now?"

"What do you mean?" I asked, suspicion filling me.

"Something else I think you'll like if you're interested in a short drive before we start on your homework."

Intrigued, I nodded.

He helped me put on my shoes, tying them for me as I set a hand on his shoulder for balance. Catching my hand when he was done, he led me out to the car and buckled me in. He'd done the same thing for me for days already, but something about it felt different. I couldn't put my finger on what though.

Just before he shut my door, he kissed my forehead. I touched the spot as he walked around the car, wondering why he was still showing me affection when he'd already agreed to let me go.

...it's always been you.

I watched him get in and realized letting me go wasn't him giving up on me. His love for me was for life.

My heart gave another odd beat that hurt more than the last one.

I reached up and rubbed my chest. He noticed the move and glanced at me as he drove down the driveway.

"Are you all right?"

"Yeah. Just feeling a little uncomfortable. Maybe I slept wrong."

As soon as I said that, I remembered how I'd slept last night, pantyless and using him as a body pillow.

"Are you going to give me any hints about where we're going?" I asked to distract myself as much as to distract him.

"It's something you've always wanted to do."

I frowned, thinking. How would Bennett know what I wanted to do? We weren't that close.

He knows you want to try new things. He knows you love running and hate skirts. He knows you want a friend and lets you leave work with Miranda whenever you want. He knows you have bad dreams and sleeps with you to stop them. He knows you felt unloved at school and is doing everything in his power to show you how loved you are now.

That last thought was an epiphany that crushed me.

Why did he have to show me now when I was done? When I was determined to be free?

"Your scent is all over the place. What's wrong? Do you want to go home?"

"No. I'm fine. Just thinking."

He didn't pry as he continued driving.

When he turned into a gas station, I was insanely curious. I'd never been to one. At least, not for as long as I could remember. He didn't pull up next to a gas pump, though. He parked in a spot in front of it.

MELISSA HAAG

I turned to him to ask what we were doing and found him holding out his credit card.

"You can go in to buy study snacks by yourself, or I can go with you and act as your arms. Up to you."

I looked from him to the card to the gas station, a smile growing on my face.

"I need you to be my arms."

His gaze swept over my face, and he darted in to brush my lips with his. He was out of the car, and his card was in my hand before I registered what he'd done. I was still trying to process how I felt about the stolen kiss when he opened the door for me and offered me a hand out.

Dazed, I slipped my hand into his without considering the consequences. His fingers gripped mine, and he pulled me so close my nose almost brushed his chest. Why did I want to lean into him and brush my cheek against his shirt?

The door closed behind me, and he released me.

I realized he'd only pulled me close to shut the door and flushed. His fingers caught my chin and tipped my head back to meet his gaze. He didn't say anything, just studied my face.

"I'm crazy for you...with you...without you. I never stood any chance. Anything you want, anything you need, it's yours. You only need to tell me. Do you understand?"

Catching the edge of my lip between my teeth, I debated whether I was just as insane because I wanted to ask him for a hug.

Me.

With Bennett.

Willingly.

His thumb brushed over my bottom lip, freeing it from the light hold of my teeth.

His pupils were going wild again.

"Can I ask you something without you shifting in public?"

He nodded.

"Can I just..." Rather than finishing the question, I shuffled a step forward and lifted my arms to wrap them around his waist. Then I rested my head against his chest like I'd wanted to do. It felt so good. Comforting.

He made a pained sound a second before his arms closed around me. Cocooned in his embrace, I let myself just exist in the moment. His shaking gave away his struggle after a minute, though.

I eased out of his hold and looked up at him.

"Thank you."

He swallowed hard and fisted his hands at his sides.

"Go inside and look around. I'll join you in a bit."

I nodded and turned toward the door. He stepped around me and opened it. Even though he was shaking and struggling for control, he stood there and held the door for me until I was inside.

When I glanced back, he was already pacing next to the car.

"You guys fighting?" the woman at the register asked, watching him with me.

"Actually, we're getting along for a change, and I think it's breaking him."

He paused, glancing at me, proving he could hear.

"I'd pay to have a man broken for me like that," the woman said. "And my husband would pay to have a new truck. Different priorities, I guess."

"You're right. Maybe you should prioritize yourself over your husband, just as he's prioritizing himself over you. It might open his eyes."

"Or he might divorce me."

"He might. But do you want to stay where you aren't valued and appreciated for your worth?"

The woman's expression closed down. Understanding that my opinion was no longer welcome, I went to browse the snacks.

Bennett joined me a few minutes later, and I had fun pointing to all the snacks I wanted to try. There were so many that Bennett had to make several trips to the counter with them. When the woman checked us out, she kept glancing at Bennett. Not in a flirty way, but an evaluating one.

It made me question the way Bennett treated me, too.

Yes, he'd made mistakes that had irrevocably hurt me. But his regret for what he'd done in ignorance was real. He was making every effort to make up for it, including finally listening to me.

I bit my lip again as he paid.

He turned suddenly, grabbed the back of my head, and sucked my bottom lip into his mouth. My stomach dipped, and my breath caught. Then his mouth was gone, and he had an arm wrapped around my shoulders as he accepted the card back from the woman.

Her gaze met mine.

"I wish I were as smart as you are when I was your age."

"It's never too late," I said. "We get one life, right?"

"We humans do." She handed the bags to Bennett, who had to release me to accept them. "I'd give anything to be a phoenix shifter and get a do-over."

"They don't get do-overs," Bennett said. "Their pasts are always with them."

He nodded and, with one arm loaded with bags, led me out of the store. I waited until we were outside.

"Do you really know a phoenix?"

"I do."

"Is it true that there aren't many of them?"

"It is. They were hunted to the brink of extinction by people who believed they could steal their ability to be reborn."

He opened the door for me and then shut it, leaving me inside while he put the snacks in the trunk. When he got in, he inhaled deeply.

"Why are you sad?" he asked.

"I was just thinking of what you said—being hunted because you can live again. I don't think I'd want to live again. It would take the magic out of living the life I'm living now."

Bennett nodded. "The one I know feels the same way. He said

that each life gets lonelier than the last because he's watched too many people he'd cared about die."

"That just makes me more sad for them. Your friend doesn't have a phoenix mate? Wife? Whatever?"

"No."

Bennett started the car and didn't say anything else until we were back home and at the table.

"Which snack would you like me to open first?" he asked.

I pointed. He obliged and then opened my laptop.

Inarguably, he was a better assistant than I was. He did everything I said without question. He got me something to drink before I realized I was thirsty and suggested a walk after the hour I spent reading the assignment.

We strolled in the backyard, talking about the class and the text. Bennett was smart and insightful. He helped me understand what I'd read and how it applied to more than the context in which it'd been given.

When we returned to the dining room, he opened a new snack for me since I didn't want to finish the previous one. At some point while I read, he disappeared to fix lunch. Nachos. Another first. It was as messy and as delicious as breakfast. I was getting better at eating with my left hand.

We took another walk after lunch, still around the back yard because I was very aware of how many pack members did not like me now.

Mom, Dad, and Grandma showed up around dinnertime.

"There's my girl," Grandma said, holding out her arms for a hug, which I quickly stood to give.

It felt good, but so different from the one I'd gotten from Bennett in the parking lot.

She pulled back, her gaze briefly flicking to Bennett, the table, then settling on me again.

"Everything seems okay now?" She said it like a question, and I knew she was referring to my panicked, middle-of-the-night call to her.

"It is. Sorry for waking you up."

She waved away my apology as Mom asked, "Did something happen?"

"I lost control," Bennett said.

Mom's stare hardened. "What do you mean, you 'lost control'?" The growl behind the words grew as her irises expanded.

Remembering the handprint on his face, the last time she'd gotten mad at him, I quickly side-stepped so I stood between her and him.

"It's not what you think, Mom. He suddenly shifted, scaring me. I'm fine. I promise."

She pulled her angry gaze from him to look down at me. I saw her surprise and joy.

"Are you defending Bennett?"

"He's more needy when you slap him. I'm just making my life easier."

Dad cleared his throat, and I knew he was trying not to laugh as Mom snorted.

"You're too good for him," she said.

"Mom, I'm your son," Bennett said, only sounding a little offended.

"I know. Where did I go wrong to raise such a thickheaded man?"

Although she said it with playful affection, I felt a stirring of bittersweet regret. I'd spent so many years thinking they didn't love me. The hurt and terror had blinded me to the truth. Every person in the room would give their lives for me.

"I love you, Mom."

She looked surprised for a second before she hugged me.

"I love you, too, Sweetheart. You can call me in the middle of the night too."

"I know. But Grandma was closer."

She jerked a little and withdrew to glare at Bennett.

"We'll change that today."

I both sighed and laughed at the growl in her voice.

"Mom, it's actually kind of nice only having to deal with Bennett's overprotectiveness. I think all of you at once would be a bit much for me. And I know that's what would happen. My track record for safety hasn't been the best." I held up my stitched arm.

She opened her mouth.

"Before you say anything, I know you only left because Bennett wanted it. I know you love me and want to be here. And I promise I won't step outside this door without an escort capable of keeping me safe."

She sighed and gave me another quick hug.

"I hate that you know me better than I know you."

"That's an easy fix. Typing will be impossible for me for a while, which means I can't go to work. How do you feel about a Mom and Wrenly day tomorrow?" I glanced at Grandma. "You're welcome too, of course."

"What about me?" Dad asked.

"Someone needs to run the company and stop Bennett from throwing things when Wrenly's not there," Mom said.

Bennett snorted, and I grinned with Grandma.

CHAPTER THIRTY-ONE

BENNETT WAS quiet as he drove us into the city. Not a moody quiet, just quiet. He'd been attentive and helpful this morning as I got ready, going so far as to brush my hair and pull it back into a ponytail. I'd pretended not to notice the way his fingers had brushed my neck before he'd stepped away. Just like I was pretending not to notice his nervous energy.

He didn't need to say he was worried. I already knew it. What I didn't know was if he'd let his fear that something *might* happen stop me from spending the day with Mom.

How was today any different than when I'd gone shopping with Miranda? Was it really just because of the stitches, or was there something else going on?

He pulled into his usual spot in the parking garage and cut the engine. But instead of getting out, he turned to me.

"Can I ask you a question?" he asked.

"Sure."

"When Dad and I were fighting, why did you run? You would have been safer if you had stayed close to us."

The direction of his thoughts and the curious concern with which he'd asked surprised me.

"I knew I couldn't stay," I said honestly. "They would have used me to distract you to hurt you, which would have distracted Dad. No matter what I chose, I was going to be hurt. By leaving, I ensured you would fight harder to win faster to get to me. Your focus kept you safe. And you being safe kept Dad and his position in the pack safe so that I wouldn't be killed on the spot."

"Is that why you said you'd get hurt Saturday before we even went there? You were sure that was going to happen and still went?"

I gave a half-hearted shrug. "Once you know a person's personality and their goals, it's not too hard to anticipate their next move."

He closed his eyes for a second.

"Hey, it's fine," I said, noticing his tremble.

"What do you see happening next?"

"Well, either you calm down so we can walk into work, or you turn into the Furminator and wreck the inside of your beautiful car and possibly me if I don't get out the door fast enough. I'm leaning toward the former by a ninety-to-ten percent probability."

He stopped shaking and opened his eyes to shake his head at me.

"I meant with the pack."

I thought about it for a second. "If Storm doesn't already know Miranda, she'll find a way to casually meet with her to gauge whether she has a chance at winning a challenge. If Storm doesn't think she has a chance, she'll possibly team up with Milena and Olivia if they know each other."

"They do," Bennett said. "And after watching Miranda fight, I don't think Storm would win."

"Then she'll find another way to get rid of me." I went quiet, considering what I knew of Storm and how badly she wanted Bennett. "She'll try to use someone else to do her dirty work. She won't risk alienating you. Having a chance to mate with you is the whole reason she wants me gone. She might try getting Milena and Olivia to help her. They might agree since they already openly challenged me. That they wouldn't back off when Dad threatened to leave the pack proves they want me out more than they want you as a mate."

"What should we do about them?"

I grinned. "Let them try."

He closed his eyes again and dropped his head back against the headrest. "You're not making it easy to let go."

I leaned toward him until my mouth was close to his ear.

"I know."

His hand was on the back of my head, and his mouth was on mine before I even saw him move. The kiss was sweet and hungry at the same time. My heart flipped at the need he conveyed with each questioning swipe of his tongue, and I found myself kissing him back with equal intensity for the first time.

He moaned into my mouth a second before he released me and gripped the steering wheel.

"Baby, can you open the door without hurting yourself?" The words were rough and strained.

Without saying anything, I got out of the car and leaned against my closed door. I wasn't waiting for him. I was waiting for my legs to stop shaking.

What the hell were you thinking, Wrenly?

I hadn't been. I'd gotten caught up in the moment and the kiss. By the moon, how could I like it so much? No, not like *it*. How could I like *him* so much?

With a heavy sigh, I rubbed my face with my good hand to shake the feeling of the kiss.

Don't fuck this up now, Wrenly. He said he'd let you go. Do you think he'll keep his word if you're suddenly actively kissing him? Idiot.

I pushed away from the car and started walking toward the elevator.

His door slammed as I reached it. I waited for him, knowing he'd only act out if I tried to avoid him. He reached around me to press the call button and threaded his fingers through mine.

"I want to pull away," I admitted. "I'm terrified showing you any affection will change your mind about letting me go."

"It won't," he said, his hold on my hand tightening.

"If it does, neither of us will survive the fallout, Bennett." I turned my head to meet his gaze so he could see my seriousness. "I will do anything and everything to live the life I want."

He nodded once, his gaze shifting to my mouth.

"No kissing at work," I said, facing forward as the elevator opened.

We rode up in silence, and I let go of his hand just as the doors opened to the main lobby. He didn't fight to keep hold but followed me out to wait for the next elevator. Walt was in line and saw me. Then he saw my arm.

"I know what you're thinking," I said with a smile. "Wulf Enterprises isn't good for my health. But I promise I was this injury-prone before coming here."

Bennett's hand brushed my back. It wasn't firm like a warning but soft like an apology.

"That was what I was thinking," Walt admitted. "What happened?"

"A knife fight gone wrong," I said.

One of the office women standing close by heard and snorted.

Walt smiled, misunderstanding the sound for humor, as if I'd been joking.

"Maybe you should take some self-defense classes. It could help with coordination, too," he said.

I laughed. "Yeah, maybe."

We got on the same elevator and continued to chat until he got off on his floor. Then it was just Bennett, me, and a bunch of female Wulf pack shifters. I could see the glare of several in the reflection of the steel in front of us.

"How many people would be laid off if headquarters moved to another city?" I asked, looking up at Bennett.

His gaze swept over my face, and the corner of his mouth lifted. The partial smile wasn't filled with humor but anger.

"Two hundred and three. Unless Miranda decides to relocate with us. Then two hundred and two."

"Moving headquarters would be expensive," I said. "I bet we'd need to sell a few subsidiaries to help fund it."

"More than a few," he said, catching on. "It doesn't make sense to own companies in a city we no longer support."

The doors opened, and he and I got off the elevator, leaving a silent group of women behind. I felt like I was walking through a gauntlet ready to spring when I passed the desks. However, that feeling vanished when we entered the office suite.

A huge chocolate cupcake with an unholy amount of frosting sat on the desk in my spot. Miranda looked up from her place beside my chair and steepled her hands under her chin.

"Please tell me you're not mad."

I grinned at her. "I'm not mad, but you might be. I'm going shopping with Mom and Grandma today, and you're stuck guarding Bennett."

She pouted. "Can't I go shopping too?"

"You can take Wrenly out tomorrow if she's feeling up to it," Bennett said.

Her expression lit up. "Deal. Go have fun, my little cublet. And if you can't find anything to buy for yourself, feel free to shop for me."

I shook my head at her and turned to Bennett.

"No yelling and no making people I like cry."

"What about the people you don't like?" Miranda asked behind me.

Bennett's smile was there and gone as he focused on me.

"Don't come back with a new injury," he said softly.

"I make no promises. Life is rough."

With a wave to both of them, I made my way back to Mom's office.

The women from the elevator were already spreading word about what we'd said, and the hostility was more subdued as they realized the enormity of what was at stake. If the Wulfs pulled their support, a lot of families would be hurting. Was their biased hate worth it? The majority would look at their quality of life and decide it wasn't. A few families who decided it was might leave the pack on their own.

I wondered how many females would still try to challenge Miranda in the hopes of getting rid of me.

Mom's office door was open, and Grandma was sitting in her chair, talking to her. Both looked pretty serious until they saw me.

"How did you sleep last night, my little Wren?" Grandma asked, standing to give me a brief hug.

"Pretty well, actually. My interactive body pillow kept my arm elevated all night."

Grandma laughed and allowed Mom to steal me for a hug. She breathed in deeply and pulled back to look at me, confusion and hesitation in her expression.

I knew what she was smelling. Bennett's lust and my interest. And I knew why she wasn't talking, too. However, what happened this weekend helped repair some of the trust I'd lost in my family due to past mistakes.

"Let's head out on our shopping day so you can ask me all the questions you want," I said.

She quickly agreed and held my good arm on the way out.

Since we were already downtown, we stopped at a place for coffee and a chat while we waited for the stores to open. It took some coaxing and reassurances that I wouldn't get mad for Mom to ask what was on her mind.

"Did you change your mind about Bennett? I could smell him on you. Lust and affection. Not just his but yours too."

"No, I didn't change my mind. He changed his. He said I can go to Coalwell and he won't force me to live with him. He still plans to live in the apartment by himself, in case I need him."

Mom and Grandma exchanged glances.

"And you're okay with that?" Grandma asked.

"He said he wouldn't interfere with my life. That's all I ever wanted. I didn't want to distance myself from any of you, but if that's the only way to get my freedom, then I would. I think he understands that now."

Mom looked unsure.

"I know. I wasn't sure he meant it, either."

"Talking to whoever I want without fear of consequences is a freedom I've never had. But this morning, I had a conversation with a man in the lobby without Bennett freaking out. That's never happened before.

"I know he's possessive and protective and wants to hold me close, but he knows doing that will break any chance he has of ever getting me to agree to him. I've already warned him that attraction doesn't mean affection.

"If he really wants to win me over, he needs my affection. And he'll never get that when I'm fighting to win every scrap of freedom everyone else is inherently allowed."

Grandma nodded. "Loving a dictator would be impossible."

"Exactly," I said. "And by not interrupting my conversation with a person of the opposite sex this morning, he proved to me that he isn't interested in being a dictator anymore."

Mom still looked nervous.

"Just say it, Mom," I said.

"I'm worried it's not going to last. That this is just his knee-jerk reaction to you being hurt this weekend."

I considered what she said, then shook my head. "His change isn't because of my stitches but what happened after. He shifted when we kissed and almost hurt me. I think it scared him to realize that his intensity is what's driving me away. He's giving us the space we both need."

Mom sighed, and Grandma reached out to pat her hand.

"Wrenly's wiser than she should be. It helps balance out Bennett's impulsivity when it comes to her."

Grandma winked at me, and I hid my grin behind a sip of my coffee.

The last thing I was giving Bennett was balance.

WE RETURNED CLOSE to the end of the workday. Grandma carried the bags to Bennett's office suite despite my protest that I could one-arm them.

"I'm old, not dead. I can still carry my granddaughter's bags. What's in this one? Bricks?"

I shook my head at her as she continued to stride through the door with the energy of a woman half her age.

Miranda's gaze lit with anticipation when she saw the bags.

"You bought stuff?" she asked. "It better not be jean shorts. Show me."

"I didn't buy anything for myself," I said.

"This one's for you from me," Grandma said, passing Miranda a bag.

"Really?" Miranda opened it and let out a squeal. "This is the one I wanted!"

She pulled out a purse that just looked like a purse to me, but had cost close to five figures, and hugged it to her face.

"Thank you so much," she said, still making love to the bag with her face.

"You're welcome," Grandma said with a laugh. "Thank you for protecting my little Wren."

Miranda immediately stopped and looked at me, her smile slowly growing. I knew I'd be hearing "my little Wren" from her in the future.

"Be nice, or I won't give you the gift from Mom," I said.

She immediately looked contrite and held out her hands. Grandma handed her the second bag. It was a pretty skirt and blouse outfit, but it had cost an insane amount of money, in my opinion.

"I'm wearing this tomorrow," Miranda said, petting the material.

"You might want this to go with it," Grandma said, handing Miranda a much smaller bag. "It's from Wrenly."

Miranda opened it and stared lovingly at the Zellon earrings I'd picked out for her.

"I promise I will answer every challenge they've issued," Miranda said.

"What do you mean?" I asked.

"Two so far," Miranda answered without hesitation. "I think they're going to end like Milena's, though. Neither has any talent or training."

"But you do?" I asked.

She didn't get offended. She laughed. "Yeah. Any parents who want their pups to mate up in rank will train them. I'm better than most."

Two she-wolves with no talent would only challenge a skilled fighter if they thought they could win, or if they thought the fight wouldn't happen.

I glanced at Bennett's closed door. He was watching me through the open blinds, but made no move to come to me.

"I need to talk to Bennett for a minute," I said.

"Go ahead. I'll leave the rest of these with Miranda and see you on Friday," Grandma said.

Nodding, I walked away from the pair and let myself into Bennett's office.

He stayed seated at his desk as I closed the door.

"It looks like you had a good day," he said.

"I did. Shopping with Mom and Grandma was fun. I didn't get to use your card, though." I held up the card he'd given me that morning and walked over to put it on his desk. "Mom paid for everything.

"How was your day?"

"All right. Miranda kept everyone away. I missed you, though."

My heart flip-flopped at his words.

"Miranda said there are two challenges so far but that neither has any training. Do you know who they are?"

He nodded.

"Do they stand a chance against her?"

He shook his head. "She'll be fine."

"I wasn't worried about her." I paused when I realized how it sounded. "That's not what I meant. I mean, I'm more worried that these challenges are just a distraction. When are they happening?"

"Saturday."

His phone rang. He glanced at it but returned his full attention to me without answering it.

"Do I need to be there?" I asked

"There's nothing in our laws that says you have to be present."

"Perfect. Once the time for accepting new challenges expires, have Dad announce that I won't be there."

His phone rang again. He frowned at it, then at me as he sent it to voicemail.

"Why?" he asked.

"I think the women will withdraw their challenges because whatever they have planned won't work. Then they'll have to come up with something else."

"Like what?"

"That'll depend on how accessible I am."

His phone started to ring again.

"Just answer it already," I said.

A mix of guilt and panic briefly appeared in his expression.

"Is it another woman harassing you?" I asked.

"No. It's Konni."

Why the guilt and panic for Konni? I reached across his desk and answered it on speaker.

"Wrenly's with me," Bennett said before Konni could speak.

"And that better not change whatever you were about to say," I said, frowning at Bennett.

"Um...I finished the thing. You need to pay up."

I looked at Bennett, expecting him to clarify Konni's vagueness. His gaze held mine, but something in his expression hinted at nervousness, which was a first.

Bennett's main traits were anger, seriousness, and possessiveness, with rare glimpses of playfulness and humor. Nervousness just wasn't part of who he was, and his reaction was only making me more curious.

Typically, the only thing that put him on edge was me. So was Konni calling about something that had to do with me, or was it something else?

I tilted my head at Bennett. "Keeping things from me in the past hasn't worked out well for either of us."

Walking around the desk, I nudged his chair back. His pupils expanded when I angled away from him and set a hand on his shoulder. A small rumble vibrated from him as I sat on his leg and turned his face toward me.

He swallowed hard as I studied him.

"You better start talking, Bennett," I said.

"The Shanes reached out to a foreign investor whom I haven't had contact with, but Konni has," he said in a rush. "I gave him five minutes to block them and call me back."

I wasn't stupid. Nothing about what he just said was the cause of his guilt and nervousness.

I narrowed my eyes at him and looked at the phone.

"What's he leaving out, Konni?"

"He promised to, um... You explain it to her, you moon-cursed ass. And hurry up. I need you."

The call disconnected.

"Hurry up...I need you?" I arched a brow at Bennett. "I'm usually pretty accurate at reading situations, but this one has me wondering so many things. Exactly how close were you and Konni at school?"

Bennett flushed.

"It's not..." He cleared his throat. "Dragons molt every three to five years. It's uncomfortable for them if they don't have help."

"Okay." I drew out the word. "So Konni's a dragon. That's interesting. I've seen a lizard molting, and assuming he's not that small when he shifts, I can see why he'd need help. But why is helping him molt making you so red?" I trailed my finger over his cheek, which grew even redder.

"It's...he..." Bennett sighed. "Dragons molt in their human form."

I slowly smiled as my imagination painted a picture for me.

"Can this be a closed topic?" he asked.

Bennett was adorable when he was uncomfortable, and there had to be something wrong with me for enjoying it so much.

"It can be. But what if I can make it worth your while to make it not a closed topic?"

He lost a hint of his embarrassment with a flicker of interest.

"What do you mean?"

"Would you be willing to consider a deal to make this an open topic?"

I watched as he weighed the wisdom of possibly telling me whatever he was hiding and leaned in to whisper in his ear.

"You're just making me want to know even more when you act like this."

He started to tremble. I stood and went to his door.

"Yes," he said. "I'm willing to make a deal."

When I looked back over my shoulder at him, he still looked torn. How big was this secret? Big enough. I knew I'd learn by making offers and watching him weigh them.

"Good. I'll think of something I'm willing to give and make a proposal tonight. Don't forget to tell Dad about the announcement."

With a smile, I left. Miranda was sitting at our desk but with her chair blatantly turned toward Bennett's office window.

"That looked fun," she said. "To quote your Grandma, 'You have him by the pebbles. Keep him unbalanced.'"

"Could you hear us?"

"No. Your Grandma and I were just watching. I'm surprised he didn't do more when you sat on his lap."

"He's afraid of hurting me with this." I held up my arm.

"Makes sense. When do the stitches come out?"

"I have an appointment next week."

"What do you think he'll do then?"

I shrugged. She gave me a speculative look as she shut down her computer and grabbed her bags.

"We'll talk tomorrow," she said. "Wear comfortable shoes and bring pain relievers."

The door opened behind me as she walked away.

Hands settled on my shoulders.

"We can leave early, too," Bennett said.

"You're the boss."

He reached around me to pick up the remaining bag.

"What did you buy?"

"Earrings for Miranda. I don't know what's in that bag. Mom got it for you and handed it to Grandma when we got here."

He looked inside it and stared for so long that I tried looking too, but he closed it and took my good hand, leading me out of the office.

"What is it?" I asked.

"Replacements for what I accidentally wrecked in your closet."

Aware that everyone was listening, I waited until we were alone in the elevator to ask, "Is that why you asked me not to go into the closet? You wrecked my clothes?"

"And the door."

I wasn't sure how I felt about that. Not the wrecking part. That I understood. Asking Mom to replace my clothes instead of me. Sure, I didn't like shopping, but I also didn't like dressing in the clothes Mom had previously bought me.

Not Mom, I silently corrected myself. *Bennett.*

"Did you warn her that I don't like anything fancy?"

"No. I told her not to purchase anything expensive. That it needed to be something you could wear at school to blend in with the other students."

That didn't sound so bad. Why had he stared at it so long, then?

Curious, I glanced at the bag that was in his opposite hand.

He shifted it back so his leg blocked my view of the bag.

CHAPTER THIRTY-TWO

MY ATTENTION WAS STILL on the bag when we reached the parking garage, so I didn't notice the familiar car idling near the elevator or Milo until he waved.

"What's Milo doing here?" I asked as Bennett steered us toward the car.

"Giving you a ride home. I promised Konni I'd help him after work." He opened the passenger door for me.

"Wait... Do I get a say in where I go after work?"

"Yes."

"Then I don't want to go home. I want to know what you and Konni do together."

He grimaced. "Not this time. You still need to make an offer."

I made a face. "But I really don't want to spend a night alone with nothing to do." I held up my arm. "I can't even go running yet."

Bennett tipped my chin to look up at him.

"Not just because of the arm, though, right? That smart mind of yours knows there are still people who would like to add to your injuries if you were to run without me, right?"

"Without you or with someone else who can protect me," I corrected. "What if I spent the night at Miranda's?"

"You just gave her earrings, a bag, and expensive clothes. She's not going to want to stay home."

"Perfect. Neither do I."

Bennett sighed and set his forehead against mine.

"Independence is important to you. I get that. But is exercising it worth your health? Your life?" He kissed my forehead and stepped back. "Milo will take you wherever you want to go."

"Thank you." I got into the car and waved as Milo pulled away.

"You have no idea how hard that was for him," Milo said.

"I have a pretty good idea. He was shaking again. I hope Konni's ready for a moody Bennett."

"Probably. Where to?"

"There's an ice cream place I've been wanting to try. Are you interested in being my wingman for that adventure?"

Milo wasn't just along for the ride. He was actually fun and didn't get ruffled by anything. He laughed at my jokes and was so sweet about tasting ice creams with me to bring his mate back something she'd like. Like everyone else in my life, he wouldn't hear of me carrying the two pints I'd selected to bring home. But we did have a lively debate about the merits of the classic butter pecan, his pick, and outrageous chocolate overload, my pick.

By the time we got home, Sandy had walking tacos waiting for us. They both joined me, and it was one of the best meals I'd had since coming home. No tension. A lot of laughter. Just normal.

Stuffed and content, I went upstairs with only a little bit of guilt poking at me because I'd felt so happy *without* my family.

It didn't take me long to change to the T-shirt I'd stolen from Bennett the night before and settle into my bed with my laptop. However, it took me forever to hunt-and-peck my way through an email to my professor regarding my assignment. I didn't mind the tediousness of the task, though. At least it was something to do.

Once I finished, I sent Sophia a text asking if she wanted to meet for lunch soon.

Sophia: Sure. My week is open. Lunch and after dinner. The club invite is standing.

Me: Lunch on Wednesday? And possibly club next Friday.

Sophia: Really? Does that mean things are better with your family?

Me: They're getting better. Fingers crossed it stays better.

Sophia: Same. See you at noon on Wednesday. I'll text the location.

I woke up with a stretch that pulled at my stitches and made me wince. The sound of my shower running registered a second later.

Reaching out, I touched the spot next to me. It was cold. Had Bennett not come home, or had he come home late and just gone to get ready for work right away? But if it was the latter, why did he use my bathroom when he had his own? It didn't make sense. But who else would be in my bathroom except him?

My thoughts spiraled to all the shit Lindi and her crew had pulled over the years.

Unsure what to think, I slipped out of bed and crept toward the bathroom, wishing I had a baseball bat or something. The water didn't shut off at my approach or when I carefully turned the doorknob.

Thankfully, the glass shower partition didn't leave the identity of my bathroom guest a mystery. It didn't leave *anything* a mystery when Bennett turned to look at me.

I spun around toward the door and made it one step before a wet body suctioned to my back.

"You have three seconds to prevent a meltdown that will ensure I don't talk to you the whole day."

"I smell like him," Bennett said roughly.

That sure stopped any freakout I'd been about to have.

"Konni?"

"Yeah."

"Did he touch you in your no-no square?"

"My what?"

"The place I was thinking about kicking a few seconds ago?"

Bennett snorted a laugh and dipped his head to kiss the side of my neck.

"I missed you. Your scent...the way you can distract me with just one word...the feel of you in my arms."

His hand moved over my good arm, which was pinned in front of me, to intertwine our fingers.

"Okay. Well, I'm here. No need to keep missing me." I meant it as more of a let go now, but he made a pained sound and kissed the side of my neck in a way that clearly showed me how he'd interpreted what I'd said.

"Are you going to let go and finish your shower, or am I going to need to start screaming?"

"Shower. I'll help you scream later."

I frowned. He released me, and the water started splashing behind me a second later. I fled before he thought I was interested in his offer.

With the back of my shirt wet, I hurried down the stairs and entered the kitchen to see Sandy making breakfast.

"Good morning," she said. "Bennett suggested French toast. Does that work for you?"

"Yeah, that's fine."

She glanced at me but did a double-take.

"Are you all right?"

"Bennett was in my shower."

"Ah. Why don't you sit, and I'll tell you about the time Milo broke my favorite vase...on purpose?"

My ass was on the island chair, and I was avidly distracted for the next ten minutes as she entertained me with a love-struck mate's woes. Hands settled on my shoulders, cutting off my laughter. Twisting, I looked back at Bennett.

His gaze dipped to my mouth, but he didn't try stealing a kiss.

"Your turn to get ready," he said. "Miranda already texted you."

I nodded and hurried from the kitchen before he tried anything. It wasn't until I reached the bedroom that I realized two things. I'd left my phone behind when I'd run earlier, and I never looked in the bag from yesterday, which was currently on my bed, along with my phone and an outfit I didn't recognize.

My gaze shifted to the closet. I still hadn't looked. Drawn forward, I opened the door and blinked at the empty space. The built-in closet was gone. A few holes from where things had been anchored were already patched. The wood floor was deeply furrowed in front of the door. Opening it wider, I stepped inside and partially closed the door to look at the back of it. The damage was primarily focused around the knob, with furrows trailing down away from it.

"I wouldn't have hurt you. I know what it looks like, but I wouldn't ever hurt you," Bennett said from my room.

Opening the door, I looked out at him. He looked guilty and upset.

"Your clothes are in my closet until yours is fixed. It shouldn't take too long. If you want to wear something else, you can take whatever you want, or I can pick something for you."

"What's there is fine," I said, stepping out of the closet.

He watched me grab my clothes from the bed and look in the bag. It was filled with underwear. Lacy, skimpy, sexy underwear.

"I asked Sandy to wash what Mom bought you yesterday," Bennett said, his voice once again rough.

Tearing my gaze from what was in the bag, I looked at him.

"Where's my other underwear?"

His face grew red.

"I wasn't thinking straight," he said.

I stared at him, letting my imagination play out. Upset and

needing my scent, he'd gone for my underwear while still in his fur and accidentally ripped it all. Or . . he'd trashed everything in my closet because he'd been mad. Or…he knew he was letting me go and hoarding his scent collection.

"Yeah, no matter what answer you give me, I think I'm going to be upset about it. So let's pretend I didn't go in there and that my mom isn't so clueless about me that she bought thongs."

Reaching into the bag, I sorted through my options and withdrew the most modest pair. Then, I closed myself in the bathroom.

Showering while keeping my arm out of the water wasn't too hard since I wasn't washing my hair. Drying off was a little harder with just one hand. I briefly tried using my other hand but learned quickly that wasn't a good idea.

By the time I tugged myself into my clothes, my arm was throbbing again.

"I hope you're standing out there with an ice pack for me," I said as I opened the door.

He was.

Greedy, I took the ice pack and set it over the bandage. The relief was almost immediate.

He stepped behind me and picked up my brush to start detangling the damp ends of my hair. I let him work without looking at him. If I met his gaze, I knew I'd question what happened to my underwear.

"Are you mad?" he asked after a prolonged silence.

"You already know I'm not. You'd smell it."

"Sometimes you're really good at hiding what you're feeling."

"Well, I'm not mad. I'm honestly trying not to overthink anything like why you were in my shower instead of your own and why you smelled like Konni. It's not my business."

The brush paused in my hair. "Because I'm not your business?"

"Because I have enough on my plate," I said diplomatically. "Stitches. Bitches. Staying out of ditches. I'm not sure how much more my plate will carry without tipping over. So what you do with Konni can't be my business."

I met his gaze in the mirror, catching his hurt look.

"Why you were in my shower is borderline my business as long as it doesn't add to my plate."

"It smells like you."

"If you wanted to smell me, why didn't you get into bed with me?"

"Because then it would have smelled like him."

"Ah," I said, understanding that he would not have been okay if I or my bed had smelled like Konni. "Are you going to be okay in the office today without Miranda?"

"Yeah." He started brushing again. "Will you stay with me tomorrow?"

"Sure. I don't think I'll be able to do much, though. I tried using my hand to dry off, and that's why I needed an ice pack."

"You should have called for me."

"And have you dry me off? I'm not stupid, Bennett. You couldn't handle it when I asked for a kiss rain check, in case it turned into something more. What do you think would happen if you saw me naked?"

He gathered my hair to one side and kissed my exposed neck.

"I already saw you naked," he said close to my skin. "And I didn't lose control then."

I frowned, remembering the towel incident. "Why didn't you lose control then? What was different?"

"You. You still didn't see me as a potential mate. Knowing you were thinking of accepting me was what—"

A tremble ran through him, and he kissed my neck again.

I wasn't as unaffected as I would have liked. The feel of his lips against my skin sent a shock of...something through me. It made me feel hot and made my stomach flip.

His hold on my hair tightened, guiding my head more to the side so he had better access.

Closing my eyes, I let myself feel what he could do to me and started to wonder what it would feel like to just let go.

My eyes snapped open.

"Stop."

He jerked back, breathing heavily. His pupils had completely devoured his irises.

"Five more minutes and I'll tell you anything you want about Konni's molting," he said, his voice edged with a pre-shift growl.

"No. You'd shift in less than three."

His hold on my hair hadn't eased, and I watched in the mirror as his gaze dipped to the red mark he'd left on my skin.

"Two minutes."

"No."

He growled. The sound was filled with frustration and annoyance.

"Let go of my hair."

He did. Then he smoothed his fingers through it and rubbed the back of my neck. His attention shifted between my eyes and the small mark he'd left on my skin. If I didn't distract him, I knew he'd find a way to kiss me again, and I wasn't sure I'd have the sense to stop it.

"I'm hungry."

I watched him inhale and melt a little. His need to give me what I needed trumped his need to touch me more. Or, it mostly trumped it, since he held my hand all the way down the stairs.

Sandy exited the kitchen a few seconds after Bennett pulled out my chair for me in the dining room. I sat in anticipation of what she'd made, but Bennett stole my plate before I could grab it. He quickly and efficiently cut through the powdered triangles, turning them into manageable bite-sized pieces.

"Thank you," I said as he set it in front of me and handed over my fork.

"You're welcome."

Breakfast took a few minutes longer than it should have, using my non-dominant hand, but I didn't quit. Miranda would understand.

Despite the delay, however, we still reached the office on time. Miranda was by our desk, decked out in yesterday's purchases. When she saw me, she grinned and did a twirl.

"Take in this look, my little ah-pWren-tice. This is what we're shopping for today, but for you. Purse. Earrings. And whatever high-end clothes you can tolerate. Now get that pretty black rectangle from your wallet-with-legs so we can get out of here."

I laughed at her and turned to Bennett with my hand out.

His gaze dipped to my smiling mouth, and I was against the office wall before I could think "wolf in heat." The hand of my hurt arm was gently pinned to the side while my other one had freedom to tangle itself in his hair.

Then his mouth was on mine, kissing the daylights out of me. He turned my thoughts to mush in seconds. I forgot where we were and who was watching until Miranda said, "She won't be happy once you're no longer kissing her."

Bennett turned his head to snarl at her. His hand that had been teasing its way up my stomach was still resting against my skin.

The break gave me clarity, and I grabbed a handful of hair, not pulling, but with enough tension to cut off his warning and draw his attention back to me.

"No growling at Miranda when she's giving you good advice," I said. "Now, please let go before I react negatively."

His frustration was plain as he removed his hand from my shirt.

"Thank you. May I have your card, or should I ask Mom for hers?"

He handed over his card, gave Miranda a terse, "Protect her with your life," then closed himself in his office a little forcefully. The blinds closed a second later.

"I bet he's touching himself."

I gave Miranda a "what's wrong with you" look and straightened my shirt.

"Since you were timely with your interruption, I won't deduct an hour of shopping time for that crass comment."

She grinned at me. "So that's how we're playing today? All right. Give cutting our shopping time your best shot. Remember, I'm stronger than you."

"Good thing because you might need to carry me by the end of today."

"This is silk. I'm not carrying you."

We walked out of the office, good-naturedly bickering, and returned eight hours later with zero bickering and a lot of whining. Only, this time, it was Miranda.

"Are we even friends anymore? How could you walk away from those heels? They were perfect. They lifted your already firm ass and put it on display in that skirt you were wearing."

"I don't like heels. I don't need my ass displayed. And I only wear skirts for weddings and funerals. Are you planning on dying soon?"

One of the office girls laughed but quickly smothered it.

Miranda growled a low warning at the group then smiled at me.

"Unless it's Bennett or your parents, I doubt anyone has what it takes to bring me down."

"Pfft. I should be on that danger list, too. One distracting Zellon's necklace and you wouldn't even know what hit you."

She laughed all the way to the office suite where Bennett's door was open. As soon as he saw us, he came out.

"That wasn't there when we left," Miranda said, pointing to a slash in the wall.

"Looks like an embedded folder mark," I said. "Who was it?"

"I'm only going to give you the name if you're going to do something about it."

"Like what? The only one who would stand still long enough for me to attempt a maiming is Miranda."

"And you don't have the necklace for it," she said, setting half the bags she carried down on the desk.

He opened his arms. "If I tell you, you have to comfort me."

I was betrayed by my shopping partner and pushed into his open arms. He caught me tight and hugged me close as he whispered every woman's name in the office except for Mom.

"And how many of them left crying?"

"Only the 'sensitive ones' would be my bet," Miranda said. "And he knows who they are and goes a little easier on them, so they don't deserve your pity."

He nuzzled my neck where he'd left the mark this morning, and I pushed at his chest even as my knees went weak.

"I'll see you two tomorrow. Push her too far, Bennett, and she'll start ignoring you again."

Bennett made a frustrated sound a second before he backed off.

He threaded his fingers through mine and picked up all the bags Miranda had left behind on the desk.

"Let's go home."

He used every excuse possible to touch me more than handholding all the way to the car, and I knew I'd be in trouble once we got home if I didn't put him in his place. But how? Avoiding him would frustrate him. Yelling at him would frustrate him. Pleading with him might work. Guilting him would definitely work.

Maybe I'd get something delicious for dinner out of it, too.

I waited until after he buckled me in and was walking around the car to unbuckle myself.

"Oops," I said, letting the seatbelt go when he got in. It snapped home with a light thud.

He glanced from it to me, suspicion in his gaze. I amped up my innocence with a few blinks. He leaned in, reaching across me. I caught the back of his head and pulled him close enough that I could brush my lips against his ear.

Locked in place, he shook, mini tremors that rocked through his entire body.

"This is why you need to stop. I'm human and break, Bennett. I don't want to end up like my closet door." I knew damn well that each word delivered softly in his ear was adding to his torture.

But this was Bennett. He seemed to like being tortured by me. Why else would he send me away instead of keeping me close?

"Wrenly..."

My name was both a whispered prayer and a curse.

I played with the hair at the back of his head.

"If I kiss your ear again, will you wolf out? Should we test it?"

He jerked away from me, and I was left sitting alone in the car with the driver's side door open. When I twisted around to look for him, I saw him pacing behind the car like a caged animal, watching me.

My heart gave a heavy beat and felt like it was turning over in my chest. Why did I like seeing him barely in control? What was wrong with me? Did I have a death wish?

Was I...

Was I turned on by this?

My heart gave another heavy beat as I quickly faced forward.

Calm down, Wrenly. If he gets back in this car and he smells your hormones screaming "Yes," you're never going to get home.

"Pizza. Burgers. Tacos. Macaroni and cheese. Hot dogs. Chicken nuggets and fries. Potato salad. Fried Chicken. Corn bread. Chicken fried steak. BBQ. The messy kind that drips out of the bun."

"What are you doing?" Bennett asked, bending down to look at me, but not getting in.

"It's my freedom food list. Things I wanted to eat once I was out of prison."

His mask slipped into place, and he got in.

"Would you like to stop for chicken nuggets and fries on the way home, or should we find somewhere with BBQ?"

"Nuggets, please."

He started the car and drove to the closest drive-thru to home.

"Can we talk about before?" he asked after I was holding our takeout order.

"Sure."

"Were you teasing me?"

"That's a complex question," I said.

"Why?"

"Technically, I was teasing you, but not to get your hopes up."

"Why then?"

"So you'd stop kissing me."

"I feel like I'm a toddler for repeating this, but…why?"

"Because there's no point. You were getting yourself all worked up for what? The result would be the same. Regardless of my role in the kiss, eventually you'd shift, and I'd potentially be hurt.

"I didn't think reminding you of what happened to the closet after a hint of acceptance would be effective, so I demonstrated."

He pulled into the garage and turned off the car. We sat in silence for a few minutes as he digested what I'd said.

"Is there any hope for us, Wrenly?"

CHAPTER THIRTY-THREE

"I DON'T KNOW," I said honestly. "The way you were before, controlling and not listening, would have been an easy no. But you're saying the right things now.

"Saying and doing are two different things, though. First, I'll need to see if you actually do them. Then, I'll need to figure out if that's enough to make me want to spend a lifetime with someone whose default is to smother me."

The truth was brutal, and I saw it in his gaze. But withholding it to spare his feelings would only hurt us more later on.

I noticed the way his hand was shaking as he got out and opened the door for me. He didn't do anything, though.

We ate dinner together without much conversation; then I went upstairs to watch a movie by myself. It was a rather boring night... until I got ready for bed. When I emerged from my bathroom with my pajamas on, Bennett was already in his spot. Awake. Watching. Waiting.

After what I'd said in the car, I thought he'd go back to his distant self. What did it mean that he was waiting for me?

He watched me watch him.

"This feels like a test," I said.

He didn't smile as he patted my empty spot.

"Are you going to pounce once I'm next to you? Because I just brushed my hair when I shouldn't have, and my arm is aching a little."

He immediately got out of bed. "I'll get the ice pack."

I hated that I liked his consideration so damn much. It softened me toward him, and I couldn't afford to be soft. I knew what waited for me.

No more cage, Wrenly, I reminded myself.

While he was gone, I hurried into bed and considered hiding his pillow. However, it would most likely encourage him to use me as a substitute rather than stop him from joining me. So, I nudged his pillow to the edge of his side of the bed instead.

He returned a few minutes later with a pain reliever and an ice pack. I took the pain reliever and settled in with the ice pack as he walked around the bed to his side. He didn't even blink at the space I'd created between our spots. He just got into bed and rolled toward me to use the edge of *my* pillow.

"Why don't you save us both time and tell me what your goal is?" I said.

"I want to fall asleep with you."

I arched a brow at him.

"That's all?"

He nodded.

"Fine. Close your eyes and go to sleep."

He grinned and looked so damn boyishly handsome that my heart did its weird, heavy beat thing.

I rolled away from him, trying to deny what my body wanted me to feel. But there was no escaping Bennett. He wrapped an arm around my waist and pulled me flush against his chest.

Moving my hair off my neck, he inhaled deeply. I knew I should move away, but I was so tired of running away from him. From myself. So, I didn't move. I waited.

I knew I was in trouble before his lips even touched me. Once they did, though, I forgot why I needed to fight what he made me feel.

Safe.

Wanted.

Loved.

His lips skimmed my neck. My breath caught, and my skin prickled in anticipation. Lips, tongue, and teeth teased the side of my neck, warming me, making me want more from him.

I moved to give him better access. He approved with a growl.

The feel of his hand on my stomach added to the heat slowly consuming me. When it slid under my tank top, I didn't think to stop him. Everything felt too good, especially as his fingers inched higher, stroking my skin and making me ache for more.

My pulse raced as I rolled toward him a few more inches.

He pulled back, and I saw his pupils were so large that his eyes seemed black.

"Ask me for anything," he said roughly.

"Kiss me."

His mouth claimed mine hungrily, surpassing the need in all his previous kisses. Raw and demanding, it consumed me. His body caged mine. I threaded my fingers into his hair, trying to pull him closer, needing more. Needing him.

I arched against him.

Our hips connected, and an electric feeling rushed through me.

I tore my mouth from his, gasping at the sensation. The sound of fabric ripping registered a second before air touched my chest. Then he was kissing me again as his hand covered my breast. The heat and pressure of his palm added to the fire slowly burning through me.

An aching throb started between my legs. He swallowed the sound I made as I arched into him again.

Warning bells rang faintly in my head, but I couldn't focus on them. Bennett's touch demanded attention.

The warning grew louder as his hand left my breast and trailed down my stomach. I tried turning my head to the side to break the kiss, needing a second to think. But his lips followed, keeping me submerged in a sea of hunger I didn't fully understand, unable to draw a breath without him filling my senses.

His fingers found the waistband of my shorts and slipped under them. He was touching me...*there*, over the thin material of my underwear.

Panic fluttered in my chest, and I pushed at his chest. Pain flared in my arm.

He growled and pulled back to look down at me.

"Don't hurt yourself, Wrenly," he warned as his fingers moved.

My breath caught at the ache his touch was creating. It felt so good. So wrong. Why was it wrong?

"Wait."

"To what? To kiss you?"

He kissed me tenderly. Then, his fingers hooked my underwear and slid underneath. His touch was feather-light as he gently stroked over my center, making me forget how to breathe.

"Why? I can smell how much you like me kissing you." His lips skimmed the corner of my mouth then my chin. "Maybe you want me to kiss you somewhere else?"

He kissed my throat again, and then his mouth closed over one of my breasts. The sound that came out of me was a blend of a sigh and a gasp. He used his tongue and teeth to melt my thoughts and my resistance as his fingers continued to tease me.

Nothing had ever made me feel so...perfect.

He used his foot to nudge my leg aside, giving his fingers more room to skim over me.

"Bennett...I...we..."

"I know, baby," he said, shifting his attention to my other breast.

My hips lifted off the bed when he sucked it into his mouth, and his fingers used the opportunity to press a little more firmly against me.

He groaned. The vibrations shook the bed.

"Wrenly, baby, open a little wider for me."

I listened and felt his fingers part me.

"You're so wet, baby. I need—"

Material ripped again, stinging my lower back, and baring me to the air. Before I could register the pain, he ducked down, and he started kissing me *there*. I grabbed his head, completely lost. His tongue flicked against a spot that made me feel feverish. The shaking grew worse. A finger stroked my opening, teasing it but not entering.

"Bennett. There. Please. I—"

Pleasure unlike anything I'd ever known shattered me from head to toe, intensifying when his finger dipped into my opening and found a spot to stroke from the inside. I screamed, tensing and curling into myself so hard that my stomach cramped. The euphoria didn't stop, though. It kept spreading out in waves, taking me away with it.

With a yawn, I stretched myself awake. The slip of the sheet against my bare skin froze me as the night before came back to me. My face flushed, and I slowly pulled the cover up over my head.

How could I let that happen? Idiot.

I frowned as I realized something very important—the bed next to me was empty.

Flipping the cover back, I sat up and scanned the room. He wasn't lurking somewhere, safely watching my response from a distance. He really was gone.

Just when I was starting to feel hurt by his abandonment, I spotted a note waiting on my bedside table, along with an ice pack that had frost on it and two pain relievers.

I wanted to stay, but I wasn't sure if you wanted the same.
Last night doesn't change anything unless you want it to. I'll

keep my word. I won't take what you're not willing to give. I'll let go.

The ice pack and pain relievers are for your arm. You used it too much yesterday.

Please tell me when you're ready to see me. I'll be downstairs until you call my name.

Bennett

I reread the note, unable to believe what I was seeing. Flopping back onto the bed, I relived what happened before I'd passed out. It'd been intense, magical, and *dangerous* because I wanted to do it again.

How had his mind not changed when mine was starting to?

Grandma's words repeated in my head.

He would try to persuade you so you're willing. He wouldn't do anything to cause you to reject him.

Was that what last night had been? A taste of how good it could be if I accepted him?

I wanted to go back to being ignorant. Back to when I thought I had no real interest in him. Just a little physical attraction. But I couldn't go back to that self-delusion. I liked Bennett. His face. His moodiness. His absolute obsession with me. I felt *wanted*. Needed. For the first time in my life. And I didn't want to walk away from that. But I didn't want his need to trap me either. Not ever again.

With a sigh, I sat up and wrapped my arms around my bent knees.

So, how did I play this then?

Pretending it hadn't happened wouldn't work for either of us. Trying to pull away would only make him want to hold me closer. Did I...accept it then? The pull I felt to be with him? And then what? Would I find myself mated and pregnant before the start of the semester? No thanks.

Setting my chin on my knees, I reached for the ice pack and continued to ponder my options.

He'd stopped metaphorically holding me too tightly when I'd stopped resisting and had instead pointed out how much he was going to hurt me by being physical. Last night had proven he could control himself, though.

I thought back to his shaking and frowned.

Had he been holding on by a claw?

My phone rang. I glanced at Miranda's name and answered.

"Good morning, my MBBF," she said.

"Shouldn't it be MBFF? My Best Friend Forever."

"Please, I'm not that sentimental, Miranda's Beautiful Bag Financer."

I snorted. "That sounds about right. Why are you calling?" I glanced at the clock. It was about the time I normally got up for work.

"To see if you're coming in today or if you want to play hooky."

"Both. I'm coming to work to play hooky. Why?"

"Just checking."

I narrowed my eyes. "Why? What's going on?"

She hummed into the phone. "Your paranoia is cute. Are you going to tell me what happened that has you acting like that, and why Bennett wanted me to call you to see if you were going to work? Because my imagination is running wild, and I can't wait to set my nose to you."

"Thanks for the reminder to wash well. Pack running clothes."

I hung up before she could say anything else and closed myself in the bathroom to scrub every inch of my skin without getting my arm wet. When I reemerged wrapped in a towel, my bed had been changed, and a fresh set of clothes waited for me. Professional clothes.

"Is there a reason for a pantsuit instead of more comfortable clothes?" I asked.

Bennett answered from the hallway. "Before lunch, Dad is going to announce the challengers, set the date and time, and say you won't be there. Mom wants to take you out somewhere to lunch afterward so you're not in the office. She suggested you wear something dressier, but wouldn't say where she planned to take you."

I thought of the plans I'd made with Sophia and knew I'd need to cancel. With the announcement forcing those plotting against me to change their plans, I didn't want to potentially put Sophia in danger.

"Is there another option than this one? It's pretty, but I'm going to have a hard time going to the bathroom in a one-piece with the stitches still in."

"There are more options. Do you want to see them?"

I could hear the hope in his voice, and I glanced down at the towel covering me.

He knew I was wearing it. Other than the clothes on the bed and what I'd slept in, I didn't have anything else in my room.

If you run, he'll chase you, I warned myself.

With a steadying inhalation, I started for the hallway.

He was leaning against the wall beside my door. His gaze swept over my face, trying to read my mood even as he slowly inhaled.

"I'll give what you want so I can get what I want, okay?" I asked.

His frown was still flickering in his expression when I closed the distance between us and hugged his waist.

"Good morning, Bennett. Thank you for last night."

For several heartbeats, he didn't move. Then his arms wrapped around me, and he kissed the top of my head. I felt his frayed control in how his shaking fingers smoothed over the damp ends of my hair.

"You don't hate me."

"Not currently, but we both know that's subject to change depending on my circumstances, right?"

He kissed the top of my head again. "How did you know a hug and reassurance is what I wanted?"

"You're pretty easy to read."

He hummed his agreement. "Tell me what you want in exchange for giving me what I needed."

I looked up at him.

"Your word that you won't mate me, no matter how willing I might seem, so that I won't need to break both our hearts after."

His gaze swept over my face as my words sank in. His shaking increased as he leaned in toward me. I read his intent, tipped my head back to better offer my lips, and stood on my toes.

The gentle way he kissed me had an edge to it.

He was barely tethered.

I stood on his feet, taking a few more inches to kiss him more aggressively.

He growled, and one of his hands captured the back of my head to meet my demand.

When I withdrew to look up at him, I could see I'd eroded his control just a bit more.

"You are what I fear most, Bennett. Or what you represent. I don't want to lose any more of my life to someone else's misguided plans for me. I'm not saying my way will be perfect, but it can't be any worse. And if I'm hurt doing things my way, then I have no one else to blame but myself."

He closed his eyes and nodded once.

"I promise," he said.

"Good." I moved to get off his feet, but he scooped me up into his arms and carried me to his room.

I didn't miss his side glance at his bed, and I knew he was considering taking me there, even as he strode toward his closet. My new clothes were neatly lined up, taking up half the space, and the old uniforms were gone.

"Letting go of your old stalker ways?" I asked as he set me down.

He turned me toward my options and started kissing my shoulder.

"You know the rule about this in public, right? Not allowed. It would embarrass me and make me want to run and hide."

He hummed an acknowledgment as his teeth scraped my skin.

Rolling my eyes, I reached back to swat his head. My towel slipped. I grabbed for it at the same time he did. While I wanted to keep it in place, I could feel the pressure in his hold to pull it away. If he really wanted to, he'd win.

I turned my head to meet his heated gaze.

"Are you willing to risk my mood the morning after you pressed for more after I said wait? I wonder what Mom's reaction will be to that news."

He released the towel and stepped back.

"You don't fight fair."

"I only fight dirty when warranted. Now, are you going to step out so I can change without provoking you, or are you going to tempt your control by staying behind me so you can watch me bend over to put my underwear on?"

A tortured sound came from him, and I watched his skin ripple.

"Don't wreck another closet, Bennett. Go for a run."

He spun on his heel and was gone.

Shaking my head, I closed the door and dressed with purpose. After last night, Bennett would be dangerous today. So, I needed to be more dangerous. Wearing comfortable summer clothes wouldn't meet the dress code for work, but I didn't care. However, I did pack the clothes I would need to go out with Mom. I didn't want to embarrass her.

When I opened the door, he was standing there, completely naked, breathing hard, and very sweaty. Refusing to look at anything except his eyes, I tilted my head as I studied him.

"Did the run help at all?"

"Not really."

"Yeah, I thought that might be the case. Last night made it worse for you. And each concession will only make you more desperate. That's why I asked for your word. Because I'm not going to fight you anymore. If you want me on that bed right now, fine. Then that's where I'll be. I'll give you my body. I'll even give you my heart. But I will never again give up my freedom, and that's exactly what you'll want as soon as you mate me.

"I'm not talking about the freedom to go to the school of my choice anymore, either. It'll be the jealousy over who I sit next to. Who I talk to. Who I accidentally make eye contact with across the room.

"I've already lived a life where I walked around in constant fear of making a mistake. I won't go live in that cage again. If freeing myself means rejecting you, I'll do it without hesitation."

"I understand," he said. But his hands were already shaking.

"You should go shower. I'll meet you downstairs. If we have enough time, can we stop somewhere for pastries? I'm in the mood for Pain au Chocolat." I said it with perfect French pronunciation.

"You make me want to—" He closed his eyes, breathed deeply, then closed himself in the bathroom.

I moved closer to the door.

"And you make me want to say yes," I said softly. "It's dangerous for both of us."

Something cracked inside the bathroom.

I left with a smirk and sent a quick reschedule text to Sophia.

If Bennett thought it'd been hell waiting for me to acknowledge him as a potential mate, he'd seriously underestimated what it would feel like to know his mate wanted him but would still walk away to get what she wanted out of life.

He came downstairs, looking dangerously composed, fifteen minutes later.

"Do you want a kiss before we leave, or would that be counterproductive?" I asked.

His steps faltered, and his gaze searched mine. Then he stalked toward me. I retreated a step before I could stop myself, and the corner of his mouth tilted. A second later, my back was against the nearest wall, and his lips were skimming my earlobe.

"Do you know what Grandma told me the day after you came home?" he whispered. "She said she told you to compliment me and that I shouldn't react. I should let you play your games until you come to the right conclusion on your own. Are you still playing games, Wrenly, or is this your conclusion?"

"I don't know what you mean." I hated that the words sounded breathy and unsteady.

"Are you purposely doing things to break my control so I mate you and break my promise? Are you so determined to leave me?"

I reached for his jacket, gripping it at his sides and turning my head to kiss his lips lightly.

"When I withdraw, you hold me tighter. When I'm accommodating, you're less smothering. When you start smothering, I go to extremes. It's that simple."

He sighed and set his forehead against mine.

"Your words tear through me better than any shifter's claws, Wrenly. Why can't you just let yourself want me? I know you do. I can smell it."

"Basically, you're asking why I can't just sit down, shut up, and do what you want me to do. Do you really want a lifeless puppet? Because that's what you'll get with your method. You told me to fight for a life I love. That's what I'm doing."

He growled and pushed back from me. But he didn't walk away. He threaded his fingers through mine and led the way out to the car. We held hands all the way to the pastry shop. I refused after though.

"If you want my continued affection, you need to let me eat," I said, already reaching into the bag.

"Don't you want to wait until we reach the office?"

"Hell no. I want to get crumbs all over your expensive car so you can find one weeks from now and think of me gorging myself on pastries." I gave him my most innocent grin then bit into the buttery flakiness I'd been craving.

He watched me for several seconds, then darted in to lick the corner of my mouth.

"What was that?" I asked after I swallowed.

"Crumb control."

He started the car and drove the rest of the way to the office.

Miranda was waiting at the desk by the time we arrived. She frowned at my casual clothes.

"Where are the clothes from yesterday?"

"Getting washed. Don't worry, I have different clothes." I pointed to the bag Bennett was carrying for me.

Miranda gave me a disapproving look. Grinning, I held out a pastry bag to her.

"I brought you a bribe."

She looked at Bennett. "Before I accept her bribe, what are the rules for today?"

He snorted. "Rules? What rules?"

Miranda and I watched him walk into his office and close the door. The blinds stayed open, though.

"It doesn't smell like you two are fighting. What happened? Why did I need to bring running clothes? I thought the doctor's instructions said no running until the stitches were removed."

"They do, and I plan to follow them. But I think Bennett is going to test me every way possible today, which might wear on my nerves. So the jogging clothes are my Plan B."

"And your Plan A?"

I grinned. "I'll tell you about it when I drag you away for a much-needed break at ten."

The office door opened.

"Wrenly, I need to speak with you, please," Bennett said.

I winked at Miranda and turned toward Bennett. "About what?"

He gestured for me to go into his office. I complied and found myself pinned to the back of the closed door.

"I said no kissing at work."

"You said no kissing in public. We're not in public. The door's closed." He reached over and shut the blinds, too.

"She's going to know what we're doing."

"So?"

"It'll embarrass me."

"Then don't leave." He dipped his head and kissed my neck.

It felt really good and brought back memories of last night. How far would he push this today? How far would I let him? My body was saying as far as he wanted.

He inhaled with a groan, and I knew I was in trouble. If I didn't distract him, he was going to press, and I was going to give. So, I did what I did best. I threw a verbal grenade.

"I'm not wearing any underwear."

The phrase was like a bomb in the room. He flung himself away from me as he shifted, and I bolted out the door.

CHAPTER THIRTY-FOUR

I LEANED against Bennett's closed office door, holding the knob just in case.

Miranda's eyes went wide as he thudded against the other side, making the door—and me—shake.

"This soundproofing is really good," I said. "I can't even hear the noise he's making." The door vibrated against my back again.

"What did you do?" she asked.

Mom came around the corner just then. Her gaze swept over us, lingering on the shaking door for a second.

"Is everything all right?"

"Depends on how sturdy this door is," I said.

"What happened?"

I hesitated, debating what to say. The door gave an aggressive lurch.

"The truth, Wrenly. So I can help."

"I told him I wasn't wearing any underwear," I mumbled, my face flushing.

Miranda fell out of her chair, laughing so hard that she was wheezing.

"Ah," was all that Mom said. "It's best if you make yourself scarce until lunch. Are you still all right with going out? We can change locations from what I suggested to Bennett."

That her gaze didn't even flicker to my clothes when she said that was a testament to Mom's poise.

"I have a change of clothes, but they're in the office...with Bennett."

"No problem. I'll get them for you once you're gone. Why don't you pick Miranda up and take her with you?"

I nodded and hurried over to grab Miranda's arm.

"Get off the floor so we can go to Zellon's," I said.

She sprang up like she'd been equipped with a pogo stick. I rolled my eyes at her weeping ones.

"Your mascara looks like it belongs on a hooker."

"What do they charge these days? Is 'no panties to work' extra?"

I shot her a look as I towed her away from the office, and she waited until we were out on the sidewalk to say anything else.

"Am I going to get the full story now? Why did you tell him you had open access under those shorts, and why was he calling me at dawn, asking me to check on you?"

"We made out last night."

"Remind me again how that advances your fight for freedom?"

"If you can't beat 'em, join 'em and then beat 'em?" I said with a shrug.

She stopped walking, all humor leaving her expression.

"You're going to mate him and reject him?"

"Only if he makes that move. I told him I was done fighting him but that, if he mates me, even if I'm willing in the heat of the moment, once the deed is done, I will reject him. He knows his options. I laid it all out for him."

"I bet you did, Miss No Knickers."

"This is a bigger test for him to keep his word. He promised he wouldn't mate with me. If he can keep that promise, no matter what I do or say, then I believe he'll keep his promise about other things. And maybe..." I shrugged, and she slowly smiled.

"He's winning you over, isn't he?"

I sighed. "Maybe. Now, what are we going to do for the next hour that it'll take him to calm down?"

"Shop, of course. It's your penance."

I groaned all the way to the ride share she ordered for us, but my mood improved when we walked through Zellon's doors and got snooty looks from the two women who were sitting at a consultation table with a jeweler.

One of the women's phones started to ring before they could say anything to us.

Miranda pulled me over to the necklace that went with her earrings.

"Mommy, mommy, if I win on Saturday, will you buy this?" Miranda begged with a grin.

"If you have to fight at all, I'll tell Mom and Dad to get it for you, but I doubt you will."

"What? Why?"

"Don't pick it up," a woman behind us said.

At first, I thought she was talking to Miranda, which was dumb of her since the necklace was in a locked glass case.

"You know what she wants," the woman continued.

I glanced over my shoulder and saw the woman with the phone in her hand sigh and answer the call on speaker. Rude, but I also sensed some brewing drama.

"Chloe, I need a favor," a familiar voice said. "Daddy froze my cards, and I need a loan for a few days."

"Sorry, Lindi. Daddy froze my card, too, after last week's party. It's going to be at least a month before I'm back in his good graces."

"I understand."

The tension in Lindi's response had me grinning along with Chloe.

"I hope we can meet up for lunch soon," Chloe said before hanging up and handing her card to the consultant. "I'll take the bracelet."

"Wait, is that *the* Lindi?" Miranda asked softly.

Turning away from the pair to study the necklace in the case, I nodded.

"But did her parents actually kick her out, or was that an act?" I wondered quietly.

"How could it be an act? We didn't even know we would be here today."

She wasn't wrong, but I had years of reasons to suspect lies from Lindi.

A sales associate approached us. While she spoke with Miranda about the necklace, I watched the woman who'd spoken to Lindi. She didn't glance at us as the jeweler wrapped her purchase.

Going to my phone, I went to check Lindi's profile. I wasn't expecting her to announce her disownment or anything like that, but I was curious if there would be a hint. She hadn't updated her profile for three days. That was a hint enough for me to text Bennett.

Me: Are you human again?
Bennett: Yes. If you want to buy something, you can put it on the store tab. I just called to confirm it.
Me: Thanks, but I just overheard a call and am more interested in finding out if the Shanes really disowned Lindi like it sounded.
Bennett: They called Monday to say they had. I told them they needed to make it public. There hasn't been any news yet.
Me: k. Thanks.
Bennett: Will you be coming back soon?
Me: Are you asking because I'm in public with no underwear and you're worried I'll talk to the opposite sex?
Bennett: No, I'm asking because I miss you. And I really like being near you when you're not wearing any underwear.

I flushed, thinking of last night.

"Let me guess…Bennett?" Miranda asked.

I looked up and found her watching me with a smirk.

"Yeah. I'm asking him to confirm what we heard. Why?"

"You smell like lust." She sighed. "He's probably going to shift again the second he sees you. Let's go."

We left the store and made it back to the office in thirty minutes. When I got out of the car, I spotted Bennett through the main lobby doors, waiting for us, proof that he'd been tracking me.

"He doesn't look much calmer," Miranda said, seeing what I was seeing.

His hands were fisted in his pockets, and he was radiating barely checked irritation, which everyone was picking up on since they were giving him a wide berth.

Why did seeing him like that make me giddy and desperate to see how far I could push him before he snapped?

"You have it so bad for him," she said. "Are you sure giving in would be the end of the world like you think?"

I met her gaze and smiled slightly. Then, without answering her, I met the gaze of a random guy on the street and smiled.

"Excuse me, do you have the time?"

He paused, glancing at his expensive watch. "Eleven-thirty-six."

"Thanks. I'm Wrenly." I held out my hand.

He seemed a little confused but shook my hand. The doors opened behind him. I didn't look at Bennett but maintained eye contact with the man who was still holding my hand.

"And you are?"

"Landel Marchel. Are you hitting on me?"

"Wrenly." That was it from Bennett, one word spoken with enough volume that my human ears could hear it.

"No, just trying to meet people," I said, ignoring the warning. "I work in administration at Wulf Enterprises. It was nice meeting you, Landel."

"You too, Wrenly," he said, letting go of my hand. "If you're ever interested in a custom piece of jewelry, give me a call. I might be able to help you out."

He handed over a business card from his pocket and walked away after a brief nod.

"He was good-looking," I said, glancing at the card. "I think you'd like him, Miranda." I held up the card that had the Zellon's logo on it.

"No way. Shit. I should have said something." She stole the card from me. "Do you think that was the designer himself? He didn't look old enough, though, did he?"

She was staring after the guy's retreating back, and I could see her debating whether or not to run after him.

"We have his card. It's better to wait and call later than to show how desperate you are now."

I glanced at Bennett as I said the last part, and he frowned at me.

"Stop drooling," I said, focusing on Miranda again. "It's almost lunchtime, and I still need to change. And you need to actually work."

"Pfft. Shows what you know. I have an unlimited shop-with-Wrenly day pass thanks to tall, dark, and scowling by the door."

I snorted a laugh and grinned at Bennett. Some of his tension melted away as I watched.

"Ah, the lovestruck mate look. I can't decide if I want one myself or want to wait now."

"What? Why would you want to wait? I thought getting a mate was the end-all be-all."

"It's supposed to be, but meeting you changed my mind."

"Because I'm difficult?"

"No, because if I had a mate, I'd be more focused on him and less focused on shopping with you."

"A travesty."

"Are we going to keep standing here, torturing him, or are you going to give him the pity hug he wants?" she asked.

"Neither."

I walked toward him, let him open the door for me, but otherwise ignored his presence until we were in his office and the door was closed.

"That's going to take some serious repair work," I said, pointing toward the back of the door.

"Mom is already ordering a new one." He didn't pin me to the wall or move toward me like I'd thought he would. He kept his hands in his pockets.

"Was waiting for you crossing a line?" he asked, surprising me.

"No."

"Was going outside crossing a line?"

I slowly shook my head, wondering where this was going.

"If I had interrupted your talk with Landel, would that have crossed a line?" He started shaking when he said "Landel."

"Yes."

His face twitched a little. "Do I get any reward for staying away?"

I fought not to smile but knew he smelled my amusement when he relaxed a little.

"Go sit in your chair."

He frowned then slowly retreated to his desk. Once he was seated, I approached with a teasing smile on my lips. His pupils devoured his irises before I even set my hands on his shoulders. When I straddled his lap, he started shaking.

"The less you take, the more I'm willing to give," I said, brushing my lips against his. "The more restrained you are, the more I want to provoke you."

I kissed his bottom lip then his chin, nudging it so he tilted his head back. When I had access to his throat, I did the same thing he'd done to me the night before. His breathing turned ragged, and the chair creaked ominously.

"Should I stop?" I asked against his skin.

"No."

The snarled word made me smile and bite his throat gently.

"Will you be okay while I'm at lunch with Mom?"

"No."

I bit him again, and he groaned.

"Mark me, Wrenly," he said harshly.

I sucked on his neck, and when I was finished leaving a small purple mark, I kissed his Adam's apple. A second later, I was on my back on the desk with Bennett looming over me. His eyes were wild as they searched mine.

Warning bells went off in my head.

"Can we stop, please? If someone comes in…"

His mask slipped into place as he plucked me off the desk and turned me toward the bathroom.

"Go change. The bag is inside."

I nodded and fled.

After splashing water on my face one-handed, I opened the bag I'd brought from home.

A note lay on top of the underwear I'd packed.

There will be a repeat of last night if you keep forgetting these.

My face flamed hot again as I quickly stripped and put on the new clothes. The tie at the back of my neck wasn't happening on my own, but I knew better than to leave the bathroom without Mom present. So I waited. And waited.

Noon came and went.

"Are you hiding, Wrenly?"

"If I were, I'd pick a better place than your bathroom."

"You're supposed to meet Mom by the elevator."

I made a face in the mirror then opened the door.

"Can you please tie my shirt without making me smell like we were just making out?"

"But we were just making out."

"You're making me regret your reward." My gaze flicked to the faded to yellow mark prominently displayed above his starched collar.

He scowled and motioned for me to turn around. Grumpy, he kept his fingers from wandering too far from the tie.

"There. Now, do I get a kiss goodbye?"

I faced him and shook my head.

"You already had one."

"Another wouldn't hurt."

I started to cross my arms, but he stopped me, kissing the back of my hand and rubbing the spot with his thumb.

"Stitches," he said. "You're going to hurt yourself."

"Ask yourself why I was crossing my arms."

He sighed and kissed my brow.

"Fine. Go. I'll see you after lunch."

I smiled as he released me. "Do you want me to bring something back for you?"

"I doubt you'll let me eat what I'm hungry for."

I blinked at him, the meaning of his words lost on me until he started to smile slowly.

"You're getting another shaken bento box."

He hurried around me to open the door so I could continue my outraged march out of his office.

Miranda looked up from her work.

"That looked pretty hot," she commented.

I glanced back and saw the blinds had been opened.

"Nope. Not going to think about that. And there won't be a next time."

She was grinning as I walked away.

Mom was waiting by the elevator, her eyes filled with worry as I approached.

"What's wrong?" I asked.

She waited until we were on the elevator alone to answer.

"Was he calm when you got back?"

"Mostly. He needs to stop taking his frustrations out on doors, though."

"Better doors than you."

"Me? What do you mean? I thought you said he would never hurt me."

She wrapped an arm around my shoulders and set her cheek on the top of my head.

"He wouldn't. I just meant in other ways you might not be open to yet." I heard her sniff. "Or maybe you are?"

"Mom..." I wormed my way out of her hold. "Can you please pretend you can't smell what you're smelling?"

She grinned at me.

"I don't know why everyone thinks work romance is okay," I grumbled.

She sighed and hugged me again. "Sending you away was a mistake on so many levels. If you'd stayed with us, you wouldn't even think twice about office sex with your mate."

The elevator doors opened on my tortured moan.

Walt stood there. Of course he did.

"Hey, Wrenly. Everything okay?"

"No. I'm going to need therapy. Mom, this is Walt, a sublet employee. Walt, this is my mom, Christine Wulf."

His brows shot up briefly before he composed himself.

"A pleasure to meet you, Mrs. Wulf," he said.

She shook hands with him, her smile polite.

"How do you two know each other?" she asked.

"My first day here, we bumped into each other at the sandwich shop down the way. He recommended the park to me."

The elevators opened to the main floor.

"Have a good lunch, Walt," I said as Mom and I headed for the garage elevator.

"So you met him on your first day?" she asked.

"Yep. And Bennett found me sitting next to him at the park. Like an uninformed idiot, I traded a week of lunches in Bennett's office in exchange for him not telling you and Dad."

She caught my hand and gave it a comforting squeeze.

"He didn't do anything inappropriate, did he?"

"Walt? Heck no. He's nice."

"I meant Bennett when he found you."

"No. Actually…" I thought about what I knew now and how he'd reacted then. "He was pretty restrained. He didn't approach but waited until I saw him."

She smiled and opened my door for me and even buckled me in like Bennett did.

"I can use my other hand, you know."

"You could, but then we'd both miss this chance to baby you like I should have been doing all these years."

"Are you going to cut up my lunch for me too?" I asked, amused and not minding her attention.

She laughed as she closed the door.

"So where are we going?" I asked when she got in behind the wheel.

"Clay and Leaf. It's a tea room where people go to be seen, which is why I'm taking you there."

She caught the face I made.

"We don't have to go, but I heard that Mrs. Shane will be there today, and I want to see how she acts when we get there."

"Well, now you're talking. Did Bennett tell you I overheard a call from Lindi today?"

"No."

I explained what I heard.

"Mr. Shane reached out to Aaron on Saturday before the run, thinking he could circumvent the conditions Bennett set." She patted my hand. "Dad quickly corrected that notion and the one that their horrible offspring's crimes don't fit the punishment."

Her words had a bit of a growl at the end.

"So we're going to the Clay and Leaf to do what?"

"I want Mrs. Shane to see how much we value you so they know you're off limits. But this isn't about just her. I want the pack to know your place in this family, too. Just because you choose not to wear expensive clothes or flaunt your wealth doesn't mean you're not part of this family."

"Technically, I have no wealth to flaunt. I still don't have my bank account."

"That will be fixed as soon as my eldest cub removes his head from his ass."

I choked on my laugh, and she grinned at me.

"I love that boy, but he's a typical male still trying to control things."

"He's getting better every day, though," I said, thinking about how he hadn't tried manipulating the situation before we'd left. Well, at least not too hard.

It took about twenty minutes to reach the tea room. As the valet drove away with Mom's car, Mom tucked my arm around hers.

"Let's remind them all that you're a Wulf."

The hint of growl in her voice didn't bode well for anyone who might mention the Wulf family taking in a poor orphan all those years ago.

I patted her arm and hugged it a little. She smiled and took a calming breath before we moved toward the attendant, who opened the door at our approach.

We walked into the quaintest entry I'd ever seen. It reminded me so much of something I might see in a Hallmark Channel movie.

"Do you have a reservation?" The woman at the antique desk asked.

"Yes. Wulf for two."

The woman glanced down at her tablet then at the woman standing next to her.

"Table Twenty-Three."

The second woman nodded and smiled at us. "Please follow me."

I noted that all the staff wore the same medium grey vest, a light grey button-up shirt with pinstripes, and a darker grey tie, paired with black slacks. The uniforms looked trendy and old-fashioned at the same time, which helped blend the vintage decor with the modern clothes of the customers we passed.

A woman wearing a hat with a plume nodded at Mom and glanced at me. I smiled.

"Nice hat."

She smiled back.

Under my breath, I said, "Shakespeare probably wants his pen back."

Mom coughed suddenly, and I patted her arm soothingly, faking concern when I knew she was trying her best to swallow her laughter.

Our attendant stopped at a table and held out a chair for me. A man quickly approached to do the same for Mom. While she ordered for us, I glanced around the room for Mrs. Shane.

"I think we're early," Mom said after the man walked away.

The words had barely left her mouth when I spotted Mrs. Shane at the door. I waited until her gaze met mine, then looked away indifferently.

"She's here," I said to Mom.

Mom smiled and watched our server approach with our tea.

A warning, "Shh. I know," from the table next to ours caught my attention, but I didn't turn to look at who was talking. With a relaxed smile of thanks, I accepted my tea and listened.

"Hurry up and finish so we can leave," a woman said.

"Why? I want to see what happens," another said.

"And I don't want to be caught up in their grudge against each other," the first one said. "I heard it's because of her."

I could feel the weight of their gazes as I took my first sip.

"This is nice," I said to Mom. "Sweet but not overly so."

She nodded and hid her smile with her cup.

"I heard the same," the other woman continued.

One of them groaned. "Too late. Here she comes. Keep your head down, and maybe we'll make it out of here without offending people we can't afford to offend."

CHAPTER THIRTY-FIVE

THANKS TO THEIR WHISPERED WARNING, I waited a few seconds before looking up. My perfect smile was in place for Mrs. Shane as she focused on me with barely a glance at Mom.

"Wrenly, you look lovely today. I think this is your first visit to Clay and Leaf, isn't it? If you could spare a few minutes, I would like to show you the garden and have a private word."

"A private word? Why? I think this is the first time I've ever spoken to you. Is this about your daughter, Lindi?"

All conversation around us stopped, and Mrs. Shane's smile grew a little more brittle. If I were a betting person, which I was, I'd bet her face was flushed under all the makeup she was wearing.

"It is. There are some concerning photos she has on her phone that I'd like to discuss with you."

I laughed. "Those? I promise I won't tell anyone about her involvement in those." I dropped my volume as if to keep the rest confidential and felt the ladies next to us lean in. "I never used her name when I went to the police. But it's still an open case that, as the victim, I'm not supposed to discuss with those involved."

Mrs. Shane wasn't good at hiding what she was thinking or

feeling. She was irate and ready to do whatever was necessary to save her daughter, but she couldn't tell if I was bluffing or not.

"Is there something else?" I asked.

"My daughter is showing you more respect and kindness than you deserve," Mom said before Mrs. Shane could answer. "Instead of wasting your time trying to intimidate her, you should focus on fixing the mess your daughter made. I heard it's starting to affect your business.

"What was the name of the investor your husband found in France again? Oh, wait, that one fell through yesterday. Today's is in India, isn't it?"

Mrs. Shane's face drained of color, and she slowly sank to her knees on the floor.

"Please." The broken word was filled with defeat.

Mom leaned in toward Mrs. Shane and spoke softly enough that I could barely hear her.

"I rented the grand ballroom at the same hotel you used to throw your daughter her welcome home banquet. Tomorrow at seven. Invite everyone you know, and make the announcement, or watch everything you covet disappear."

When Mom straightened, she looked at me.

"We should go before Bennett starts to worry."

I stepped around Mrs. Shane and left with Mom.

She kept it together until we were in the car then unleashed her outrage in a verbal deluge.

"How dare she try to threaten you with those pictures again! They've pushed too far. I don't care if they do disown their daughter. They're never coming back from this. I will spend every penny we have to make them pay. I'll haunt them for the rest of their lives."

She pressed a button on her steering wheel.

"Call Bennett."

The phone started to ring through the speaker.

"Um, maybe you shouldn't be driving mad," I said just as Bennett picked up.

"What's wrong? Are you okay, Wrenly?"

"I'm fine. Mom's mad."

"Use whatever resources you need to add more pressure on the Shanes. If they don't use that room tomorrow at seven to announce they've severed all ties with their daughter, I want them to wake up to an eviction on their house."

"What happened?"

"That woman tried to use those pictures to coerce Wrenly into speaking with her in private."

"I didn't," I said quickly so Bennett wouldn't start freaking out too. "I stayed with Mom."

"Good girl."

I blinked at the tone in which the praise had been delivered and felt an immediate flush consume my body.

Mom sniffed. All the anger evaporated from her body as she glanced at me with a smile.

"We'll be back in fifteen minutes," Mom said before hanging up.

I rolled down my window and let the wind clear out whatever Mom had smelled and my growing worry. Why had I reacted like that? When did Bennett's praise start to matter? Why was I even worried?

My state of confused apprehension lasted all the way to the office, where Mom watched me hesitate to get out of the car after she opened the door.

"Do you want to talk about it?" she asked.

"Yes, but I'm not even sure what's bothering me. All I know is that I don't want to face Bennett right now."

"Why?"

"Because I think he's going to go too far and I won't hate it." Admitting the truth didn't make me feel any better.

She gently tugged me out of the car and hugged me. "My poor sweetheart. It's not easy dealing with an obsessed mate. Especially when they're so good at being loving after the initial insanity settles down."

"Has it settled down? He still sleeps with me at night and wants to touch me all the time."

"That's normal, not insanity. The insanity was not telling you the truth, stealing your bed, hoarding your old clothes, and sending his brothers away."

She withdrew as she said the last part and caught my frown.

"He told them to come back. They're waiting for you to reach out to them, though."

I snorted. "I'm not going to invite them back into my life. They left because Bennett told them to, despite what I needed. If they want back in, they can earn it. I'm not going to beg for it."

"Can I let them know that?"

I shrugged indifferently.

"Do you want to sit in my office for a while?"

I sighed and shook my head. "He's worse when I avoid him."

She gave me a reassuring smile as we walked to the elevator. When we reached our floor, we parted ways. She went to talk to Dad, and I slowly traversed the path to Bennett's suite.

Turning the corner, I saw him pacing in front of his desk.

"Finally," Miranda. "He's like a caged wolf."

"Has anyone bothered him while I was gone?"

"After Mr. Wulf sent out the pack announcement about the challenges for your position, a few women came by, but they took one look at him and decided to ask me why you wouldn't be there instead."

"And what did you say?"

"That it was a waste of your time to spectate when you could be out shopping for me instead. I'll make sure to narrow down my wishlist so you don't have to shop for too long."

I shook my head at her, amused.

When I glanced at Bennett through the windows again, he wasn't pacing. He was staring right at me.

"Are you thinking about going in there?" she asked, humor lacing the words.

"I don't think I have a choice."

"You could try running, but I'm betting you wouldn't even reach Olivia's desk."

"You're not helpful."

"Do you want me to try to trip him or something?"

"Tempting, but no. I think you're risking enough for me. Set the timer, and get me in five minutes."

"You got it."

As I approached the door, he closed the blinds. Miranda laughed behind me.

"Have fun."

"Timer," I said before I opened the door.

Bennett had me pinned to the wall and the door shut again before I'd even opened it a foot.

"One of these days, you're going to hurt me."

"Never," he said, easing up on his already gentle hold on my hands.

"Did you miss me?"

He groaned and dipped his head to inhale near my neck.

"Yes, but this isn't just about missing you. I hate those pictures. I hate what they did to you...what I did to you." He started to shake.

"Regret wastes the present by dwelling on a past that can't be changed. Why do something that's useless?"

"Everything I've done feels useless. Clothes. Jewelry. Makeup. Dates. The car. What's useful?"

Each word created an exhale that teased my skin, warming me from the inside.

"I like the car. And the dates when you weren't being a moody ass."

He let out a frustrated breath, and I closed my eyes against the sensation.

"I have a nose. You didn't like anything but the car. And what good is the car when you can't use it?" The fingers of one hand traced along the bandage on my arm.

"You should let me go," I said, trying not to react to how much I liked my current pinned position and his frustration.

I knew it was too late when he slowly inhaled.

"Wrenly, you are the most confusing female I've ever—"

Turning my head, I kissed him. He released my good hand when I tugged at his hold and groaned as my fingers speared through his hair. His tongue met mine, stroke for stroke, distracting me so much that I didn't at first notice the arm he slipped around my waist until he started walking with me.

"Wait," I said, breaking the kiss when I realized he was headed for the couch.

"For what?"

"Miranda is going to come in here in five minutes."

He veered and locked the door.

"Not what I meant, Bennett."

He kissed me again. Hungrily.

I wrapped my legs around his waist to prevent him from setting me down. It certainly had the desired effect. One hand clasped my thigh as the other captured the back of my head. He kissed me so thoroughly that I forgot where we were and why making out with him was a bad idea until he pulled away and set his forehead against mine.

"This is me listening, Wrenly. I'm stopping now, not because I want to but because you'll be embarrassed if I do what I want to do here. Tonight. When we're home. We'll do this again."

Struggling to catch my breath, I nodded without fully understanding his words. It wasn't until he set me on my feet by the door and opened it for me that I understood what I'd agreed to.

Miranda, who was standing just on the other side of the door, watched my eyes go wide, and looked from me to Bennett.

"You sure know how to stress her out. Come on, my little ah-pWren-tice. Let's look at some spreadsheets together."

She led me away from him before I could say anything. The door closed behind us.

"You're sending off 'what have I done' and 'I'd like another helping' scents at the same time. Breathe. Whatever happened in there is over. However, if you'd like to discuss it, I'm more than happy to listen. The more detailed, the better."

Her ridiculous comment broke through the muddle in my mind, and I managed a short laugh before settling into my spot.

"Let's just focus on work."

It was easy to say but hard to do. Scrolling through columns of numbers with my non-dominant hand was frustrating and made it hard to concentrate on what I was seeing. However, I had no problem dwelling on what happened behind Bennett's door, which remained firmly shut until five.

Just as I was turning off my computer, he walked out with my bag of clothes in one hand. The other he extended for me. He was almost vibrating with his caged energy.

"Do you feel like fast food tonight?" he asked.

He didn't sound like himself either.

When I glanced at Miranda, she kept her head down as if she were still working.

"Wrenly? Do you need to eat?"

His voice had gotten rougher, and when I looked at him, his pupils were fully expanded.

If I didn't turn around his mood, we'd never make it out of the parking lot. What had he done the whole afternoon? Sit in his office and think about making out with me? Probably.

"What kind of dumb question is that? Of course I need to eat. And no, I don't want fast food. I want pizza. And ice cream. And I'm tired of these stitches, and I want to go for a run!"

The anger and frustration I'd managed to churn up snapped him out of his haze. I watched his pupils slowly return to normal as he gently took my hand. His show of concern made it easy for me to turn on my sad face and a wobbly bottom lip.

"And I want to watch a movie with gas station snacks."

"Okay. Then that's what we'll do. We'll stop for pizza and ice cream on the way home."

I nodded and let him lead me away from Miranda.

When I glanced back at her, she was silently applauding. I winked, then turned around and focused on being frustrated, sad, hungry Wrenly, who needed pampering and not a make-out session in the parking garage.

We made it all the way home before his eyes started flipping out. It was my own fault. I'd moaned while eating the pizza, but it'd been too good not to make some kind of noise in appreciation.

Bennett didn't say anything as he held my gaze.

My enjoyment faded. After swallowing, I set aside the rest of my piece with a sigh.

"You at least waited until we were home and I had something to eat. Have at me." I spread my arms and closed my eyes without leaving my seat.

"What movie do you want to watch?" he said after a few seconds of silence.

I cracked an eye open to frown at him.

"Are you toying with me, or are you going to wait until I'm excited to watch something, then rip the rug out from under me?"

"No. The less I take, the more you give. The more restrained I am, the more you want to provoke me," he said, using my words. "I really want you to provoke me, Wrenly."

I had no control over the slow smile his words produced, and I saw what my reaction to his words did to him.

"We're just feeding off of each other now," I said.

"Yeah."

"Are you sure you're okay with that?"

"Play your games, baby. As long as they're with me, I'm okay with it."

"Does that mean you knew I was distracting you back at the office when I demanded pizza and a movie?"

"When you want something..." he exhaled heavily and gave up

the pretext of eating. "You're always distracting, Wrenly. But when you look at me with sad eyes and ask for something, nothing else exists in this world but you and getting you what you want."

I stuck my bottom lip out.

"I need my bankbook. Please, Bennett. Pretty, pretty please." My tone had enough syrup in it to top a sundae. But apparently, Bennett really liked me sweet.

His pupils opened wide before he swept a hand over his face as if hoping that would help dilute my effect on him.

I waited until he glanced at me again to bat my lashes innocently and beg a little harder with my lower lip. His chair fell backward, and he was gone, only to return a second later with a credit card.

"This is yours."

"I don't want your credit card."

"It's not mine, and it's not a credit card. It's your bank card. The pin is your birthday."

Curious, I took it from him and then used my phone to check the balance. I didn't believe what I was seeing.

"One...two...three..." I looked up at him. "How do I have over nine million dollars in my bank account, Bennett? I just started working a few weeks ago. Please tell me that's not what this is all from."

His gaze searched my upturned face before he caught the back of my head with a hand and bent down, setting his forehead against mine.

"Will you still watch a movie with me even if you don't like the answer?"

"Now, I have to know. Spill it, Bennett."

"Promise first."

I pulled back enough to meet his gaze. He let me see his concern and his need.

"I can do better than just a promise to watch a movie. Let me finish eating, then we'll go to that couch, and while I'm sitting on your lap, you can tell me about the money. And after, we'll watch a movie together."

Fine tremors started to race through his arms. I felt it in his fingers at the back of my head.

"With you still sitting on my lap?"

"That depends. Are you going to sit down and finish eating?"

He slowly straightened away from me and, after a measured look, returned to his chair, which he had to pick up. Not trusting his patience, I ate quickly. He stopped eating when I did, and we took everything to the kitchen together.

"I'll clean up later," he said, picking me up when I would have started rinsing the plates.

He carried me to the couch and sat with me in his lap. Why did sitting like this feel like I was home more than actually being home? Exhaling contentedly, I snuggled in a little more and looked up at him expectantly.

Instead of giving me an explanation, he kissed me. The brief brush of his lips was there and gone before I would have liked. The precedent of previous kisses had obviously left me expecting more, which was the only reason I could come up with for my immediate scowl.

He slowly smiled in response.

"I opened the account for you once I turned eighteen. I was still at school and doing everything I could to distract myself from being without you."

"Like helping your brother from another mother with his sheds?"

He made a pained face. "You're mean when you don't get what you want."

I shrugged. "What were you doing to distract yourself?"

"Challenges. From anyone dumb enough to issue one. Konni would encourage our classmates to bet. I made some money that I needed to hide or I'd have to explain to Mom and Dad what I was doing." A smile ghosted his lips. "Putting it in your account was a way to get away with it if I ever got caught. Then, when I started to see the amount grow, the reason for adding to it changed.

"Everything I have is yours. No questions. No arguments. But I wanted you to have something that was just yours, too."

I looked down at the number again, touched by what he'd done, but also worried.

"It's not all from fighting, is it?"

"No. I've made money on investments too."

He dipped his head and brushed his lips against mine again. "I can smell your relief."

"Yeah, well, I was starting to worry my potential mate was an idiot who likes fighting. First school. Then bullying people in the office, including women and his brothers. Add to that mess the fact that he's his best friend's primary contact for shedding season, and it's not looking good for you."

"You won't ever let me forget that, will you?"

I grinned at him. "No. Not any time soon. So when it comes to his bits, do you assist with that too?"

His hand covered my mouth, and he looked me in the eyes, his gaze pleading with me.

"I'll double the amount in that account by the end of the year if you don't talk about Konni's shedding until then."

My tongue flicked against Bennett's palm. His pupils dilated as his expression turned tortured.

"Triple," he pleaded.

I pulled his hand away from my mouth.

"You can go to sleep with me every night, and I'll kiss you every morning if you let me bring it up as much as I want."

He flipped us and had my back against the couch with my hands pinned near my head.

"Yes." The rough word was little more than a drawn-out growl.

I knew I was walking a fine line again, but my attraction to Bennet made it so damn hard to resist provoking him, especially when he was on edge like this.

"And if you tell me in detail how you help him with the shed, I might consider reenacting it with you."

Bennett's heated expression turned shocked then worried and disturbed.

I laughed. I couldn't help it.

"No deal to the second part," he said.

"And the first part?"

His hesitation to agree had me tilting my head to steal a quick kiss. When he didn't respond, I kissed his chin. His gaze said I was on my way to convincing him, but not quite there yet. So I kissed my way down his neck until I found the spot I'd marked earlier. I kissed the area gently, tracing it with my tongue, then scraping it with my teeth.

By the time I finished, he was shaking like a purse pooch who got into mommy's magic dust.

"Say yes, Bennett," I said between nips.

"Make me."

Those two words made my insides go hot and cold in anticipation. I wasn't the type to back down from anything. I plotted. I waited for the right time, maybe. But I never backed down when things got hard. And they were getting hard. I had no doubt about that.

And he was giving me permission to keep pushing at his control.

"Switch spots with me."

He flipped us again, and my hands were free to smooth over his chest as I leaned in to nuzzle his neck like he had mine. His shaking grew more pronounced with each passing second.

His hands settled on my hips, locking me in place just a few inches above his hips. It was a clear indication that he was on the verge of breaking. If I pushed down, I doubted he'd resist much. But would I be able to handle the fallout?

I debated a safer way to push him over the edge.

"Where should I mark you next?" I asked against his throat. "Here? Or..." The fingers of my good hand plucked open one of the buttons on his shirt, and I slipped my hand inside to tease his chest. "Should I kiss you here tomorrow morning when there's no shirt in the way?

"Yes," he said. "To the first part. To the kisses in the morning."

"Are you sure there's nothing I can do to make you say yes to the second part?"

I made the mistake of lifting my head and looking at him. The look in his eyes was one of desperation and determination.

"Make me yours, Wrenly, and I'll do anything you want."

CHAPTER THIRTY-SIX

HIS PLEA SET off a chain reaction inside of me. It felt like my heart was trying to turn over in my chest. My insides went hot and cold. And I desperately wanted to lean into him and keep kissing.

Fighting it all, I straightened away from him with a sigh.

"No deal, then. I'm not willing to trade my freedom for a fleeting sense of enlightenment. Besides, you've already told me that I own you and you do pretty much what I want...except for this, apparently."

He didn't get mad about the no and didn't try to hold onto me as I got off his lap.

"You keep saying you want your freedom, but what if it's not freedom you want? What if it's control?" he asked as I sat next to him.

His words made me pause and consider the last few weeks.

I'd had freedom to do what I wanted at home...as long as I told them what I was doing. When they said no to something, no matter how justified the reason, that was when I lost my temper. That was when I reacted. Did I really just not like being told what to do? I hadn't liked Mom arranging the job for me, but I'd accepted it to play nice so they would be more willing to let me go. However, when Bennett had tried to force me to go to work with him by taking the keys, I'd reacted. When he tried forcing me to wear clothes I didn't like without giving me a reason, I'd reacted.

"I think you're right."

"Do you want to hear another thought?"

"Sure."

He wrapped his arm around my shoulders and pulled me close to his side. I rested my head against him, waiting.

"I'm willing to let you control whatever you want, and I'm willing to give up whatever control I have to be with you."

My heart gave a wild thump against my ribcage.

"What do you mean?"

"You already know I'm willing to hand over anything to you. Properties. Bank accounts. Cars. It's all yours. It's the other stuff you're worried about. Now that we know, we can adjust accordingly.

"You don't want me to control who you talk to or where you go, so I won't. Will I get jealous? Yes. Will I need reassurance? Yes. But I won't interfere. You want to go to school without me following you? Okay. We can talk on the phone, and I'll be able to see where you are during the week. And maybe, when you can, you come home on the weekends to see me."

I tipped my head back to look at him, a tightness gathering in my chest.

"Are you serious?"

"Yes."

I searched his gaze and saw no hesitation there, but his mask was in place.

"Will you need to go back to keeping my old clothes?"

"Maybe. But that's my problem, not yours...unless I take something of yours that you like."

"What about mating? Are you willing to wait, or are you just saying this to get me to say yes to mating?"

He kissed my forehead. "I'm not stupid. I know what will happen if I claim you and go back on my word. Rejection can happen at any time, not just in the beginning."

"So what are we saying?"

"I'm saying I'll be anything you need me to be and do anything you need me to do for even just a small chance to remain in your life."

His mask slipped, showing me his sincerity and hope. It was a hope I shared, but I was a realist too. Being with Bennett wasn't just about the two of us.

"Us being together isn't just about me accepting you," I said. "We both know I've already pretty much done that. Why else would I be kissing you?" A tremor ran through him. "If the pack can't accept me, we'll never have a day of peace in our lives.

"You've seen the mental scars I have from school. Nightmares. Startling easily. Swinging first, checking to see who it is after. I don't want to keep living my life constantly being on guard. I want to heal and move on. I want to be happy, Bennett."

He crushed me in a fierce hug. Thankfully, my arm was out of the way.

"That's what I want for you, too. If the pack doesn't accept you, we leave. It's that simple. I will always choose you over the pack."

He was saying all the right things, but I still wasn't convinced that staying with him was the right choice for both of us.

"Let's wait and see how things go on Saturday before making any promises, okay?"

He slowly shook his head. "No. My promise stands. You're first, Wrenly. Always. I thought I was putting you first by sending you away to school to give you time and space to mature, but I see how messed up that was. I wasn't listening, and I won't do that a second time. We'll communicate and listen to each other and find ways to meet both our needs without either of us sacrificing more than we're willing to give."

He kissed my mouth again and lifted the TV remote, which I hadn't seen him grab.

"Now, what movie do you want to watch?"

I WOKE up with a leisurely stretch against Bennett's side.

"What time is it?" I asked without opening my eyes or moving away.

"Time to pay up. Where's my morning kiss?"

I snorted and kissed his chest. Just a peck, nothing more, but I still found myself pinned under him a second later.

"I will pee this bed if you don't let me up."

Chuckling, he kissed my forehead and got off of me.

"Two minutes, then I demand a redo."

I bolted for the bathroom and took five minutes. When I returned, the bed was made, and Bennett was missing.

Curious, I checked the hallway. He wasn't there either. I went to his room and heard his shower running.

"Am I supposed to come in there and kiss you while you're showering?" I asked through the door.

The door opened, and Bennett yanked me inside. I collided with his wet chest and looked up at him in shock. Soap suds were running from his hair to his eyes. I reached up to wipe them away before they reached them.

"I was kidding," I said.

"Too late."

He kissed me hard. A second later, warm water hit my back, soaking my pajamas. I broke away from the kiss, quick to keep my stitches out of the water.

"Bennett!"

"I'll help."

He tugged my shirt over my head and threw it aside with a wet plop. I crossed my good arm over my chest and glared at him.

"You know that's not what I wanted."

His slow smile made my stomach do flips.

"I think it is. Remember not to use your hand."

He took a knee and had my shorts and underwear around my ankles as I pushed at his shoulders.

"Keep it out of the water, Wrenly," he said, his voice rough. "Last warning."

Then he leaned in and buried his face between my legs. I had to brace my good hand on his shoulder and my stitched one on the wall out of the water to keep my balance as he slowly shattered my world.

As the pulsing stopped, he reached around me, shut off the water, then picked me up.

"What are you doing?" I asked, leaning against him.

"I'm making sure my bed will smell like you for a long time."

Still wet, he tumbled us sideways onto the bed, rolling at the last second so I was on top of him.

"Mark me," he said, his hands already capturing my face to draw my mouth to his chest.

Too relaxed to resist, I kissed his chest and left the mark he craved right over his heart.

I lifted my head. "Are you going to wear your shirt unbuttoned to show this one off, too?"

"No. But I wouldn't mind if you left your mark on my neck again. Yesterday's faded."

I pulled myself a little higher up his body to reach his neck. Our hips aligned. He groaned, and his hands gripped my backside, jostling me partially to the side. Without thinking, I moved to brace my knees on the bed, opening myself to him to prevent a fall he would have never let happen in the first place.

We both froze at the contact.

"Don't wolf out," I said.

"Don't move," he gritted out.

I didn't. I held perfectly still as his grip on my backside slowly loosened, then slid up my back only to travel down again. It felt nice. His hands. Not the hard ridge I was straddling.

"Can I move off of you, yet?"

"Not yet."

The words were strained. If I didn't do something to distract him, we would both be in trouble.

"We're going to be late for work," I said.

He made a sound between a laugh and a groan. "We don't need more money."

He wasn't wrong.

My stomach growled, giving me a perfect opportunity. Sticking out my bottom lip, I gave him a sad look.

"I'm so hungry…"

He moved fast, catching my bottom lip between his and sucking it lightly before lifting me off of him.

"Go to my closet. Don't come out until you're dressed."

I slipped off the bed and closed myself inside then listened at the door for a few seconds before dressing. Since the clothes I'd purchased with Miranda were in there and clean, I grabbed those. The top was lightweight and pretty, and the slacks were easy to pull down with one hand. Plus, Mom and Miranda would approve.

When I stepped out, Bennett was on the bed but sitting, and with a towel wrapped around his waist. His hair looked wet again, too.

The mark on his chest stood out like a misplaced third nipple, making me smirk. But it was already getting lighter.

"Nice hickey," I said.

"Thanks." He studied me for a moment. "I think today is going to be a struggle for me."

"How so?"

"I don't want to go to work. I want to stay here with you and keep doing the things we were doing." He closed his eyes and frowned briefly. "I can still feel you and it's—"

He rubbed a hand over his face and opened his eyes. His pupils were spasming between fully dilated and pinpoint. I crossed the room, and when I reached him, he spread his knees to pull me closer.

I tipped his head back and marked his neck the way he'd wanted me to do earlier. When I drew back, his pupils were fully dilated and he was back to looking more desperate than tortured.

"Don't let today be a bad day because of what we did."

"It won't be a bad day because of what we did or because of what we didn't do…yet. But it will be a day that tests my control. I want you so much it hurts. I just want to—"

He leaned in suddenly so his lips could skim my neck as he inhaled my scent.

"This. Non-stop. You're the oxygen I need to breathe, Wrenly. Without you, I'm slowly suffocating."

I pulled back enough to capture his face.

"Go put some clothes on. I'll meet you in the kitchen and let you buy me breakfast on the way into work."

He closed his eyes and nodded. I kissed his nose and whirled out of his hold when he tried to tip back into bed. Laughing, I left him to dress.

The time on my phone when I collected my things made me cringe. I'd either woken up late, or we'd taken more time in the shower than I'd thought. Either way, Miranda had already sent a message.

Miranda: Coming in today?
Me: Yep. We're running late. Leaving the house in a few minutes and stopping for something to eat on the way.

She sent the location of a bagel place that was on the way.

Miranda: Best bagels you'll ever eat. Just in case you haven't decided yet.
Me: LOL what's your order?
Miranda: Everything with avocado and smoked salmon for me. I recommend the French Toast bagel for you.

I liked her text and looked up as Bennett walked into the kitchen.

He was neatly dressed in his usual suit ensemble, but missing his tie today. The collar of his shirt was unbuttoned and proudly displaying the mark on his neck.

"Most people try to hide those," I said.

"First, how would you know that? Second, most people didn't have to wait twelve years for their mate to acknowledge them."

I rolled my eyes at him.

"You already know I escaped my prison as often as possible. It was an all-girls school, not a convent. The dick pic you saw was proof of that."

"It would be better for everyone if you don't bring that up too often."

"Noted. Miranda sent me the location of a bagel place for breakfast. Ready?"

We arrived at work exactly an hour late. A few women muttered under their breath until Bennett shot them dark looks. Miranda didn't mind our late arrival, though. She made grabby hands for the bag I held.

"Good call on the bagels. It was good," I said, handing over her order.

"I'm going to work in Bennett's office today. The door and blinds will stay open for self-preservation, not welcome. Deflect everyone."

She grinned at me. "On it, boss lady."

I turned to Bennett. "Would you mind setting up my laptop on the coffee table?"

His slow smile accompanied his quick compliance.

FRIDAY MORNING DAWNED with a shower of kisses on my stomach, which is where Bennett had kissed just before I'd fallen asleep. Naked. He'd been pretty persistent about reciprocating the kisses I'd promised.

He veered south of my belly button, and I caught him by the hair.

"Wait."

"For what?"

"I need five minutes again."

"I'll give you two. Turn the shower on when you're ready for me to join you."

I hurried out of bed and shut myself in the bathroom. When I glanced at the mirror, I saw I had several kiss marks on my body. One over my heart. One on my neck. One just under my belly button, and when I looked down, I saw two on the inside of my thighs from when he'd been down there last night.

He seemed to really like kissing me *there*. I definitely didn't mind it since it always ended with me feeling good and nicely relaxed.

"You're wasting time," he said from the other side of the door.

"I'm going to kick you out of my room if you're going to stand right outside the bathroom."

"Two minutes. Leaving now."

I hurried to do my business and turned on the water. He didn't come in until I'd already quickly washed some important parts. But when he did walk in, he was completely nude.

This time, I didn't look away. I took in the sight of his broad, muscled shoulders, chiseled torso, and...I swallowed hard at what lay not-so-limply between his powerful thighs.

"You're frowning," he said.

I stopped and turned away from him to wet my face.

His hands stroked down my back.

"Why were you frowning?" he asked, kissing my shoulder that wasn't in the water since I was still making an effort to keep the bandage covering my stitches dry.

"I was thinking that sex with you might not be comfortable initially."

His hands stalled briefly on my back, and he made a sound between a growl and a purr.

"Was that a happy noise or a mad noise?"

"Happy. Definitely happy. My mate is thinking about the next step. I'm over the moon. But will you promise me something?"

Facing him, I watched his eyes do their mood swing thing.

"Promise you'll tell me if I do anything that doesn't feel good when the time comes."

"You're both wanting it and afraid of it, aren't you?" I asked. "Sex with me, I mean."

"I am."

"Me too. Probably for different reasons."

"Not really. I'm afraid sex will change everything and result in you leaving me."

"Hmm. I think I've tabled that and am more afraid that it's going to hurt."

He kissed my cheek, my nose, then my mouth. When he finished, I couldn't remember why I'd been nervous.

"I'll pre-pay by making you feel good every day so that, when you're ready, you won't be worried about any pain."

"That sounds nice. What's nicer is knowing that it won't hurt for long. At least, that's what Grandma told me when I went to the first pack run."

He hugged me close, smoothing a hand over my wet hair.

"I want to make the world a perfect place for you, Wrenly."

"It doesn't need to be perfect. Bad days are okay. We all have them. I just want to know that someone is there for me. Unconditionally. And…" I swallowed hard, debating whether I was ready to admit the truth. Honesty won. "I think you might be my best option for having that."

Pulling back so his hungry, intense gaze could see what his nose was already telling him—that I wasn't lying—he nodded to my bad arm. "Keep your hand on the wall again."

That was the only warning he gave me before he did his best to make me forget my name with his mouth and his hands.

Like the day before, we were an hour late to work.

Miranda grinned and accepted another bagel.

"It was good enough to go back for seconds, huh?"

I nodded and flushed, knowing she wasn't talking about breakfast. She had a nose and could probably smell what we'd done not only today but yesterday, too. Ignoring her silent applause, I followed Bennett into his office.

He took calls for the first hour, and I worked on spreadsheets until I got annoyed with using my left hand and stood, needing a break. Bennett watched me stretch, his gaze hungry.

I shook my head at him, and he grinned.

"I'm going to grab Miranda for a walk," I said quietly.

He nodded.

Miranda looked up from her work as the door opened.

"You busy?" I asked.

"For you? Never."

"Want to take a walk around the block?"

She was quick to lock her computer and join me. She seemed to sense that something was on my mind because neither of us said anything until we reached the street.

"What's up, my horny little buttercup?" she asked.

"How bad is it?" I asked.

"It's pretty strong, but from him. I can just smell him all over you and a little bit of your lust occasionally."

"Not that," I said, making an 'ew' face at her. "The fallout from saying I won't be at the challenge. Bennett's been keeping me purposefully distracted, and no one's said a thing. Which either means the challengers honestly thought they had a chance against you, or that everyone is trying to hide something from me. We both know it's not the former."

She grinned. "I was wondering if they were actually fooling you."

"What was that necklace you wanted again?"

"The challengers have already backed out, so there's no point in going. Mr. Wulf has announced that this is the end of the challenges, but he started a petition for anyone who wants you out of the pack to sign. If it gets half the pack's signatures, the Wulfs will leave the pack and start the process of relocating headquarters. So far, no one's signing it."

I wasn't the type to think my parents were leaving everything behind because of me. They were willing to leave because they'd lost faith in the people they'd spent their lives helping.

"When did he start the petition?" I asked.

"The day he announced you wouldn't be at the challenge." She glanced at me. "Bennett told me you thought the challenges were just a distraction. What do you think is going to happen?"

"Nothing good. Dad's forced the people opposing me into a corner. They'll need to choose between their hate for me and their need for the Wulf family's benefits, which, after seeing the numbers for these past few weeks, are too considerable for any smart person to give up just for the sake of a bias. But it's not just about bias. It's about status and money. Why should a lowly human have the coveted place of Mrs. Wulf, future Luna, when a fur-born female could hold that place and distribute even more wealth back into the pack?"

"Kind of twisted thinking since most fur-borns—I like that phrase by the way—are likely to spend more on themselves than you ever will."

I shrugged. "Everyone makes dumb decisions in their life. Theirs is thinking someone is better just because of their race."

"What dumb decisions did you make?"

"Ha. Don't you remember pinning me to the bathroom door?"

"I still cringe whenever I think about Bennett hearing about that."

Grinning, I said, "I'll keep it our dirty little secret until you get your necklace."

"And this is why we're friends."

"Is there anything else I don't know?"

"The Shanes publicly disowned Lindi last night."

She took out her phone and showed me the articles about their fallout. They hadn't just disowned her. They'd given reasons. Physical and financial victimization of her peers. No remorse or plans for atonement for past actions. And a complete disregard for her parents' repeated pleas for rehabilitation. The Shanes had publicly apologized on behalf of their daughter to anyone she had victimized and said the only way they could compensate for her actions was to cut ties completely. Anyone who wanted to press charges should do so.

"Wow. That's better than I'd hoped," I said. "Now the pack just needs to make up its mind whether or not getting rid of me is worth losing the Wulfs' money."

"Or maybe we can have both," a familiar voice said from behind us.

Miranda spun around fast, meeting Storm's lunge head-on. I backpedaled quickly, getting out of their way.

As Storm started to shift in broad daylight—something shifters typically didn't do because it freaked out humans—people around us were starting to yell and run. Tires screeched on the road, too.

Miranda growled and shifted, tearing her clothes and bending the bracelet that had been on her wrist. The way she went after Storm said she was pissed about it, too. Storm wasn't like the other women who'd challenged her, though. She was a fighter, and Miranda had to work to keep away from her teeth and claws while still trying to counterattack.

They moved so fast and everything was so chaotic that I didn't realize someone was behind me until a hand covered my mouth and I was lifted off the ground. My eyes went wide. I thrust back an elbow as I tipped my head forward. When they grunted, I flung my head back as hard as I could.

Something stung my arm as whoever had me groaned but held firm.

I kicked back with my heel, missing the leg. I tried to use my stitched arm to pull the hand away, but I was either too weak, or whoever had me was strong.

Things started to get fuzzy. I tried to fight as my vision swam, but I knew I was going under from whatever they'd given me.

Miranda continued to fight Storm, unaware of the growing space between us as I was dragged away.

Whoever had me threw me into the side door of the van as my vision started to tunnel.

I was so fucked.

CHAPTER THIRTY-SEVEN

MY GROGGY THOUGHTS matched my unresponsive eyelids as consciousness returned by degrees.

"You're hurting me," a woman cried.

"Shut up and fucking take it. You owe me."

The shuffling noises and the grunts set off warning bells in my head. Despite the throbbing in my arm, I had to fight the urge to sink back into the void. Whatever they'd given me was strong. The more alert I became, the more I heard and felt. Someone was having rough sex nearby, and my hands and feet were tied. Wherever I was, I was in trouble and needed to find a way out.

It took a few more seconds for me to open my eyes successfully. I quickly closed them after a glimpse.

I was sitting on the dirty cement floor of an abandoned building. In the large, open space in front of me, someone had set up a makeshift table, which Lindi was currently bent over. The metal barrels serving as table supports were scraping against the floor with the force of the man's thrusts into her. She wasn't making the same happy noises she'd made when getting railed at school, though.

The two men standing beside me were watching them and not me, but for how long?

Someone swore. The scraping stopped.

"I don't know why I thought rich pussy would be better than what I get now," the man who spoke earlier said. "It's not."

"It should be bubble gum flavored or something," one of the men next to me said, making the other two laugh.

What kind of idiots had Lindi found now?

I heard a soft, pained sound.

"I'm bleeding," Lindi said.

"Yeah, well, so was I. I think you said, 'Don't worry, I'll pay to get it fixed when this is done.' Does that make it hurt less?"

"I told you she can fight and to watch out. What happened to your nose isn't my fault; it's hers. You should have made her bleed."

"Not until we know whether or not she's one of *them*."

"She's not. She's human like us."

"Then why was she with one of them?"

"A rich, well-connected family adopted her to make themselves look good. She likes to pretend she has connections, but she's no one important and not one of them. If she were, do you think that shifter would have let us take her?"

I let out a laugh and opened my eyes to look at her.

"Is that how you get everyone to believe your lies? A little bit of sex to drain their brains first?" I looked at the man with the swollen nose. "Do you know her?"

"Yeah. Lindi Shane. One of the city's elite families."

"Did she say who my family is?"

Lindi marched over and slapped me hard across the face. It stung like a bitch, but I didn't show it as I glared up at her.

"The Wulfs, backed by the Steeles—"

Her hand lashed out and cracked across the same cheek.

"—made her family kick her out. Look at the newsfeeds. Why would either of those families do that for someone unimportant?"

She seethed at me, hating that her pathetic attempts to shut me up hadn't worked.

One of the two next to me pulled out his phone while the other one looked at the man with the swollen nose. He'd been the one railing Lindi. I saw a bit of blood on the zipper of his pants.

"She's right about the Shanes disowning their daughter," the man said after a moment.

"They were forced to post that to save their business," Lindi said. "It doesn't change anything. Once this bitch is dead, I'll pay you."

I laughed again. "With what money? I know your parents cut off funds and that you were calling people you thought were friends for a loan earlier in the week. Was someone dumb enough to lend you some?"

Lindi's expression turned cold, and she smiled as she leaned down to softly say, "Borrowing from friends means there's no paper trail to tie me or them to this once you're gone, bitch."

She straightened away from me and looked at the zipper guy.

"I sent you a picture of the money. If you need more proof, we can do a video call with the person holding it. Up to you. But before you kill her, I want all three of you to make her bleed worse than I am."

"Wouldn't recommend it," I said. "Right now, the worst I've suffered are Lindi's slaps. He'll smell that it was her, and she'll pay for it. If he smells that you've done worse to me…" I shook my head. "Why do you think he made her parents' business almost go under? Didn't she show you pictures of what she did to me last time?"

Zipper guy was glancing between the pair of us.

"Who are you talking about? Who is *he*?" he finally asked.

"Bennett Wulf."

Lindi scoffed. "He's only nice to her because his parents adopted her. He doesn't like her. I heard him say she's not his sister."

The man watched my slow smile.

"Who is he to you?" he asked.

"The better question is, who am I to him? I'm his potential mate. He's one of *them*. And I'm the orphan girl he found when I was six and he was thirteen. He's waited twelve long years to bring me home to claim me."

I looked at Lindi.

"When he found out I wasn't the perfectly protected princess he thought I'd been, he didn't get mad at me, Lindi, did he? No, he got mad at you while making me promises that you'd pay. And he did make you pay. He took everything you ever flaunted away from you."

I focused on the lead guy again.

"What do you think will happen if he finds me raped and dead in a ditch? Because he will find me. He has the nose for it. He will hunt you down and kill all of you, but not before you regret ever listening to her. And then, he'll go after her.

"He won't care about human laws. He'll use pack laws for all of you. Murdering someone's mate means that the pack will hunt you down and tear you apart like the animals you are.

"So, save yourselves, and walk away. Let him find Lindi here." I met her gaze. "We both know you won't walk away, no matter what they do. Are you crazy enough to kill me yourself, though?" I slowly shook my head. "No, you need them to do it for you. They'll be the sacrifice. That's why it's a cash payment. Nothing in or out of your accounts to pin the blame on you. I bet you haven't even been using your phone to contact them."

"Any recorded calls to cover your ass?" I asked the man. "Because it's going to look like a self-defense rape case when you're found dead if you just did a pump and dump."

He frowned and looked at Lindi.

"Yeah, a condom would have been your friend with her," I added.

He took out his phone and took a picture of her, but she was fast, changing her hardened expression to something soft and pitiful at the last second. I knew right when he figured out she was setting him up.

"Bitch." He hit her hard. Not a slap like she delivered me but a solid fist to the face.

I wasn't a good person. I didn't feel bad for her.

"You think you can set me up?"

"No, that's not—"

His next swing knocked her down at my feet. He kicked her twice in the stomach. She was sobbing and curled in a ball when he spat on her and focused on me.

"I know what you're thinking. Witnesses are bad. But in this case, I'm good.

"He's going to smell you, no matter what you do. Gasoline and a match will only cover up the bodies, not the trail he's been following from where you kidnapped me. Your scent is in his nose. In his memory. He'll never stop until he has answers.

"He'll have someone pull the surveillance from the stores in the area so he has faces to go with the scents. If you were smart enough to mask, he has the van you used. He'll use all his resources to keep pulling surveillance until he has the face of whoever was driving. Then he'll find known associates for that person. You'll be on that list. He won't discriminate. He'll hunt everyone down, even if it takes his whole life.

"I'm exhausted just thinking about it, but he won't be. He'll be fueled by his rage.

"Unless…"

"You're as annoying as she is," the man said.

I grinned. "Oh, I'm way more annoying, which should tell you a little bit about how obsessed my mate would have to be to still want me. And how grateful he'd be when he learns that you were tricked into kidnapping me and stopped Lindi before I was seriously hurt."

"Don't listen to her," Lindi said, trying to push herself up. "She's a liar. Everyone knows you can't lie to a shifter. They can smell a lie. He'd know she was trying to lie for you. A million if you kill her now."

She managed to sit up, but didn't try to stand.

"A million? That's it? And I wouldn't be lying. Did you tell them who I was to the Wulfs? No. You didn't even know who I was to them. Have they hurt me? No. You're the one who slapped me.

"Do you have my phone?" I asked. "We can call Bennett right now and ask him."

"No. We tossed it."

"Okay. Not a problem. I remember his number. Call him and put him on speaker. You'll know within thirty seconds if I'm telling the truth."

"Don't do it," Lindi said. "They'll trace your number." She didn't cower when the guy looked at her, but she didn't have her usual haughtiness either.

"Do you think I don't use a burner phone, given my line of work?"

He pulled out his phone, and I quickly rattled off Bennett's number.

He answered on the first ring.

"Bennett, it's me," I said.

"Where are you? Are you safe?"

"I don't know where I am. Lindi tricked some people into kidnapping me. He hit her pretty hard when he found out. I'm safe, though."

"Are they listening?" he asked.

"Yes."

"Tell me where you are and I'll compensate you for keeping my mate safe. More if you ensure Lindi is still there when I get there. I'd prefer no police involvement." The last bit had enough growl in it not to leave any ambiguity about how Bennett felt about Lindi.

"Done," the man said before hanging up.

"Untie that one and use the ropes on her," he said as he tapped his screen.

Lindi tried to stand. Zipper man kicked her down. She didn't try to get up again as the other two untied me and tied her.

Zipper man glanced at me when his phone pinged, then handed it over.

"Check the pictures," he said.

I did. He only had one of Lindi. I looked up at him in question.

"No picture of you," he clarified. "Check theirs."

"Why?"

"We weren't here. We didn't see anything. We don't know anything. Especially where some rich bitch disowned by her family disappeared to. We might be connected to kidnapping you, but like you said, nothing is tying us to working with her."

I nodded, understanding.

"Tell him the million he sent is more than enough." He looked at the guy to my right. "Leave your phone with her."

He handed it over.

"Hope I never see you around," he said.

"I'll pretend I don't know you if you do."

He nodded and walked away with the other two.

I looked at Lindi. She was lying on her side with her hands tied behind her back. She was staring straight ahead, bitterness and hate etched into her features.

I knew I shouldn't ask...that the answer wouldn't change anything, but I asked anyway.

"Was there even a reason why you started targeting me?"

"Other than you liked acting like you were better than the rest of us, and we didn't matter? No."

I shook my head and slowly got to my feet. Not once had I acted better than anyone. I'd ignored people and minded my own business until they made themselves my business. However, I didn't bother saying any of that. Nothing would get through to her. And, honestly, she didn't matter anymore.

Instead, I walked over to the table where Lindi's designer purse was being defiled by the dirty surface and pulled out her phone. Her face wasn't too swollen for facial recognition, thankfully, so I was able to read through her recent messages.

I found the conversation between her and Storm, as I'd suspected.

"So how do you know Storm?" I asked.

"I didn't. She reached out to me last night and suggested we work together."

It aligned with the texts that I'd read. Storm had promised to contact Lindi when I left the office, which meant that either Storm had been watching outside or that someone inside had tipped Storm off that we were leaving.

"Did you know she was a shifter going into it?"

"No. Will that save me?"

"You paid people to kidnap, rape, and kill his mate. What do you think?"

"I think you're just as heartless as me. Only you don't show it."

"I'm only heartless when I need to be. You're heartless when you *want* to be. That's the difference between a 'live and let live' person and a 'kill them all because they disagree with me' person."

Something banged somewhere in the building, and I heard Bennett shout my name a second later.

"Here!" I called back.

Bennett and Konni crashed through the doors, looking more threatening than I could have ever imagined. Fur rippled along Bennett's skin, and his expression screamed mayhem and murder. Beside him, Konni's eyes were glittering with gold flecks, and the air around him looked like heat waves were warping it. He had scales covering his face and hands, too.

"Please, no shifting inside, Konni. I heard dragons are big, and I don't trust the ceiling if you bump it."

His scales immediately vanished along with the weird waves in the air around him.

Bennett didn't calm down, though, as his gaze swept over me, then lingered on my face, specifically the cheek that felt hot and throbbed with my heartbeat.

"I'm fine," I said.

"I'm not." He crossed the space and pulled me into his arms. I felt him shaking as I hugged him back.

"I know," I said, using my hand to smooth over the material of his shirt. "But you need to hold off on your need to lock me in a room for now. I have to show you something."

He pulled back to look at me, and I showed him Lindi's conversation with Storm.

"Storm was either waiting for us, or she was working with someone inside," I said when he'd read it all.

He pulled out his phone and called Dad on speaker.

"Storm plotted with Lindi to kill Wrenly."

A growl echoed over the phone.

"I demand blood for blood," Mom said.

"I'll put out the call for a hunt tonight," Dad said.

"Wait. Where's Storm now?"

"In your mom's office," Dad said. "Miranda brought her back to get answers."

"And did you find out if she was working alone or if someone in the office was helping her?" I asked.

"Olivia was working with her," Mom said. "Don't worry. We already know who to hold responsible and will make an example of them before we leave."

"Leave?" I looked at Bennett. "Did that many people sign the petition?"

He shook his head.

"No, Sweetheart," Mom said. "We won't stay where the entire pack doesn't love you as much as we do."

My eyes watered as Bennett kissed my forehead. I hadn't realized how much I'd needed them to put me first for a change. I thought I'd moved beyond that, but knowing they were willing to give up everything for me, not because they'd lost faith in their pack, almost broke me.

Bennett inhaled as I pressed my face into his chest.

"Mom. Dad. We'll talk more at the house." He hung up and scooped me into his arms, holding me close and comforting us both.

"You can head to the car," Konni said. "I'll follow with this one after I clean up in here."

"Thank you," Bennett said.

We'd just cleared the doors outside when the windows farther down on the second level exploded with flames. I watched the glass rain down as Bennett put me into the front seat.

"Konni?" I asked.

"It's okay. He's cleaning the scene with dragon fire. If anyone can trace Lindi to the building, they'll think she died there." His fingers brushed over my cheek. "Are you really okay?"

I looked into his loving eyes and nodded.

For the first time in my life, I genuinely believed I could have the future I wanted, filled with love, laughter, and family.

THE WOODS WERE QUIET, as if all the animals in the area knew what was about to happen.

Lindi, Storm, and Olivia knelt in front of several of Mom and Dad's supporters. This time, more people were standing behind Mom and Dad than those who weren't. The people who stood opposite didn't look as angry as they had last Saturday.

I glanced at Storm's parents, who were off to the side. Her dad was silently crying. Her mom wasn't doing anything, just staring straight ahead, pale and vacant.

"The people in front of us attacked me outside of a challenge with the intent to kill our future alpha's mate," Miranda said. "I demand blood for blood."

"She wasn't killed," someone from the other side said.

Grandma stepped forward. "Storm and Olivia turned against our own outside of a challenge."

"She's a human," Storm growled. "She'll never be our own."

"She's human," Grandma said. "Just like the human you worked with to try to kill her. The world is filled with them. Trying to deny them their place is like trying to deny the air you need to breathe. Our laws exist for a reason. We do not harm humans unless in defense for a reason.

"The hatred that you carry for humans won't fade. It will warp and grow until humans notice and tear this pack apart. To save the pack, we need to cleanse it. I demand blood for blood."

"Blood for blood has been called according to our laws," Dad said. "All are required to witness. Those who don't are exiled from the pack."

Everyone started to undress. Storm's dad turned to his wife and started to help her out of her clothes.

I looked at Grandma. She took my hand, patted it, and shook her head discreetly.

"I'll walk with you rather than run," she said.

"So will we," a voice called from the trees. I watched my brothers stride through the opposing people. Tall with dark hair and dark eyes, they looked so much like Bennett. But with more laugh lines.

Emotions hit me hard. I wanted to run and jump on them and hug them hard. But I also wanted to hit them just as hard for leaving me when I'd needed them.

"She's mad," Aiden said to Karter.

"I have eyes," Karter said. Then he stepped behind Aiden and pushed Aiden at me.

It was a ploy to hug me without me having time to react, and it worked. His smell was exactly how I'd remembered. I hugged him and sniffled.

"I hate you," I whispered.

"I know," he said back.

"Not you, Aiden," I said, turning my head and looking at Bennett. "Never take them away from me again."

"I won't," he promised.

Karter tugged Aiden away to hug me, too. Neither of them undressed, thankfully, as the rest of the pack finished up. But Bennett did. I watched him strip and saw his anger and aggression. Mom and Dad's was close but not quite to his level of rage.

When he turned and locked gazes with me, his softened.

"Tonight, they pay. Tomorrow, the world will be a little better because of it."

I didn't say anything. The human in me had a hard time following pack law, especially when it meant violence and death. But I knew Lindi had no problem with either. She'd proven it so many times. She'd had plenty of opportunities to reform and hadn't taken them. She'd only gotten worse. And while Storm had always been a pain in my ass, I'd never believed she was a killer. She'd proven me wrong by working with Lindi, knowing what Lindi meant to do to me. Olivia, I didn't know well, only that she'd never liked me.

Bennett kissed my forehead. "Everyone needs to witness."

I nodded, understanding what he was saying—if I wanted to have a place in the pack, whether as a daughter, sister, or mate, I couldn't turn away from what was about to happen.

"You have a five-second head start," Dad said.

Olivia and Storm sprang to their feet.

Lindi didn't move. Instead, she looked me in the eye and said, "I hope you wake up feeling like you're being suffocated for the rest of your life."

"Five," Mom said before shifting.

The rest of the pack shifted and sprang for the woods.

Mom tore out Lindi's throat where she still knelt, making sure to keep her body between me and Lindi. She blocked my view to spare me, and I thanked her by not looking away.

Bennett chuffed to gain my attention then sprinted for the trees.

"Come on, my little Wren," Grandma said.

She led the way with Aiden and Karter trailing behind me.

"So, did either of you find your mates?" I asked as we walked.

"No," Aiden said.

"We weren't really trying," Karter said. "I heard you hoped we'd mate with a Rottweiler."

"Not nice, by the way," Aiden said.

"Wasn't meant to be."

"What's it going to take to earn your forgiveness?" Karter asked.

"Bennett gave me nine million dollars. What do you have?"

"Nine?" Karter asked. "How did he manage that? All I have is my car, some stock in Wulf Enterprises, and about two hundred and fifty thousand from working the last three years."

"Same."

"You'll have to ask Bennett," I said. "But I'll take your salary, and you can keep your car so you can go back to work as Bennett's lackey."

"You're quitting?" Grandma asked from in front of me.

"Yep. The end of August. Then I'm going to school to get my degree."

A chorus of howls rang out ahead of us, followed by snarls.

"Better pick up the pace," Grandma said, walking faster.

We caught up just as Bennett ended Storm and Dad ended Olivia.

I didn't look away.

EPILOGUE

Music thumped loudly in the bar, and I grinned at Sophia as she plopped down next to me, holding out a cocktail.

"Here's to you," she said. "For getting your degree in just three years. I really wish I'd gone to your school and had credits when I started college so I wouldn't be looking at another year come this fall."

I clinked glasses with her. "No, you don't. We both would have been tortured."

She leaned in and kissed my cheek. "For you, it would have been worth it."

Winking at her, I took a sip of my drink.

The years I'd spent feeling abandoned and alone felt like a distant memory. Sophia was one of my closest friends. She knew all about my past and about who Bennett was to me.

It would have been hard to keep either of them from her. We'd roomed together the first year in the dorms then moved into the place Bennett had renovated. She'd witnessed the trauma my years of school had left me with and hadn't turned away from it. She'd accepted me, my screaming nightmares, and how easily I could startle under the right circumstances. And she'd helped me heal with that acceptance.

Sophia had also been a great friend whenever I'd needed to talk about my fears of a future with Bennett, which hadn't been very often because he'd been nearly perfect at adapting to what I needed, to get what he needed...me. Although he'd shown up occasionally, he'd otherwise kept his word. He hadn't moved with me.

He'd called nightly and messaged throughout the day. He was always present. Always there for me. But not in a caging way. In a supportive one. During the first two months of school, I'd gone home every weekend, leaving after my last class on Friday. After that, I'd started leaving Saturday morning.

He'd struggled with the separation a few times, but when he did, he'd reach out, asking for some in-person time. He never interfered with who I talked to. Never said anything about who he smelled on me. He would just hold me, tell me he missed me, and usually spend the night in my bed.

He'd learned to let go. And so had I. I'd gone to parties and other social events with Sophia and made more friends. None as close as her, though. Or as close as Miranda, who'd messaged daily without fail. Sometimes it was office gossip. Sometimes pack gossip. Sometimes it was a random picture of whatever jewelry or bag she was lusting after.

"I'm surprised your furred wonder let you out for some fun on your first night home," Sophia said, bringing me back to the present.

"He promised that he'd stay away until I texted him for a ride home, and I promised to be his for twenty-four hours in return."

She paused mid-sip. "As in his-his? As in you're finally saying yes?"

I just smiled and took another sip.

"Wow. So, like, is this your bachelorette party? Shit, I should have ordered some guys. Call Miranda and tell her to come out."

She pressed her hands together, silently pleading with me. After meeting, the pair had hit it off, mostly because Sophia and Miranda both shared a love for fashion and enjoyed having fun. I was a little worried about the fun part, though.

"If I call her, do you promise not to order any male models?"

"I swear."

I sent a text.

Me: Sophia and I are at a club downtown. Want to join us?
Miranda: Send me the address. I'll be right there.

Sophia cheered and waved down a server to order a line of shots. She knew the only time I let loose was when I had a trusted designated sober person with us, whether we had a ride or not. And thanks to Miranda's wolfy tolerance, getting drunk was nearly impossible for her.

The shots were lined up and waiting for us by the time Miranda walked into the busy club.

"Look at you getting ready to misbehave," Miranda said when she saw what was waiting. "What's the occasion?"

"Wrenly's going to say yes tonight," Sophia said. "Our sisterhood of singularity is about to be cut to two."

Miranda's gaze cut to mine. "Seriously? You're accepting his mark?"

"Yes, unless you say or do something to freak me out."

She quickly picked up a shot and handed it to me.

"Hell no. You're going to make him the happiest mate ever tonight. Does he know? No. He can't know, or you wouldn't be sitting here drinking. Hurry up. Take the shot before he shows up."

I laughed at her and downed the shot. It burned. "He'll blame you if I get too drunk. Keep that in mind."

"Oh, I will." She focused on Sophia, eyeing her clothes. "I know you have better taste than that. Did you have some kind of home emergency that forced you to evacuate without packing and borrow from Wrenly's closet?"

Sophia laughed and plucked at her T-shirt and jean shorts.

"These are now my standard clubbing clothes. Less attention in these."

"And why do we want less attention?" Miranda asked.

"I'm not the till-death-do-us-part type, and we've hit the age where men start craving seeing us in a white dress. Unless it's a fuck-boy looking for a good time, I'm telling them all I'm currently gender transitioning and that I'll call them after I'm healed from surgery. No one's left their number with me yet."

Miranda nearly died laughing. While I knew Sophia wasn't serious about transitioning, she was very serious about avoiding commitment because of how badly her dad had screwed over her mom in their messy divorce.

"Not all men are scumbags," I said. "Look at Bennett. He's waited fifteen years for me."

"He's a unicorn," Sophia said.

"Something will be pointy on him tonight, but it won't be on his forehead," Miranda said.

I made an "ew" face. "How can you dress so nice and have no class?"

Miranda winked at me. Sophia laughed and handed us all the second round of shots. It didn't burn as much this time, and when they dragged me out to the dance floor, I was ready for the packed, body-to-body bumping and grinding.

Sophia used me as her dance partner, getting dirty with her moves, which entertained me and more than a few guys watching us. I lost myself to the music until Sophia motioned she was thirsty. Apparently, grinding on me like a perv was dehydrating. That, or she was craving a better buzz.

We left the floor and ordered another round of drinks, not shots, and sat at our reserved table.

"So where are you staying now that you're back?" Miranda asked as we sipped.

"Bennett has a downtown flat that'll be near the welfare center," I said. "We're going back there tonight."

"Smart since the rest of your family is back at the old house," Sophia said. "I hear the mating sessions with a shifter can be pretty intense."

Miranda shot her a warning look, and Sophia shrugged.

"Wrenly's the one who told me."

"He won't be intense with you," Miranda said. "He won't do anything to scare you."

A guy approached our table, looking at Sophia. "I saw your moves and would like to experience them firsthand. Interested?"

The guy was so blatant about what he was after, I thought for sure Sophia would agree.

"Give me five more days, and I'll be cleared to use what the doctor reconstructed for me. I've heard that having a vagina is way better than having a dick and can't wait to try it out." She held out her phone. "Your number?"

He shook his head and walked away without saying anything else.

Miranda howled with laughter, and Sophia smacked her arm.

"You're going to give away the lie if you're obvious like that."

"Oh, he knew you were lying. Trust me. Next time, ask if they're bi and into trans. It'll be more impactful and leave them in more doubt."

Sophia looked suitably impressed and did a silent toast in thanks.

I was taking another sip when the second guy approached. He wasn't looking at Sophia, though. He was looking at me.

"Would you like to dance? With me?"

He was so shy and so cute about it that I felt bad about having to turn him down.

"Yes," Sophia said.

"She'd love to dance," Miranda added, tugging me to my feet and pushing me toward the guy.

He caught me and immediately backed away, leaving a respectful amount of space.

"Would you?" he asked again, obviously aware that I'd been forced.

"Sure."

Bennett had been great about all my interactions with the opposite sex, rarely showing any sign of jealousy. However, that wasn't why I was dancing with this guy. This one looked like he'd put some effort into himself. No name brands like half the people here, but still nice clothes, light on the cologne, and a trendy hair style that looked freshly cut. And I had a feeling he'd go home and never try going to a bar again if he got turned down right now.

So I followed him out to the dance floor and had a good time for three dances before another girl joined us. Then another. I smiled at him and waved with a wink and a nod to my table before leaving him with his actual options.

"How did you do that?" Sophia asked.

"I didn't do anything. He did it by not grinding on me like someone else I danced with today. Girls like guys who can be present and not have to dominate."

"Wait. Say that again so I can send that to Bennett, too," Miranda said.

When I looked at her, she was holding her phone up.

"Too? What did you do?" I asked.

She grinned and showed me her phone. She'd sent a recording of me dancing with the guy along with a message saying it was time to pick me up before someone else did.

"Why do you have to stir up trouble?" I asked.

"Trouble? Tipping him off will get me the bracelet I've been wanting."

"The one you sent me last week?" Sophia asked. "Your willpower is commendable."

I snorted at them and settled into my chair to wait for Bennett.

"As fun as this is, I think I'm going to bail before the green monster gets here. He's frisky when he's jealous, and I don't want to witness the good times I'm trying to avoid, or I'll wake up in a tiara and dressed in white."

Miranda waved her off and stayed with me until Bennett showed up with Konni almost fifteen minutes later. The pair made heads turn.

Miranda made a sound beside me. "Now that's a fine specimen there."

I knew she wasn't talking about Bennett, but Konni.

"He's single," I said, "and will steal my man soon for inappropriate things we're not allowed to talk about."

Bennett was close enough to hear me despite the loud music and frowned as he closed the distance. Konni flushed. Feeling guilty, I stood and hugged him before I hugged Bennett.

"No hard feelings," I said. "I'll loan him out to you whenever you need, as long as there aren't any women involved. Unless you need me to witness whatever it is you two do."

I pulled back and arched a brow at him, thinking I was being funny. However, the look in Konni's eyes wasn't amused. He was looking a lot like Bennett had when I'd first come home. Intense, expanded pupils, and barely in control.

"Who were you with?" he asked, his voice rough.

Bennett had me out of Konni's arms and in his a second later.

"You need to calm down, Konni," he said. "You're going to scare Wrenly."

He wasn't scaring me, but I didn't correct Bennett. Instead, I watched Konni take a slow breath and close his eyes.

"I'm sorry. The scent on you is...confusing."

Bennett leaned in and smelled me.

"Her friend, Sophia, a male I haven't met, and Miranda. That's all I smell."

"Ooh! Me! Pick me!" Miranda said, popping up from her place on the sofa. She pulled her hair aside to expose the long line of her neck and the Zellon's necklace resting there. "You can sniff me right here."

Konni glanced at her and shook his head slightly. "It's not you. I'm sorry."

And he did sound sorry.

"It's all right," Miranda said with a shrug. "My knight will come along someday. But if you're not interested in me, that means you're either interested in the man on the dance floor or a woman who was just talking about gender transitioning. Good luck." She patted his arm as she walked by him on her way out.

Konni looked at Bennett.

"She wasn't lying," Bennett confirmed.

"Wait, can't Konni smell lies?" I asked.

"His nose is good, but he has a harder time with the subtleties emotions can cause in someone's scent. Is your friend actually thinking about a gender transition?"

I thought of Sophia's stance on committed relationships. Her parents had divorced when she was younger, and she'd confided that marriage had ruined her mom in ways she never wanted to experience herself. Loss of self-worth. Fear of men. Questioning herself on every decision she made, no matter how small it was.

Any man who approached Sophia with the intent of a serious relationship was always met with rejection. She told me she would never make herself smaller for a man to feel bigger.

Knowing what Konni was, I understood that his interest in Sophia was exactly the kind she was trying to avoid. So I answered like a best friend should.

"She's not thinking about it; she's already talked to several people about it."

Konni nodded, but his eyes had lost their focus. I knew he was thinking, but about what?

"She's been through a lot, Konni, and just wants to be free to be whoever she wants to be."

"I understand." He looked at Bennett. "Thanks for the drink. Enjoy your night."

I watched him walk away and felt a tinge of guilt. I knew what it meant for their kind to find a mate, but I also knew how Sophia felt.

"It's not your problem," Bennett said, kissing my temple. "He'll be fine. Are you ready to go home?"

My stomach did a little flip, and I quickly threaded my fingers through Bennett's to lead the way out. When we reached the sidewalk, he stopped me.

"You're nervous. Why? Because you danced with another man?"

I grinned at him and shook my head.

"No. I know you won't be mad about that."

He looked down, and I knew he was struggling with his jealousy.

"It was a pity dance. He just needed a little courage to get out on the dance floor, and I probably looked like the person least likely to be mean about turning him down."

Bennett crushed me in a hug. "Thank you for explaining when you didn't have to."

I wrapped my arms around him, running my fingers through the hair at the back of his neck.

"My poor, needy mate. Why don't you take me home so I can reassure you in private?"

He made a pained sound and had me buckled in the car less than a minute later. I was laughing and breathless from how he'd carried me, which seemed to provoke him because he paused to kiss me as soon as he took his seat.

"We're never going to get home this way," I teased.

The intensity in his gaze heated my blood, and the unspoken promise in mine had him smoothly navigating the lingering traffic to get us home in fifteen minutes.

We started kissing in the elevator and didn't stop until the backs of my knees hit the bed.

Drawing away, I smirked at him.

"If that was the tour you promised me, I think I blinked and missed it."

"Tour later. I need to taste you again. Now."

He reached for my dress pants, and I caught his hands.

"What if I want more than a taste tonight?"

His gaze filled with torment. "You know more is dangerous. The last time—" He swallowed hard. "I don't think I can feel you come apart around me again and not mark you, Wrenly. No more sex until you're ready to be my mate."

Sex with Bennett had been amazing, the handful of times he'd allowed it. But it had tested his control and his promise to me. And I'd loved how he'd kept his word but had been driven wild because of it.

"What if I told you that I am ready?"

"What?" he rasped. His gaze sparked with hope as it searched mine.

"I'm ready for you to mark me, Bennett. I want to spend the rest of my life being loved by you and loving you back."

I saw fear extinguish his surge of excitement.

"Maybe we should wait. You just graduated. You start your new job—"

I covered his mouth with my hand.

"We promised honesty. No lies. No holding back information. Remember?"

His shoulders slumped, and he set his forehead against mine. I removed my hand.

"I've hurt you unintentionally so many times. The thought of hurting you intentionally...I don't think I can."

"Then don't. What we're doing tonight isn't about the hurt but the result. I choose you, Bennett. Be my mate. I've waited long enough, and you've waited longer."

He groaned and kissed me. While he was tentative, I wasn't. I kissed him hungrily, showing him how much I wanted him and how sure I was of my decision.

We fell back onto the bed, a fumble of hands and clothes. And when he finally entered me, it felt like I'd found my way home to where I was meant to be. He did everything he knew I loved until I was begging him not to stop. I toppled over, and as I floated in that bliss, he carefully bit me.

It hurt, but I'd never felt more connected to him than in that moment.

He was my everything. And I was his.

"I love you, Bennett. Thank you for waiting for me."

"From beginning to end, you were always mine. I would have waited a lifetime for you if you needed it. Thank you for loving me and agreeing to be my mate. I love you, Wrenly. Now and forever."

Smiling, I relaxed into his arms, glad Bennett had found me and even happier that I'd given him a chance.

* * *

Thank you for reading *His White Moonlight*. If you're hungry for another story in this world, check out *His Flash Mate*, Sophia and Konni's story. (And, yes, you will learn what happens when a dragon molts!)

AUTHOR'S NOTE

Thank you for diving into *His White Moonlight*! If it felt longer than my usual books... you're not imagining it. This labor of love took nearly a year to write and packs in the word count of *two* of my "usual" stories. I poured my heart into every page, and I hope you enjoyed Wrenly and Bennett's journey as much as I loved bringing it to life.

From the moment they met, their connection was undeniable. Bennett embraced their bond without hesitation, but Wrenly? She fought it every step of the way—and who could blame her after everything she's endured? That push-and-pull is what made their romance burn so brightly.

Now, I'm beyond excited to turn the page to my next couple: Sophia and Konni in *His Flash Mate* (already up for pre-order!). And yes... you'll *finally* find out what happens when a dragon molts.

If you enjoyed this story, I'd be incredibly grateful if you left a review, shared it with your book-loving friends, or even requested it at your local library. Your support is what keeps these worlds alive. And while you're at it, pop over to my shop at melissahaag.com to snag some snarky Wrenly merch—you know she'd approve.

Until next time—happy reading!
Melissa

THE MANTIRUM WORLD

OF FATES AND FURIES

Join the Academy!

BOOK 1: FURY FRAYED

Raised to believe she's human, Megan must discover the truth about who and what she is to stop a murderer after her mom abandons her in Uttira, a town filled with mythological creatures posing as humans.

BOOK 2: FURY FOCUSED

With a new boyfriend and new responsibilities, Megan's life is more complicated than ever. As new abilities start to emerge, she must learn to control them or risk never being able to leave Uttira again.

BOOK 3: FURY FREED

Discovering the Book of Fury forces Megan down a path she never thought she'd travel. It's a race against time to discover a way to obtain her powers without sacrificing who she's become and those she loves.

THE  MANTIRUM WORLD

By Kiss and Claw

Run with the wolves!

BOOK 1: THE HOWL

A young succubus struggles to accept what she is and how she must feed in this hilarious yet emotional paranormal coming of age story filled with love, lust, and a brownie too horny to trust.

BOOK 2: THE HUNT

Eliana lost her chance at a peaceful life the moment her mom returned to Uttira and vowed to help her overcome her feeding disorder. Seeking to escape the pressure, she retreats to a cabin in the woods, but something is stalking her. Whatever beast is out there is about to become the hunted, because Eliana's had enough playing by everyone else's rules.

BOOK 3: THE HUNGER

Eliana has the one thing she thought she'd never have. Fenris. But in order to keep him, she'll need to unleash the last piece of herself that she's been hiding and fully embrace all that she is. And, the world will fall on its knees when she's done.

JUDGEMENT OF THE SIX

BOOK 1:   HOPE(LESS)

With her abilities, Gabby discovers the existence of werewolves and others like her. She is the spark that ignites an inescapable fate for six uniquely gifted women, a fate that will claim her life and her heart.

BOOK 2:   (MIS)FORTUNE

Tormented by her predictions, Michelle escapes from the creatures who seek to use her only to run straight into the arms of another beast. However, this one isn't what he seems, and with his help, she might be able to free herself forever.

BOOK 3:   (UN)WISE

Bethi, the keeper of past lives, fights the truth of who she is and what she needs to do when one of the werewolves finds her. But there's no hiding from her destiny. She is the key to bring them all together.

BOOK 4:   (UN)BIDDEN

Charlene has more power than she knows and all the strength that the werewolves need. And if she decides the werewolves are worth saving, she'll need to claim one of them as her own.

BOOK 5:   (DIS)CONENT

An emotional syphon, Isabelle deals the best way she can — with her fists. When a werewolf comes crashing through friend's bar, Isabelle is forced into a game she doesn't want to play with new friends she doesn't really like.

BOOK 6:   (SUR)REAL

Olivia is blind, yet sees. What she sees, she keeps to herself as he father plots for control. She does her own plotting, working with forces that only she understands. Her time is running out to save her sisters and the world.

JUDGEMENT OF THE SIX

COMPANIONS

Join the heroes!

BOOK 1: CLAY'S HOPE

A werewolf more comfortable in his fur than his skin, Clay only thinks he knows what it means to be human. Until he meets Gabby, his unique human Mate. The Claiming rules have changed and learning has never been harder...

BOOK 2: EMMITT'S TREASURE

The story of finding my Mate starts like a bad bar joke–a woman walked into a diner. If only the punch line made it better. But it doesn't. She's running and scared and keeping a secret. One of my kind, a werewolf, had kept her prisoner for years. What he did is unforgivable. What I'll do when I find him will be far worse.

BOOK 3: LUKE'S DREAM

Luke's been kicked in the teeth by fate enough to know: nice guys finish last. Yet, he still finds himself driving across the country to look for someone because Gabby asked him to. It's his one last nice deed. Afterward, he's going Mate hunting and nothing will stop him from Claiming what's his.

BOOK 4: THOMAS' HEART

Thomas vows no human would go unpunished for the destruction of his world. His mission to rid the north of every one of them comes to a halt when he meets Charlene. He wants her, but can't have her. She's unique. And she's changing everything.

BOOK 5: CARLOS' PEACE

My earliest memory holds a secret that haunts me. Driven not to repeat the mistake of my past, I've molded myself to become what's needed, a protector of my race. But even that might be taken from me.